The thought of laying a hand on someone brings back a world of memories, feelings, a flush of power I experience only when I make contact with skin not immune to my own. It's a rush of invincibility; a tormented kind of euphoria; a wave of intensity flooding every pore in my body. I don't know what it will do to me. I don't know if I can trust myself to take pleasure in someone else's pain.

All I know is that Warner's last words are caught in my chest and I can't cough out the cold of the truth hacking at the back of my throat.

Adam has no idea that Warner can touch me.

No one does.

Warner was supposed to be dead. Warner was supposed to be dead because I was supposed to have shot him but no one supposed I'd need to know how to fire a gun so now I suppose he's come to find me.

He's come to fight.

For me.

BOOKS BY TAHEREH MAFI

Shatter Me: Series One

BOOK 1: *Shatter Me*

BOOK 2: *Unravel Me*

BOOK 3: *Ignite Me*

BOOK 4: *Restore Me*

BOOK 5: *Defy Me*

BOOK 6: *Imagine Me*

Shatter Me: Series One Novellas

BOOK 1.5: *Destroy Me*

BOOK 2.5: *Fracture Me*

BOOK 4.5: *Shadow Me*

BOOK 5.5: *Reveal Me*

BOOK 6.5: *Believe Me*

Shatter Me: Series One Novella Collections

Unite Me

Find Me

Shatter Me: Series Two

BOOK 1: *Watch Me*

BOOK 2: *Release Me*

The Woven Kingdom Series

BOOK 1: *This Woven Kingdom*

BOOK 2: *These Infinite Threads*

BOOK 3: *All This Twisted Glory*

BOOK 4: *Every Spiral of Fate*

An Emotion of Great Delight

A Very Large Expanse of Sea

UNRAVEL ME

SHATTER ME: SERIES ONE

BOOK TWO

TAHEREH MAFI

STORYTIDE
An Imprint of HarperCollins*Publishers*

HarperCollins Children's Books,
a division of HarperCollins Publishers,
195 Broadway, New York, NY 10007

HarperCollins Publishers, Macken House,
39/40 Mayor Street Upper, Dublin 1, D01 C9W8, Ireland

Storytide is an imprint of HarperCollins Publishers.

Unravel Me

harpercollins.com

Library of Congress Cataloging-in-Publication Data
Mafi, Tahereh.
Unravel me / Tahereh Mafi. — 1st ed.
p. cm.
Summary: "Juliette has escaped to Omega Point, the headquarters of the rebel resistance and a safe haven for people with abilities like hers. She is finally free from The Reestablishment and their plans to use her as a weapon, but Warner, her former captor, won't let her go without a fight." —Provided by publisher.
ISBN 978-0-06-349766-5
[1. Science fiction. 2. Ability—Fiction. 3. Love—Fiction. 4. Soldiers—Fiction. 5. Dictatorship—Fiction.] I. Title.
PZ7.M2695Un 2013 2012028389
[Fic]—dc23 CIP
AC

Typography by Ray Shappell
26 27 28 29 30 RTLO 10 9 8 7 6 5 4 3 2 1

SPECIAL EDITION, 2026

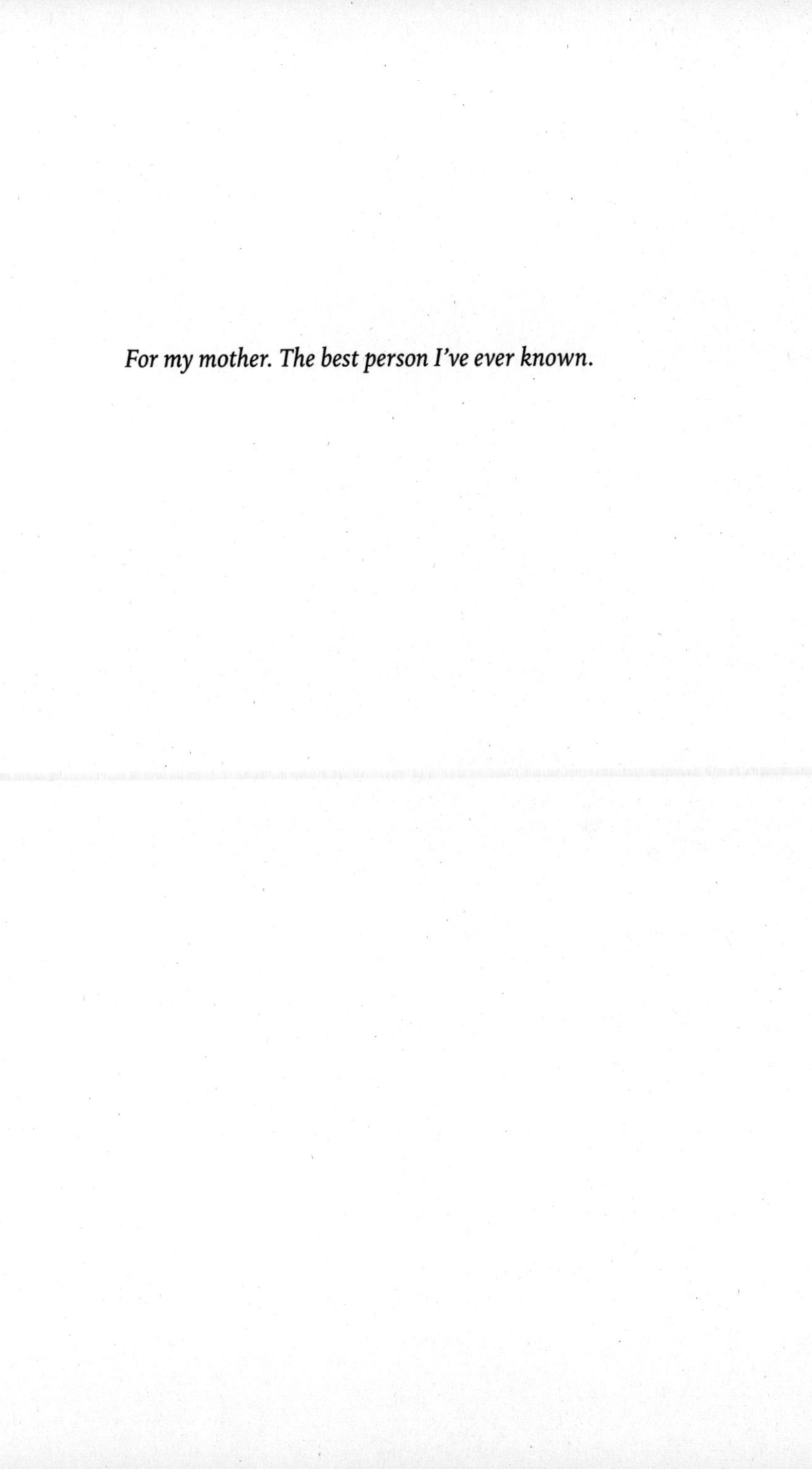

For my mother. The best person I've ever known.

Dear Reader:

The strikethroughs in the Shatter Me books are intentional. The writing in this series is occasionally as erratic as its main character, and serves as a visual representation of the chaos in Juliette's mind. The repetition, the hyperbolic language, the obsession with numbers—these are not errors on the page. As our heroine grows and evolves, so too does the prose, and as she finds her voice, the strikethroughs disappear, the language softens, the repetition dissolves, and the numerals ease into written words. This is, ultimately, a story of change. Thank you so much for reading.

ONE

The world might be sunny-side up today.

The big ball of yellow might be spilling into the clouds, runny and yolky and blurring into the bluest sky, bright with cold hope and false promises about fond memories, real families, hearty breakfasts, stacks of pancakes drizzled in maple syrup sitting on a plate in a world that doesn't exist anymore.

Or maybe not.

Maybe it's dark and wet today, whistling wind so sharp it stings the skin off the knuckles of grown men. Maybe it's snowing, maybe it's raining, I don't know maybe it's freezing it's hailing it's a hurricane slip slipping into a tornado and the earth is quaking apart to make room for our mistakes.

I wouldn't have any idea.

I don't have a window anymore. I don't have a view. It's a million degrees below zero in my blood and I'm buried 50 feet underground in a training room that's become my second home lately. Every day I stare at these 4 walls and remind myself *I'm not a prisoner I'm not a prisoner I'm not a prisoner* but sometimes the old fears streak across my skin and I can't seem to break free of the claustrophobia clutching at my throat.

I made so many promises when I arrived here.

Now I'm not so sure. Now I'm worried. Now my mind is a traitor because my thoughts crawl out of bed every morning with darting eyes and sweating palms and nervous giggles that sit in my chest, build in my chest, threaten to burst through my chest, and the pressure is tightening and tightening and *tightening*

Life around here isn't what I expected it to be.

My new world is etched in gunmetal, sealed in silver, drowning in the scents of stone and steel. The air is icy, the mats are orange; the lights and switches beep and flicker, electronic and electric, neon bright. It's busy here, busy with bodies, busy with halls stuffed full of whispers and shouts, pounding feet and thoughtful footsteps. If I listen closely I can hear the sounds of brains working and foreheads pinching and fingers tap tapping at chins and lips and furrowed brows. Ideas are carried in pockets, thoughts propped up on the tips of every tongue; eyes are narrowed in concentration, in careful planning I should want to know about.

But nothing is working and all my parts are broken.

I'm supposed to harness my Energy, Castle said. Our gifts are different forms of Energy. Matter is never created or destroyed, he said to me, and as our world changed, so did the Energy within it. Our abilities are taken from the universe, from other matter, from other Energies. We are not anomalies. We are inevitabilities of the perverse manipulations of our Earth. Our Energy came from somewhere, he said. And somewhere is in the chaos all around us.

It makes sense. I remember what the world looked like when I left it.

I remember the pissed-off skies and the sequence of sunsets collapsing beneath the moon. I remember the cracked earth and the scratchy bushes and the used-to-be-greens that are now too close to brown. I think about the water we can't drink and the birds that don't fly and how human civilization has been reduced to nothing but a series of compounds stretched out over what's left of our ravaged land.

This planet is a broken bone that didn't set right, a hundred pieces of crystal glued together. We've been shattered and reconstructed, told to make an effort every single day to pretend we still function the way we're supposed to. But it's a lie, it's all a lie.

I do not function properly.

I am nothing more than the consequence of catastrophe.

2 weeks have collapsed at the side of the road, abandoned, already forgotten. 2 weeks I've been here and in 2 weeks I've taken up residence on a bed of eggshells, wondering when something is going to break, when I'll be the first to break it, wondering when everything is going to fall apart. In 2 weeks I should've been happier, healthier, sleeping better, more soundly in this safe space. Instead I worry about what will happen ~~when~~ if I can't get this right, if I don't figure out how to train properly, if I hurt someone ~~on purpose~~ by accident.

We're preparing for a bloody war.

That's why I'm training. We're all trying to prepare

ourselves to take down Warner and his men. To win one battle at a time. To show the citizens of our world that there is hope yet—that they do not have to acquiesce to the demands of The Reestablishment and become slaves to a regime that wants nothing more than to exploit them for power. And I agreed to fight. To be a warrior. To use my power against my better judgment. But the thought of laying a hand on someone brings back a world of memories, feelings, a flush of power I experience only when I make contact with skin not immune to my own. It's a rush of invincibility; a tormented kind of euphoria; a wave of intensity flooding every pore in my body. I don't know what it will do to me. I don't know if I can trust myself to take pleasure in someone else's pain.

All I know is that Warner's last words are caught in my chest and I can't cough out the cold or the truth hacking at the back of my throat.

Adam has no idea that Warner can touch me.

No one does.

Warner was supposed to be dead. Warner was supposed to be dead because I was supposed to have shot him but no one supposed I'd need to know how to fire a gun so now I suppose he's come to find me.

He's come to fight.

For me.

TWO

A sharp knock and the door flies open.

"Ah, Ms. Ferrars. I don't know what you hope to accomplish by sitting in the corner." Castle's easy grin dances into the room before he does.

I take a tight breath and try to make myself look at Castle but I can't. Instead I whisper an apology and listen to the sorry sound my words make in this large room. I feel my shaking fingers clench against the thick, padded mats spread out across the floor and think about how I've accomplished nothing since I've been here. It's humiliating, so humiliating to disappoint one of the only people who's ever been kind to me.

Castle stands directly in front of me, waits until I finally look up. "There's no need to apologize," he says. His sharp, clear brown eyes and friendly smile make it easy to forget he's the leader of Omega Point. The leader of this entire underground movement dedicated to fighting The Reestablishment. His voice is too gentle, too kind, and it's almost worse. ~~Sometimes I wish he would just yell at me.~~ "But," he continues, "you do have to learn how to harness your Energy, Ms. Ferrars."

A pause.

A pace.

His hands rest on the stack of bricks I was supposed to have destroyed. He pretends not to notice the red rims around my eyes or the metal pipes I threw across the room. His gaze carefully avoids the bloody smears on the wooden planks set off to the side; his questions don't ask me why my fists are clenched so tight and whether or not I've injured myself again. He cocks his head in my direction but he's staring at a spot directly behind me and his voice is soft when he speaks. "I know this is difficult for you," he says. "But you must learn. You have to. Your life will depend upon it."

I nod, lean back against the wall, welcome the cold and the pain of the brick digging into my spine. I pull my knees up to my chest and feel my feet press into the protective mats covering the ground. I'm so close to tears I'm afraid I might scream. "I just don't know how," I finally say to him. "I don't know any of this. I don't even know what I'm supposed to be doing." I stare at the ceiling and blink blink blink. My eyes feel shiny, damp. "I don't know how to make things happen."

"Then you have to think," Castle says, undeterred. He picks up a discarded metal pipe. Weighs it in his hands. "You have to find links between the events that transpired. When you broke through the concrete in Warner's torture chamber—when you punched through the steel door to save Mr. Kent—what happened? Why in those two instances were you able to react in such an extraordinary way?" He sits down some feet away from me. Pushes the pipe in my direction. "I need you to analyze your abilities, Ms. Ferrars. You have to focus."

Focus.

It's one word but it's enough, it's all it takes to make me feel sick. Everyone, it seems, needs me to focus. First Warner needed me to focus, and now Castle needs me to focus.

I've never been able to follow through.

Castle's deep, sad sigh brings me back to the present. He gets to his feet. He smooths out the only navy-blue blazer he seems to own and I catch a glimpse of the silver Omega symbol embroidered into the back. An absent hand touches the end of his ponytail; he always ties his dreads in a clean knot at the base of his neck. "You are resisting yourself," he says, though he says it gently. "Maybe you should work with someone else for a change. Maybe a partner will help you work things out—to discover the connection between these two events."

My shoulders stiffen, surprised. "I thought you said I had to work alone."

He squints past me. Scratches a spot beneath his ear, shoves his other hand into a pocket. "I didn't actually want you to work alone," he says. "But no one volunteered for the task."

I don't know why I suck in my breath, why I'm so surprised. I shouldn't be surprised. Not everyone is Adam.

Not everyone is safe from me the way he is. No one but

Adam has ever touched me and enjoyed it. ~~No one except for Warner.~~ But despite Adam's best intentions, he can't train with me. He's busy with other things.

Things no one wants to tell me about.

But Castle is staring at me with hopeful eyes, generous eyes, eyes that have no idea that these new words he's offered me are so much worse. Worse because as much as I know the truth, it still hurts to hear it. It hurts to remember that though I might live in a warm bubble with Adam, the rest of the world still sees me as a threat. A monster. An abomination.

~~Warner was right. No matter where I go, I can't seem to run from this.~~

"What's changed?" I ask him. "Who's willing to train me now?" I pause. "You?"

Castle smiles.

It's the kind of smile that flushes humiliated heat up my neck and spears my pride right through the vertebrae. I have to resist the urge to bolt out the door.

~~Please please please do not pity me, is what I want to say.~~

"I wish I had the time," Castle says to me. "But Kenji is finally free—we were able to reorganize his schedule—and he said he'd be happy to work with you." A moment of hesitation. "That is, if that's all right with you."

Kenji.

I want to laugh out loud. Kenji *would* be the only one willing to risk working with me. I injured him once. By accident. But he and I haven't spent much time together since he first led our expedition into Omega Point. It was like he was just doing a task, fulfilling a mission; once complete, he went back to his own life. Apparently Kenji is important around here. He has a million things to do. Things to regulate. People seem to like him, respect him, even.

I wonder if they've ever known him as the obnoxious, foul-mouthed Kenji I first met.

"Sure," I tell Castle, attempting a pleasant expression for the first time since he arrived. "That sounds great."

Castle stands up. His eyes are bright, eager, easily pleased. "Perfect. I'll have him meet you at breakfast tomorrow. You can eat together and go from there."

"Oh but I usually—"

"I know." Castle cuts me off. His smile is pressed into a thin line now, his forehead creased with concern. "You like to eat your meals with Mr. Kent. I know this. But you've hardly spent any time with the others, Ms. Ferrars, and if you're going to be here, you need to start trusting us. The people of Omega Point feel close to Kenji. He can vouch for you. If everyone sees you spending time together, they'll feel less intimidated by your presence. It will help you adjust."

Heat like hot oil spatters across my face; I flinch, feel my fingers twitch, try to find a place to look, try to pretend I can't feel the pain caught in my chest. "They're—they're afraid of me," I tell him, I whisper, I trail off. "I don't—I didn't want to bother anyone. I didn't want to get in their way. . . ."

Castle sighs, long and loud. He looks down and up,

scratches the soft spot beneath his chin. "They're only afraid," he says finally, "because they don't know you. If you just tried a little harder—if you made even the smallest effort to get to know anyone—" He stops. Frowns. "Ms. Ferrars, you have been here two weeks and you hardly even speak to your roommates."

"But that's not—I think they're great—"

"And yet you ignore them? You spend no time with them? Why?"

~~Because I've never had girl friends before. Because I'm afraid I'll do something wrong, say something wrong and they'll end up hating me like all the other girls I've known. And I like them too much, which will make their inevitable rejection so much harder to endure.~~

I say nothing.

Castle shakes his head. "You did so well the first day you arrived. You seemed almost *friendly* with Brendan. I don't know what happened," Castle continues. "I thought you would do well here."

Brendan. The thin boy with platinum-blond hair and electric currents running through his veins. I remember him. He was nice to me. "I like Brendan," I tell Castle, bewildered. "Is he upset with me?"

"*Upset*?" Castle shakes his head, laughs out loud. He doesn't answer my question. "I don't understand, Ms. Ferrars. I've tried to be patient with you, I've tried to give you time, but I confess I'm quite perplexed. You were so different when you first arrived—you were excited to be here! But it took less than a week for you to withdraw completely. You don't even look at anyone when you walk through the halls. What happened to conversation? To friendship?"

Yes.

It took 1 day for me to settle in. 1 day for me to look around. 1 day for me to get excited about a different life and 1 day for everyone to find out who I am and what I've done.

Castle doesn't say anything about the mothers who see me walking down the hall and yank their children out of my way. He doesn't mention the hostile stares and the unwelcoming words I've endured since I've arrived. He doesn't say anything about the kids who've been warned to stay far, far away, and the handful of elderly people who watch me too closely. I can only imagine what they've heard, where they got their stories from.

Juliette.

A girl with a lethal touch that saps the strength and energy of human beings until they're limp, paralyzed carcasses wheezing on the floor. A girl who spent most of her life in hospitals and juvenile detention centers, a girl who was cast off by her own parents, labeled as certifiably insane, and sentenced to isolation in an asylum where even the rats were afraid to live.

A girl.

So power hungry that she killed a small child. She tortured a toddler. She brought a grown man gasping to his knees. She doesn't even have the decency to kill herself.

None of it is a lie.

So I look at Castle with spots of color on my cheeks and unspoken letters on my lips and eyes that refuse to reveal their secrets.

He sighs.

He almost says something. He tries to speak but his eyes inspect my face and he changes his mind. He only offers me a quick nod, a deep breath, taps his watch, says, "Three hours until lights-out," and turns to go.

Pauses in the doorway.

"Ms. Ferrars," he says suddenly, softly, without turning around. "You've chosen to stay with us, to fight with us, to become a member of Omega Point." A pause. "We're going to need your help. And I'm afraid we're running out of time."

I watch him leave.

I listen to his departing footsteps and lean my head back against the wall. Close my eyes against the ceiling. Hear his voice, solemn and steady, ringing in my ears.

We're running out of time, he said.

As if time were the kind of thing you could run out of, as if it were measured into bowls that were handed to us at birth and if we ate too much or too fast or right before jumping into the water then our time would be lost, wasted, already spent.

But time is beyond our finite comprehension. It's endless, it exists outside of us; we cannot run out of it or lose track of it or find a way to hold on to it. Time goes on even when we do not.

We have plenty of time, is what Castle should have said.

We have all the time in the world, is what he should have said to me. But he didn't because what he meant *tick tock* is that our time *tick tock* is shifting. It's hurtling forward heading in an entirely new direction slamming face-first into something else and

tick
tick
tick
tick
tick
it's almost

time for war.

THREE

I could touch him from here.

His eyes, dark blue. His hair, dark brown. His shirt, too tight in all the right places and his lips, his lips twitch up to flick the switch that lights the fire in my heart and I don't even have time to blink and exhale before I'm caught in his arms.

Adam.

"Hey, you," he whispers, right up against my neck.

I bite back a shiver as the blood rushes up to blush my cheeks and for a moment, just for this moment, I drop my bones and allow him to hold me together. "Hey." I smile, inhaling the scent of him.

Luxurious, is what this is.

We rarely ever see each other alone. Adam is staying in Kenji's room with his little brother, James, and I bunk with the healer twins. We probably have less than 20 minutes before the girls get back to this room, and I intend to make the most of this opportunity.

My eyes fall shut.

Adam's arms wrap around my waist, pulling me closer, and the pleasure is so tremendous I can hardly keep myself from shaking. It's like my skin and bones have been craving contact, warm affection, human interaction for so many years that I don't know how to pace myself. I'm a starving child trying to stuff my stomach, gorging my senses on the decadence of these moments as if I'll wake up in the morning and realize I'm still sweeping cinders for my stepmother.

But then Adam's lips press against my head and my worries put on a fancy dress and pretend to be something else for a while.

"How are you?" I ask, and it's so embarrassing because my words are already unsteady even though he's hardly held me but I can't make myself let go.

Laughter shakes the shape of his body, soft and rich and indulgent. But he doesn't respond to my question and I know he won't.

We've tried so many times to sneak off together, only to be caught and chastised for our negligence. We are not allowed outside of our rooms after lights-out. Once our grace period—a leniency granted on account of our very abrupt arrival—ended, Adam and I had to follow the rules just like everyone else. And there are a lot of rules to follow.

These security measures—cameras everywhere, around every corner, in every hallway—exist to prepare us in the case of an attack. Guards patrol at night, looking for any suspicious noise, activity, or sign of a breach. Castle and his team are vigilant in protecting Omega Point, and they're unwilling to take even the slightest risks; if trespassers get too close to this hideout, someone has to do anything and everything necessary to keep them away.

Castle claims it's their very vigilance that's kept them from discovery for so long, and if I'm perfectly honest, I can see his rationale in being so strict about it. But these same strict measures keep me and Adam apart. He and I never see each other except during mealtimes, when we're always surrounded by other people, and any free time I have is spent locked in a training room where I'm supposed to "harness my Energy." Adam is just as unhappy about it as I am.

I touch his cheek.

He takes a tight breath. Turns to me. Tells me too much with his eyes, so much that I have to look away because I feel it all too acutely. My skin is hypersensitive, finally finally finally awake and thrumming with life, humming with feelings so intense it's almost indecent.

I can't even hide it.

He sees what he does to me, what happens to me when his fingers graze my skin, when his lips get too close to my face, when the heat of his body against mine forces my eyes to close and my limbs to tremble and my knees to buckle under pressure. I see what it does to him, too, to know that he has that effect on me. He tortures me sometimes, smiling as he takes too long to bridge the gap between us, reveling in the sound of my heart slamming against my chest, in the sharp breaths I fight so hard to control, in the way I swallow a hundred times just before he moves to kiss me. I can't even look at him without reliving every moment we've had together, every memory of his lips, his touch, his scent, his skin. It's too much for me, too much, so much, so new, so many exquisite sensations I've never known, never felt, never even had access to before.

~~Sometimes I'm afraid it will kill me.~~

I break free of his arms; I'm hot and cold and feeling unsteady, hoping I can get myself under control, hoping he'll forget how easily he affects me, and I know I need a moment to pull myself together. I stumble backward; I cover my face with my hands and try to think of something to say but everything is shaking and I catch him looking at me, looking like he might inhale the length of me in one breath.

No is the word I think I hear him whisper.

All I know next are his arms, the desperate edge to his voice when he says my name, and I'm unraveling in his embrace, I'm frayed and falling apart and I'm making no effort to control the tremors in my bones and he's so hot his skin is so hot and I don't even know where I am anymore.

His right hand slides up my spine and tugs on the zipper holding my suit together until it's halfway down my back and I don't care. I have 17 years to make up for and I want to feel everything. I'm not interested in waiting around and risking the who-knows and the what-ifs and the huge regrets. I want to feel all of it because what if I wake up to find this phenomenon has passed, that the expiration date has arrived, that my chance came and went and would never return. That these hands will feel this warmth never again.

I can't.

I won't.

I don't even realize I've pressed myself into him until

I feel every contour of his frame under the thin cotton of his clothes. My hands slip up under his shirt and I hear his strained breath; I look up to find his eyes squeezed shut, his features caught in an expression resembling some kind of pain and suddenly his hands are in my hair, desperate, his lips so close. He leans in and gravity moves out of his way and my feet leave the floor and I'm floating, I'm flying, I'm anchored by nothing but this hurricane in my lungs and this heart beating a skip a skip a skip too fast.

Our lips

touch

and I know I'm going to split at the seams. He's kissing me like he's lost me and he's found me and I'm slipping away and he's never going to let me go. I want to scream, sometimes, I want to collapse, sometimes, I want to die knowing that I've known what it was like to live with this kiss, this heart, this soft soft explosion that makes me feel like I've taken a sip of the sun, like I've eaten clouds 8, 9, and 10.

This.

This makes me ache everywhere.

He pulls away, he's breathing hard, his hands slip under the soft material of my suit and he's so hot his skin is so hot and I think I've already said that but I can't remember and I'm so distracted that when he speaks I don't quite understand.

But it's something.

Words, deep and husky in my ear but I catch little more than an unintelligible utterance, consonants and vowels and broken syllables all mixed together. His heartbeats crash through his chest and topple into mine. His fingers are tracing secret messages on my body. His hands glide down the smooth, satiny material of this suit, slipping down the insides of my thighs, around the backs of my knees and up and up and up and I wonder if it's possible to faint and still be conscious at the same time and I'm betting this is what it feels like to hyper, to hyperventilate when he tugs us backward. He slams his back into the wall. Finds a firm grip on my hips. Pulls me hard against his body.

I gasp.

His lips are on my neck. His lashes tickle the skin under my chin and he says something, something that sounds like my name and he kisses up and down my collarbone, kisses along the arc of my shoulder, and his lips, his lips and his hands and his lips are searching the curves and slopes of my body and his chest is heaving when he swears and he stops and he says *God you feel so good*

and my heart has flown to the moon without me.

I love it when he says that to me. I love it when he tells me that he likes the way I feel because it goes against everything I've heard my entire life and I wish I could put his words in my pocket just to touch them once in a while and remind myself that they exist.

"Juliette."

I can hardly breathe.

I can hardly look up and look straight and see anything but the absolute perfection of this moment but none of that even matters because he's smiling. He's smiling like someone's strung the stars across his lips and he's looking at me, looking at me like I'm *everything* and I want to weep.

"Close your eyes," he whispers.

And I trust him.

So I do.

My eyes fall closed and he kisses one, then the other. Then my chin, my nose, my forehead. My cheeks. Both temples.

Every

inch

of my neck

and

he pulls back so quickly he bangs his head against the rough wall. A few choice words slip out before he can stop them. I'm frozen, startled and suddenly scared. "What happened?" I whisper, and I don't know why I'm whispering. "Are you okay?"

Adam fights not to grimace but he's breathing hard and looking around and stammering "S-sorry" as he clutches the back of his head. "That was—I mean I thought—" He looks away. Clears his throat. "I—I think—I thought I heard something. I thought someone was about to come inside."

Of course.

Adam is not allowed to be in here.

The guys and the girls stay in different wings at Omega Point. Castle says it's mostly to make sure the girls feel safe and comfortable in their living quarters—especially because we have communal bathrooms—so for the most part, I don't have a problem with it. It's nice not to have to shower with old men. But it makes it hard for the two of us to find any time together—and during whatever time we do manage to scrounge up, we're always hyperaware of being discovered.

Adam leans back against the wall and winces. I reach up to touch his head.

He flinches.

I freeze.

"Are you okay . . . ?"

"Yeah." He sighs. "I just—I mean—" He shakes his head. "I don't know." Drops his voice. His eyes. "I don't know what the hell is wrong with me."

"Hey." I brush my fingertips against his stomach. The cotton of his shirt is still warm from his body heat and I have to resist the urge to bury my face in it. "It's okay," I tell him. "You were just being careful."

He smiles a strange, sad sort of smile. "I'm not talking about my head."

I stare at him.

He opens his mouth. Closes it. Pries it open again. "It's—I mean, *this*—" He motions between us.

He won't finish. He won't look at me.

"I don't understand—"

"I'm losing my *mind*," he says, but whispers it like he's not sure he's even saying it out loud.

I look at him. I look and blink and trip on words I can't

see and can't find and can't speak.

He's shaking his head.

He grips the back of his skull, hard, and he looks embarrassed and I'm struggling to understand why. Adam doesn't get embarrassed. Adam never gets embarrassed.

His voice is thick when he finally speaks. "I've waited so long to be with you," he says. "I've wanted this—I've wanted *you* for so long and now, after everything—"

"Adam, what are y—"

"I can't *sleep*. I can't sleep and I think about you all—all the time and I can't—" He stops. Presses the heels of his hands to his forehead. Squeezes his eyes shut. Turns toward the wall so I can't see his face. "You should know—you have to know," he says, the words raw, seeming to drain him, "that I have never wanted anything like I've wanted you. Nothing. Because this—this—I mean, God, I *want* you, Juliette, I want—I want—"

His words falter as he turns to me, eyes too bright, emotion flushing up the planes of his face. His gaze lingers along the lines of my body, long enough to strike a match to the lighter fluid flowing in my veins.

I ignite.

I want to say something, something right and steady and reassuring. I want to tell him that I understand, that I want the same thing, that I want him, too, but the moment feels so charged and urgent that I'm half convinced I'm dreaming. It's like I'm down to my last letters and all I have are Qs and Zs and I've only just remembered that someone invented a dictionary when he finally rips his eyes away from me.

He swallows, hard, his eyes down. Looks away again. One of his hands is caught in his hair, the other is curled into a fist against the wall. "You have no idea," he says, his voice ragged, "what you do to me. What you make me feel. When you *touch* me—" He runs a shaky hand across his face. He almost laughs, but his breathing is heavy and uneven; he won't meet my eyes. He steps back, swears under his breath. Pumps his fist against his forehead. "Jesus. What the hell am I saying. Shit. *Shit*. I'm sorry—forget that—forget I said anything—I should go—"

I try to stop him, try to find my voice, try to say, It's all right, it's okay, but I'm nervous now, so nervous, so confused, because none of this makes any sense. I don't understand what's happening or why he seems so uncertain about me and us and him and me and he and I and all of those pronouns put together. I'm not rejecting him. I've never rejected him. My feelings for him have always been so clear—he has no reason to feel unsure about me or around me and I don't know why he's looking at me like something is *wrong*—

"I'm so sorry," he says. "I'm—I shouldn't have said anything. I'm just—I'm—*shit*. I shouldn't have come. I should go—I have to go—"

"What? Adam, what happened? What are you talking about?"

"This was a bad idea," he says. "I'm so stupid—I shouldn't have even been here—"

"You are *not* stupid—it's okay—everything is okay—"

He laughs, loud, hollow. The echo of an uncomfortable smile lingers on his face as he stops, stares at a point directly behind my head. He says nothing for a long time, until finally he does. "Well," he says. He tries to sound upbeat. "That's not what Castle thinks."

"What?" I breathe, caught off guard. I know we're not talking about our relationship anymore.

"Yeah." His hands are in his pockets.

"No."

Adam nods. Shrugs. Looks at me and looks away. "I don't know. I think so."

"But the testing—it's—I mean"—I can't stop shaking my head—"has he found something?"

Adam won't look at me.

"Oh my God," I say, and I whisper it like if I whisper, it'll somehow make this easier. "So it's true? Castle's right?" My voice is inching higher and my muscles are beginning to tighten and I don't know why this feels like fear, this feeling slithering up my back. I shouldn't be afraid if Adam has a gift like I do; I should've known it couldn't have been that easy, that it couldn't have been so simple. This was Castle's theory all along—that Adam can touch me because he too has some kind of Energy that allows it. Castle never thought Adam's immunity from my ability was a happy coincidence. He thought it had to be bigger than that, more scientific than that, more specific than that. ~~I always wanted to believe I just got lucky.~~

And Adam wanted to know. He was excited about finding out, actually.

But once he started testing with Castle, Adam stopped wanting to talk about it. He's never given me more than the barest status updates. The excitement of the experience faded far too fast for him.

Something is wrong.

Something is *wrong*.

~~Of course it is.~~

"We don't know anything conclusive," Adam tells me, but I can see he's holding back. "I have to do a couple more sessions—Castle says there are a few more things he needs to . . . examine."

I don't miss the mechanical way Adam is delivering this information. Something isn't right and I can't believe I didn't notice the signs until just now. I haven't wanted to, I realize. I haven't wanted to admit to myself that Adam looks more exhausted, more strained, more tightly wound than I've ever seen him. Anxiety has built a home on his shoulders.

"Adam—"

"Don't worry about me." His words aren't harsh, but there's an undercurrent of urgency in his tone I can't ignore, and he pulls me into his arms before I find a chance to speak. His fingers work to zip up my suit. "I'm fine," he says. "Really. I just want to know you're okay. If you're all right here, then I am too. Everything is fine." His breath catches. "Okay? Everything is going to be fine." The shaky smile on his face is making my pulse forget it has a job to do.

"Okay." It takes me a moment to find my voice. "Okay sure but—"

The door opens and Sonya and Sara are halfway into the room before they freeze, eyes fixed on our bodies wound together.

"Oh!" Sara says.

"Um." Sonya looks down.

Adam swears under his breath.

"We can come back later—," the twins say together.

They're headed out the door when I stop them. I won't kick them out of their own room.

I ask them not to leave.

They ask me if I'm sure.

I take one look at Adam's face and know I'm going to regret forfeiting even a minute of our time together, but I also know I can't take advantage of my roommates. This is their personal space, and it's almost time for lights-out. They can't be wandering the corridors.

Adam isn't looking at me anymore, but he's not letting go, either. I lean forward and leave a light kiss on his heart. He finally meets my eyes. Offers me a small, pained smile.

"I love you," I tell him, quietly, so only he can hear me.

He exhales a short, uneven breath. Whispers, "You have no idea," and pulls himself away. Pivots on one heel. Heads out the door.

My heart is beating in my throat.

The girls are staring at me. Concerned.
Sonya is about to speak, but then

a switch
a click
a flicker

and the lights are out.

FOUR

The dreams are back.

They'd left me for a while, shortly after I'd been freshly imprisoned on base with Warner. I thought I'd lost the bird, the white bird, the bird with streaks of gold like a crown atop its head. It used to meet me in my dreams, flying strong and smooth, sailing over the world like it knew better, like it had secrets we'd never suspect, like it was leading me somewhere safe. It was my one piece of hope in the bitter darkness of the asylum, just until I met its twin tattooed on Adam's chest.

It was like it flew right out of my dreams only to rest atop his heart. I thought it was a signal, a message telling me I was finally safe. That I'd flown away and finally found peace, sanctuary.

I didn't expect to see the bird again.

But now it's back and looks exactly the same. It's the same white bird in the same blue sky with the same yellow crown. Only this time, it's frozen. Flapping its wings in place like it's been caught in an invisible cage, like it's destined to repeat the same motion forever. The bird *seems* to be flying: it's in the air; its wings work. It looks as if it's free to soar through the skies. But it's stuck.

Unable to fly upward.

Unable to fall.

I've had the same dream every night for the past week, and all 7 mornings I've woken up shaking, shuddering into the earthy, icy air, struggling to steady the bleating in my chest.

Struggling to understand what this means.

I crawl out of bed and slip into the same suit I wear every day; the only article of clothing I own anymore. It's the richest shade of purple, so plum it's almost black. It has a slight sheen, a bit of a shimmer in the light. It's one piece from neck to wrists to ankles and it's skintight without being tight at all.

I move like a gymnast in this outfit.

I have springy leather ankle boots that mold to the shape of my feet and render me soundless as I pad across the floor. I have black leather gloves that prevent me from touching something I'm not supposed to. Sonya and Sara lent me one of their hair ties and for the first time in years I've been able to pull my hair out of my face. I wear it in a high ponytail and I've learned to zip myself up without help from anyone. This suit makes me feel extraordinary. It makes me feel invincible.

It was a gift from Castle.

He had it custom-made for me before I arrived at Omega Point. He thought I might like to finally have an outfit that would protect me from myself and others while simultaneously offering me the option of *hurting* others. If I wanted to. Or needed to. The suit is made of some kind of special material that's supposed to keep me cool in the heat and keep me warm in the cold. So far it's been perfect.

~~So far so far so far~~

I head to breakfast by myself.

Sonya and Sara are always gone by the time I'm awake. Their work in the medical wing is never-ending—not only are they able to heal the wounded but they also spend their days trying to create antidotes and ointments. The one time we ever had a conversation, Sonya explained to me how some Energies can be depleted if we exert ourselves too much—how we can exhaust our bodies enough that they'll just break down. The girls say that they want to be able to create medicines to use in the case of multiple injuries they can't heal all at once. They are, after all, only 2 people. And war seems imminent.

Heads still spin in my direction when I walk into the dining hall.

I am a spectacle, an anomaly even among the anomalies. I should be used to it by now, after all these years. I should be tougher, jaded, indifferent to the opinions of others.

~~I should be a lot of things.~~

I clear my eyes and keep my hands to my sides and pretend I'm unable to make eye contact with anything but that spot, that little mark on the wall 50 feet from where I'm standing.

I pretend I'm just a number.

No emotions on my face. Lips perfectly still. Back straight, hands unclenched. I am a robot, a ghost slipping through the crowds.

6 steps forward. 15 tables to pass. 42 43 44 seconds and counting.

~~I am scared~~

~~I am scared~~

~~I am scared~~

I am strong.

Food is served at only 3 times throughout the day: breakfast from 7:00 to 8:00 a.m., lunch from 12:00 to 1:00 p.m., and dinner from 5:00 to 7:00 p.m. Dinner is an hour longer because it's at the end of the day; it's like our reward for working hard. But mealtimes aren't a fancy, luxurious event—the experience is very different from dining with Warner. Here we just stand in a long line, pick up our prefilled bowls, and head toward the eating area—which is nothing more than a series of rectangular tables arranged in parallel lines across the room. Nothing superfluous so nothing is wasted.

I spot Adam standing in line and head in his direction.

68 69 70 seconds and counting.

"Hey, gorgeous." Something lumpy hits me in the back. Falls to the floor. I turn around, my face flexing the 43 muscles required to frown before I see him.

Kenji.

Big, easy smile. Eyes the color of onyx. Hair even darker, sharper, stick-straight and slipping into his eyes. His jaw is twitching and his lips are twitching and the impressive lines of his cheekbones are appled up into a smile struggling to stay suppressed. He's looking at me like I've been walking around with toilet paper in my hair and I can't help but wonder why I haven't spent time with him since we got here. He did, on a purely technical level, save my life. And Adam's life. James', too.

Kenji bends down to pick up what looks like a wadded ball of socks. He weighs them in his hand like he's considering throwing them at me again. "Where are you going?" he says. "I thought you were supposed to meet me here? Castle said—"

"Why did you bring a pair of socks in here?" I cut him off. "People are trying to eat."

He freezes for only a split second before he rolls his eyes. Pulls up beside me. Tugs on my ponytail. "I was running late to meet *you*, your highness. I didn't have time to put my socks on." He gestures to the socks in his hand and the boots on his feet.

"That's so gross."

"You know, you have a really strange way of telling me you're attracted to me."

I shake my head, try to bite back my amusement. Kenji is a walking paradox of Unflinchingly Serious Person and 12-Year-Old Boy Going Through Puberty all rolled into one. But I'd forgotten how much easier it is to breathe around him; it seems natural to laugh when he's near. So I keep walking and I'm careful not to say a word, but a smile is still tugging at my lips as I grab a tray and head into the heart of the kitchen.

Kenji is half a step behind me. "So. We're working together today."

"Yup."

"So, what—you just walk right past me? Don't even say hello?" He clutches the socks to his chest. "I'm crushed. I saved us a table and everything."

I glance at him. Keep walking.

He catches up. "I'm serious. Do you have any idea how awkward it is to wave at someone and have them ignore you? And then you're just looking around like a jackass, trying to be all, 'No, really, I swear, I know that girl' and no one believes y—"

"Are you kidding?" I stop in the middle of the kitchen. Spin around. My face is pulled together in disbelief. "You've spoken to me maybe *once* in the two weeks I've been here. I hardly even notice you anymore."

"Okay, hold up," he says, turning to block my path. "We *both* know there's no way you haven't noticed all of *this*"—he gestures to himself—"so if you're trying to play games with me, I should let you know up front that it's not going to work."

"What?" I frown. "What are you talking abou—"

"You can't play hard to get, kid." He raises an eyebrow. "I can't even *touch* you. Takes 'hard to get' to a whole new level, if you know what I mean."

"Oh my God," I mouth, eyes closed, shaking my head. "You are *insane*."

He falls to his knees. "Insane for your sweet, sweet love!"

"Kenji!" I can't lift my eyes because I'm afraid to look around, but I'm desperate for him to stop talking. To put an entire room between us at all times. I know he's joking, but I might be the only one.

"What?" he says, his voice booming around the room. "Does my love embarrass you?"

"Please—*please* get up—and lower your *voice*—"

"Hell no."

"Why not?" I'm pleading now.

"Because if I lower my voice, I won't be able to hear myself speak. And that," he says, "is my favorite part."

I can't even look at him.

"Don't deny me, Juliette. I'm a lonely man."

"What is *wrong* with you?"

"You're breaking my heart." His voice is even louder now, his arms making sad, sweeping gestures that almost hit me as I back away, panicked. But then I realize everyone is watching him.

Entertained.

I manage an awkward smile as I glance around the room and I'm surprised to find that no one is looking at me now. They're all grinning, clearly accustomed to Kenji's antics, staring at him with a mixture of adoration and something else.

Adam is staring, too. He's standing with his tray in his hands, his head cocked and his eyes confused. He smiles a tentative sort of smile when our gazes meet.

I head toward him.

"Hey—wait up, kid." Kenji jumps up to grab my arm. "You know I was just messing with—" He follows my eyes to where Adam is standing. Slaps a palm to his forehead. "Of *course*! How could I forget? You're in love with my roommate."

I turn to face him. "Listen, I'm grateful you're going to help me train now—really, I am. Thank you for that. But you can't go around proclaiming your fake love to me—especially not in front of Adam—and you have to let me cross this room before the breakfast hour is over, okay? I hardly ever get to see him."

Kenji nods very slowly, looks a little solemn. "You're right. I'm sorry. I get it."

"Thank you."

"Adam is jealous of our love."

"Just go get your food!" I push him, hard, fighting back an exasperated laugh.

Kenji is one of the only people here—with the exception of Adam, of course—who isn't afraid to touch me. In truth, no one really has anything to fear when I'm wearing this suit, but I usually take my gloves off when I eat and my reputation is always walking 5 feet ahead of me. People keep their distance. And even though I accidentally attacked Kenji once, he's not afraid. I think it would take an astronomical amount of something horrible to get him down.

I admire that about him.

Adam doesn't say much when we meet. He doesn't have

to say more than "Hey," because his lips quirk up on one side and I can already see him standing a little taller, a little tighter, a little tenser. And I don't know much about anything in this world but I do know how to read the book written in his eyes.

The way he looks at me.

His eyes are heavy now in a way that worries me, but his gaze is still so tender, so focused and full of feeling that I can hardly keep myself out of his arms when I'm around him. I find myself watching him do the simplest things—shifting his weight, grabbing a tray, nodding good morning to someone—just to track the movement of his body. My moments with him are so few that my chest is always too tight, my heart too spastic. He makes me want to be impractical all the time.

He never lets go of my hand.

"You okay?" I ask him, still feeling a little apprehensive about the night before.

He nods. Tries to smile. "Yeah. I, uh . . ." Clears his throat. Takes a deep breath. Looks away. "Yeah, I'm sorry about last night. I kind of . . . I freaked out a little."

"About what, though?"

He's looking over my shoulder. Frowning.

"Adam . . . ?"

"Yeah?"

"Why were you freaked out?"

His eyes meet mine again. Wide. Round. "What? Nothing."

"I don't understa—"

"Why the hell are you guys taking so long?"

I spin around. Kenji is standing just behind me, so much food piled on his tray I'm surprised no one said anything. He must've convinced the cooks to give him extra.

"Well?" Kenji is staring, unblinking, waiting for us to respond. He finally cocks his head backward, in a motion that says *follow me,* before walking away.

Adam blows out his breath and looks so distracted that I decide to drop the subject of last night. Soon. We'll talk soon. I'm sure it's nothing. I'm sure it's nothing at all.

We'll talk soon and everything is going to be fine.

FIVE

Kenji is waiting for us at an empty table.

James used to join us at mealtimes, but now he's friends with the handful of younger kids at Omega Point, and prefers sitting with them. He seems the happiest of all of us to be here—and I'm happy he's happy—but I have to admit I miss his company. I'm afraid to mention it though; sometimes I'm not sure if I want to know why he doesn't spend time with Adam when I'm around. ~~I don't think I want to know if the other kids managed to convince him that I'm dangerous. I mean, I *am* dangerous, but I just~~

Adam sits down on the bench seat and I slide in next to him. Kenji sits across from us. Adam and I hide our linked hands under the table and I allow myself to enjoy the simple luxury of his proximity. I'm still wearing my gloves but just being this close to him is enough; flowers are blooming in my stomach, the soft petals tickling every inch of my nervous system. It's like I've been granted 3 wishes: to touch, to taste, to feel. It's the strangest phenomenon. A crazy happy impossibility wrapped in tissue paper, tied with a bow, tucked away in my heart.

~~It often feels like a privilege I don't deserve.~~

Adam shifts so the length of his leg is pressed against mine.

I look up to find him smiling at me, a secret, tiny sort of smile that says so many things, the kinds of things no one should be saying at a breakfast table. I force myself to breathe as I suppress a grin. I turn to focus on my food. Hope I'm not blushing.

Adam leans into my ear. I feel the soft whispers of his breath just before he begins to speak.

"You guys are disgusting, you know that, right?"

I look up, startled, and find Kenji frozen midmovement, his spoon halfway to his mouth, his head cocked in our direction. He gestures with his spoon at our faces. "What the hell is this? You guys playing footsie under the table or someshit?"

Adam moves away from me, just an inch or 2, and exhales a deep, irritated sigh. "You know, if you don't like it, you can leave." He nods at the tables around us. "No one asked you to sit here."

This is Adam making a concerted effort to be nice to Kenji. The 2 of them were friends back on base, but somehow Kenji knows exactly how to provoke Adam. I almost forget for a moment that they're roommates.

I wonder what it must be like for them to live together.

"That's bullshit and you know it," Kenji says. "I told you this morning that I had to sit with you guys. Castle wants me to help the two of you *adjust*." He snorts. Nods in my direction. "Listen, I don't have a clue what you see in this guy," he says, "but you should try living with him. The man is moody as hell."

"I am not *moody*—"

"Yeah, bro." Kenji puts his utensils down. "You are *moody*. It's always 'Shut up, Kenji.' 'Go to sleep, Kenji.' 'No one wants to see you naked, Kenji.' When I know for a *fact* that there are thousands of people who would love to see me naked—"

"How long do you have to sit here?" Adam looks away, rubs his eyes with his free hand.

Kenji sits up straighter. Picks up his spoon only to stab it through the air again. "*You* should consider yourself lucky that I'm sitting at your table. I'm making you cool by association."

I feel Adam tense beside me and decide to intervene. "Hey, can we talk about something else?"

Kenji grunts. Rolls his eyes. Shovels another spoonful of breakfast into his mouth.

I'm worried.

Now that I'm paying closer attention, I can see the weariness in Adam's eyes, the heaviness in his brow, the stiff set of his shoulders. I can't help but wonder what he's going through. What he's not telling me. I tug on Adam's hand a little and he turns to me.

"You sure you're okay?" I whisper. I feel like I keep asking him the same question over and over and over

His eyes immediately soften, looking tired but slightly amused. His hand releases mine under the table just to rest on my lap, just to slip down my thigh, and I almost lose control of my vocabulary before he leaves a light kiss in my hair. I swallow too hard, almost drop my fork on the floor. It takes me a moment to remember that he hasn't actually answered my question. It's not until he's looked away, staring at his food, when he finally nods, says, "I'm okay." But I'm not breathing and his hand is still tracing patterns on my leg.

"Ms. Ferrars? Mr. Kent?"

I sit up so fast I slam my knuckles under the table at the sound of Castle's voice. There's something about his presence that makes me feel like he's my teacher, like I've been caught misbehaving in class. Adam, on the other hand, doesn't seem remotely startled.

I cling to Adam's fingers as I lift my head.

Castle is standing over our table and Kenji is leaving to deposit his bowl in the kitchen. He claps Castle on the back like they're old friends and Castle flashes Kenji a warm smile as he passes.

"I'll be right back," Kenji shouts over his shoulder, twisting to flash us an overly enthusiastic thumbs-up. "Try not to get naked in front of everyone, okay? There are kids in here."

I cringe and glance at Adam but he seems oddly focused on his food. He hasn't said a word since Castle arrived.

I decide to answer for the both of us. Paste on a bright smile. "Good morning."

Castle nods, touches the lapel of his blazer; his stature is strong and poised. He beams at me. "I just came to say hello and to check in. I'm so happy to see that you're expanding your circle of friends, Ms. Ferrars."

"Oh. Thank you. But I can't take credit for the idea," I point out. "You're the one who told me to sit with Kenji."

Castle's smile is a little too tight. "Yes. Well," he says, "I'm happy to see that you took my advice."

I nod at my food. Rub absently at my forehead. Adam looks like he's not even breathing. I'm about to say something when Castle cuts me off. "So, Mr. Kent," he says. "Did Ms. Ferrars tell you she'll be training with Kenji now? I'm hoping it will help her progress."

Adam doesn't answer.

Castle soldiers on. "I actually thought it might be interesting for her to work with you, too. As long as I'm there to supervise."

Adam's eyes snap up to attention. Alarmed. "What are you talking about?"

"Well—" Castle pauses. I watch his gaze shift between the two of us. "I thought it would be interesting to run some tests on you and her. Together."

Adam stands up so quickly he almost bangs his knee into the table. "Absolutely not."

"Mr. Kent—," Castle starts.

"There's no chance in *hell*—"

"It's her choice to make—"

"I don't want to discuss this here—"

I jump to my feet. Adam looks ready to set something on fire. His fists are clenched at his sides, his eyes narrowed into a tight glare; his forehead is taut, his entire frame shaking with energy and anxiety.

"What is going on?" I demand.

Castle shakes his head. He's not addressing me when he speaks. "I only want to see what happens when she touches you. That's it."

"Are you *insane*—"

"This is for *her*," Castle continues, his voice careful, extra calm. "It has nothing to do with your progress—"

"What progress?" I cut in.

"We're just trying to help her figure out how to affect nonliving organisms," Castle is saying. "Animals and humans we've figured out—we know one touch is sufficient. Plants don't seem to factor into her abilities at all. But everything else? It's . . . different. She doesn't know how to handle that part yet, and I want to help her. That's all we're doing," he says. "Helping Ms. Ferrars."

Adam takes a step closer to me. "If you're helping her figure out how to destroy nonliving things, why do you need me?"

For a second Castle actually looks defeated. "I don't really know," he says. "The unique nature of your relationship—it's quite fascinating. Especially with everything we've learned so far, it's—"

"What have you learned?" I jump in again.

"—entirely possible," Castle is still saying, "that everything is connected in a way we don't yet understand."

Adam looks unconvinced. His lips are pressed into a thin line. He doesn't look like he wants to answer.

Castle turns to me. Tries to sound excited. "What do you think? Are you interested?"

"Interested?" I look at Castle. "I don't even know what you're talking about. And I want to know why no one is answering my questions. What have you discovered about Adam?" I ask. "What's wrong? Is something wrong?" Adam is breathing extra hard and trying not to show it; his hands keep clenching and unclenching. "Someone, please, tell me what's going on."

Castle frowns.

He's studying me, confused, his eyebrows pulled together. "Mr. Kent," he says, still looking at me. "Am I to understand that you have not yet shared our discoveries with Ms. Ferrars?"

"What discoveries?" My heart is racing hard now, so hard it's beginning to hurt.

"Mr. Kent—"

"That's none of your business," Adam snaps.

"She should *know*—"

"We don't know anything yet!"

"We know enough."

"Bullshit. We're not done yet—"

"The only thing left is to test the two of you together—"

Adam steps directly in front of Castle, grabbing his breakfast tray with a little too much strength. "Maybe," he says very, very carefully, "some other time."

He turns to leave.

I touch his arm.

He stops. Drops his tray, pivots in my direction. There's less than half an inch between us and I almost forget we're standing in a crowded room. His breath is hot and his breathing shallow and the heat from his body is melting my blood only to splash it across my cheeks.

Panic is doing backflips in my bones.

"Everything is fine," he says. "Everything is going to be fine. I promise."

"But—"

"I promise," he says again, grabbing my hand. "I swear. I'm going to fix this—"

"Fix this?" I think I'm dreaming. I think I'm dying. "Fix what?" Something is breaking in my brain and something is happening without my permission and I'm lost, I'm so lost, I'm so much everything confused and I'm drowning in confusion. "Adam, I don't underst—"

"I mean, really though?" Kenji is making his way back to our group. "You're going to do that here? In front of everyone? Because these tables aren't as comfortable as they look—"

Adam pulls back and slams into Kenji's shoulder on his way out.

"Don't."

Is all I hear him say before he disappears.

SIX

Kenji lets out a low whistle.

Castle is calling Adam's name, asking him to slow down, to speak to him, to discuss things in a rational manner. Adam never looks back.

"I told you he was moody," Kenji mutters.

"He's not moody," I hear myself say, but the words feel distant, disconnected from my lips. I feel numb, like my arms have been hollowed out.

Where did I leave my voice I can't find my voice I can't find my

"So! You and me, huh?" Kenji claps his hands together. "Ready to get your ass kicked?"

"Kenji."

"Yeah?"

"I want you to take me to wherever they went."

Kenji is looking at me like I've just asked him to kick himself in the face. "Uh, yeah—how about a warm *hell no* to that request? Does that work for you? Because it works for me."

"I need to know what's going on." I turn to him, desperate, feeling stupid. "You know, don't you? You know what's wrong—"

"Of course I know." He crosses his arms. Levels a look at me. "I *live* with that poor bastard and I practically run this place. I know everything."

"So why won't you tell me? Kenji, *please*—"

"Yeah, um, I'm going to pass on that, but you know what I will do? I *will* help you to remove yourself the hell out of this dining hall where everyone is listening to *everything we say*." This last bit he says extra loudly, looking around at the room, shaking his head. "Get back to your breakfasts, people. Nothing to see here."

It's only then that I realize what a spectacle we've made. Every eye in the room is blinking at me. I attempt a weak smile and a twitchy wave before allowing Kenji to shuffle me out of the room.

"No need to wave at the people, princess. It's not a coronation ceremony." He pulls me into one of the many long, dimly lit corridors.

"Tell me what's happening." I have to blink several times before my eyes adjust to the lighting. "This isn't fair—everyone knows what's going on except for me."

He shrugs, leans one shoulder against the wall. "It's not my place to tell. I mean, I like to mess with the guy, but I'm not an asshole. He asked me not to say anything. So I'm not going to say anything."

"But—I mean—is he okay? Can you at least tell me if he's okay?"

Kenji runs a hand over his eyes; exhales, annoyed. Shoots me a look. Says, "All right, like, have you ever seen a train wreck?" He doesn't wait for me to answer. "I saw one when I was a kid. It was one of those big, crazy trains with a billion cars all hitched up together, totally derailed, half exploded. Shit was on fire and everyone was screaming and you just *know* people are either dead or they're about to die and you really don't want to watch but you just can't look away, you know?" He nods. Bites the inside of his cheek. "This is kind of like that. Your boy is a freaking train wreck."

I can't feel my legs.

"I mean, I don't know," Kenji goes on. "Personally? I think he's overreacting. Worse things have happened, right? Hell, aren't we up to our earlobes in crazier shit? But no, Mr. Adam Kent doesn't seem to know that. I don't even think he sleeps anymore. And you know what," he adds, leaning in, "I think he's starting to freak James out a little, and to be honest it's starting to piss me off because that kid is way too nice and way too cool to have to deal with Adam's drama—"

But I'm not listening anymore.

I'm envisioning the worst possible scenarios, the worst possible outcomes. Horrible, terrifying things that all end with Adam dying in some miserable way. He must be sick, or he must have some kind of terrible affliction, or something that causes him to do things he can't control or oh, God, *no*

"You have to tell me."

I don't recognize my own voice. Kenji is looking at me, shocked, wide-eyed, genuine fear written across his features and it's only then that I realize I've pinned him against the wall. My 10 fingers are curled into his shirt, fistfuls of fabric clenched in each hand, and I can only imagine what I must look like to him right now.

The scariest part is that I don't even care.

"You're going to tell me *something*, Kenji. You have to. I need to know."

"You, uh"—he licks his lips, looks around, laughs a nervous laugh—"you want to let go of me, maybe?"

"Will you help me?"

He scratches behind his hear. Cringes a little. "No?"

I slam him harder into the wall, recognize a rush of some wild kind of adrenaline burning in my veins. It's strange, but I feel as though I could rip through the ground with my bare hands.

It seems like it would be easy. So easy.

"Okay—all right—god*damn*." Kenji is holding his arms up, breathing a little fast. "Just—how about you let me go, and I'll, uh, I'll take you to the research labs."

"The research labs."

"Yeah, that's where they do the testing. It's where we do all of our testing."

"You promise you'll take me if I let go?"

"Are you going to bash my brain into the wall if I don't?"

"Probably," I lie.

"Then yeah. I'll take you. *Damn*."

I drop him and stumble backward; make an effort to pull myself together. I feel a little embarrassed now that I've let go of him. Some part of me feels like I must've overreacted.

"I'm sorry about that," I tell him. "But thank you. I appreciate your help." I try to lift my chin with some dignity.

Kenji snorts. He's looking at me like he has no idea who I am, like he's not sure if he should laugh or applaud or run like hell in the opposite direction. He rubs the back of his neck, eyes intent on my face. He won't stop staring.

"What?" I ask.

"How much do you weigh?"

"Wow. Is that how you talk to every girl you meet? That explains so much."

"I'm about one hundred seventy-five pounds," he says. "Of muscle."

I stare at him. "Would you like an award?"

"Well, well, well," he says, cocking his head, the barest hint of a smile flickering across his face. "Look who's the smart-ass now."

"I think you're rubbing off on me," I say.

But he's not smiling anymore.

"Listen," he says. "I'm not trying to flatter myself by pointing this out, but I could toss you across the room with my pinkie finger. You weigh, like, less than nothing. I'm almost twice your body mass." He pauses. "So how the hell did you pin me against the wall?"

"What?" I frown. "What are you talking about?"

"I'm talking about *you*"—he points at me—"pinning *me*"—he points at himself—"against the wall." He points at the wall.

"You mean you *actually* couldn't move?" I blink. "I thought you were just afraid of touching me."

"No," he says. "I legit could not move. I could hardly breathe."

"You're kidding."

"Have you ever done that before?"

"No." I'm shaking my head. "I mean I don't think I . . ." I gasp, as the memory of Warner and his torture chamber rushes to the forefront of my mind; I have to close my eyes against the influx of images. The barest recollection of that event is enough to make me feel unbearably nauseous; I can already feel my skin break into a cold sweat. Warner was testing me, trying to put me in a position where I'd be forced to use my power on a toddler. I was so horrified, so enraged that I crashed through the concrete barrier to get to Warner, who was waiting on the other side. I'd pinned *him* against the wall, too. Only I didn't realize he was cowed by my strength. I thought he was afraid to move because I'd gotten too close to touching him.

I guess I was wrong.

"Yeah," Kenji says, nodding at something he must see on my face. "Well. That's what I thought. We'll have to remember this juicy tidbit when we get around to our real training sessions." He throws me a loaded look. "Whenever that actually happens."

I'm nodding, not really paying attention. "Sure. Fine. But first, take me to the research rooms."

Kenji sighs. Waves his hand with a bow and a flourish. "After you, princess."

SEVEN

We're trailing down a series of corridors I've never seen before.

We're passing all of the regular halls and wings, past the training room I normally occupy, and for the first time since I've been here, I'm really paying attention to my surroundings. All of a sudden my senses feel sharper, clearer; my entire being feels like it's humming with a renewed kind of energy.

I am electric.

This entire hideout has been dug out of the ground—it's nothing but cavernous tunnels and interconnected passageways, all powered by supplies and electricity stolen from secret storage units belonging to The Reestablishment. This space is invaluable. Castle told us once that it took him at least a decade to design it, and a decade more to get the work done. By then he'd also managed to recruit all of the other members of this underground world. I can understand why he's so relentless about security down here, why he's not willing to let anything happen to it. I don't think I would either.

Kenji stops.

We reach what looks like a dead end—what could be the

very end of Omega Point.

Kenji pulls out a key card I didn't know he was hiding, and his hand fumbles for a panel buried in the stone. He slides the panel open. Does something I can't see. Swipes the key card. Hits a switch.

The entire wall rumbles to life.

The pieces are coming apart, shifting out of place until they reveal a hole big enough for our bodies to clamber through. Kenji motions for me to follow his lead and I scramble through the entryway, glancing back to watch the wall close up behind me.

My feet hit the ground on the other side.

It's like a cave. Massive, wide, separated into 3 longitudinal sections. The middle section is the most narrow and serves as a walkway; square glass rooms fit with slim glass doors make up the left and right sections. Each clear wall acts as a partition to rooms on either side—everything is see-through. There's an electric aura engulfing the entire space; each cube is bright with white light and blinking machinery; sharp and dull hums of energy pulse through the vast dimensions.

There are at least 20 rooms down here.

10 on either side, all of them unobstructed from view. I recognize a number of faces from the dining hall down here, some of them strapped to machines, needles stuck in their bodies, monitors beeping about some kind of information I can't understand. Doors slide open and closed open and closed open and closed; words and whispers and

footsteps, hand gestures and half-formed thoughts collect in the air.

This.

This is where everything happens.

Castle told me 2 weeks ago—the day after I arrived—that he had a pretty good idea why we are the way we are. He said that they'd been doing research for years.

Research.

I see figures running, gasping on what resemble inordinately fast treadmills. I see a woman reloading a gun in a room bursting with weapons and I see a man holding something that emits a bright blue flame. I see a person standing in a chamber full of nothing but water and there are ropes stacked high and strung across the ceiling and all kinds of liquids, chemicals, contraptions I can't name and my brain won't stop screaming and my lungs keep catching fire and it's too much too much too much too much

Too many machines, too many lights, too many people in too many rooms taking notes, talking amongst themselves, glancing at the clocks every few seconds and I'm stumbling forward, looking too closely and not closely enough and then I hear it. I try so hard not to but it's barely contained behind these thick glass walls and there it is again.

The low, guttural sound of human agony.

It hits me right in the face. Punches me right in the stomach. Realization jumps on my back and explodes in my skin and rakes its fingernails down my neck and I'm choking on impossibility.

Adam.

I see him. He's already here, in one of the glass rooms. Shirtless. Strapped down to a gurney, arms and legs clamped in place, wires from a nearby machine taped to his temples, his forehead, just below his collarbone. His eyes are pressed shut, his fists are clenched, his jaw is tight, his face too taut from the effort not to scream.

I don't understand what they're doing to him.

I don't know what's happening I don't understand *why* it's happening or why he needs a machine or why it keeps blinking or beeping and I can't seem to move or breathe and I'm trying to remember my voice, my hands, my head, and my feet and then he

jerks.

He convulses against the stays, strains against the pain until his fists are pounding the padding of the gurney and I hear him cry out in anguish and for a moment the world stops, everything slows down, sounds are strangled, colors look smeared and the floor seems set on its side and I think wow, I think I'm actually going to die. I'm going to drop dead or

I'm going to kill the person responsible for this.

It's one or the other.

That's when I see Castle. Castle, standing in the corner of Adam's room, watching in silence as this 18-year-old boy rages in agony while he does nothing. Nothing except watch, except to take notes in his little book, to purse his lips as he tilts his head to the side. To glance at the monitor on the beeping machine.

And the thought is so simple when it slips into my head. So calm. So easy.

So, *so* easy.

I'm going to kill him.

"Juliette—*no*—"

Kenji grabs me by the waist, arms like bands of iron around me and I think I'm screaming, I think I'm saying things I've never heard myself say before and Kenji is telling me to calm down, he's saying, "This is *exactly* why I didn't want to bring you in here—you don't understand—it's not what it looks like—"

And I decide I should probably kill Kenji, too. Just for being an idiot.

"LET GO OF ME—"

"Stop *kicking* me—"

"I'm going to *murder* him—"

"Yeah, you should really stop saying that out loud, okay? You're not doing yourself any favors—"

"LET GO OF ME, KENJI, I SWEAR TO GOD—"

"Ms. Ferrars!"

Castle is standing at the end of the walkway, a few feet from Adam's glass room. The door is open. Adam isn't jerking anymore, but he doesn't appear to be conscious, either.

White, hot rage.

It's all I know right now. The world looks so black-and-white from here, so easy to demolish and conquer. This is anger like nothing I've known before. It's an anger so raw, so potent it's actually calming, like a feeling that's finally found its place, a feeling that finally sits comfortably as it settles into my bones.

I've become a mold for liquid metal; thick, searing heat distributes itself throughout my body and the excess coats my hands, forging my fists with a strength so breathtaking, an energy so intense I think it might engulf me. I'm light-headed from the rush of it.

I could do anything.

Anything.

Kenji's arms drop away from me. I don't have to look at him to know that he's stumbling back. Afraid. Confused. Probably disturbed.

I don't care.

"So this is where you've been," I say to Castle, and I'm surprised by the cool, fluid tone of my voice. "This is what you've been doing."

Castle steps closer and appears to regret it. He looks startled, surprised by something he sees on my face. He tries to speak and I cut him off.

"What have you done to him?" I demand. "What have you been *doing to him*—"

"Ms. Ferrars, please—"

"He is not your *experiment*!" I explode, and the composure is gone, the steadiness in my voice is gone and I'm suddenly so unstable again I can hardly keep my hands from shaking. "You think you can just use him for your *research*—"

"Ms. Ferrars, please, you must calm yourself—"

"Don't tell me to calm down!" I can't imagine what they must have done to him down here, testing him, treating him like some kind of specimen.

They're *torturing* him.

"I would not have expected you to have such an adverse reaction to this room," Castle says. He's trying to be conversational. Reasonable. Charismatic, even. It makes me wonder what I must look like right now. I wonder if he's afraid of me. "I thought you understood the importance of the research we do at Omega Point," he says. "Without it, how could we possibly hope to understand our origins?"

"You're hurting him—you're *killing* him! What have you done—"

"Nothing he hasn't asked to be a part of." Castle's voice is tight and his lips are tight and I can see his patience is starting to wear thin. "Ms. Ferrars, if you are insinuating that I've used him for my own personal experimentation, I would recommend you take a closer look at the situation." He says the last few syllables with a little too much emphasis, a little too much fire, and I realize I've never seen him angry before.

"I know that you've been struggling here," Castle continues. "I know you are unaccustomed to seeing yourself as part of a group, and I've made an effort to understand where you might be coming from—I've tried to help you adjust. But you must look around!" He gestures toward the glass walls and the people behind them. "We are all the same. We are working on the same team! I have subjected

Adam to nothing I have not undergone myself. We are simply running tests to see where his supernatural abilities lie. We cannot know for certain what he is capable of if we do not test him first." His voice drops an octave or 2. "And we do not have the luxury of waiting several years until he accidentally discovers something that might be useful to our cause right now."

And it's strange.

Because it's like a real thing, this anger.

I feel it wrapping itself around my fingers like I could fling it at his face. I feel it coiling itself around my spine, planting itself in my stomach and shooting branches down my legs, up my arms, through my neck. It's choking me. Choking me because it needs release, needs relief. Needs it now.

"You," I tell him, and I can hardly spit the words out. "You think you're any better than The Reestablishment if you're just *using us*—experimenting on us to further your cause—"

"MS. FERRARS!" Castle bellows. His eyes are flashing bright, too bright, and I realize everyone in this underground tunnel is now staring at us. His fingers are in fists at his sides and his jaw is unmistakably set and I feel Kenji's hand on my back before I realize the earth is vibrating under my feet. The glass walls are beginning to tremble and Castle is planted right in the middle of everything, rigid, raw with anger and indignation and I remember that he has an impossibly advanced level of psychokinesis.

I remember that he can move things with his mind.

He lifts his right hand, palm splayed outward, and the glass panel not a few feet away begins to shake, shudder, and I realize I'm not even breathing.

"You do not want to upset me." Castle's voice is far too calm for his eyes. "If you have a problem with my methods, I would gladly invite you to state your claims in a rational manner. I will not tolerate you speaking to me in such a fashion. My concerns for the future of our world may be more than you can fathom, but you should not fault me for your own ignorance!" He drops his right hand and the glass buckles back just in time.

"My *ignorance?*" I'm breathing hard again. "You think because I don't understand why you would subject anyone to—to *this*—" I wave a hand around the room. "You think that means I'm *ignorant*—?"

"Hey, Juliette, it's okay—," Kenji starts.

"Take her away," Castle says. "Take her back to her training quarters." He shoots an unhappy look at Kenji. "And you and I—we will discuss this later. What were you *thinking,* bringing her here? She's not ready to see this—she can hardly even handle *herself* right now—"

He's right.

I can't handle this. I can't hear anything but the sounds of machines beeping, screeching in my head, can't see anything but Adam's limp form lying on a thin mattress. I can't stop imagining what he must've been going through, what he had to endure just to understand what he might be and I realize it's all my fault.

It's my fault he's here, it's my fault he's in danger, it's my fault Warner wants to kill him and Castle wants to test him and if it weren't for me he'd still be living with James in a home that hasn't been destroyed; he'd be safe and comfortable and free from the chaos I've introduced to his life.

I brought him here. If he'd never touched me none of this would've happened. He'd be healthy and strong and he wouldn't be suffering, wouldn't be hiding, wouldn't be trapped 50 feet underground. He wouldn't be spending his days strapped to a gurney.

~~It's my fault it's my fault it's my fault it's my fault~~ it's all my fault

I snap.

It's like I've been stuffed full of twigs and all I have to do is bend and my entire body will break. All the guilt, the anger, the frustration, the pent-up aggression inside of me has found an outlet and now it can't be controlled. Energy is coursing through me with a vigor I've never felt before and I'm not even thinking but I have to do *something* I have to touch *something* and I'm curling my fingers and bending my knees and pulling back my arm and

punching

my

fist

right

through

the

floor.

The earth fissures under my fingers and the reverberations surge through my being, ricocheting through my bones until my skull is spinning and my heart is a pendulum slamming into my rib cage. My eyesight fades in and out of focus and I have to blink a hundred times to clear it only to see a crack creaking under my feet, a thin line splintering the ground. Everything around me is suddenly off-balance. The stone is groaning under our weight and the glass walls are rattling and the machines arc shifting out of place and the water is sloshing against its container and the people—

The people.

The people are frozen in terror and horror and the fear in their expressions rips me apart.

I fall backward, cradling my right fist to my chest and try to remind myself I am not a monster, I do not have to be a monster, I do not want to hurt people I do not want to hurt people *I do not want to hurt people*

and it's not working.

Because it's all a lie.

Because this was me, trying to help.

I look around.

At the ground.

At what I've done.

And I understand, for the first time, that I have the power to destroy everything.

EIGHT

Castle is limp.

His jaw is unhinged. His arms are slack at his sides, his eyes wide with worry and wonder and a sliver of intimidation and though he moves his lips he can't seem to make a sound.

I feel like now might be a good time to jump off a cliff.

Kenji touches my arm and I turn to face him only to realize I'm petrified. I'm always waiting for him and Adam and Castle to realize that being kind to me is a mistake, that it'll end badly, that I'm not worth it, that I'm nothing more than a tool, a weapon, a closet murderer.

But he takes my right fist in his hand so gently. Takes care not to touch my skin as he slips off the now-tattered leather glove and sucks in his breath at the sight of my knuckles. The skin is torn and blood is everywhere and I can't move my fingers.

I realize I am in *agony.*

I blink and stars explode and a new torture rages through my limbs in such a hurry I can no longer speak.

I gasp

and
the
world

d i s a p p e a r s

NINE

My mouth tastes like death.

I manage to pry my eyes open and immediately feel the wrath of hell ripping through my right arm. My hand has been bandaged in so many layers of gauze it's rendered my 5 fingers immobile and I find I'm grateful for it. I'm so exhausted I don't have the energy to cry.

I blink.

Try to look around but my neck is too stiff.

Fingers brush my shoulder and I discover myself wanting to exhale. I blink again. Once more. A girl's face blurs in and out of focus. I turn my head to get a better view and blink blink blink some more.

"How're you feeling?" she whispers.

"I'm okay," I say to the blur, but I think I'm lying. "Who are you?"

"It's me," she says. Even without seeing her clearly I can hear the kindness in her voice. "Sonya."

Of course.

Sara is probably here, too. I must be in the medical wing.

"What happened?" I ask. "How long have I been out?"

She doesn't answer and I wonder if she didn't hear me.

"Sonya?" I try to meet her eyes. "How long have I been sleeping?"

"You've been really sick," she says. "Your body needed time—"

"How long?" My voice drops to a whisper.

"Three days."

I sit straight up and know I'm going to be sick.

Luckily, Sonya's had the foresight to anticipate my needs. A bucket appears just in time for me to empty the meager contents of my stomach into it and then I'm dry-heaving into what is not my suit but some kind of hospital gown and someone is wiping a hot, damp cloth across my face.

Sonya and Sara are hovering over me, the hot cloths in their hands, wiping down my bare limbs, making soothing sounds and telling me I'm going to be fine, I just need to rest, I'm finally awake long enough to eat something, I shouldn't be worried because there's nothing to worry about and they're going to take care of me.

But then I look more closely.

I notice their hands, so carefully sheathed in latex gloves; I notice the IV stuck in my arm; I notice the urgent but cautious way they approach me and then I realize the problem.

The healers can't touch me.

TEN

They've never had to deal with a problem like me before.

Injuries are always treated by the healers. They can set broken bones and repair bullet wounds and revive collapsed lungs and mend even the worst kinds of cuts—I know this because Adam had to be carried into Omega Point on a stretcher when we arrived. He'd suffered at the hands of Warner and his men after we escaped the military base and I thought his body would be scarred forever. But he's perfect. Brand-new. It took all of 1 day to put him back together; it was like magic.

But there are no magic medicines for me.

No miracles.

Sonya and Sara explain that I must've suffered some kind of immense shock. They say my body overloaded on its own abilities and it's a miracle I even managed to survive. They also think my body has been passed out long enough to have repaired most of the psychological damage, though I'm not so sure that's true. I think it'd take quite a lot to fix that sort of thing. ~~I've been psychologically damaged for a very long time.~~ But at least the physical pain has settled. It's little more than a steady throbbing that I'm able to ignore for short periods of time.

I remember something.

"Before," I tell them. "In Warner's torture rooms, and then with Adam and the steel door—I never—this never happened—I never injured myself—"

"Castle told us about that," Sonya tells me. "But breaking through one door or one wall is very different from trying to split the earth in two." She attempts a smile. "We're pretty sure this can't even compare to what you did before. This was a lot stronger—we all felt it when it happened. We actually thought explosives had gone off. The tunnels," she says. "They almost collapsed in on themselves."

"No." My stomach turns to stone.

"It's okay," Sara tries to reassure me. "You pulled back just in time."

I can't catch my breath.

"You couldn't have known—," Sonya starts.

"I almost killed—I almost killed all of you—"

Sonya shakes her head. "You have an amazing amount of power. It's not your fault. You didn't know what you were capable of."

"I could've killed you. I could've killed Adam—I could've—" My head whips around. "Is he here? Is Adam here?"

The girls stare at me. Stare at each other.

I hear a throat clear and I jerk toward the sound.

Kenji steps out of the corner. He waves a half wave, offers me a crooked smile that doesn't reach his eyes. "Sorry," he says to me, "but we had to keep him out of here."

"Why?" I ask, but I'm afraid to know the answer.

Kenji pushes his hair out of his eyes. Considers my question. "Well. Where should I begin?" He counts off on his fingers. "After he found out what happened, he tried to *kill* me, he went ballistic on Castle, he refused to leave the medical wing, and then he wou—"

"Please." I stop him. I squeeze my eyes shut. "Never mind. Don't. I can't."

"You asked."

"Where is he?" I open my eyes. "Is he okay?"

Kenji rubs the back of his neck. Looks away. "He'll be all right."

"Can I see him?"

Kenji sighs. Turns to the girls. Says, "Hey, can we get a second alone?" and the 2 of them are suddenly in a hurry to go.

"Of course," Sara says.

"No problem," Sonya says.

"We'll give you some privacy," they say at the same time.

And they leave.

Kenji grabs 1 of the chairs pushed up against the wall and carries it over to my bed. Sits down. Props the ankle of 1 foot on the knee of the other and leans back. Links his hands behind his head. Looks at me.

I shift on the mattress so I'm better seated to see him. "What is it?"

"You and Kent need to talk."

"Oh." I swallow. "Yes. I know."

"Do you?"

"Of course."

"Good." He nods. Looks away. Taps his foot too fast against the floor.

"What?" I ask after a moment. "What are you not telling me?"

His foot stops tapping but he doesn't meet my eyes. He covers his mouth with his left hand. Drops it. "That was some crazy shit you pulled back there."

All at once I feel humiliated. "I'm sorry, Kenji. I'm so sorry—I didn't think—I didn't know—"

He turns to face me and the look in his eyes stops me in place. He's trying to read me. Trying to figure me out. Trying, I realize, to decide whether or not he can trust me. Whether or not the rumors about the monster in me are true.

"I've never done that before," I hear myself whisper. "I swear—I didn't mean for that to happen—"

"Are you sure?"

"What?"

"It's a question, Juliette. It's a legitimate question." I've never seen him so serious. "I brought you here because Castle wanted you here. Because he thought we could help you—he thought we could provide you with a safe place to live. To get you away from the assholes trying to use you for their own benefit. But you come here and you don't even seem to want to be a part of anything. You don't talk to people. You don't make any progress with your training. You do nothing, basically."

"I'm sorry, I really—"

"And then I believe Castle when he says he's worried about you. He tells me you're not adjusting, that you're having a hard time fitting in. That people heard negative things about you and they're not being as welcoming as they should be. And I should kick my own ass for it, but I feel sorry for you. So I tell him I'll help. I rearrange my entire goddamn schedule just to help you deal with your issues. Because I think you're a nice girl who's just a little misunderstood. Because Castle is the most decent guy I've ever known and I want to help him out."

My heart is pounding so hard I'm surprised it's not bleeding.

"So I'm wondering," he says to me. He drops the foot he was resting on his knee. Leans forward. Props his elbows on his thighs. "I'm wondering if it's possible that all of this is just *coincidence*. I mean, was it just some crazy *coincidence* that I ended up working with you? Me? One of the very few people here who have access to that room? Or was it coincidence that you managed to threaten me into taking you down to the research labs? That you then, somehow, accidentally, coincidentally, unknowingly punched a fist into the ground that shook this place so hard we all thought the walls were caving in?" He stares at me, hard. "Was it a coincidence," he says, "that if you'd held on for just a few more seconds, this entire place would've collapsed in on itself?"

My eyes are wide, horrified, caught.

He leans back. Looks down. Presses 2 fingers to his lips.

"Do you actually want to be here?" he asks. "Or are you just trying to bring us down from the inside?"

"What?" I gasp. "No—"

"Because you either know *exactly* what you're doing—and you're a hell of a lot sneakier than you pretend to be—or you really have no *clue* what you're doing and you just have really shitty luck. I haven't decided yet."

"Kenji, I swear, I never—I n-never—" I have to bite back the words to blink back the tears. It's crippling, this feeling, this not knowing how to prove your own innocence. It's my entire life replayed over and over and over again, trying to convince people that I'm not dangerous, that I never meant to hurt anyone, that I didn't intend for things to turn out this way. That I'm not a bad person.

~~But it never seems to work out.~~

"I'm so sorry," I choke, the tears flowing fast now. I'm so disgusted with myself. I tried so hard to be different, to be better, to be *good,* and I just went and ruined everything and lost everything all over again and I don't even know how to tell him he's wrong.

~~Because he might be right.~~

I knew I was angry. I knew I wanted to hurt Castle and I didn't care. In that moment, I meant it. In the anger of that moment, I really, truly meant it. I don't know what I would've done if Kenji hadn't been there to hold me back. I don't know. I have no idea. I don't even understand what I'm capable of.

~~*How many times,* I hear a voice whisper in my head, *how*~~

~~*many times will you apologize for who you are?*~~

I hear Kenji sigh. Shift in his seat. I don't dare lift my eyes.

"I had to ask, Juliette." Kenji sounds uncomfortable. "I'm sorry you're crying but I'm not sorry I asked. It's my job to constantly be thinking of our safety—and that means I have to look at every possible angle. No one knows what you can do yet. Not even you. But you keep trying to act like what you're capable of isn't a big deal, and it's not helping anything. You need to stop trying to pretend you're not dangerous."

I look up too fast. "But I'm not—I'm n-not trying to hurt anyone—"

"That doesn't matter," he says, standing up. "Good intentions are great, but they don't change the facts. You *are* dangerous. Shit, you're *scary* dangerous. More dangerous than me and everyone else in here. So don't ask me to act like that knowledge, in and of itself, isn't a threat to us. If you're going to stay here," he says to me, "you have to learn how to control what you do—how to contain it. You have to deal with who you are and you have to figure out how to live with it. Just like the rest of us."

3 knocks at the door.

Kenji is still staring at me. Waiting.

"Okay," I whisper.

"And you and Kent need to sort out your drama ASAP," he adds, just as Sonya and Sara walk back into the room. "I don't have the time, the energy, or the interest to deal with your problems. I like to mess with you from time to time because, well, let's face it"—he shrugs—"the world is going to hell out there and I suppose if I'm going to be shot dead before I'm twenty-five, I'd at least like to remember what it's like to laugh before I do. But that does not make me your clown or your babysitter. At the end of the day I do not give two shits about whether or not you and Kent are going steady. We have a million things to take care of down here, and less than none of them involve your love life." A pause. "Is that clear?"

I nod, not trusting myself to speak.

"So are you in?" he says.

Another nod.

"I want to hear you say it. If you're in, you're all in. No more feeling sorry for yourself. No more sitting in the training room all day, crying because you can't break a metal pipe—"

"How did you kn—"

"Are you *in*?"

"I'm in," I tell him. "I'm in. I promise."

He takes a deep breath. Runs a hand through his hair. "Good. Meet me outside of the dining hall tomorrow morning at six a.m."

"But my hand—"

He waves my words away. "Your hand, nothing. You'll be fine. You didn't even break anything. You messed up your knuckles and your brain freaked out a little and basically you just fell asleep for three days. I don't call that an injury," he says. "I call that a goddamn vacation." He stops to consider something. "Do you have any idea how long it's been since I've gone on *vacation*—"

"But aren't we training?" I interrupt him. "I can't do anything if my hand is wrapped up, can I?"

"Trust me." He cocks his head. "You'll be fine. This . . . is going to be a little different."

I stare at him. Wait.

"You can consider it your official welcome to Omega Point," he says.

"But—"

"Tomorrow. Six a.m."

I open my mouth to ask another question but he presses a finger to his lips, offers me a 2-finger salute, and walks backward toward the exit just as Sonya and Sara head over to my bed.

I watch as he nods good-bye to both of them, pivots on 1 foot, and strides out the door.

6:00 a.m.

ELEVEN

I catch a glimpse of the clock on the wall and realize it's only 2:00 in the afternoon.

Which means 6:00 a.m. is 16 hours from now.

Which means I have a lot of hours to fill.

Which means I have to get dressed.

Because I need to get out of here.

And I really need to talk to Adam.

"Juliette?"

I jolt out of my own head and back to the present moment to find Sonya and Sara staring at me. "Can we get you anything?" they ask. "Are you feeling well enough to get out of bed?"

But I look from one set of eyes to another and back again, and instead of answering their questions, I feel a crippling sense of shame dig into my soul and I can't help but revert back to another version of myself. A scared little girl who wants to keep folding herself in half until she can't be found anymore.

I keep saying, "Sorry, I'm so sorry, I'm sorry about everything, for all of this, for all the trouble, for all the damage, really, I'm so, so sorry—"

I hear myself go on and on and on and I can't get myself to stop.

It's like a button in my brain is broken, like I've developed a disease that forces me to apologize for everything, for existing, for wanting more than what I've been given, and I can't stop.

It's what I do.

I'm always apologizing. Forever apologizing. For who I am and what I never meant to be and for this body I was born into, this DNA I never asked for, this person I can't unbecome. 17 years I've spent trying to be different. Every single day. Trying to be someone else for someone else.

And it never seems to matter.

But then I realize they're talking to me.

"There's nothing to apologize for—"

"Please, it's all right—"

Both of them are trying to speak to me, but Sara is closer.

I dare to meet her eyes and I'm surprised to see how soft they are. Gentle and green and squinty from smiling. She sits down on the right side of my bed. Pats my bare arm with her latex glove, unafraid. Unflinching. Sonya stands just next to her, looking at me like she's worried, like she's sad for me, and I don't have long to dwell on it because I'm distracted. I smell the scent of jasmine filling the room, just as it did the very first time I stepped in here. When we first arrived at Omega Point. When Adam was injured. Dying.

He was dying and they saved his life. These 2 girls in front of me. They saved his life and I've been living with them for 2 weeks and I realize, right then, exactly how selfish I've been.

So I decide to try a new set of words.

"Thank you," I whisper.

I feel myself begin to blush and I wonder at my inability to be so free with words and feelings. I wonder at my incapacity for easy banter, smooth conversation, empty words to fill awkward moments. I don't have a closet filled with umms and ellipses ready to insert at the beginnings and ends of sentences. I don't know how to be a verb, an adverb, any kind of modifier. I'm a noun through and through.

Stuffed so full of people places things and ideas that I don't know how to break out of my own brain. How to start a conversation.

I want to trust but it scares the skin off my bones.

But then I remember my promise to Castle and my promise to Kenji and my worries over Adam and I think maybe I should take a risk. Maybe I should try to find a new friend or 2. And I think of how wonderful it would be to be friends with a girl. A girl, just like me.

I've never had one of those before.

So when Sonya and Sara smile and tell me they're "happy to help" and they're here "anytime" and that they're always around if I "need someone to talk to," I tell them I'd love that.

I tell them I'd really appreciate that.

I tell them I'd love to have a friend to talk to.

Maybe sometime.

TWELVE

"Let's get you back into your suit," Sara says to me.

The air down here is cool and cold and often damp, the winter winds relentless as they whip the world above our heads into submission. Even in my suit I feel the chill, especially early in the morning, especially right now. Sonya and Sara are helping me out of this hospital dress and back into my normal uniform and I'm shaking in my skin. Only once they've zipped me up does the material begin to react to my body temperature, but I'm still so weak from being in bed for so long that I'm struggling to stay upright.

"I really don't need a wheelchair," I tell Sara for the third time. "Thank you—really—I-I appreciate it," I stammer, "but I need to get the blood flowing in my legs. I have to be strong on my feet." I have to be strong, period.

Castle and Adam are waiting for me in my room.

Sonya told me that while I was talking to Kenji, she and Sara went to notify Castle that I was awake. So. Now they're there. Waiting for me. In the room I share with Sonya and Sara. And I'm so afraid of what is about to happen that I'm worried I might conveniently forget how to get to my own room. Because I'm fairly certain that whatever I'm about to hear isn't going to be good.

"You can't walk back to the room by yourself," Sara is saying. "You can hardly stand on your own—"

"I'm okay," I insist. I try to smile. "Really, I should be able to manage as long as I can stay close to the wall. I'm sure I'll be back to normal just as soon as I start moving."

Sonya and Sara glance at each other before scrutinizing my face. "How's your hand?" they ask at the same time.

"It's okay," I tell them, this time more earnestly. "It feels a lot better. Really. Thank you so much."

The cuts are practically healed and I can actually move my fingers now. I inspect the brand-new, thinner bandage they've wrapped across my knuckles. The girls explained to me that most of the damage was internal; it seems I traumatized whatever invisible bone in my body is responsible for my ~~curse~~ "gift."

"All right. Let's go," Sara says, shaking her head. "We're walking you back to the room."

"No—please—it's okay—" I try to protest but they're already grabbing my arms and I'm too feeble to fight back. "This is unnecessary—"

"You're being ridiculous," they chorus.

"I don't want you to have to go through the trouble—"

"You're being ridiculous," they chorus again.

"I—I'm really not—" But they're already leading me out of the room and down the hall and I'm hobbling along between them. "I promise I'm fine," I tell them. "Really."

Sonya and Sara share a loaded look before they smile at me, not unkindly, but there's an awkward silence between us as we move through the halls. I spot people walking past us and immediately duck my head. I don't want to make eye contact with anyone right now. I can't even imagine what they must've heard about the damage I've caused. I know I've managed to confirm all of their worst fears about me.

"They're only afraid of you because they don't know you," Sara says quietly.

"Really," Sonya adds. "We barely know you and we think you're great."

I'm blushing fiercely, wondering why embarrassment always feels like ice water in my veins. It's like all of my insides are freezing even though my skin is burning hot too hot.

~~I *hate* this.~~

~~I *hate* this feeling.~~

Sonya and Sara stop abruptly. "Here we are," they say together.

We're in front of our bedroom door. I try to unlatch myself from their arms but they stop me. Insist on staying with me until they're sure I've gotten inside okay.

So I stay with them.

And I knock on my own door, because I'm not sure what else to do.

Once.

Twice.

I'm waiting just a few seconds, just a few moments for fate to answer when I realize the full impact of Sonya's and Sara's presence beside me. They're offering me smiles that are supposed to be encouraging, bracing, reinforcing. They're trying to lend me their strength because they know I'm about to face something that isn't going to make me happy.

And this thought makes me happy.

If only for a fleeting moment.

Because I think wow, I imagine this is what it's like to have friends.

"Ms. Ferrars."

Castle opens the door just enough for me to see his face. He nods at me. Glances down at my injured hand. Back up at my face. "Very good," he says, mostly to himself. "Good, good. I'm happy to see you're doing better."

"Yes," I manage to say. "I—th-thank you, I—"

"Girls," he says to Sonya and Sara. He offers them a bright, genuine smile. "Thank you for all you've done. I'll take it from here."

They nod. Squeeze my arms once before letting go and I sway for just a second before I find my footing. "I'm all right," I tell them as they try to reach for me. "I'll be fine."

They nod again. Wave, just a little, as they back away.

"Come inside," Castle says to me.

I follow him in.

THIRTEEN

1 bunk bed on one side of the wall.

1 single bed on the other side.

That's all this room consists of.

That, and Adam, who is sitting on my single bed, elbows propped up on his knees, face in his hands. Castle shuts the door behind us, and Adam startles. Jumps up.

"Juliette," he says, but he's not looking at me; he's looking at all of me. His eyes are searching my body as if to ensure I'm still intact, arms and legs and everything in between. It's only when he finds my face that he meets my gaze; I step into the sea of blue in his eyes, dive right in and drown. I feel like someone's punched a fist into my lungs and snatched up all my oxygen.

"Please, have a seat, Ms. Ferrars." Castle gestures to Sonya's bottom bunk, the bed right across from where Adam is sitting. I make my way over slowly, trying not to betray the dizziness, the nausea I'm feeling. My chest is rising and falling too quickly.

I drop my hands into my lap.

I feel Adam's presence in this room like a real weight against my chest but I choose to study the careful wrapping of my new bandage—the gauze stretched tight across the knuckles of my right hand—because I'm too much of a coward to look up. I want nothing more than to go to him, to have him hold me, to transport me back to the few moments of bliss I've ever known in my life but there's something gnawing at my core, scraping at my insides, telling me that something is wrong and it's probably best if I stay exactly where I am.

Castle is standing in the space between the beds, between me and Adam. He's staring at the wall, hands clasped behind his back. His voice is quiet when he says, "I am very, very disappointed in your behavior, Ms. Ferrars."

Hot, terrible shame creeps up my neck and forces my head down again.

"I'm sorry," I whisper.

Castle takes a deep breath. Exhales very slowly. "I have to be frank with you," he says, "and admit that I'm not ready to discuss what happened just yet. I am still too upset to be able to speak about the matter calmly. Your actions," he says, "were childish. Selfish. *Thoughtless!* The damage you caused—the years of work that went into building and planning that room, I can't even begin to tell you—"

He catches himself, swallows hard.

"That will be a subject," he says steadily, "for another time. Perhaps just between the two of us. But I am here today because Mr. Kent asked me to be here."

I look up. Look at Castle. Look at Adam.

Adam looks like he wants to run.

I decide I can't wait any longer. "You've learned something

about him," I say, and it's less of a question than it is a fact. It's so obvious. There's no other reason why Adam would bring Castle here to talk to me.

Something terrible has already happened. Something terrible is about to happen.

I can feel it.

Adam is staring at me now, unblinking, his hands in fists pressed into his thighs. He looks nervous; scared. I don't know what to do except to stare back at him. I don't know how to offer him comfort. I don't even know how to smile right now. I feel like I'm trapped in someone else's story.

Castle nods, once, slowly.

Says, "Yes. Yes, we've discovered the very intriguing nature of Mr. Kent's ability." He walks toward the wall and leans against it, allowing me a clearer view of Adam. "We believe we now understand why he's able to touch you, Ms. Ferrars."

Adam turns away, presses one of his fists to his mouth. His hand looks like it might be shaking but he, at least, seems to be doing better than I am. Because my insides are screaming and my head is on fire and panic is stepping on my throat, suffocating me to death. Bad news offers no returns once received.

"What is it?" I fix my eyes on the floor and count stones and sounds and cracks and nothing.

1

2, 3, 4

1

2, 3, 4

1

2, 3, 4

"He . . . can disable things," Castle says to me.

5, 6, 7, 8 million times I blink, confused. All my numbers crash to the floor, adding and subtracting and multiplying and dividing. "What?" I ask him.

This news is wrong. This news doesn't sound horrible at all.

"The discovery was quite accidental, actually," Castle explains. "We weren't having much luck with any of the tests we'd been running. But then one day I was in the middle of a training exercise, and Mr. Kent was trying to get my attention. He touched my shoulder."

Wait for it.

"And . . . suddenly," Castle says, pulling in a breath, "I couldn't perform. It was as if—as if a wire inside of my body had been cut. I felt it right away. He wanted my attention and he inadvertently shut me off in an attempt to redirect my focus. It was unlike anything I've ever seen." He shakes his head. "We've now been working with him to see if he can control his ability at will. And," Castle adds, excited, "we want to see if he can *project*.

"You see, Mr. Kent does not need to make contact with the skin—I was wearing my blazer when he touched my arm. So this means he's already projecting, if only just a little bit. And I believe, with some work, he'll be able to extend his gift to a greater surface area."

I have no idea what that means.

I try to meet Adam's eyes; I want him to tell me these things himself but he won't look up. He won't speak and I don't understand. This doesn't seem like bad news. In fact, it sounds quite good, which can't be right. I turn to Castle. "So Adam can just make someone else's power—their *gift*—whatever it is—he can just make it stop? He can turn it off?"

"I appears that way, yes."

"Have you tested this on anyone else?"

Castle looks offended. "Of course we have. We've tried it on every gifted member at Omega Point."

But something isn't making sense.

"What about when he arrived?" I ask. "And he was injured? And the girls were able to heal him? Why didn't he cut off their abilities?"

"Ah." Castle nods. Clears his throat. "Yes. Very astute, Ms. Ferrars." He paces the length of the room. "This . . . is where the explanation gets a little tricky. After much study, we've been able to conclude that his ability is a kind of . . . *defense* mechanism. One that he does not yet know how to control. It's something that's been working on autopilot his entire life, even though it only works to disable other preternatural abilities. If there was ever a risk, if Mr. Kent was ever in any state of danger, in any situation where his body was on high alert, feeling threatened or at risk of injury, his ability automatically set in."

He stops. Looks at me. Really looks at me.

"When you first met, for example, Mr. Kent was working

as a soldier, on guard, always aware of the risks in his surroundings. He was in a constant state of *electricum*—a term we use to define when our Energy is 'on,' so to speak—because he was always in a state of danger." Castle tucks his hands into his blazer pockets. "A series of tests have further shown that his body temperature rises when he is in a state of *electricum*—just a couple of degrees higher than normal. His elevated body temperature indicates that he is exerting more energy than usual to sustain this. And, in short," Castle says, "this constant exertion has been exhausting him. Weakening his defenses, his immune system, his self-control."

His elevated body temperature.

That's why Adam's skin was always so hot when we were together. Why it was always so intense when he was with me. His ability was working to fight mine. His energy was working to *defuse* mine.

It was *exhausting him. Weakening his defenses.*

Oh.

God.

"Your physical relationship with Mr. Kent," Castle says, "is, in truth, none of my business. But because of the very unique nature of your gifts, it's been of great interest to me on a purely scientific level. But you must know, Ms. Ferrars, that though these new developments no doubt fascinate me, I take absolutely no pleasure in them. You've made it clear that you do not think much of my character, but you must believe that I would never find joy in your troubles."

My troubles.

My troubles have arrived fashionably late to this conversation, inconsiderate beasts that they are.

"Please," I whisper. "Please just tell me what the problem is. There's a problem, isn't there? Something is wrong." I look at Adam but he's still staring away, at the wall, at everything but at my face, and I feel myself rising to my feet, trying to get his attention. "Adam? Do you know? Do you know what he's talking about? *Please*—"

"Ms. Ferrars," Castle says quickly. "I beg you to sit down. I know this must be difficult for you, but you must let me finish. I've asked Mr. Kent not to speak until I'm done explaining everything. Someone needs to deliver this information in a clear, rational manner, and I'm afraid he is in no position to do so."

I fall back onto the bed.

Castle lets out a breath. "You brought up an excellent point earlier—about why Mr. Kent was able to interact with our healer twins when he first arrived. But it was different with them," Castle says. "He was weak; he knew he needed help. His body would not—and, more importantly, could not—refuse that kind of medical attention. He was vulnerable and therefore unable to defend himself even if he wanted to. The last of his Energy was depleted when he arrived. He felt safe and he was seeking aid; his body was out of immediate danger and therefore unafraid, not primed for a defensive strategy."

Castle looks up. Looks me in the eye.

"Mr. Kent has begun having a similar problem with you."

"What?" I gasp.

"I'm afraid he doesn't know how to control his abilities yet. It's something we're hoping we can work on, but it will take a lot of time—a lot of energy and focus—"

"What do you mean," I hear myself ask, my words heavy with panic, "that he has *already begun* having a similar problem with me?"

Castle takes a small breath. "It—it seems that he is weakest when he is with you. The more time he spends in your company, the less threatened he feels. And the more . . . intimate you become," Castle says, looking distinctly uncomfortable, "the less control he has over his body." A pause. "He is too open, too vulnerable with you. And in the few moments his defenses have slipped thus far, he's already felt the very distinct pain associated with your touch."

There it is.

There's my head, lying on the floor, cracked right open, my brain spilling out in every direction and I can't I don't I can't even I'm sitting here, struck, numb, slightly dizzy.

Horrified.

Adam is *not* immune to me.

Adam has to *work* to defend himself against me and I'm exhausting him. I'm making him sick and I'm weakening his body and if he ever slips again. If he ever forgets. If he ever makes a mistake or loses focus or becomes too aware of the fact that he's using his *gift* to control what I might do—

I could hurt him.

I could *kill* him.

FOURTEEN

Castle is staring at me.

Waiting for my reaction.

I haven't been able to spit the chalk out of my mouth long enough to string a sentence together.

"Ms. Ferrars," he says, rushing to speak now, "we are working with Mr. Kent to help him control his abilities. He's going to train—just as you are—to learn how to exercise this particular element of who he is. It will take some time until we can be certain he'll be safe with you, but it will be all right, I assure you—"

"No." I'm standing up. "No no no no no." I'm tripping sideways. "NO."

I'm staring at my feet and at my hands and at these walls and I want to scream. I want to run. I want to fall to my knees. I want to curse the world for cursing me, for torturing me, for taking away the only good thing I've ever known and I'm stumbling toward the door, searching for an outlet, for escape from this nightmare that is my life and

"Juliette—please—"

The sound of Adam's voice stops my heart. I force myself to turn around. To face him.

But the moment he meets my eyes his mouth falls closed.

His arm is outstretched toward me, trying to stop me from 10 feet away and I want to sob and laugh at the same time, at the terrible hilarity of it all.

He will not touch me.

I will not allow him to touch me.

Never again.

"Ms. Ferrars," Castle says gently. "I'm sure it's hard to stomach right now, but I've already told you this isn't permanent. With enough training—"

"When you touch me," I ask Adam, my voice breaking, "is it an effort for you? Does it exhaust you? Does it drain you to have to constantly be fighting me and what I am?"

Adam tries to answer. He tries to say something but instead he says nothing and his unspoken words are so much worse.

I spin in Castle's direction. "That's what you said, isn't it?" My voice is even shakier now, too close to tears. "That he's using his Energy to extinguish mine, and that if he ever forgets—if he ever gets c-carried away or t-too vulnerable—that I could hurt him—that I've *already* h-hurt him—"

"Ms. Ferrars, please—"

"Just answer the question!"

"Well yes," he says, "for now, at least, that's all we know—"

"Oh, God, I—I can't—" I'm tripping to reach the door again but my legs are still weak, my head is still spinning, my eyes are blurring and the world is being washed of all its color when I feel familiar arms wrap around my waist, tugging me backward.

"Juliette," he says, so urgently, "please, we have to talk about this—"

"Let go of me." My voice is barely a breath. "Adam, please—I can't—"

"Castle." Adam cuts me off. "Do you think you can give us some time alone?"

"Oh." He startles. "Of course," he says, just a beat too late. "Sure, yes, yes, of course." He walks to the door. Hesitates. "I will—well, right. Yes. You know where to find me when you're ready." He nods at both of us, offers me a strained sort of smile, and leaves the room. The door clicks shut behind him.

Silence pours into the space between us.

"Adam, please," I finally say, and hate myself for saying it. "Let go of me."

"No."

I feel his breath on the back of my neck and it's killing me to be so close to him. It's killing me to know that I have to rebuild the walls I'd so carelessly demolished the moment he came back into my life.

"Let's talk about this," he says. "Don't go anywhere. Please. Just talk to me."

I'm rooted in place.

"Please," he says again, this time more softly, and my resolve runs out the door without me.

I follow him back to the beds. He sits on one side of the room. I sit on the other.

He stares at me. His eyes are too tired, too strained. He looks like he hasn't been eating enough, like he hasn't slept in weeks. He hesitates, licks his lips before pressing them tight, before he speaks. "I'm sorry," he says. "I'm so sorry I didn't tell you. I never meant to upset you."

And I want to laugh and laugh and laugh until the tears dissolve me.

"I understand why you didn't tell me," I whisper. "It makes perfect sense. You wanted to avoid all of *this*." I wave a limp hand around the room.

"You're not mad?" His eyes are so terribly hopeful. He looks like he wants to walk over to me and I have to hold out a hand to stop him.

The smile on my face is literally killing me.

"How could I be mad at you? You were torturing yourself down there just to figure out what was happening to you. You're torturing yourself right now just trying to find a way to fix this."

He looks relieved.

Relieved and confused and afraid to be happy all at the same time. "But something's wrong," he says. "You're crying. Why are you crying if you're not upset?"

I actually laugh this time. Out loud. Laugh and hiccup and want to die, so desperately. "Because I was an idiot for thinking things could be different," I tell him. "For thinking you were a fluke. For thinking my life could ever be better than it was, that *I* could ever be better than I was." I try to speak again but instead clamp a hand over my mouth like I can't believe what I'm about to say. I force myself to swallow the stone in my throat. I drop my hand. "Adam." My voice is raw, aching. "This isn't going to work."

"What?" He's frozen in place, his eyes too wide, his chest rising and falling too fast. "What are you talking about?"

"You can't touch me," I tell him. "You can't touch me and I've already hurt you—"

"No—Juliette—" Adam is up, he's cleared the room, he's on his knees next to me and he reaches for my hands but I have to snatch them back because my gloves were ruined, ruined in the research lab and now my fingers are bare.

Dangerous.

Adam stares at the hands I've hidden behind my back like I've slapped him across the face. "What are you doing?" he asks, but he's not looking at me. He's still staring at my hands. Barely breathing.

"I can't do this to you." I shake my head too hard. "I don't want to be the reason why you're hurting yourself or weakening yourself and I don't want you to always have to worry that I might accidentally *kill* you—"

"No, Juliette, listen to me." He's desperate now, his eyes up, searching my face. "I was worried too, okay? I was worried too. Really worried. I thought—I thought that maybe—I don't know, I thought maybe it would be bad or that maybe we wouldn't be able to work through it but I talked to Castle. I talked to him and explained everything and he said that I just have to learn to control it. I'll learn how to turn it on and off—"

"Except when you're with me? Except when we're together—"

"No—what? No, *especially* when we're together!"

"Touching me—being with me—it takes a physical toll on you! You run a *fever* when we're together, Adam, did you realize that? You'd get sick just trying to fight me off—"

"You're not hearing me—please—I'm telling you, I'll learn to control all of that—"

"When?" I ask, and I can actually feel my bones breaking, 1 by 1.

"What? What do you mean? I'll learn now—I'm learning *now*—"

"And how's it going? Is it easy?"

His mouth falls closed but he's looking at me, struggling with some kind of emotion, struggling to find composure. "What are you trying to say?" he finally asks. "Are you"—he's breathing hard—"are you—I mean—you don't want to make this work?"

"Adam—"

"What are you *saying*, Juliette?" He's up now, a shaky hand caught in his hair. "You don't—you don't want to be with me?"

I'm on my feet, blinking back the tears burning my eyes, desperate to run to him but unable to move. My voice breaks when I speak. "Of course I want to be with you."

He drops his hand from his hair. Looks at me with eyes so open and vulnerable but his jaw is tight, his muscles are tense, his upper body is heaving from the effort to inhale, exhale. "Then what's happening right now? Because something is happening right now and it doesn't feel okay," he says, his voice catching. "It doesn't feel okay, Juliette, it feels like the opposite of whatever the hell okay is and I really just want to hold you—"

"I don't want to h-hurt you—"

"You're not going to hurt me," he says, and then he's in front of me, looking at me, pleading with me. "I swear. It'll be fine—we'll be fine—and I'm better now. I've been working on it and I'm stronger—"

"It's too dangerous, Adam, please." I'm begging him, backing away, wiping furiously at the tears escaping down my face. "It's better for you this way. It's better for you to just stay away from me—"

"But that's not what I want—you're not asking me what *I* want—," he says, following me as I dodge his advances. "I want to be with you and I don't give a damn if it's hard. I still want it. I still want you."

I'm trapped.

I'm caught between him and the wall and I have nowhere to go and I wouldn't want to go even if I could. I don't want to have to fight this even though there's something inside of me screaming that it's wrong to be so selfish, to allow him to be with me if it'll only end up hurting him. But he's looking at me, looking at me like I'm *killing* him and I realize I'm hurting him more by trying to stay away.

I'm shaking. Wanting him so desperately and knowing now, more than ever, that what I want will have to wait. And I hate that it has to be this way. I hate it so much I could scream.

But maybe we can try.

"Juliette." Adam's voice is hoarse, broken with feeling. His hands are at my waist, trembling just a little, waiting for my permission. "Please."

And I don't protest.

He's breathing harder now, leaning into me, resting his forehead against my shoulder. He places his hands flat against the center of my stomach, only to inch them down my body, slowly, so slowly and I gasp.

There's an earthquake happening in my bones, tectonic plates shifting from panic to pleasure as his fingers take their time moving around my thighs, up my back, over my shoulders and down my arms. He hesitates at my wrists. This is where the fabric ends, where my skin begins.

But he takes a breath.

And he takes my hands.

For a moment I'm paralyzed, searching his face for any sign of pain or danger but then we both exhale and I see him attempt a smile with new hope, a new optimism that maybe everything is going to work out.

But then he blinks and his eyes change.

His eyes are deeper now. Desperate. Hungry. He's searching me like he's trying to read the words etched inside of me and I can already feel the heat of his body, the power in his limbs, the strength in his chest and I don't have time to stop him before he's kissing me.

His left hand is cupping the back of my head, his right tightening around my waist, pressing me hard against him and destroying every rational thought I've ever had. It's deep. So strong. It's an introduction to a side of him I've never known before and I'm gasping gasping gasping for air.

It's hot rain and humid days and broken thermostats. It's screaming teakettles and raging steam engines and wanting to take your clothes off just to feel a breeze.

It's the kind of kiss that makes you realize oxygen is overrated.

And I know I shouldn't be doing this. I know it's probably stupid and irresponsible after everything we've just learned but someone would have to shoot me to make me want to stop.

I'm pulling at his shirt, desperate for a raft or a life preserver or something, anything to anchor me to reality but he breaks away to catch his breath and rips off his shirt, tosses it to the floor, pulls me into his arms and we both fall onto my bed.

Somehow I end up on top of him.

He reaches up only to pull me down and he's kissing me, my throat, my cheeks, and my hands are searching his body, exploring the lines, the planes, the muscle and he pulls back, his forehead is pressed against my own and his eyes are squeezed shut when he says, "How is it possible," he says, "that I'm this close to you and it's killing me that you're still so far away?"

And I remember I promised him, 2 weeks ago, that once he got better, once he'd healed, I would memorize every inch of his body with my lips.

I figure now is probably a good time to fulfill that promise.

I start at his mouth, move to his cheek, under his jawline, down his neck to his shoulders and his arms, which are wrapped around me. His hands are skimming my suit and he's so hot, so tense from the effort to remain still but I can hear his heart beating hard, too fast against his chest.

Against mine.

I trace the white bird soaring across his skin, a tattoo of the one impossible thing I hope to see in my life. A bird. White with streaks of gold like a crown atop its head.

It will fly.

Birds don't fly, is what the scientists say, but history says they used to. And one day I want to see it. I want to touch it. I want to watch it fly like it should, like it hasn't been able to in my dreams.

I dip down to kiss the yellow crown of its head, tattooed deep into Adam's chest. I hear the spike in his breathing.

"I love this tattoo," I tell him, looking up to meet his eyes. "I haven't seen it since we got here. I haven't seen you without a shirt on since we got here," I whisper. "Do you still sleep without your shirt on?"

But Adam answers with a strange smile, like he's laughing at his own private joke.

He takes my hand from his chest and tugs me down so we're facing each other, and it's strange, because I haven't felt a breeze since we got here, but it's like the wind has found a home in my body and it's funneling through my lungs, blowing through my blood, mingling with my breath and making it hard for me to breathe.

"I can't sleep at all," he says to me, his voice so low I have to strain to hear it. "It doesn't feel right to be without you every night." His left hand is threaded in my hair, his right wrapped around me. "God I've missed you," he says, his words a husky whisper in my ear. "Juliette."

I am

lit

on fire.

It's like swimming in molasses, this kiss, it's like being dipped in gold, this kiss, it's like I'm diving into an ocean of emotion and I'm too swept up in the current to realize I'm drowning and nothing even matters anymore. Not my hand which no longer seems to hurt, not this room that isn't entirely mine, not this war we're supposed to be fighting, not my worries about who or what I am and what I might become.

This is the only thing that matters.

This.

This moment. These lips. This strong body pressed against me and these firm hands finding a way to bring me closer and I know I want so much more of him, I want all of him, I want to feel the beauty of this love with the tips of my fingers and the palms of my hands and every fiber and bone in my being.

I want all of it.

My hands are in his hair and I'm reeling him in until

he's practically on top of me and he breaks for air but I pull him back, kissing his neck, his shoulders, his chest, running my hands down his back and the sides of his torso and it's incredible, the energy, the unbelievable power I feel in just *being* with him, touching him, holding him like this. I'm alive with a rush of adrenaline so potent, so euphoric that I feel rejuvenated, indestructible—

I jerk back.

Push away so quickly that I'm scrambling and I fall off the bed only to slam my head into the stone floor and I'm swaying as I attempt to stand, struggling to hear the sound of his voice but all I hear are wheezing, paralyzed breaths and I can't think straight, I can't see anything and everything is blurry and I can't, I refuse to believe this is actually happening—

"J-Jul—" He tries to speak. "I-I c-ca—"

And I fall to my knees.

Screaming.

Screaming like I've never screamed in my entire life.

FIFTEEN

I count everything.

Even numbers, odd numbers, multiples of 10. I count the ticks of the clock I count the tocks of the clock I count the lines between the lines on a sheet of paper. I count the broken beats of my heart I count my pulse and my blinks and the number of tries it takes to inhale enough oxygen for my lungs. I stay like this I stand like this I count like this until the feeling stops. Until the tears stop spilling, until my fists stop shaking, until my heart stops aching.

There are never enough numbers.

Adam is in the medical wing.

He is in the medical wing and I have been asked not to visit him. I have been asked to give him space, to give him time to heal, ~~to leave him the hell alone.~~ He is going to be okay, is what Sonya and Sara told me. They told me not to worry, that everything would be fine, but their smiles were a little less exuberant than they usually are and I'm beginning to wonder if they, too, are finally beginning to see me for what I truly am.

A horrible, selfish, pathetic monster.

I took what I wanted. I knew better and I took it anyway. Adam couldn't have known, he could never have known what it would be like to really suffer at my hands. He was innocent of the depth of it, of the cruel reality of it. He'd only felt bursts of my power, according to Castle. He'd only felt small stabs of it and was able and aware enough to let go without feeling the full effects.

But I knew better.

I knew what I was capable of. I knew what the risks were and I did it anyway. I allowed myself to forget, to be reckless, to be greedy and stupid because I wanted what I couldn't have. I wanted to believe in fairy tales and happy endings and pure possibility. I wanted to pretend that I was a better person than I actually am but instead I managed to out myself as the terror I've always been accused of being.

~~My parents were right to get rid of me.~~

Castle isn't even speaking to me.

Kenji, however, still expects me to show up at 6:00 a.m. for whatever it is we're supposed to be doing tomorrow, and I find I'm actually kind of grateful for the distraction. I only wish it would come sooner. Life will be solitary for me from now on, just as it always has been, and it's best if I find a way to fill my time.

To forget.

It keeps hitting me, over and over and over again, this complete and utter loneliness. This absence of him in my life, this realization that I will never know the warmth of his body, the tenderness of his touch ever again. This reminder of who I am and what I've done and where I belong.

But I've accepted the terms and conditions of my new reality.

I cannot be with him. I will not be with him. I won't risk

hurting him again, won't risk becoming the creature he's always afraid of, too scared to touch, to kiss, to hold. I don't want to keep him from having a normal life with someone who isn't going to accidentally kill him all the time.

So I have to cut myself out of his world. Cut him out of mine.

It's much harder now. So much harder to resign myself to an existence of ice and emptiness now that I've known heat, urgency, tenderness, and passion; the extraordinary comfort of being able to touch another being.

It's humiliating.

That I thought I could slip into the role of a regular girl with a regular boyfriend; that I thought I could live out the stories I'd read in so many books as a child.

Me.

Juliette with a dream.

Just the thought of it is enough to fill me with mortification. How embarrassing for me, that I thought I could change what I'd been dealt. That I looked in the mirror and actually liked the pale face staring back at me.

How sad.

I always dared to identify with the princess, the one who runs away and finds a fairy godmother to transform her into a beautiful girl with a bright future. I clung to something like hope, to a thread of maybes and possiblys and perhapses. But I should've listened when my parents told me that things like me aren't allowed to have dreams. ~~Things like me are better off destroyed, is what my mother said to me.~~

And I'm beginning to think they were right. I'm

beginning to wonder if I should just bury myself in the ground before I remember that technically, I already am. I never even needed a shovel.

It's strange.

How hollow I feel.

Like there might be echoes inside of me. Like I'm one of those chocolate rabbits they used to sell around Easter, the ones that were nothing more than a sweet shell encapsulating a world of nothing. I'm like that.

I encapsulate a world of nothing.

Everyone here hates me. The tenuous bonds of friendship I'd begun to form have now been destroyed. Kenji is tired of me. Castle is disgusted, disappointed, angry, even. I've caused nothing but trouble since I arrived and the 1 person who's ever tried to see good in me is now paying for it with his life.

The 1 person who's ever dared to touch me.

Well. 1 of 2.

I find myself thinking about Warner too much.

I remember his eyes and his odd kindness and his cruel, calculating demeanor. I remember the way he looked at me when I first jumped out the window to escape and I remember the horror on his face when I pointed his own gun at his heart and then I wonder at my preoccupation with this person who is nothing like me ~~and still so similar.~~

I wonder if I will have to face him again, sometime soon, and I wonder how he will greet me. I have no idea if he wants to keep me alive anymore, especially not after

I tried to kill him, and I have no idea what could propel a 19-year-old man boy person into such a miserable, murderous lifestyle and then I realize I'm lying to myself. Because I do know. Because I might be the only person who could ever understand him.

And this is what I've learned:

I know that he is a tortured soul who, like me, never grew up with the warmth of friendship or love or peaceful coexistence. I know that his father is the leader of The Reestablishment and applauds his son's murders instead of condemning them and I know that Warner has no idea what it's like to be normal.

~~Neither do I.~~

He's spent his life fighting to fulfill his father's expectations of global domination without questioning why, without considering the repercussions, without stopping long enough to weigh the worth of a human life. He has a power, a strength, a position in society that enables him to do too much damage and he owns it with pride. He kills without remorse or regret and he wants me to join him. He sees me for what I am and expects me to live up to that potential.

Scary, monstrous girl with a lethal touch. Sad, pathetic girl with nothing else to contribute to this world. Good for nothing but a weapon, a tool for torture and taking control. That's what he wants from me.

And lately I'm not sure if he's wrong. Lately, I'm not sure of anything. Lately, I don't know anything about anything

I've ever believed in, not anymore, and I know the least about who I am. Warner's whispers pace the space in my head, telling me I could be more, I could be stronger, I could be everything; I could be so much more than a scared little girl.

He says I could be power.

But still, I hesitate.

Still, I see no appeal in the life he's offered. I see no future in it. I take no pleasure in it. Still, I tell myself, despite everything, I know that I do not *want* to hurt people. It's not something I crave. And even if the world hates me, even if they never stop hating me, I will never avenge myself on an innocent person. If I die, if I am killed, if I am murdered in my sleep, I will at least die with a shred of dignity. A piece of humanity that is still entirely mine, entirely under my control. And I will not allow anyone to take that from me.

So I have to keep remembering that Warner and I are 2 different words.

We are synonyms but not the same.

Synonyms know each other like old colleagues, like a set of friends who've seen the world together. They swap stories, reminisce about their origins and forget that though they are similar, they are entirely different, and though they share a certain set of attributes, one can never be the other. Because a quiet night is not the same as a silent one, a firm man is not the same as a steady one, and a bright light is not the same as a brilliant one because the way they wedge themselves into a sentence changes everything.

They are not the same.

I've spent my entire life fighting to be better. Fighting to be stronger. Because unlike Warner I don't want to be a terror on this Earth. I don't want to hurt people.

I don't want to use my power to cripple anyone.

But then I look at my own 2 hands and I remember exactly what I'm capable of. I remember exactly what I've done and I'm too aware of what I might do. Because it's so difficult to fight what you cannot control and right now I can't even control my own imagination as it grips my hair and drags me into the dark.

SIXTEEN

Loneliness is a strange sort of thing.

It creeps up on you, quiet and still, sits by your side in the dark, strokes your hair as you sleep. It wraps itself around your bones, squeezing so tight you almost can't breathe. It leaves lies in your heart, lies next to you at night, leaches the light out from every corner. It's a constant companion, clasping your hand only to yank you down when you're struggling to stand up.

You wake up in the morning and wonder who you are. You fail to fall asleep at night and tremble in your skin. You doubt you doubt you doubt

do I

don't I

should I

why won't I

And even when you're ready to let go. When you're ready to break free. When you're ready to be brand-new. Loneliness is an old friend standing beside you in the mirror, looking you in the eye, challenging you to live your life without it. You can't find the words to fight yourself, to fight the words screaming that you're not enough never enough never ever enough.

Loneliness is a bitter, wretched companion.

Sometimes it just won't let go.

"Hellooooo?"

I blink and gasp and flinch away from the fingers snapping in front of my face as the familiar stone walls of Omega Point come back into focus. I manage to spin around.

Kenji is staring at me.

"What?" I shoot him a panicked, nervous look as I clasp and unclasp my ungloved hands, wishing I had something warm to wrap my fingers in. This suit does not come with pockets and I wasn't able to salvage the gloves I ruined in the research rooms. I haven't received any replacements, either.

"You're early," Kenji says to me, cocking his head, watching me with eyes both surprised and curious.

I shrug and try to hide my face, unwilling to admit that I hardly slept through the night. I've been awake since 3:00 a.m., fully dressed and ready to go by 4:00. I've been dying for an excuse to fill my mind with things that have nothing to do with my own thoughts. "I'm excited," I lie. "What are we doing today?"

He shakes his head a bit. Squints at something over my shoulder as he speaks to me. "You, um"—he clears his throat—"you okay?"

"Yes, of course."

"Huh."

"What?"

"Nothing," he says quickly. "Just, you know." A haphazard gesture toward my face. "You don't look so good, princess. You look kind of like you did that first day you showed up with Warner back on base. All scared and dead-looking and, no offense, but you look like you could use a shower."

I smile and pretend I can't feel my face shaking from the effort. I try to relax my shoulders, try to look normal, calm, when I say, "I'm fine. Really." I drop my eyes. "I'm just—it's a little cold down here, that's all. I'm not used to being without my gloves."

Kenji is nodding, still not looking at me. "Right. Well. He's going to be okay, you know."

"What?" Breathing. I'm so bad at breathing.

"Kent." He turns to me. "Your boyfriend. *Adam*. He's going to be fine."

1 word, 1 simple, stupid reminder of him startles the butterflies sleeping in my stomach before I remember that Adam is not my boyfriend anymore. He's not my anything anymore. He can't be.

And the butterflies drop dead.

~~This.~~

~~I can't do this.~~

"So," I say too brightly. "Shouldn't we get going? We should get going, right?"

Kenji shoots me an odd look but doesn't comment. "Yeah," he says. "Yeah, sure. Follow me."

SEVENTEEN

Kenji leads me to a door I've never seen before. A door belonging to a room I've never been in before.

I hear voices inside.

Kenji knocks twice before turning the handle and all at once the cacophony overwhelms me. We're walking into a room bursting with people, faces I've only ever seen from far away, people sharing smiles and laughter I've never been welcome to. There are individual desks with individual chairs set up in the vast space so that it resembles a classroom. There's a whiteboard built into the wall next to a monitor blinking with information. I spot Castle. Standing in the corner, looking over a clipboard with such focus that he doesn't even notice our entry until Kenji shouts a greeting.

Castle's entire face lights up.

I'd noticed it before, the connection between them, but it's now becoming increasingly apparent to me that Castle harbors a special kind of affection for Kenji. A sweet, proud sort of affection that's usually reserved for parents. It makes me wonder about the nature of their relationship. Where it began, how it began, what must've happened to bring them together. It makes me wonder at how little I know about the people of Omega Point.

I look around at their eager faces, men and women, youthful and middle-aged, all different ethnicities, shapes, and sizes. They're interacting with one another like they're part of a family and I feel a strange sort of pain stabbing at my side, poking holes in me until I deflate.

It's like my face is pressed up against the glass, watching a scene from far, far away, wishing and wanting to be a part of something I know I'll never really be a part of. I forget, sometimes, that there are people out there who still manage to smile every day, despite everything.

They haven't lost hope yet.

Suddenly I feel sheepish, ashamed, even. Daylight makes my thoughts look dark and sad and I want to pretend I'm still optimistic, I want to believe that I'll find a way to live. That maybe, somehow, there's still a chance for me somewhere.

Someone whistles.

"All right, everyone," Kenji calls out, hands cupped around his mouth. "Everyone take a seat, okay? We're doing another orientation for those of you who've never done this before, and I need all of you to get settled for a bit." He scans the crowd. "Right. Yeah. Everyone just take a seat. Wherever is fine. Lily—you don't have to—okay, fine, that's fine. Just settle down. We're going to get started in five minutes, okay?" He holds up an open palm, fingers splayed. "Five minutes."

I slip into the closest empty seat without looking around. I keep my head down, my eyes focused on the individual grains of wood on the desk as everyone collapses into chairs around me. Finally, I dare to glance to my right. Bright white hair and snow-white skin and clear blue eyes blink back at me.

Brendan. The electricity boy.

He smiles. Offers me a 2-finger wave.

I duck my head.

"Oh—hey," I hear someone say. "What are you doing here?"

I jerk toward my left to find sandy-blond hair and black plastic glasses sitting on a crooked nose. An ironic smile twisted onto a pale face. *Winston*. I remember him. He interviewed me when I first arrived at Omega Point. Said he was some kind of psychologist. But he also happens to be the one who designed the suit I'm wearing. The gloves I destroyed.

I think he's some kind of genius. I'm not sure.

Right now, he's chewing on the cap of his pen, staring at me. He uses an index finger to push his glasses up the bridge of his nose. I remember he's asked me a question and I make an effort to answer.

"I'm not actually sure," I tell him. "Kenji brought me here but didn't tell me why."

Winston doesn't seem surprised. He rolls his eyes. "Him with the freaking mysteries all the time. I don't know why he thinks it's such a good idea to keep people in suspense. It's like the guy thinks his life is a movie or something. Always so dramatic about everything. It's irritating as hell."

I have no idea what I'm supposed to say to that. ~~I can't help thinking that Adam would agree with him and then I can't help thinking about Adam and then I.~~

"Ah, don't listen to him." An English accent steps into

the conversation. I turn around to see Brendan still smiling at me. "Winston's always a bit beastly this early in the morning."

"Jesus. How early *is* it?" Winston asks. "I would kick a soldier in the crotch for a cup of coffee right now."

"It's your own fault you never sleep, mate," Brendan counters. "You think you can survive on three hours a night? You're mad."

Winston drops his chewed-up pen on the desk. Runs a tired hand through his hair. Tugs his glasses off and rubs at his face. "It's the freaking patrols. Every goddamn night. Something is going on and it's getting intense out there. So many soldiers just walking around? What the hell are they doing? I have to actually be *awake* the whole time—"

"What are you talking about?" I ask before I can stop myself. My ears are perked and my interest is piqued. News from the outside is something I've never had the opportunity to hear before. Castle was so intent on me focusing all my energy on training that I never heard much more than his constant reminders that *we're running out of time* and that I *need to learn before it's too late.* I'm beginning to wonder if things are worse than I thought.

"The patrols?" Brendan asks. He waves a knowing hand. "Oh, it's just, we work in shifts, right? In pairs—take turns keeping watch at night," he explains. "Most of the time it's no problem, just routine, nothing too serious."

"But it's been weird lately," Winston cuts in. "It's like they're *really* searching for us now. Like it's not just some crazy theory anymore. They know we're a real threat and it's like they actually have a clue where we are." He shakes his head. "But that's impossible."

"Apparently not, mate."

"Well, whatever it is, it's starting to freak me out," Winston says. "There are soldiers all over the place, way too close to where we are. We see them on camera," he says to me, noticing my confusion. "And the weirdest part," he adds, leaning in, lowering his voice, "is that Warner is always with them. Every single night. Walking around, issuing orders I can't hear. And his arm is still injured. He walks around with it in a sling."

"Warner?" My eyes go wide. "He's with them? Is that—is that . . . unusual?"

"It's quite odd," Brendan says. "He's CCR—chief commander and regent—of Sector 45. In normal circumstances he would delegate this task to a colonel, a lieutenant, even. His priorities should be on base, overseeing his soldiers." Brendan shakes his head. "He's a bit daft, I think, taking a risk like that. Spending time away from his own camp. Seems strange that he'd be able to get away so many nights."

"Right," Winston says, nodding his head. "Exactly." He points at the 2 of us, stabbing at the air. "And it makes you wonder who he's leaving in charge. The guy doesn't trust anyone—he's not known for his delegation skills to begin with—so for him to leave the base behind every night?" A pause. "It doesn't add up. Something is going on."

"Do you think," I ask, feeling scared and feeling brave,

"that maybe he's looking for ~~someone~~ something?"

"Yup." Winston exhales. Scratches the side of his nose. "That's exactly what I think. And I'd love to know what the hell he's looking for."

"Us, obviously," Brendan says. "He's looking for us."

Winston seems unconvinced. "I don't know," he says. "This is different. They've been searching for us for years, but they've never done anything like this. Never spent so much manpower on this kind of a mission. And they've never gotten this close."

"Wow," I whisper, not trusting myself to posit any of my own theories. Not wanting to think too hard about ~~who~~ what it is, exactly, Warner is searching for. And all the time wondering why these 2 guys are speaking to me so freely, as if I'm trustworthy, as if I'm one of their own.

I don't dare mention it.

"Yeah," Winston says, picking up his chewed-up pen again. "Crazy. Anyway, if we don't get a fresh batch of coffee today, I am seriously going to lose my shit."

I look around the room. I don't see coffee anywhere. No food, either. I wonder what that means for Winston. "Are we going to have breakfast before we start?"

"Nah," he says. "Today we get to eat on a different schedule. Besides, we'll have plenty to choose from when we get back. We get first picks. It's the only perk."

"Get back from where?"

"Outside," Brendan says, leaning back in his chair. He points up at the ceiling. "We're going up and out."

"What?" I gasp, feeling true excitement for the first time. "Really?"

"Yup." Winston puts his glasses back on. "And it looks like you're about to get your first introduction to what it is we do here." He nods at the front of the room, and I see Kenji hauling a huge trunk onto a table.

"What do you mean?" I ask. "What are we doing?"

"Oh, you know." Winston shrugs. Clasps his hands behind his head. "Grand larceny. Armed robbery. That sort of thing."

I begin to laugh when Brendan stops me. He actually puts his hand on my shoulder and for a moment I'm mildly terrified. Wondering if he's lost his mind.

"He's not joking," Brendan says to me. "And I hope you know how to use a gun."

EIGHTEEN

We look homeless.

Which means we look like civilians.

We've moved out of the classroom and into the hallway, and we're all wearing a similar sort of ensemble, tattered and grayish and frayed. Everyone is adjusting their outfits as we go; Winston slips off his glasses and shoves them into his jacket only to zip up his coat. The collar comes up to his chin and he huddles into it. Lily, one of the other girls among us, wraps a thick scarf around her mouth and pulls the hood of her coat over her head. I see Kenji pull on a pair of gloves and readjust his cargo pants to better hide the gun tucked inside.

Brendan shifts beside me.

He pulls a skullcap out of his pocket and tugs it on over his head, zipping his coat up to his neck. It's startling the way the blackness of the beanie offsets the blue in his eyes to make them even brighter, sharper than they looked before. He flashes me a smile when he catches me watching. Then he tosses me a pair of old gloves 2 sizes too big before bending down to tighten the laces on his boots.

I take a small breath.

I try to focus all my energy on where I am, on what I'm

doing and what I'm about to do. I tell myself not to think of Adam, not to think about what he's doing or how he's healing or what he must be feeling right now. I beg myself not to dwell on my last moments with him, the way he touched me, how he held me, his lips and his hands and his breaths coming in too fast—

I fail.

I can't help but think about how he always tried to protect me, how he nearly lost his life in the process. He was always defending me, always watching out for me, never realizing that it was *me,* it was always *me* who was the biggest threat. The most dangerous. He thinks too highly of me, places me on a pedestal I've never deserved.

I definitely don't need protection.

I don't need anyone to worry for me or wonder about me or risk falling in love with me. I ~~am unstable. I need to be avoided. It's right that people fear me~~.

~~They should.~~

"Hey." Kenji stops beside me, grabs my elbow. "You ready?"

I nod. Offer him a small smile.

The clothes I'm wearing are borrowed. The card hanging from my neck, hidden under my suit, is brand-new. Today I was given a fake RR card—a Reestablishment Registration card. It's proof that I work and live on the compounds; proof that I'm registered as a citizen in regulated territory. Every legal citizen has one. I never did, because I was tossed into an asylum; it was never necessary for someone like me. In fact, I'm fairly certain they just expected me to die in there. Identification was not necessary.

But this RR card is special.

Not everyone at Omega Point receives a counterfeit card. Apparently they're extremely difficult to replicate. They're thin rectangles made out of a very rare type of titanium, laser-etched with a bar code as well as the owner's biographical data, and contain a tracking device that monitors the whereabouts of the citizen.

"RR cards track everything," Castle explained. "They're necessary for entering and exiting compounds, necessary for entering and exiting a person's place of work. Citizens are paid in REST dollars—wages based on a complicated algorithm that calculates the difficulty of their profession, as well as the number of hours they spend working, in order to determine how much their efforts are worth. This electronic currency is dispensed in weekly installments and automatically uploaded to a chip built into their RR cards. REST dollars can then be exchanged at Supply Centers for food and basic necessities. Losing an RR card," he said, "means losing your livelihood, your earnings, your legal status as a registered citizen.

"If you're stopped by a soldier and asked for proof of identification," Castle continued, "you must present your RR card. Failure to present your card," he said, "will result in . . . very unhappy consequences. Citizens who walk around without their cards are considered a threat to The Reestablishment. They are seen as purposely defying the law, as characters worthy of suspicion. Being uncooperative in any way—even if that means you simply do not want your every movement to be tracked and monitored—makes you seem sympathetic to rebel parties. And that makes you a threat. A threat," he said, "that The Reestablishment has no qualms about removing.

"Therefore," he said, taking a deep breath, "you cannot, and you will not, lose your RR card. Our counterfeit cards do not have the tracking device nor the chip necessary for monitoring REST dollars, because we don't have the need for either. But! That does not mean they are not just as valuable as decoys," he said. "And while for citizens on regulated territory, RR cards are part of a life sentence, at Omega Point, they are considered a privilege. And you will treat them as such."

A privilege.

Among the many things I learned in our meeting this morning, I discovered that these cards are only granted to those who go on missions outside of Omega Point. All of the people in that room today were hand-selected as being the best, the strongest, the most trustworthy. Inviting me to be in that room was a bold move on Kenji's part. I realize now that it was his way of telling me he trusts me. Despite everything, he's telling me—and everyone else—that I'm welcome here. Which explains why Winston and Brendan felt so comfortable opening up to me. Because they trust the system at Omega Point. And they trust Kenji if he says he trusts me.

So now I am one of them.

And as my first official act as a member?

I'm supposed to be a thief.

NINETEEN

We're heading up.

Castle should be joining us any moment now to lead our group out of this underground city and into the real world. It will be my first opportunity to see what's happened to our society in almost 3 years.

I was 14 when I was dragged away from home for killing an innocent child. I spent 2 years bouncing from hospital to law office to detention center to psych ward until they finally decided to put me away for good. Sticking me in the asylum was worse than sending me to prison~~; smarter, according to my parents.~~ If I'd been sent to prison, the guards would've had to treat me like a human being; instead, I spent the past year of my life treated like a rabid animal, trapped in a dark hole with no link to the outside world. Most everything I've witnessed of our planet thus far has been out of a window or while running for my life. And now I'm not sure what to expect.

But I want to see it.

I need to see it.

I'm tired of being blind and I'm tired of relying on my memories of the past and the bits and pieces I've managed to scrape together of our present.

All I really know is that The Reestablishment has been a household name for 10 years.

I know this because they began campaigning when I was 7 years old. I'll never forget the beginning of our falling apart. I remember the days when things were still fairly normal, when people were only sort-of dying all the time, when there was enough food for those with enough money to pay for it. This was before cancer became a common illness and the weather became a turbulent, angry creature. I remember how excited everyone was about The Reestablishment. I remember the hope in my teachers' faces and the announcements we were forced to watch in the middle of the school day. I remember those things.

And just 4 months before my 14-year-old self committed an unforgivable crime, The Reestablishment was elected by the people of our world to lead us into a better future.

Hope. They had so much hope. My parents, my neighbors, my teachers and classmates. Everyone was hoping for the best when they cheered for The Reestablishment and promised their unflagging support.

Hope can make people do terrible things.

I remember seeing the protests just before I was taken away. I remember seeing the streets flooded with angry mobs who wanted a refund on their purchase. I remember how The Reestablishment painted the protesters red from head to toe and told them they should've read the fine print before they left their houses that morning.

All sales are final.

Castle and Kenji are allowing me on this expedition because they're trying to welcome me into the heart of Omega Point. They want me to join them, to really accept them, to understand why their mission is so important. Castle wants me to fight against The Reestablishment and what they have planned for the world. The books, the artifacts, the language and history they plan on destroying; the simple, empty, monochromatic life they want to force upon the upcoming generations. He wants me to see that our Earth is still not so damaged as to be irreparable; he wants to prove that our future is salvageable, that things can get better as long as power is put in the right hands.

He wants me to trust.

I *want* to trust.

But I get scared, sometimes. In my very limited experience I've already found that people seeking power are not to be trusted. People with lofty goals and fancy speeches and easy smiles have done nothing to calm my heart. Men with guns have never put me at ease no matter how many times they promised they were killing for good reason.

It has not gone past my notice that the people of Omega Point are very excellently armed.

But I'm curious. I'm so desperately curious.

So I'm camouflaged in old, ragged clothes and a thick woolen hat that nearly covers my eyes. I wear a heavy jacket that must've belonged to a man and my leather boots are almost hidden by the too-large pants puddling around my ankles. I look like a civilian. A poor, tortured civilian struggling to find food for her family.

A door clicks shut and we all turn at once. Castle beams. Looks around at the group of us.

Me. Winston. Kenji. Brendan. The girl named Lily. 10 other people I still don't really know. We're 16 altogether, including Castle. A perfectly even number.

"All right, everyone," Castle says, clapping his hands together. I notice he's wearing gloves, too. Everyone is. Today, I'm just a girl in a group wearing normal clothes and normal gloves. Today, I'm just a number. No one of significance. Just an ordinary person. Just for today.

It's so absurd I feel like smiling.

And then I remember how I nearly killed Adam yesterday and suddenly I'm not sure how to move my lips.

"Are we ready?" Castle looks around. "Don't forget what we discussed," he says. A pause. A careful glance. Eye contact with each one of us. Eyes on me for a moment too long. "Okay then. Follow me."

No one really speaks as we follow Castle down these corridors, and I'm left to wonder how easy it would be to just disappear in this inconspicuous outfit. I could run away, blend into the background and never be found again.

~~Like a coward.~~

I search for something to say to shake the silence. "So how are we getting there?" I ask anyone.

"We walk," Winston says.

Our feet pound the floors in response.

"Most civilians don't have cars," Kenji explains. "And we sure as hell can't be caught in a tank. If we want to blend in, we have to do as the people do. And walk."

I lose track of which tunnels break off in which directions as Castle leads us toward the exit. I'm increasingly aware of how little I understand about this place, how little I've seen of it. Although if I'm perfectly honest, I'll admit I haven't made much of an effort to explore anything.

I need to do something about that.

It's only when the terrain under my feet changes that I realize how close we are to getting outside. We're walking uphill, up a series of stone stairs stacked into the ground. I can see what looks like a small square of a metal door from here. It has a latch.

I realize I'm a little nervous.

Anxious.

Eager and afraid.

Today I will see the world as a civilian, really see things up close for the very first time. I will see what the people of this new society must endure now.

~~See what my parents must be experiencing wherever they are.~~

Castle pauses at the door, which looks small enough to be a window. Turns to face us. "Who are you?" he demands.

No one answers.

Castle draws himself up to his full height. Crosses his arms. "Lily," he says. "Name. ID. Age. Sector and occupation. *Now.*"

Lily tugs the scarf away from her mouth. She sounds slightly robotic when she says, “My name is Erica Fontaine, 1117-52QZ. I’m twenty-six years old. I live in Sector 45.”

“Occupation,” Castle says again, a hint of impatience creeping into his voice.

“Textile. Factory 19A-XC2.”

“Winston,” Castle orders.

“My name is Keith Hunter, 4556-65DS,” Winston says. “Thirty-four years old. Sector 45. I work in Metal. Factory 15B-XC2.”

Kenji doesn’t wait for a prompt when he says, “Hiro Yamasaki, 8891-11DX. Age twenty. Sector 45. Artillery. 13A-XC2.”

Castle nods as everyone takes turns regurgitating the information etched into their fake RR cards. He smiles, satisfied. Then he focuses his eyes on me until everyone is staring, watching, waiting to see if I screw it up.

“Delia Dupont,” I say, the words slipping from my lips more easily than I expected.

We’re not planning on being stopped, but this is an extra precaution in the event that we’re asked to identify ourselves; we have to know the information on our RR cards as if it were our own. Kenji also said that even though the soldiers overseeing the compounds are from Sector 45, they’re always different from the guards back on base. He doesn’t think we’ll run into anyone who will recognize us.

But.

Just in case.

I clear my throat. "ID number 1223-99SX. Seventeen years old. Sector 45. I work in Metal. Factory 15A-XC2."

Castle stares at me for just a second too long.

Finally, he nods. Looks around at all of us. "And what," he says, his voice deep and clear and booming, "are the three things you will ask yourself before you speak?"

Again, no one answers. Though it's not because we don't know the answer.

Castle counts off on his fingers. "First! *Does this need to be said?* Second! *Does this need to be said by me?* And third! *Does this need to be said by me right now?*"

Still, no one says a word.

"We do not speak unless absolutely necessary," Castle says. "We do not laugh, we do not smile. We do not make eye contact with one another if we can help it. We will not act as if we know each other. We are to do nothing at all to encourage extra glances in our direction. We do not draw attention to ourselves." A pause. "You understand this, yes? This is clear?"

We nod.

"And if something goes wrong?"

"We scatter." Kenji clears his throat. "We run. We hide. We think of only ourselves. And we never, ever betray the location of Omega Point."

Everyone takes a deep breath at the same time.

Castle pushes the small door open. Peeks outside before motioning for us to follow him, and we do. We scramble through, one by one, silent as the words we don't speak.

I haven't been aboveground in almost 3 weeks. It feels

like it's been 3 months.

The moment my face hits the air, I feel the wind snap against my skin in a way that's familiar, admonishing. It's as if the wind is scolding me for being away for so long.

We're in the middle of a frozen wasteland. The air is icy and sharp, dead leaves dancing around us. The few trees still standing are waving in the wind, their broken, lonely branches begging for companionship. I look left. I look right. I look straight ahead.

There is nothing.

Castle told us this area used to be covered in lush, dense vegetation. He said when he first sought out a hiding place for Omega Point, this particular stretch of ground was ideal. But that was so long ago—decades ago—that now everything has changed. Nature itself has changed. And it's too late to move this hideout.

So we do what we can.

This part, he said, is the hardest. Out here, we're vulnerable. Easy to spot even as civilians because we're out of place. Civilians have no business being anywhere outside of the compounds; they do not leave the regulated grounds deemed safe by The Reestablishment. Being caught anywhere on unregulated turf is considered a breach of the laws set in place by our new pseudogovernment, and the consequences are severe.

So we have to get ourselves to the compounds as quickly as possible.

The plan is for Kenji—whose gift enables him to blend

into any background—to travel ahead of the pack, making himself invisible as he checks to make sure our paths are clear. The rest of us hang back, careful, completely silent. We keep a few feet of distance between ourselves, ready to run, to save ourselves if necessary. It's strange, considering the tight-knit nature of the community at Omega Point, that Castle wouldn't encourage us to stay together. But this, he explained, is for the good of the majority. It's a sacrifice. One of us has to be willing to get caught in order for the others to escape.

Take one for the team.

Our path is clear.

We've been walking for at least half an hour and no one seems to be guarding this deserted piece of land. Soon, the compounds come into view. Blocks and blocks and blocks of metal boxes, cubes clustered in heaps across the ancient, wheezing ground. I clutch my coat closer to my body as the wind flips on its side just to fillet our human flesh.

It's too cold to be alive today.

I'm wearing my suit—which regulates my body heat—under this outfit and I'm still freezing. I can't imagine what everyone else must be going through right now. I glance at Brendan only to find him already doing the same. Our eyes meet for less than a second but I could swear he smiled at me, his cheeks slapped into pinks and reds by a wind jealous of his wandering eyes.

Blue. So blue.

Such a different, lighter, almost transparent shade of blue but still, so very, very blue. Blue eyes will always remind me of Adam, I think. And it hits me again. Hits me so hard, right in the core of my very being.

The ache.

"Hurry!" Kenji's voice reaches us through the wind, but his body is nowhere in sight. We're not 5 feet from setting foot in the first cluster of compounds, but I'm somehow frozen in place, blood and ice and broken forks running down my back.

"MOVE!" Kenji's voice booms again. "Get close to the compounds and keep your faces covered! Soldiers at three o'clock!"

We all jump up at once, rushing forward while trying to remain inconspicuous and soon we've ducked behind the side of a metal housing unit; we get low, each pretending to be one of the many people picking scraps of steel and iron out from the heaps of trash stacked in piles all over the ground.

The compounds are set in one big field of waste. Garbage and plastic and mangled bits of metal sprinkled like craft confetti all over a child's floor. There's a fine layer of snow powdered over everything, as if the Earth was making a weak attempt to cover up its ugly bits just before we arrived.

I look up.

Look over my shoulder.

Look around in ways I'm not supposed to but I can't help it. I'm supposed to keep my eyes on the ground like I live here, like there's nothing new to see, like I can't stand to lift my face only to have it stung by the cold. I should be huddled into myself like all the other strangers trying to stay warm. But there's so much to see. So much to observe. So much I've never been exposed to before.

So I dare to lift my head.

And the wind grabs me by the throat.

TWENTY

Warner is standing not 20 feet away from me.

His suit is tailor-made and closely fitted to his form in a shade of black so rich it's almost blinding. His shoulders are draped in an open peacoat the color of mossy trunks 5 shades darker than his green, green eyes; the bright gold buttons are the perfect complement to his golden hair. He's wearing a black tie. Black leather gloves. Shiny black boots.

He looks immaculate.

Flawless, especially as he stands here among the dirt and destruction, surrounded by the bleakest colors this landscape has to offer. He's a vision of emerald and onyx, silhouetted in the sunlight in the most deceiving way. He could be glowing. That could be a halo around his head. This could be the world's way of making an example out of irony. Because Warner is beautiful in ways even Adam isn't.

Because Warner is not human.

Nothing about him is normal.

He's looking around, eyes squinting against the morning light, and the wind blows open his unbuttoned coat long enough for me to catch a glimpse of his arm underneath. Bandaged. Bound in a sling.

So close.

I was so close.

The soldiers hovering around him are waiting for orders, waiting for something, and I can't tear my eyes away. I can't help but experience a strange thrill in being so close to him, and yet so far away. It feels almost like an advantage—being able to study him without his knowledge.

He is a strange, strange, twisted boy.

I don't know if I can forget what he did to me. What he made me do. How I came so close to killing all over again. I will hate him forever for it even though I'm sure I'll have to face him again.

One day.

I never thought I'd see Warner on the compounds. I had no idea he even visited the civilians—though, in truth, I never knew much about how he spent his days unless he spent them with me. I have no idea what he's doing here.

He finally says something to the soldiers and they nod, once, quickly. Then disappear.

I pretend to be focused on something just to the right of him, careful to keep my head down and cocked slightly to the side so he can't catch a glimpse of my face even if he does look in my direction. My left hand reaches up to tug my hat down over my ears, and my right hand pretends to sort trash, pretends to pick out pieces of scraps to salvage for the day.

This is how some people make their living. Another miserable occupation.

Warner runs his good hand over his face, covering his eyes for just a moment before his hand rests on his mouth, pressing against his lips as though he has something he can't bear to say.

His eyes look almost . . . worried. Though I'm sure I'm just reading him wrong.

I watch him as he watches the people around him. I watch him closely enough to be able to notice that his gaze lingers on the small children, the way they run after each other with an innocence that says they have no idea what kind of world they've lost. This bleak, dark place is the only thing they've ever known.

I try to read Warner's expression as he studies them, but he's careful to keep himself completely neutral. He doesn't do more than blink as he stands perfectly still, a statue in the wind.

A stray dog is heading straight toward him.

I'm suddenly petrified. I'm worried for this scrappy creature, this weak, frozen little animal probably seeking out small bits of food, something to keep it from starving for the next few hours. My heart starts racing in my chest, the blood pumping too fast and too hard and

I don't know why I feel like something terrible is about to happen.

The dog bolts right into the backs of Warner's legs, as if it's half blind and can't see where it's going. It's panting hard, tongue lolling to the side like it doesn't know how to get it back in. It whines and whimpers a little, slobbering all over Warner's very exquisite pants and I'm holding my breath as the golden boy turns around. I half expect him to take out his gun and shoot the dog right in the head.

I've already seen him do it to a human being.

But Warner's face breaks apart at the sight of the small dog, cracks forming in the perfect cast of his features, surprise lifting his eyebrows and widening his gaze for just a moment. Long enough for me to notice.

He looks around, his eyes swift as they survey his surroundings before he scoops the animal into his arms and disappears around a low fence—one of the short, squat fences that are used to section off squares of land for each compound. I'm suddenly desperate to see what he's going to do and I'm feeling anxious, so anxious, still unable to breathe.

I've seen what Warner can do to a person. I've seen his callous heart and his unfeeling eyes and his complete indifference, his cool, collected demeanor unshaken after killing a man in cold blood. I can only imagine what he has planned for an innocent dog.

I have to see it for myself.

I have to get his face out of my head and this is exactly what I need. It's proof that he's sick, twisted, that he's wrong, and will always be wrong.

If only I could stand up, I could see him. I could see what he's doing to that poor animal and maybe I could find a way to stop him before it's too late but I hear Castle's voice, a loud whisper calling us. Telling us the coast is clear to move forward now that Warner is out of sight. "We all move, and we move separately," he says. "Stick to the plan! No one trails anyone else. We all meet at the drop-off. If you don't make it, we will leave you behind. You have thirty minutes."

Kenji is tugging on my arm, telling me to get to my feet, to focus, to look in the right direction. I look up long enough to see that the rest of the group has already dispersed; Kenji, however, refuses to budge. He curses under his breath until finally I stand up. I nod. I tell him I understand the plan and motion for him to move on without me. I remind him that we can't be seen together. That we cannot walk in groups or pairs. We cannot be conspicuous.

Finally, finally, he turns to go.

I watch Kenji leave. Then I take a few steps forward only to spin around and dart back to the corner of the compound, sliding my back up against the wall, hidden from view.

My eyes scan the area until I spot the fence where I last saw Warner; I tip up on my toes to peer over.

I have to cover my mouth to keep from gasping out loud.

Warner is crouched on the ground, feeding something to the dog with his good hand. The animal's quivering, bony body is huddled inside of Warner's open coat, shivering as its stubby limbs try to find warmth after being frozen for so long. The dog wags its tail hard, pulling back to look Warner in the eye only to plow into the warmth of his jacket again. I hear Warner laugh.

I see him smile.

It's the kind of smile that transforms him into someone else entirely, the kind of smile that puts stars in his eyes and a dazzle on his lips and I realize I've never seen him like this before. I've never even seen his teeth—so straight, so white, nothing less than perfect. A flawless, flawless exterior for a boy with a black, black heart. It's hard to believe there's blood on the hands of the person I'm staring at. He looks soft and vulnerable—so human. His eyes are squinting from all his grinning and his cheeks are pink from the cold.

He has *dimples*.

He's easily the most beautiful thing I've ever seen.

And I wish I'd never seen it.

Because something inside of my heart is ripping apart and it feels like fear, it tastes like panic and anxiety and desperation and I don't know how to understand the image in front of me. I don't want to see Warner like this. I don't want to think of him as anything other than a monster.

This isn't right.

I shift too fast and too far in the wrong direction, suddenly too stupid to find my footing and hating myself for wasting time I could've used to escape. I know Castle and Kenji would be ready to kill me for taking such a risk but they don't understand what it's like in my head right now, they don't understand what I'm—

"Hey!" he barks. "You there—"

I look up without intending to, without realizing that I've responded to Warner's voice until it's too late. He's up, frozen in place, staring straight into my eyes, his good hand paused midmovement until it falls limp at his side, his jaw slack; stunned, temporarily stupefied.

I watch as the words die in his throat.

I'm paralyzed, caught in his gaze as he stands there, his chest heaving so hard and his lips ready to form the words that will surely sentence me to my death, all because of my stupid, senseless, idiotic—

"Whatever you do, don't scream."

Someone closes a hand over my mouth.

TWENTY-ONE

I don't move.

"I'm going to let go of you, okay? I want you to take my hand."

I reach out without looking down and feel our gloved hands fit together. Kenji lets go of my face.

"You are such an *idiot*," he says to me, but I'm still staring at Warner. Warner who's now looking around like he's just seen a ghost, blinking and rubbing his eyes like he's confused, glancing at the dog like maybe the little animal managed to bewitch him. He grabs a tight hold of his blond hair, mussing it out of its perfect state, and stalks off so fast my eyes don't know how to follow him.

"What the hell is wrong with you?" Kenji is saying to me. "Are you even listening to me? Are you *insane*?"

"What did you just do? Why didn't he—oh my God," I gasp, sparing a look at my own body.

I'm completely invisible.

"You're welcome," Kenji snaps, dragging me away from the compound. "And keep your voice down. Being invisible doesn't mean the world can't hear you."

"You can *do* that?" I try to find his face but I might as well be speaking to the air.

"Yeah—it's called projecting, remember? Didn't Castle explain this to you already?" he asks, eager to rush through the explanation so he can get back to yelling at me. "Not everyone can do it—not all abilities are the same—but maybe if you manage to stop being a *dumbass* long enough not to *die*, I might be able to teach you one day."

"You came back for me," I say to him, struggling to keep up with his brisk pace and not at all offended by his anger. "Why'd you come back for me?"

"Because you're a *dumbass,*" he says again.

"I know. I'm so sorry. I couldn't help it."

"Well, help it," he says, his voice gruff as he yanks me by the arm. "We're going to have to run to recover all the time you just wasted."

"Why'd you come back, Kenji?" I ask again, undeterred. "How'd you know I was still here?"

"I was watching you," he says.

"What? What do you—"

"I watch you," he says, his words rushing out again, impatient. "It's part of what I do. It's what I've been doing since day one. I enlisted in Warner's army for you and only you. It's what Castle sent me for. You were my job." His voice is clipped, fast, unfeeling. "I already told you this."

"Wait, what do you mean, you *watch* me?" I hesitate, tugging on his invisible arm to slow him down a little. "You follow me around everywhere? Even now? Even at Omega Point?"

He doesn't answer right away. When he does, his words are reluctant. "Sort of."

"But why? I'm here. Your job is done, isn't it?"

"We've already had this conversation," he says. "Remember? Castle wanted me to make sure you were okay. He told me to keep an eye on you—nothing serious—just, you know, make sure you weren't having any psychotic breakdowns or anything." I hear him sigh. "You've been through a lot. He's a little worried about you. Especially now—after what just happened? You don't look okay. You look like you want to throw yourself in front of a tank."

"I would never do something like that," I say to him.

"Yeah," he says. "Fine. Whatever. I'm just pointing out the obvious. You only function on two settings: you're either moping or you're making out with Adam—and I have to say, I kind of prefer the moping—"

"Kenji!" I nearly yank my hand out of his. His grip tightens around my fingers.

"Don't let go," he snaps at me again. "You can't let go or it breaks the connection." Kenji is dragging me through the middle of a clearing. We're far enough from the compounds now that we won't be overheard, but we're still too far from the drop-off to be considered safe just yet. Luckily the snow isn't sticking enough for us to leave tracks.

"I can't believe you spied on us!"

"I was not *spying* on you, okay? Damn. Calm down. Hell, both of you need to calm down. Adam was already all up in my face about it—"

"What?" I feel the pieces of this puzzle finally beginning

to fit together. "Is that why he was being mean to you at breakfast last week?"

Kenji slows our pace a little. He takes a deep, long breath. "He thought I was, like, taking *advantage* of the situation." He says *advantage* like it's a strange, dirty word. "He thinks I get invisible just to see you naked or something. Listen—I don't even know, okay? He was being an idiot about it. I'm just doing my job."

"But—you're not, right? You're not trying to see me naked or anything?"

Kenji snorts, chokes on his laughter. "Listen, Juliette," he says through another laugh, "I'm not blind, okay? On a purely physical level? Yeah, you're pretty sexy—and that suit you have to wear all the time doesn't hurt. But even if you didn't have that whole 'I kill you if I touch you' thing going on, you are *definitely* not my type. And more importantly, I'm not some perverted asshole," he says. "I take my job seriously. I get real shit done in this world, and I like to think people respect me for it. But your boy Adam is a little too blinded by his pants to think straight. Maybe you should do something about that."

I drop my eyes. Say nothing for a moment. Then: "I don't think you'll have to worry about that anymore."

"Ah, shit." Kenji sighs, like he can't believe he got stuck listening to problems about my love life. "I just walked right into that, didn't I?"

"We can go, Kenji. We don't have to talk about this."

An irritated breath. "It's not that I don't *care* about what you're going through," he says. "It's not like I want to see you all depressed or whatever. It's just that this life is messed up enough as it is," he says. "And I'm sick of you being so caught up in your own little world all the time. You act like this whole thing—everything we do—is a joke. You don't take any of it seriously—"

"What?" I cut him off. "That's not true—I do take this seriously—"

"*Bullshit*." He laughs a short, sharp, angry laugh. "All you do is sit around and think about your *feelings*. You've got *problems*. Boo-freaking-hoo," he says. "Your parents hate you and it's so hard but you have to wear gloves for the rest of your life because you kill people when you touch them. Who *gives* a shit?" He's breathing hard enough for me to hear him. "As far as I can tell, you've got food in your mouth and clothes on your back and a place to pee in peace whenever you feel like it. Those aren't problems. That's called living like a king. And I'd really appreciate it if you'd grow the hell up and stop walking around like the world crapped on your only roll of toilet paper. Because it's stupid," he says, barely reining in his temper. "It's stupid, and it's ungrateful. You don't have a clue what everyone else in the world is going through right now. You don't have a clue, Juliette. And you don't seem to give a damn, either."

I swallow, so hard.

"Now I am *trying*," he says, "to give you a chance to fix things. I keep giving you opportunities to do things differently. To see past the sad little girl you used to be—the sad little girl you keep clinging to—and stand up for yourself. Stop crying. Stop sitting in the dark counting out all your individual feelings about how sad and lonely you are. Wake up," he says. "You're not the only person in this world who doesn't want to get out of bed in the morning. You're not the only one with daddy issues and severely screwed-up DNA. You can be whoever the hell you want to be now. You're not with your shitty parents anymore. You're not in that shitty asylum, and you're no longer stuck being Warner's shitty little experiment. So make a choice," he says. "Make a choice and stop wasting everyone's time. Stop wasting your own time. Okay?"

Shame is pooling in every inch of my body.

Heat has flamed its way up my core, singeing me from the inside out. I'm so horrified, so terrified to hear the truth in his words.

"Let's go," he says, but his voice is just a tiny bit gentler. "We have to run."

And I nod even though he can't see me.

I nod and nod and nod and I'm so happy no one can see my face right now.

TWENTY-TWO

"Stop throwing boxes at me, jackass. That's my job." Winston laughs and grabs a package heavily bandaged in cellophane only to chuck it at another guy's head. The guy standing right next to me.

I duck.

The other guy grunts as he catches the package, and then grins as he offers Winston an excellent view of his middle finger.

"Keep it classy, Sanchez," Winston says as he tosses him another package.

Sanchez. His name is Ian Sanchez. I just learned this a few minutes ago when he and I and a few others were grouped together to form an assembly line.

We are currently standing in one of the official storage compounds of The Reestablishment.

Kenji and I managed to catch up to everyone else just in time. We all congregated at the drop-off (which turned out to be little more than a glorified ditch), and then Kenji gave me a sharp look, pointed at me, grinned, and left me with the rest of the group while he and Castle communicated about the next part of our mission.

Which was getting into the storage compound.

The irony, however, is that we traveled aboveground for supplies only to have to go back underground to get them. The storage compounds are, for all intents and purposes, invisible.

They're underground cellars filled with just about everything imaginable: food, medicine, weapons. All the things needed to survive. Castle explained everything in our orientation this morning. He said that while having supplies buried underground is a clever method of concealment against the civilians, it actually worked out in his favor. Castle said he can sense—and move—objects from a great distance, even if that distance is 25 feet belowground. He said that when he approaches one of the storage facilities he can feel the difference immediately, because he can recognize the energy in each object. This, he explained, is what allows him to move things with his mind: he's able to touch the inherent energy in everything. Castle and Kenji have managed to track down 5 compounds within 20 miles of Omega Point just by walking around; Castle sensing, Kenji projecting to keep them invisible. They've located 5 more within 50 miles.

The storage compounds they access are on a rotation. They never take the same things and never in the same quantity, and they take from as many different facilities as possible. The farther the compound, the more intricate the mission becomes. This particular compound is closest, and therefore the mission is, relatively speaking, the easiest. That explains why I was allowed to come along.

All the legwork has already been done.

Brendan already knows how to confuse the electrical system in order to deactivate all the sensors and security cameras; Kenji acquired the pass code simply by shadowing a soldier who punched in the right numbers. All of this gives us a 30-minute window of time to work as quickly as possible to get everything we need into the drop-off, where we'll spend most of the day waiting to load our stolen supplies into vehicles that will carry the items away.

The system they use is fascinating.

There are 6 vans altogether, each slightly different in appearance, and all scheduled to arrive at different times. This way there are fewer chances of everyone being caught, and there's a higher probability that at least 1 of the vans will get back to Omega Point without a problem. Castle outlined what seemed like 100 different contingency plans in case of danger.

I'm the only one here, however, who appears even remotely nervous about what we're doing. In fact, with the exception of me and 3 others, everyone here has visited this particular compound several times, so they're walking around like it's familiar territory. Everyone is careful and efficient, but they feel comfortable enough to laugh and joke around, too. They know exactly what they're doing. The moment we got inside, they split themselves into 2 groups: 1 team formed the assembly line, and the other collected the things we need.

Others have more important tasks.

Lily has a photographic memory that puts photographs to shame. She walked in before the rest of us and immediately scanned the room, collecting and cataloging every minute detail. She's the one who will make sure that we leave nothing behind when we exit, and that, aside from the things we take, nothing else is missing or out of place. Brendan is our backup generator. He's managed to shut off power to the security system while still lighting the dark dimensions of this room. Winston is overseeing our 2 groups, mediating between the givers and the takers, making sure we're securing the right items and the right quantities. His arms and legs have the elastic ability to stretch at will, which enables him to reach both sides of the room quickly and easily.

Castle is the one who moves our supplies outside. He stands at the very end of the assembly line, in constant radio contact with Kenji. And as long as the area is clear, Castle needs to use only one hand to direct the hundreds of pounds of supplies we've hoarded into the drop-off.

Kenji, of course, is standing as lookout.

If it weren't for Kenji, the rest of this wouldn't even be possible. He's our invisible eyes and ears. Without him, we'd have no way of being so secure, so sure that we'll be safe on such a dangerous mission.

Not for the first time today, I'm beginning to realize why he's so important.

"Hey, Winston, can you get someone to check if they have any chocolate in here?" Emory—another guy on my assembly team—is smiling at Winston like he's hoping for good news. But then, Emory is always smiling. I've only known him for a few hours, but he's been smiling since 6:00 a.m., when we all met in the orientation room this morning. He's super tall, super bulky, and he has a super-huge afro that somehow manages to fall into his eyes a lot. He's moving boxes down the line like they're full of cotton.

Winston is shaking his head, trying not to laugh as he passes the question along. "Seriously?" He shoots a look at Emory, nudging his plastic glasses up his nose at the same time. "Of all the things in here, you want *chocolate*?"

Emory's smile vanishes. "Shut up, man, you know my mom loves that stuff."

"You say that every time."

"That's because it's true every time."

Winston says something to someone about grabbing another box of soap before turning back to Emory. "You know, I don't think I've ever seen your mom eat a piece of chocolate before."

Emory tells Winston to do something very inappropriate with his preternaturally flexible limbs, and I glance down at the box Ian has just handed to me, pausing to study the packaging carefully before passing it on.

"Hey, do you know why these are all stamped with the letters *R N W*?"

Ian turns around. Stunned. Looks at me like I've just asked him to take his clothes off. "Well, I'll be damned," he says. "She speaks."

"Of course I speak," I say, no longer interested in speaking at all.

Ian passes me another box. Shrugs. "Well, now I know."

"Now you do."

"The mystery has been solved."

"You really didn't think I could speak?" I ask after a moment. "Like, you thought I was mute?" I wonder what other things people are saying about me around here.

Ian looks over his shoulder at me, smiles like he's trying not to laugh. Shakes his head and doesn't answer me. "The stamp," he says, "is just regulation. They stamp everything RNW so they can track it. It's nothing fancy."

"But what does RNW mean? Who's stamping it?"

"RNW," he says, repeating the 3 letters like I'm supposed to recognize them. "Reestablished Nations of the World. Everything's gone global, you know. They all trade commodities. And that," he says, "is something no one really knows. It's another reason why the whole Reestablishment thing is a pile of crap. They've monopolized the resources of the entire planet and they're just keeping it all for themselves."

I remember some of this. I remember talking to Adam about this when he and I were locked in the asylum together. ~~Back before I knew what it was like to touch him. To be with him. To hurt him.~~ The Reestablishment has always been a global movement. I just didn't realize it had a name.

"Right," I say to Ian, suddenly distracted. "Of course."

Ian pauses as he hands me another package. "So is it true?" he asks, studying my face. "That you really have no clue what's happened to everything?"

"I know some things." I bristle. "I'm just not clear on all the details."

"Well," Ian says, "if you still remember how to speak when we get back to Point, maybe you should join us at lunch sometime. We can fill you in."

"Really?" I turn to face him.

"Yeah, kid." He laughs, tosses me another box. "Really. We don't bite."

TWENTY-THREE

Sometimes I wonder about glue.

No one ever stops to ask glue how it's holding up. If it's tired of sticking things together or worried about falling apart or wondering how it will pay its bills next week.

Kenji is kind of like that.

He's like glue. He works behind the scenes to keep things together and I've never stopped to think about what his story might be. Why he hides behind the jokes and the snark and the snide remarks.

But he was right. Everything he said to me was right.

Yesterday was a good idea. I needed to get away, to get out, to be productive. And now I need to take Kenji's advice and get over myself. I need to get my head straight. I need to focus on my priorities. I need to figure out what I'm doing here and how I can help. And if I care at all about Adam, I'll try to stay out of his life.

Part of me wishes I could see him; I want to make sure he's really going to be okay, that he's recovering well and eating enough and getting sleep at night. But another part of me is afraid to see him now. Because seeing Adam means saying good-bye. It means really recognizing that I can't be with him anymore and knowing that I have to find a new life for myself. Alone.

But at least at Omega Point I'll have options. And maybe if I can find a way to stop being scared, I'll actually figure out how to make friends. To be strong. To stop wallowing in my own problems.

Things have to be different now.

I grab my food and manage to lift my head; I nod hello to the faces I recognize from yesterday. Not everyone knows about my being on the trip—the invitations to go on missions outside of Omega Point are exclusive—but people, in general, seem to be a little less tense around me. I think.

I might be imagining it.

I try to find a place to sit down but then I see Kenji waving me over. Brendan and Winston and Emory are sitting at his table. I feel a smile tug at my lips as I approach them.

Brendan scoots over on the bench seat to make room for me. Winston and Emory nod hello as they shovel food into their mouths. Kenji shoots me a half smile, his eyes laughing at my surprise to be welcomed at his table.

I'm feeling okay. Like maybe things are going to be okay.

"Juliette?"

And suddenly I'm going to tip over.

I turn very, very slowly, half convinced that the voice I'm hearing belongs to a ghost, because there's no way Adam could've been released from the medical wing so soon. I wasn't expecting to have to face him so soon. I didn't think we'd have to have this talk so soon. Not here. Not in the middle of the dining hall.

I'm not prepared. I'm not *prepared*.

Adam looks terrible. He's pale. Unsteady. His hands are stuffed in his pockets and his lips are pressed together and his eyes are weary, tortured, deep and bottomless wells. His hair is messy. His T-shirt is straining across his chest, his tattooed forearms more pronounced than ever.

I want nothing more than to dive into his arms.

Instead, I'm sitting here, reminding myself to breathe.

"Can I talk to you?" he says, looking like he's half afraid to hear my answer. "Alone?"

I nod, still unable to speak. Abandon my food without looking back at Kenji or Winston or Brendan or Emory so I have no idea what they must be thinking right now. I don't even care.

Adam.

Adam is here and he's in front of me and he wants to talk to me and I have to tell him things that will surely be the death of me.

But I follow him out the door anyway. Into the hall. Down a dark corridor.

Finally we stop.

Adam looks at me like he knows what I'm going to say so I don't bother saying it. I don't want to say anything unless it becomes absolutely necessary. I'd rather just stand here and stare at him, shamelessly drink in the sight of him one last time without having to speak a word. Without having to say anything at all.

He swallows, hard. Looks up. Looks away. Blows out

a breath and rubs the back of his neck, clasps both hands behind his head and turns around so I can't see his face. But the effort causes his shirt to ride up his torso and I have to actually clench my fingers to keep from touching the sliver of skin exposed low on his abdomen, his lower back.

He's still looking away from me when he says, "I really—I really need you to say something." And the sound of his voice—so wretched, so agonized—makes me want to fall to my knees.

Still, I do not speak.

And he turns.

Faces me.

"There has to be something," he says, his hands in his hair now, gripping his skull. "Some kind of compromise—something I can say to convince you to make this work. Tell me there's *something*."

And I'm so scared. So scared I'm going to start sobbing in front of him.

"Please," he says, and he looks like he's about to crack, like he's done, like this is it he's about to fall apart and he says, "say something, I'm begging you—"

I bite my trembling lip.

He freezes in place, watching me, waiting.

"Adam," I breathe, trying to keep my voice steady. "I will always, a-always love you—"

"No," he says. "No, don't say that—don't say that—"

And I'm shaking my head, shaking it fast and hard, so hard it's making me dizzy but I can't stop. I can't say another word unless I want to start screaming and I can't look at his face, I can't bear to see what I'm doing to him—

"No, Juliette—*Juliette*—"

I'm backing away, stumbling, tripping over my own feet as I reach blindly for the wall when I feel his arms around me. I try to pull away but he's too strong, he's holding me too tight and his voice is choked when he says, "It was my fault—this is my fault—I shouldn't have kissed you—you tried to tell me but I didn't listen and I'm so—I'm so sorry," he says, gasping the words. "I should've listened to you. I wasn't strong enough. But it'll be different this time, I swear," he says, burying his face in my shoulder. "I'll never forgive myself for this. You were willing to give it a shot and I screwed everything up and I'm sorry, I'm so sorry—"

I have officially, absolutely collapsed inside.

I hate myself for what happened, hate myself for what I have to do, hate that I can't take his pain away, that I can't tell him we can try, that it'll be hard but we'll make it work anyway. Because this isn't a normal relationship. Because our problems aren't fixable.

Because my skin will never change.

All the training in the world won't remove the very real possibility that I could hurt him. Kill him, if we ever got carried away. I will always be a threat to him. Especially during the most tender moments, the most important, vulnerable moments. The moments I want most. Those are the things I can never have with him, and he deserves so much more than me, than this tortured person with so little to offer.

But I'd rather stand here and feel his arms around me than say a single thing. Because I'm weak, I'm so weak and I want him so much it's killing me. I can't stop shaking, I can't see straight, I can't see through the curtain of tears obscuring my vision.

And he won't let go of me.

He keeps whispering "Please" and I want to die.

But I think if I stay here any longer I will actually go insane.

So I raise a trembling hand to his chest and feel him stiffen, pull back, and I don't dare look at his eyes, I can't stand to see him looking hopeful, even if it's for only a second.

I take advantage of his momentary surprise and slackened arms to slip away, out of the shelter of his warmth, away from his beating heart. And I hold out my hand to stop him from reaching for me again.

"Adam," I whisper. "Please don't. I can't—I c-can't—"

"There's never been anyone else," he says, not bothering to keep his voice down anymore, not caring that his words are echoing through these tunnels. His hand is shaking as he covers his mouth, as he drags it across his face, through his hair. "There's never going to be anyone else—I'm never going to want anyone else—"

"Stop it—you have to stop—" I can't breathe I can't breathe I can't *breathe* "You don't want this—you don't want to be with someone like me—someone who will only end up h-hurting you—"

"*Dammit,* Juliette"—he turns to slam his palms against

the wall, his chest heaving, his head down, his voice broken, catching on every other syllable—"you're hurting me *now*," he says. "You're *killing* me—"

"Adam—"

"Don't walk away," he says, his voice tight, his eyes squeezed shut like he already knows I'm going to. Like he can't bear to see it happen. "Please," he whispers, tormented. "Don't walk away from this."

"I-I wish," I tell him, shaking violently now, "I wish I d-didn't have to. I wish I could love you less."

And I hear him call after me as I bolt down the corridor. I hear him shouting my name but I'm running, running away, running past the huge crowd gathered outside the dining hall, watching, listening to everything. I'm running to hide even though I know it will be impossible.

I will have to see him every single day.

Wanting him from a million miles away.

And I remember Kenji's words, his demands for me to wake up and stop crying and make a change, and I realize fulfilling my new promises might take a little longer than I expected.

Because I can't think of anything I'd rather do right now than find a dark corner and cry.

TWENTY-FOUR

Kenji finds me first.

He's standing in the middle of my training room. Looking around like he's never seen the place before, even though I'm sure that can't be true. I still don't know exactly what he does, but it's at least become clear to me that Kenji is one of the most important people at Omega Point. He's always on the move. Always busy. No one—except for me, and only lately—really sees him for more than a few moments at a time.

It's almost as if he spends the majority of his days . . . invisible.

"So," he says, nodding his head slowly, taking his time walking around the room with his hands clasped behind his back. "That was one hell of a show back there. That's the kind of entertainment we never really get underground."

Mortification.

I'm draped in it. Painted in it. Buried in it.

"I mean, I just have to say—that last line? 'I wish I could love you less'? That was genius. Really, really nice. I think Winston actually shed a tear—"

"SHUT UP, KENJI."

"I'm serious!" he says to me, offended. "That was, I don't

know. It was kind of beautiful. I had no idea you guys were so intense."

I pull my knees up to my chest, burrow deeper into the corner of this room, bury my face in my arms. "No offense, but I really don't want to t-talk to you right now, okay?"

"Nope. Not okay," he says. "You and me, we have work to do."

"No."

"Come on," he says. "Get. *Up*." He grabs my elbow, tugging me to my feet as I try to take a swipe at him.

I wipe angrily at my cheeks, scrub at the stains my tears left behind. "I'm not in the mood for your jokes, Kenji. Please just go away. Leave me alone."

"No one," he says, "is joking." Kenji picks up one of the bricks stacked against the wall. "And the world isn't going to stop waging war against itself just because you broke up with your boyfriend."

I stare at him, fists shaking, wanting to scream.

He doesn't seem concerned. "So what do you do in here?" he asks. "You just sit around trying to . . . what?" He weighs the brick in his hand. "Break this stuff?"

I give up, defeated. Fold myself onto the floor.

"I don't know," I tell him. I sniff away the last of my tears. Try to wipe my nose. "Castle kept telling me to 'focus' and 'harness my Energy.'" I use air quotes to illustrate my point. "But all I know about myself is that I *can* break things—I don't know why it happens. So I don't know how he expects me to replicate what I've already done. I had no idea what

I was doing then, and I don't know what I'm doing now, either. Nothing's changed."

"Hold up," Kenji says, dropping the brick back onto the stack before falling on the mats across from me. He splays out on the ground, body stretched out, arms folded behind his head as he stares up at the ceiling. "What are we talking about again? What events are you supposed to be replicating?"

I lie back against the mats, too; mimic Kenji's position. Our heads are only a few inches apart. "Remember? The concrete I broke back in Warner's psycho room. The metal door I attacked when I was looking for A-Adam." My voice catches and I have to squeeze my eyes shut to quell the pain.

~~I can't even say his name right now.~~

Kenji grunts. I feel him nodding his head on the mats. "All right. Well, what Castle told me is that he thinks there's more to you than just the touching thing. That maybe you also have this weird superhuman strength or something." A pause. "That sound about right to you?"

"I guess."

"So what happened?" he asks, tilting his head back to get a good look at me. "When you went all psycho-monster on everything? Do you remember if there was a trigger?"

I shake my head. "I don't really know. When it happens, it's like—it's like I really am completely out of my mind," I tell him. "Something changes in my head and it makes me . . . it makes me crazy. Like, really, legitimately insane."

I glance over at him but his face betrays no emotion. He just blinks, waiting for me to finish. So I take a deep breath and continue. "It's like I can't think straight. I'm just so paralyzed by the adrenaline and I can't stop it; I can't control it. Once that crazy feeling takes over, it *needs* an outlet. I have to touch something. I have to release it."

Kenji props himself up on one elbow. Looks at me. "So what gets you all crazy, though?" he asks. "What were you feeling? Does it only happen when you're really pissed off?"

I take a second to think about it before I say, "No. Not always." I hesitate. "The first time," I tell him, my voice a little unsteady, "I wanted to kill Warner because of what he made me do to that little kid. I was so devastated. I was angry—I was *really* angry—but I was also . . . so sad." I trail off. "And then when I was looking for Adam?" Deep breaths. "I was desperate. Really desperate. I had to save him."

"And what about when you went all Superman on me? Slamming me into the wall like that?"

"I was scared."

"And then? In the research labs?"

"Angry," I whisper, my eyes unfocused as I stare up at the ceiling, remembering the rage of that day. "I was angrier than I've ever been in my entire life. I never even knew I could feel that way. To be *so* mad. And I felt guilty," I add, so quietly. "Guilty for being the reason why Adam was in there at all."

Kenji takes a deep, long breath. Pulls himself up into a sitting position and leans against the wall. He says nothing.

"What are you thinking . . . ?" I ask, shifting to sit up and join him.

"I don't know," Kenji finally says. "But it's obvious that all of these incidents were the result of really intense emotions. Makes me think the whole system must be pretty straightforward."

"What do you mean?"

"Like there has to be some kind of trigger involved," he says. "Like, when you lose control, your body goes into automatic self-protect mode, you know?"

"No?"

Kenji turns so he's facing me. Crosses his legs underneath him. Leans back on his hands. "Like, listen. When I first found out I could do this invisible thing? I mean, it was an accident. I was nine years old. Scared out of my mind. Fast-forward through all the shitty details and my point is this: I needed a place to hide and couldn't find one. But I was so freaked out that my body, like, automatically did it for me. I just disappeared into the wall. Blended or whatever." He laughs. "Tripped me the hell out, because I didn't realize what'd happened for a good ten minutes. And then I didn't know how to turn myself back to normal. It was crazy. I actually thought I was dead for a couple of days."

"No way," I gasp.

"Yup."

"That's *crazy*."

"That's what I said."

"So . . . so, what? You think my body taps into its

defense mode when I freak out?"

"Pretty much."

"Okay." I think. "Well, how am I supposed to tap into my defense mode? How did you figure yours out?"

He shrugs. "Once I realized I wasn't some kind of ghost and I wasn't hallucinating, it actually became kind of cool. I was a kid, you know? I was excited, like I could tie on a cape and kill bad guys or something. I liked it. And it became this part of me that I could access whenever I wanted. But," he adds, "it wasn't until I really started training that I learned how to control and maintain it for long periods of time. That took a lot of work. A lot of focus."

"A lot of work."

"Yeah—I mean, all of this takes a lot of work to figure out. But once I accepted it as a part of me, it became easier to manage."

"Well," I say, leaning back again, blowing out an exasperated breath, "I've already accepted it. But it definitely hasn't made things easier."

Kenji laughs out loud. "My ass you've accepted it. You haven't accepted anything."

"I've been like this my entire *life*, Kenji—I'm pretty sure I've accepted it—"

"No." He cuts me off. "*Hell* no. You hate being in your own skin. You can't stand it. That's not called acceptance. That's called—I don't know—the opposite of acceptance. You," he says, pointing a finger at me, "you are the *opposite* of acceptance."

"What are you trying to say?" I shoot back. "That I have to *like* being this way?" I don't give him a chance to respond before I say, "You have no *idea* what it's like to be stuck in my skin—to be trapped in my body, afraid to breathe too close to anything with a beating heart. If you did, you'd never ask me to be *happy* to live like this."

"Come on, Juliette—I'm just saying—"

"No. Let me make this clear for you, Kenji. I *kill* people. I *kill* them. That's what my 'special' power is. I don't blend into backgrounds or move things with my mind or have really stretchy arms. You touch me for too long and you *die*. Try living like that for seventeen years and then tell me how easy it is to accept myself."

I taste too much bitterness on my tongue.

It's new for me.

"Listen," he says, his voice noticeably softer. "I'm not trying to judge, okay? I'm just trying to point out that because you don't *want* it, you might subconsciously be sabotaging your efforts to figure it out." He puts his hands up in mock defeat. "Just my two cents. I mean, obviously you've got some crazy powers going on. You touch people and bam, done. But then you can crush through walls and shit, too? I mean, hell, I'd want to learn how to do *that*, are you kidding me? That would be insane."

"Yeah," I say, slumping against the wall. "I guess that part wouldn't be so bad."

"Right?" Kenji perks up. "That would be awesome. And then—you know, if you leave your gloves on—you could just crush random stuff without actually killing anyone. Then you wouldn't feel so bad, right?"

"I guess not."

"So. Great. You just need to relax." He gets to his feet. Grabs the brick he was toying with earlier. "Come on," he says. "Get up. Come over here."

I walk over to his side of the room and stare at the brick he's holding. He gives it to me like he's handing over some kind of family heirloom. "Now," he says. "You have to let yourself get comfortable, okay? Allow your body to touch base with its core. Stop blocking your own Energy. You've probably got a million mental blocks in your head. You can't hold back anymore."

"I don't have *mental blocks*—"

"Yeah you do." He snorts. "You definitely do. You have severe mental constipation."

"Mental *what*—"

"Focus your anger on the brick. On the *brick*," he says to me. "Remember. Open mind. You *want* to crush the brick. Remind yourself that this is what you want. It's *your* choice. You're not doing this for Castle, you're not doing it for me, you're not doing it to fight anyone. This is just something you feel like doing. For fun. Because you feel like it. Let your mind and body take over. Okay?"

I take a deep breath. Nod a few times. "Okay. I think I'm—"

"Ho-ly *shit*." He lets out a low whistle.

"What?" I spin around. "What happened—"

"How did you not just feel that?"

"Feel what—"

"Look in your hand!"

I gasp. Stumble backward. My hand is full of what looks like red sand and brown clay pulverized into tiny particles. The bigger chunks of brick crumble to the floor and I let the debris slip through the cracks between my fingers only to lift the guilty hand to my face.

I look up.

Kenji is shaking his head, shaking with laughter. "I am so jealous right now you have no idea."

"Oh my God."

"I know. I KNOW. So badass. Now think about it: if you can do that to a *brick*, imagine what you could do to the human *body*—"

That wasn't the right thing to say.

Not now. Not after Adam. Not after trying to pick up the pieces of my hopes and dreams and fumbling to glue them back together. Because now there's nothing left. Because now I realize that somewhere, deep down, I was harboring a small hope that Adam and I would find a way to work things out.

Somewhere, deep down, I was still clinging to possibility.

And now that's gone.

Because now it's not just my skin Adam has to be afraid of. It's not just my touch but my grip, my hugs, my hands, a kiss—anything I do could injure him. I'd have to be careful just holding his *hand*. And this new knowledge, this new information about just exactly how deadly I am—

It leaves me with no alternative.

I will forever and ever and ever be alone because no one is safe from me.

I fall to the floor, my mind whirring, my own brain no longer a safe space to inhabit because I can't stop thinking, I can't stop wondering, I can't stop anything and it's like I'm caught in what could be a head-on collision and I'm not the innocent bystander.

I'm the train.

I'm the one careening out of control.

Because sometimes you see yourself—you see yourself the way you *could* be—the way you *might* be if things were different. And if you look too closely, what you see will scare you, it'll make you wonder what you might do if given the opportunity. You know there's a different side of yourself you don't want to recognize, a side you don't want to see in the daylight. You spend your whole life doing everything to push it down and away, out of sight, out of mind. You pretend that a piece of yourself doesn't exist.

You live like that for a long time.

For a long time, you're safe.

And then you're not.

TWENTY-FIVE

Another morning.

Another meal.

I'm headed to breakfast to meet Kenji before our next training session.

He came to a conclusion about my abilities yesterday: he thinks that the inhuman power in my touch is just an evolved form of my Energy. That skin-to-skin contact is simply the rawest form of my ability—that my true gift is actually a kind of all-consuming strength that manifests itself in every part of my body.

My bones, my blood, my skin.

I told him it was an interesting theory. I told him I'd always seen myself as some sick version of a Venus flytrap and he said, "OH MY GOD. Yes. YES. You are exactly like that. Holy shit, yes."

Beautiful enough to lure in your prey, he said.

Strong enough to clamp down and destroy, he said.

Poisonous enough to digest your victims when the flesh makes contact.

"You *digest* your prey," he said to me, laughing as though it was amusing, as though it was funny, as if it was perfectly acceptable to compare a girl to a carnivorous plant. Flattering, even. "Right? You said that when you touch people, it's, like, you're taking their energy, right? It makes you feel stronger?"

I didn't respond.

"So you're *exactly* like a Venus flytrap. You reel 'em in. Clamp 'em down. Eat 'em up."

I didn't respond.

"Mmmmmmm," he said. "You're like a sexy, super-scary plant."

I closed my eyes. Covered my mouth in horror.

"Why is that so wrong?" he said. Bent down to meet my gaze. Tugged on a lock of my hair to get me to look up. "Why does this have to be so horrible? Why can't you see how *awesome* this is?" He shook his head at me. "You are seriously missing out, you know that? This could be so cool if you would just *own* it."

Own it.

Yes.

How easy it would be to just clamp down on the world around me. Suck up its life force and leave it dead in the street just because someone tells me I should. Because someone points a finger and says "Those are the bad guys. Those men over there." Kill, they say. Kill because you trust us. Kill because you're fighting for the right team. Kill because they're bad, and we're good. Kill because we tell you to. Because some people are so stupid that they actually think there are thick neon lines separating good and evil. That it's easy to make that kind of distinction and go to sleep at night with a clear conscience. Because it's okay.

It's okay to kill a man if someone else deems him unfit to live.

What I really want to say is who the hell are you and who are you to decide who gets to die. Who are you to decide who should be killed. Who are you to tell me which father I should destroy and which child I should orphan and which mother should be left without her son, which brother should be left without a sister, which grandmother should spend the rest of her life crying in the early hours of the morning because the body of her grandchild was buried in the ground before her own.

What I really want to say is who the hell do you think you are to tell me that it's awesome to be able to kill a living thing, that it's interesting to be able to ensnare another soul, that it's fair to choose a victim simply because I'm capable of killing without a gun. I want to say mean things and angry things and hurtful things and I want to throw expletives in the air and run far, far away; I want to disappear into the horizon and I want to dump myself on the side of the road if only it will bring me toward some semblance of freedom but I don't know where to go. I have nowhere else to go.

And I feel responsible.

Because there are times when the anger bleeds away until it's nothing but a raw ache in the pit of my stomach and I see the world and wonder about its people and what it's become and I think about hope and maybe and possibly and possibility and potential. I think about glasses half full and glasses to see the world clearly. I think about sacrifice.

And compromise. I think about what will happen if no one fights back. I think about a world where no one stands up to injustice.

And I wonder if maybe everyone here is right.

If maybe it's time to fight.

I wonder if it's ever actually possible to justify killing as a means to an end and then I think of Kenji. I think of what he said. And I wonder if he would still call it awesome if I decided to make *him* my prey.

I'm guessing not.

TWENTY-SIX

Kenji is already waiting for me.

He and Winston and Brendan are sitting at the same table again, and I slide into my seat with a distracted nod and eyes that refuse to focus in front of me.

"He's not here," Kenji says, shoving a spoonful of breakfast into his mouth.

"What?" Oh how fascinating look at this fork and this spoon and this table. "What do y—"

"Not here," he says, his mouth still half full of food.

Winston clears his throat, scratches the back of his head. Brendan shifts in his seat beside me.

"Oh. I—I, um—" Heat flushes up my neck as I look around at the 3 guys sitting at this table. I want to ask Kenji where Adam is, why he isn't here, how he's doing, if he's okay, if he's been eating regularly. I want to ask a million questions I shouldn't be asking but it's blatantly clear that none of them want to talk about the awkward details of my personal life. And I don't want to be that sad, pathetic girl. I don't want pity. I don't want to see the uncomfortable sympathy in their eyes.

So I sit up. Clear my throat.

"What's going on with the patrols?" I ask Winston.

"Is it getting any worse?"

Winston looks up midchew, surprised. He swallows down the food too quickly and coughs once, twice. Takes a sip of his coffee—tar black—and leans forward, looking eager. "It's getting weirder," he says.

"Really?"

"Yeah, so, remember how I told you guys that Warner was showing up every night?"

~~Warner. I can't get the image of his smiling, laughing face out of my head.~~

We nod.

"Well." He leans back in his chair. Holds up his hands. "Last night? Nothing."

"Nothing?" Brendan's eyebrows are high on his forehead. "What do you mean, nothing?"

"I mean no one was there." He shrugs. Picks up his fork. Stabs at a piece of food. "Not Warner, not a single soldier. Night before last?" He looks around at us. "Fifty, maybe seventy-five soldiers. Last night, zero."

"Did you tell Castle about this?" Kenji isn't eating anymore. He's staring at Winston with a focused, too-serious look on his face. It's worrying me.

"Yeah." Winston nods as he takes another sip of his coffee. "I turned in my report about an hour ago."

"You mean you haven't gone to sleep yet?" I ask, eyes wide.

"I slept yesterday," he says, waving a haphazard hand at me. "Or the day before yesterday. I can't remember. God, this coffee is disgusting," he says, gulping it down.

"Right. Maybe you should lay off the coffee, yeah?" Brendan tries to grab Winston's cup.

Winston slaps at his hand, shoots him a dark look. "Not all of us have electricity running through our veins," he says. "I'm not a freaking powerhouse of energy like you are."

"I only did that once—"

"Twice!"

"—and it was an emergency," he says, looking a little sheepish.

"What are you guys talking about?" I ask.

"This guy"—Kenji jerks a thumb at Brendan—"can, like, *literally* recharge his own body. He doesn't need to sleep. It's insane."

"It's not fair," Winston mutters, ripping a piece of bread in half.

I turn to Brendan, jaw unhinged. "No way."

He nods. Shrugs. "I've only done it once."

"Twice!" Winston says again. "And he's a freaking fetus," he says to me. "He's already got way too much energy as it is—shit, all of you kids do—and yet he's the one who comes with a rechargeable battery life."

"I am not a *fetus*," Brendan says, spluttering, glancing at me as heat colors his cheeks. "He's—that's not—you're *mad*," he says, glaring at Winston.

"Yeah," Winston says, nodding, his mouth full of food again. "I am mad. I'm pissed off." He swallows. "And I'm cranky as hell because I'm tired. And I'm hungry. And I need more coffee." He shoves away from the table. Stands up. "I'm going to go get more coffee."

"I thought you said it was disgusting."

He levels a look at me. "Yes, but I am a sad, sad man with very low standards."

"It's true," Brendan says.

"Shut up, fetus."

"You're only allowed one cup," Kenji points out, looking up to meet Winston's eyes.

"Don't worry, I always tell them I'm taking yours," he says, and stalks off.

Kenji is laughing, shoulders shaking.

Brendan is mumbling "I am *not* a fetus" under his breath, stabbing at his food with renewed vigor.

"How old *are* you?" I ask, curious. He's so white-blond and pale-blue-eyed that he doesn't seem real. He looks like the kind of person who could never age, who would remain forever preserved in this ethereal form.

"Twenty-four," he says, looking grateful for a chance at validation. "Just turned twenty-four, actually. Had my birthday last week."

"Oh, wow." I'm surprised. He doesn't look much older than 18. I wonder what it must be like to celebrate a birthday at Omega Point. "Well, happy birthday," I say, smiling at him. "I hope—I hope you have a very good year. And"—I try to think of something nice to say—"and a lot of happy days."

He's staring back at me now, amused, looking straight into my eyes. Grinning. He says, "Thanks." Smiles a bit wider. "Thanks very much." And he doesn't look away.

My face is hot.

I'm struggling to understand why he's still smiling at me, why he doesn't stop smiling even when he finally looks away, why Kenji keeps glancing at me like he's trying to hold in a laugh and I'm flustered, feeling oddly embarrassed and searching for something to say.

"So what are we going to do today?" I ask Kenji, hoping my voice sounds neutral, normal.

Kenji drains his water cup. Wipes his mouth. "Today," he says, "I'm going to teach you how to shoot."

"A gun?"

"Yup." He grabs his tray. Grabs mine, too. "Wait here, I'm gonna drop these off." He moves to go before he stops, turns back, glances at Brendan and says, "Put it out of your head, bro."

Brendan looks up, confused. "What?"

"It's not going to happen."

"Wha—"

Kenji stares at him, eyebrows raised.

Brendan's mouth falls closed. His cheeks are pink again. "I know that."

"Uh-huh." Kenji shakes his head, and walks away.

Brendan is suddenly in a hurry to go about his day.

TWENTY-SEVEN

"Juliette? Juliette!"

"Please wake up—"

I gasp as I sit straight up in bed, heart pounding, eyes blinking too fast as they try to focus. I blink blink blink. "What's going on? What's happening?"

"Kenji is outside," Sonya says.

"He says he needs you," Sara adds, "that something happened—"

I'm tripping out of bed so fast I pull the covers down with me. I'm groping around in the dark, trying to find my suit—I sleep in a pajama set I borrowed from Sara—and making an effort not to panic. "Do you know what's going on?" I ask. "Do you know—did he tell you anything—"

Sonya is shoving my suit into my arms, saying, "No, he just said that it was urgent, that something happened, that we should wake you up right away."

"Okay. I'm sure it's going to be okay," I tell them, though I don't know why I'm saying it, or how I could possibly be of any reassurance to them. I wish I could turn on a light but all the lights are controlled by the same switch. It's one of the ways they conserve power—and one of the ways they manage to maintain the semblance of night and day down here—by only using it during specific hours.

I finally manage to slip into my suit and I'm zipping it up, heading for the door when I hear Sara call my name. She's holding my boots.

"Thank you—thank you both," I say.

They nod several times.

And I'm tugging on my boots and running out the door.

I slam face-first into something solid.

Something human. Male.

I hear his sharp intake of breath, feel his hands steady my frame, feel the blood in my body run right out from under me. "Adam," I gasp.

He hasn't let go of me. I can hear his heart beating fast and hard and loud in the silence between us and he feels too still, too tense, like he's trying to maintain some kind of control over his body.

"Hi," he whispers, but it sounds like he can't really breathe.

My heart is failing.

"Adam, I—"

"I can't let go," he says, and I feel his hands shake, just a little, as if the effort to keep them in one place is too much for him. "I can't let go of you. I'm trying, but I—"

"Well, it's a good thing I'm here then, isn't it?" Kenji yanks me out of Adam's arms and takes a deep, uneven breath. "Jesus. Are you guys done here? We have to go."

"What—what's going on?" I stammer, trying to cover

up my embarrassment. I really wish Kenji weren't always catching me in the middle of such vulnerable moments. I wish he could see me being strong and confident. And then I wonder when I began caring about Kenji's opinion of me. "Is everything okay?"

"I have no idea," Kenji says as he strides down the dark halls. He must have these tunnels memorized, I think, because I can't see a thing. I have to practically run to keep up with him. "But," he says, "I'm assuming some kind of shit has officially hit the fan. Castle sent me a message about fifteen minutes ago—said to get me and you and Kent up to his office ASAP. So," he says, "that's what I'm doing."

"But—now? In the middle of the night?"

"Shit hitting the fan doesn't work around your schedule, princess."

I decide to stop talking.

We follow Kenji to a single solitary door at the end of a narrow tunnel.

He knocks twice, pauses. Knocks 3 times, pauses. Knocks once.

I wonder if I need to remember that.

The door creaks open on its own and Castle waves us in.

"Close the door, please," he says from behind his desk. I have to blink several times to readjust to the light in here. There's a traditional reading lamp on Castle's desk with just enough wattage to illuminate this small space. I use the moment to look around.

Castle's office is nothing more than a room with a few bookcases and a simple table that doubles as a workstation. Everything is made of recycled metal. His desk looks like it used to be a pickup truck.

There are heaps of books and papers stacked all over the floor; diagrams, machinery, and computer parts shoved onto the bookcases, thousands of wires and electrical units peeking out of their metal bodies; they must either be damaged or broken or perhaps part of a project Castle is working on.

In other words: his office is a mess.

Not something I was expecting from someone so incredibly put-together.

"Have a seat," he says to us. I look around for chairs but only find two upside-down garbage cans and a stool. "I'll be right with you. Give me one moment."

We nod. We sit. We wait. We look around.

Only then do I realize why Castle doesn't care about the disorganized nature of his office.

He seems to be in the middle of something, but I can't see what it is, and it doesn't really matter. I'm too focused on watching him work. His hands shift up and down, flick from side to side, and everything he needs or wants simply gravitates toward him. A particular piece of paper? A notepad? The clock buried under the pile of books farthest from his desk? He looks for a pencil and lifts his hand to catch it. He's searching for his notes and lifts his fingers to find them.

He doesn't need to be organized. He has a system of his own.

Incredible.

He finally looks up. Puts his pencil down. Nods. Nods again. "Good. Good; you're all here."

"Yes, sir," Kenji says. "You said you needed to speak with us."

"Indeed I do." Castle folds his hands over his desk. "Indeed I do." Takes a careful breath. "The supreme commander," he says, "has arrived at the headquarters of Sector 45."

Kenji swears.

Adam is frozen.

I'm confused. "Who's the supreme commander?"

Castle's gaze rests on me. "Warner's father." His eyes narrow, scrutinizing me. "You didn't know that Warner's father is the supreme commander of The Reestablishment?"

"Oh," I gasp, unable to imagine the monster that must be Warner's father. "I—yes—I knew that," I tell him. "I just didn't know what his title was."

"Yes," Castle says. "There are six supreme commanders around the world, one for each of the six divisions: North America, South America, Europe, Asia, Africa, and Oceania. Each section is divided into 555 sectors for a total of 3,330 sectors around the globe. Warner's father is not only in charge of this continent, he is also one of the founders of The Reestablishment, and currently our biggest threat."

"But I thought there were 3,333 sectors," I tell Castle,

"not 3,330. Am I remembering that wrong?"

"The other three are capitals," Kenji says to me. "We're pretty sure that one of them is somewhere in North America, but no one knows for certain where any of them are located. So yeah," he adds, "you're remembering right. The Reestablishment has some crazy fascination with exact numbers. 3,333 sectors altogether and 555 sectors each. Everyone gets the same thing, regardless of size. They think it shows how equally they've divided everything, but it's just a bunch of bullshit."

"Wow." Every single day I'm floored by how much I still need to learn. I look at Castle. "So is this the emergency? That Warner's dad is here and not at one of the capitals?"

Castle nods. "Yes, he . . ." He hesitates. Clears his throat. "Well. Let me start from the beginning. It is imperative that you be aware of all the details."

"We're listening," Kenji says, back straight, eyes alert, muscles tensed for action. "Go on."

"Apparently," Castle says, "he's been in town for some time now—he arrived very quietly, very discreetly, a couple of weeks ago. It seems he heard what his son has been up to lately, and he wasn't thrilled about it. He . . ." Castle takes a deep, steady breath. "He is . . . particularly angry about what happened with you, Ms. Ferrars."

"Me?" Heart pounding. Heart pounding. Heart pounding.

"Yes," Castle says. "Our sources say that he's angry Warner allowed you to escape. And, of course, that he lost two of his soldiers in the process." He nods in Adam and Kenji's direction. "Worse still, rumors are now circulating among the citizens about this defecting girl and her strange ability and they're starting to put the pieces together; they're starting to realize there's another movement—*our movement*—preparing to fight back. It's creating unrest and resistance among the civilians, who are all too eager to get involved.

"So." Castle clasps his hands. "Warner's father has undoubtedly arrived to spearhead this war and remove all doubt of The Reestablishment's power." He pauses to look at each of us. "In other words, he's arrived to punish us and his son at the same time."

"But that doesn't change our plans, does it?" Kenji asks.

"Not exactly. We've always known that a fight would be inevitable, but this . . . changes things. Now that Warner's father is in town, this war is going to happen a lot sooner than we hoped," Castle says. "And it's going to be a lot bigger than we anticipated." He levels his gaze at me, looking grave. "Ms. Ferrars, I'm afraid we're going to need your help."

I'm staring at him, struck. "Me?"

"Yes."

"Aren't—aren't you still angry with me?"

"You are not a child, Ms. Ferrars. I would not fault you for an overreaction. Kenji says he believes that your behavior lately has been the result of ignorance and not malicious intent, and I trust his judgment. I trust his word. But I do want you to understand that we are a team," he says, "and we need your strength. What you can do—your power—it is unparalleled. Especially now that you've been working with Kenji and have at least some knowledge of what you're capable of, we're going to need you. We'll do whatever we can to support you—we'll reinforce your suit, provide you with weapons and armor. And Winston—" He stops. His breath catches. "Winston," he says, quieter now, "just finished making you a new pair of gloves." He looks into my face. "We want you on our team," he says. "And if you cooperate with me, I promise you will see results."

"Of course," I whisper. I match his steady, solemn gaze. "Of course I'll help."

"Good," Castle says. "That is very good." He looks distracted as he leans back in his chair, runs a tired hand across his face. "Thank you."

"Sir," Kenji says, "I hate to be so blunt, but would you please tell me what the hell is going on?"

Castle nods. "Yes," he says. "Yes, yes, of course. I—forgive me. It's been a difficult night."

Kenji's voice is tight. "What happened?"

"He . . . has sent word."

"Warner's father?" I ask. "Warner's father sent word? To us?" I glance around at Adam and Kenji. Adam is blinking fast, lips just barely parted in shock. Kenji looks like he's about to be sick.

I'm beginning to panic.

"Yes," Castle says to me. "Warner's father. He wants to meet. He wants . . . to talk."

Kenji jumps to his feet. His entire face is leached of color.

"No—sir—this is a setup—he doesn't want to *talk*, you must know he's lying—"

"He's taken four of our men hostage, Kenji. I'm afraid we don't have another choice."

TWENTY-EIGHT

"What?" Kenji has gone limp. His voice is a horrified rasp. "Who? *How—*"

"Winston and Brendan were patrolling topside tonight." Castle shakes his head. "I don't know what happened. They must've been ambushed. They were too far out of range and the security footage only shows us that Emory and Ian noticed a disturbance and tried to investigate. We don't see anything in the tapes after that. Emory and Ian," he says, "never came back either."

Kenji is back in his chair again, his face in his hands. He looks up with a sudden burst of hope. "But Winston and Brendan—maybe they can find a way out, right? They could do something—they have enough power between the two of them to figure something out."

Castle offers Kenji a sympathetic smile. "I don't know where he's taken them or how they're being treated. If he's beaten them, or if he's already"—he hesitates—"if he's already tortured them, shot them—if they're bleeding to death—they certainly won't be able to fight back. And even if the two of them could save themselves," he says after a moment, "they wouldn't leave the others behind."

Kenji presses his fists into his thighs.

"So. He wants to talk." It's the first time Adam has said a word.

Castle nods. "Lily found this package where they'd disappeared." He tosses us a small knapsack and we take turns rummaging through it. It contains only Winston's broken glasses and Brendan's radio. Smeared in blood.

I have to grip my hands to keep them from shaking.

I was just getting to know these guys. I'd only just met Emory and Ian. I was just learning to build new friendships, to feel comfortable with the people of Omega Point. I just had *breakfast* with Brendan and Winston. I glance at the clock on Castle's wall; it's 3:31 a.m. I last saw them about 20 hours ago.

Brendan's birthday was last week.

"Winston knew," I hear myself say out loud. "He knew something was wrong. He knew there was something weird about all those soldiers everywhere—"

"I know," Castle says, shaking his head. "I've been reading and rereading all of his reports." He pinches the bridge of his nose with his thumb and index finger. Closes his eyes. "I'd only just begun to piece it all together. But it was too late. I was too late."

"What do you think they were planning?" Kenji asks. "Do you have a theory?"

Castle sighs. Drops his hand from his face. "Well, now we know why Warner was out with his soldiers every night—how he was able to leave the base for as long as he did for so many days."

"His father," Kenji says.

Castle nods. "Yes. It's my opinion that the supreme sent Warner out himself. That he wanted Warner to begin hunting us more aggressively. He's always known about us," Castle says to me. "He's never been a stupid man, the supreme. He's always believed the rumors about us, always known that we were out here. But we've never been a threat to him before. Not until now," he says. "Because now that the civilians are talking about us, it's upsetting the balance of power. The people are reenergized—looking for hope in our resistance. And that's not something The Reestablishment can afford right now.

"Anyway," he goes on, "I think it's clear that they couldn't find the entrance to Omega Point, and settled for taking hostages, hoping to provoke us to come out on our own." Castle retrieves a piece of paper from his pile. Holds it up. It's a note. "But there are conditions," he says. "The supreme has given us very specific directions on how next to proceed."

"And?" Kenji is rigid with intensity.

"The three of you will go. Alone."

Holy crap.

"What?" Adam gapes at Castle, astonished. "Why us?"

"He hasn't asked to see me," Castle says. "I'm not the one he's interested in."

"And you're just going to agree to that?" Adam asks. "You're just going to throw us at him?"

Castle leans forward. "Of course not."

"You have a plan?" I ask.

"The supreme wants to meet with you at exactly twelve p.m. tomorrow—well, today, technically—at a specific location on unregulated turf. The details are in the note." He takes a deep breath. "And, even though I know this is exactly what he wants, I think we should all be ready to go. We should move together. This is, after all, what we've been training for. I've no doubt he has bad intentions, and I *highly* doubt he's inviting you to chat over a cup of tea. So I think we should be ready to defend against an offensive attack. I imagine his own men will be armed and ready to fight, and I'm fully prepared to lead mine into battle."

"So we're the *bait*?" Kenji asks, his eyebrows pulled together. "We don't even get to fight—we're just the distraction?"

"Kenji—"

"This is bullshit," Adam says, and I'm surprised to see such emotion from him. "There *has* to be another way. We shouldn't be playing by his rules. We should be using this opportunity to ambush them or—I don't know—create a diversion or a distraction so *we* can attack offensively! I mean, hell, doesn't anyone burst into flames or something? Don't we have anyone who can do something crazy enough to throw everything off? To give us an advantage?"

Castle turns to stare at me.

Adam looks like he might punch Castle in the face. "You are *out* of your mind—"

"Then no," he says. "No, we don't have anyone else that can do something so . . . earth-shattering."

"You think that's *funny*?" Adam snaps.

"I'm afraid I'm not trying to be funny, Mr. Kent. And your anger is not helping our situation. You may opt out if you like, but I *will*—respectfully—request Ms. Ferrars' assistance in this matter. She is the only one the supreme actually wants to see. Sending the two of you with her was my idea."

"What?"

All 3 of us are stunned.

"Why me?"

"I really wish I could tell you," Castle says to me. "I wish I knew more. As of right now, I can only do my best to extrapolate from the information I have, and all I've concluded thus far is that Warner has made a glaring error that needs to be set right. Somehow you managed to get caught in the middle." A pause. "Warner's father," he says, "has asked very specifically for *you* in exchange for the hostages. He says if you do not arrive at the appointed time, he will kill our men. And I have no reason to doubt his word. Murdering the innocent is something that comes very naturally to him."

"And you were just going to let her walk into that!" Adam knocks over his garbage can as he jumps to his feet. "You weren't even going to say anything? You were going to let us assume that she wasn't a *target*? Are you insane?"

Castle rubs his forehead. Takes a few calming breaths. "No," he says, his voice carefully measured. "I was not going to let her walk right into anything. What I'm saying is that we will *all* fight together, but you two will go with Ms. Ferrars. The three of you have worked together before, and both you and Kenji have military training. You're more familiar with the rules, the techniques, the strategy they might employ. You would help keep her safe and embody the element of surprise—your presence could be what gives us an advantage in this situation. If he wants her badly enough, he'll have to find a way to juggle the three of you—"

"*Or*—you know, I don't know," Kenji says, affecting nonchalance, "maybe he'll just shoot us both in the face and drag Juliette away while we're too busy being dead to stop him."

"It's okay," I say. "I'll do it. I'll go."

"What?" Adam is looking at me, panic forcing his eyes wide. "Juliette—no—"

"Yeah, you might want to think about this for a second," Kenji cuts in, sounding a little nervous.

"You don't have to come if you don't want to," I tell them. "But I'll go."

Castle smiles, relief written across his features.

"This is what we're here for, right?" I look around. "We're supposed to fight back. This is our chance."

Castle is beaming, his eyes bright with something that might be pride. "We will be with you every step of the way, Ms. Ferrars. You can count on it."

I nod.

And I realize this is probably what I'm meant to do. Maybe this is exactly why I'm here.

Maybe I'm just supposed to die.

TWENTY-NINE

The morning is a blur.

There's so much to do, so much to prepare for, and there are so many people getting ready. But I know that ultimately this is *my* battle; I have unfinished business to deal with. I know this meeting has nothing to do with the supreme commander. He has no reason to care so much about me. I've never even met the man; I should be nothing more than expendable to him.

This is Warner's move.

It has to be Warner who asked for me. This has something and everything to do with him; it's a smoke signal telling me he still wants me and he's not yet given up. And I have to face him.

I only wonder how he managed to get his father to pull these strings for him.

I guess I'll find out soon enough.

Someone is calling my name.

I stop in place.

Spin around.

James.

He runs up to me just outside the dining hall. His hair, so blond; his eyes, so blue, just like his older brother's. But I've missed his face in a way that has nothing to do with how much he reminds me of Adam.

James is a special kid. A sharp kid. The kind of 10-year-old who is always underestimated. And he's asking me if we can talk. He points to one of the many corridors.

I nod. Follow him into an empty tunnel.

He stops walking and turns away for a moment. Stands there looking uncomfortable. I'm stunned he even wants to talk to me; I haven't spoken a single word to him in 3 weeks. He started spending time with the other kids at Omega Point shortly after we arrived, and then things somehow got awkward between us. He stopped smiling when he'd see me, stopped waving hello from across the dining hall. I always imagined he'd heard rumors about me from the other kids and decided he was better off staying away. And now, after everything that's happened with Adam—after our very public display in the tunnel—I'm shocked he wants to say anything to me.

His head is still down when he whispers, "I was really, really mad at you."

And the stitches in my heart begin to pop. One by one.

He looks up. Looks at me like he's trying to gauge whether or not his opening words have upset me, whether or not I'm going to yell at him for being honest with me. And I don't know what he sees in my face but it seems to disarm him. He shoves his hands into his pockets. Rubs his sneaker in circles on the floor. Says, "You didn't tell me you killed someone before."

I take an unsteady breath and wonder if there will ever be a proper way to respond to a statement like that. I wonder if anyone other than James will ever even say something like that to me. I think not. So I just nod. And say, "I'm really sorry. I should've told y—"

"Then why didn't you?" he shouts, shocking me. "Why didn't you tell me? Why did everyone else know except for me?"

And I'm floored for a moment, floored by the hurt in his voice, the anger in his eyes. I never knew he considered me a friend, and I realize I should have. James hasn't known many people in his life; Adam is his entire world. Kenji and I were 2 of the only people he'd ever really met before we got to Omega Point. And for an orphaned child in his circumstances, it must've meant a lot to have new friends. But I've been so concerned with my own issues that it never occurred to me that James would care so much. I never realized my omission would've seemed like a betrayal to him. That the rumors he heard from the other children must've hurt him just as much as they hurt me.

So I decide to sit down, right there in the tunnel. I make room for him to sit down beside me. And I tell him the truth. "I didn't want you to hate me."

He glares at the floor. Says, "I don't hate you."

"No?"

He picks at his shoelaces. Sighs. Shakes his head. "And I didn't like what they were saying about you," he says, quieter now. "The other kids. They said you were mean and nasty and I told them you weren't. I told them you were quiet and nice. And that you have nice hair. And they told me I was lying."

I swallow, hard, punched in the heart. "You think I have nice hair?"

"Why did you kill him?" James asks me, eyes so open, so ready to be understanding. "Was he trying to hurt you? Were you scared?"

I take a few breaths before I answer.

"Do you remember," I say to him, feeling unsteady now, "what Adam told you about me? About how I can't touch anyone without hurting them?"

James nods.

"Well, that's what happened," I say. "I touched him and he died."

"But why?" he asks. "Why'd you touch him? Because you wanted him to die?"

My face feels like cracked china. "No," I tell him, shaking my head. "I was young—only a couple of years older than you, actually. I didn't know what I was doing. I didn't know that I could kill people by touching them. He'd fallen down at the grocery store and I was just trying to help him get to his feet." A long pause. "It was an accident."

James is silent for a while.

He takes turns looking at me, looking at his shoes, at the knees he's tucked up against his chest. He's staring at the ground when he finally whispers, "I'm sorry I was mad at you."

"I'm sorry I didn't tell you the truth," I whisper back.

He nods. Scratches a spot on his nose. Looks at me. "So can we be friends again?"

"You want to be friends with me?" I blink hard against the stinging in my eyes. "You're not afraid of me?"

"Are you going to be mean to me?"

"Never."

"Then why would I be afraid of you?"

And I laugh, mostly because I don't want to cry. I nod too many times. "Yes," I say to him. "Let's be friends again."

"Good," he says, and gets to his feet. "Because I don't want to eat lunch with those other kids anymore."

I stand up. Dust off the back of my suit. "Eat with us," I tell him. "You can always sit at our table."

"Okay." He nods. Looks away again. Tugs on his ear a little. "So did you know Adam is really sad all the time?" He turns his blue eyes on me.

I can't speak. Can't speak at all.

"Adam says he's sad because of you." James looks at me like he's waiting for me to deny it. "Did you hurt him by accident too? He was in the medical wing, did you know that? He was sick."

And I think I'm going to fall apart, right there, but somehow I don't. I can't lie to him. "Yes," I tell James. "I hurt him by accident, but now—n-now I stay away from him. So I can't hurt him anymore."

"Then why's he still so sad? If you're not hurting him anymore?"

I'm shaking my head, pressing my lips together because I don't want to cry and I don't know what to say. And James seems to understand.

He throws his arms around me.

Right around my waist. Hugs me and tells me not to cry because he believes me. He believes I only hurt Adam by accident. And the little boy, too. And then he says, "But be careful today, okay? And kick some ass, too."

I'm so stunned that it takes me a moment to realize that not only did he use a bad word, he just touched me for the very first time. I try to hold on for as long as I can without making things awkward between us, but I think my heart is still in a puddle somewhere on the floor.

And that's when I realize: everyone knows.

James and I walk into the dining hall together and I can already tell that the stares are different now. Their faces are full of pride, strength, and acknowledgment when they look at me. No fear. No suspicion. I've officially become one of them. I will fight with them, for them, against the same enemy.

I can see what's in their eyes because I'm beginning to remember what it feels like.

Hope.

It's like a drop of honey, a field of tulips blooming in the springtime. It's fresh rain, a whispered promise, a cloudless sky, the perfect punctuation mark at the end of a sentence.

And it's the only thing in the world keeping me afloat.

THIRTY

"This isn't how we wanted it to happen," Castle says to me, "but these things never usually go according to plan." Adam and Kenji and I are being fitted for battle. We're camped out in one of the larger training rooms with 5 others I've never met before. They're in charge of weapons and armor. It's incredible how every single person at Omega Point has a job. Everyone contributes. Everyone has a task.

They all work together.

"Now, we still don't know yet *exactly* why or how you can do what you do, Ms. Ferrars, but I'm hoping that when the time comes, your Energy will present itself. These kinds of high-stress situations are perfect for provoking our abilities—in fact, seventy-eight percent of Point members reported initial discovery of their ability while in critical, high-risk circumstances."

Yup, I don't say to him. That sounds about right.

Castle takes something from one of the women in the room—Alia, I think is her name. "And you shouldn't worry about a thing," he says. "We'll be right there in case something should happen."

I don't point out that I never once said I was worried. Not out loud, anyway.

"These are your new gloves," Castle says, handing them to me. "Try them on."

These new gloves are shorter, softer: they stop precisely at my wrist and fasten with a snap-button. They feel thicker, a little heavier, but they fit my fingers perfectly. I curl my hand into a fist. Smile a little. "These are incredible," I tell him. "Didn't you say Winston designed them?"

Castle's face falls. "Yes," he says quietly. "He finished them just yesterday."

Winston.

His was the very first face I saw when I woke up at Omega Point. His crooked nose, his plastic glasses, his sandy-blond hair and his background in psychology. His need for disgusting coffee.

I remember the broken glasses we found in the knapsack.

I have no idea what's happened to him.

Alia returns with a leather contraption in her hands. It looks like a harness. She asks me to lift my arms and helps me slip into the piece, and I recognize it as a holster. There are thick leather shoulder straps that intersect in the center of my back, and 50 different straps of very thin black leather overlapping around the highest part of my waist—just underneath my chest—like some kind of incomplete bustier. It's like a bra with no cups. Alia has to buckle everything together for me and I still don't really understand what I'm wearing. I'm waiting for some kind of explanation.

Then I see the guns.

"There was nothing in the note about arriving unarmed," Castle says as Alia passes him two automatic handguns in a shape and size I've come to recognize. I practiced shooting with these just yesterday.

I was terrible at it.

"And I see no reason for you to be without a weapon," Castle is saying. He shows me where the holsters are on either side of my rib cage. Teaches me how the guns fit, how to snap the holder into place, where the extra cartridges go.

I don't bother to mention that I have no idea how to reload a weapon. Kenji and I never got to that part in our lesson. He was too busy trying to remind me not to use a gun to gesticulate while asking questions.

"I'm hoping the firearms will be a last resort," Castle says to me. "You have enough weapons in your personal arsenal—you shouldn't need to shoot anyone. And, just in case you find yourself using your gift to destroy something, I suggest you wear these." He holds up a set of what look like elaborate variations on brass knuckles. "Alia designed these for you."

I look from her to Castle to the foreign objects in his hand. He's beaming. I thank Alia for taking the time to create something for me and she stammers out an incoherent response, blushing like she can't believe I'm talking to her.

I'm baffled.

I take the pieces from Castle and inspect them. The underside is made up of 4 concentric circles welded together, big enough in diameter to fit like a set of rings, snug over my gloves. I slip my fingers through the holes and turn my hand over to inspect the upper part. It's like a mini shield, a million pieces of gunmetal that cover my knuckles, my fingers, the entire back of my hand. I can curl my fist and the metal moves with the motion of my joints. It's not nearly as heavy as it looks.

I slip the other piece on. Curl my fingers. Reach for the guns now strapped to my body.

Easy.

I can do this.

"Do you like it?" Castle asks. I've never seen him smile so wide before.

"I love it," I tell him. "Everything is perfect. Thank you."

"Very good. I'm so pleased. Now," he says, "if you'll excuse me, I must attend to a few other details before we leave. I will return shortly." He offers me a curt nod before heading out the door. Everyone but me, Kenji, and Adam leaves the room.

I turn to see how the guys are doing.

Kenji is wearing a suit.

Some kind of bodysuit. He's black from head to toe, his jet-black hair and eyes a perfect match for the outfit molded to every contour of his body. The suit seems to have a synthetic feel to it, almost like plastic; it gleams in the fluorescent lighting of the room and looks like it'd be too stiff to move around in. But then I see him stretching his arms and rolling back and forth on the balls of his feet and the suit suddenly looks fluid, like it moves with him. He's wearing boots but no gloves, and a harness, just like me. But his is different: it has simple holsters that sling over his arms like the straps of a backpack.

And Adam.

Adam is ~~gorgeous~~ wearing a long-sleeved T-shirt, dark blue and dangerously tight across his chest. I can't help but linger over the details of his outfit, can't help but remember what it was like to be held against him, in his arms. ~~He's standing right in front of me and I miss him like I haven't seen him in years.~~ His black cargo pants are tucked into the same pair of black boots he was wearing when I first met him in the asylum, shin-high and sleek, created from smooth leather that fits him so perfectly it's a surprise they weren't made for his body. But there are no weapons on his person.

And I'm curious enough to ask.

"Adam?"

He lifts his head to look up and freezes. Blinks, eyebrows up, lips parted. His eyes travel down every inch of my body, pausing to study the harness framing my chest, the guns slung close to my waist.

He says nothing. He runs a hand through his hair, presses the heel of his palm to his forehead and says something about being right back. He leaves the room.

I feel sick.

Kenji clears his throat, loud. Shakes his head. Says, "Wow. I mean, really, are you trying to kill the guy?"

"What?"

Kenji is looking at me like I'm an idiot. "You can't just go around all 'Oh, Adam, look at me, look at how sexy I am in my new outfit' and bat your eyelashes—"

"Bat my eyelashes?" I balk at him. "What are you talking about? I'm not *batting* my eyelashes at him! And this is the same outfit I've worn every day—"

Kenji grunts. Shrugs and says, "Yeah, well, it looks different."

"You're crazy."

"I am just *saying,*" he says, hands up in mock surrender, "that if I were him? And you were my girl? And you were walking around looking like that, and I couldn't touch you?" He looks away. Shrugs again. "I am just saying I do not envy the poor bastard."

"I don't know what to do," I whisper. "I'm not trying to hurt him—"

"Oh hell. Forget I said anything," he says, waving his hands around. "Seriously. It is *none* of my business." He shoots me a look. "And do *not* consider this an invitation for you to start telling me all of your secret feelings now."

I narrow my eyes at him. "I'm not going to tell you anything about my feelings."

"Good. Because I don't want to know."

"Have you ever had a girlfriend, Kenji?"

"What?" He looks mortally offended. "Do I *look* like the kind of guy who's never had a girlfriend? Have you even *met* me?"

I roll my eyes. "Forget I asked."

"I can't even believe you just said that."

"You're the one who's always going on about not wanting to talk about your feelings," I snap.

"No," he says. "I said I don't want to talk about *your* feelings." He points at me. "I have zero problem talking about my own."

"So do you want to talk about your feelings?"

"Hell no."

"Bu—"

"No."

"Fine." I look away. Pull at the straps tugging at my back. "So what's up with your suit?" I ask him.

"What do you mean, *what's up with it?*" He frowns. He runs his hands down his outfit. "This suit is badass."

I bite back a smile. "I just meant, why are you wearing a suit? Why do you get one and Adam doesn't?"

He shrugs. "Adam doesn't need one. Few people do—it all depends on what kind of gift we have. For me, this suit makes my life a hell of a lot easier. I don't always use it, but when I need to get serious about a mission, it really helps. Like, when I need to blend into a background," he explains, "it's less complicated if I'm shifting one solid color—hence, the black. And if I have too many layers and too many extra pieces floating around my body, I have to focus that much more on making sure I blend all the details. If I'm one solid piece and one solid color, I'm a much better chameleon. Besides," he adds, stretching out the muscles in his arms, "I look sexy as hell in this outfit."

It takes all the self-control I have not to burst into laughter.

"So, but what about Adam?" I ask him. "Adam doesn't need a suit *or* guns? That doesn't seem right."

"I do have guns," Adam says as he walks back into the room. His eyes are focused on the fists he's clenching and unclenching in front of him. "You just can't see them."

I can't stop looking at him, can't stop staring.

"Invisible guns, huh?" Kenji smirks. "That's cute. I don't think I ever went through that phase."

Adam glares at Kenji. "I have nine different weapons concealed on my body right now. Would you like to choose the one I use to shoot you in the face? Or should I?"

"It was a *joke,* Kent. Damn. I was *joking*—"

"All right, everyone."

We all spin around at the sound of Castle's voice.

He examines the 3 of us. "Are you ready?"

I say, "Yes."

Adam nods.

Kenji says, "Let's do this shit."

Castle says, "Follow me."

THIRTY-ONE

It's 10:32 a.m.

We have exactly 1 hour and 28 minutes before we're supposed to meet the supreme commander.

This is the plan:

Castle and every able body from Omega Point are already in position. They left half an hour ago. They're hiding in the abandoned buildings skirting the circumference of the meeting point indicated in the note. They will be ready to engage in an offensive strike just as soon as Castle gives the signal—and Castle will only give that signal if he senses we're in danger.

Adam and Kenji and I are going to travel by foot.

Kenji and Adam are familiar with unregulated turf because as soldiers, they were required to know which sections of land were strictly off-limits. No one is allowed to trespass on the grounds of our past world. The strange alleyways, side streets, old restaurants and office buildings are forbidden territory.

Kenji says our meeting point is in one of the few suburban areas still standing; he says he knows it well. Apparently as a soldier he was sent on several errands in this area, each time required to drop off unmarked packages in an abandoned mailbox. The packages were never explained, and he wasn't stupid enough to ask.

He says it's odd that any of these old houses are even functional, especially considering how strict The Reestablishment is about making sure the civilians never try to go back. In fact, most of the residential neighborhoods were torn down immediately after the initial takeover. So it's very, very rare to find sections left untouched. But there it is, written on the note in too-tight capital letters:

1542 SYCAMORE

We're meeting the supreme commander inside of what used to be someone's home.

"So what do you think we should do? Just ring the doorbell?" Kenji is leading us toward the exit of Omega Point. I'm staring straight ahead in the dim light of this tunnel, trying not to focus on the woodpeckers in my stomach. "What do you think?" Kenji asks again. "Would that be too much? Maybe we should just knock?"

I try to laugh, but the effort is halfhearted at best.

Adam doesn't say a word.

"All right, all right," Kenji says, all seriousness now. "Once we get out there, you know the drill. We link hands. I project to blend the three of us. One of you on either side of me. Got it?"

I'm nodding, trying not to look at Adam as I do.

This is going to be one of the first tests for him and his ability; he'll have to be able to turn off his Energy just as long as he's linked to Kenji. If he can't manage it, Kenji's projection won't work on Adam, and Adam will be exposed. In danger.

"Kent," Kenji says, "you understand the risks, right? If you can't pull this off?"

Adam nods. His face is unflinching. He says he's been training every day, working with Castle to get himself under control. He says he's going to be fine.

He looks at me as he says it.

My emotions jump out of a plane.

I hardly even notice we're nearing the surface when Kenji motions for us to follow him up a ladder. I climb and try to think at the same time, going over and over the plan we spent the early hours of the morning strategizing.

Getting there is the easy part.

Getting inside is where things get tricky.

We're supposed to pretend we're doing a swap—our hostages are supposed to be with the supreme commander, and I'm supposed to oversee their release. It's supposed to be an exchange.

Me for them.

But the truth is that we have no idea what will actually happen. We don't know, for example, who will answer the door. We don't know if *anyone* will answer the door. We don't even know if we're actually meeting inside the house or if we're simply meeting outside of it. We also don't know how they'll react to seeing Adam and Kenji and the makeshift armory we have strapped to our bodies.

We don't know if they'll start shooting right away.

This is the part that scares me. I'm not worried for myself as much as I am for Adam and Kenji. They are the twist in this plan. They are the element of surprise. They're either the unexpected pieces that give us the only advantage we can afford right now, or they're the unexpected pieces that end up dead the minute they're spotted. And I'm starting to think this was a very bad idea.

I'm starting to wonder if I was wrong. If maybe I can't handle this.

But it's too late to turn back now.

THIRTY-TWO

"Wait here."

Kenji tells us to lie low as he pops his head out of the exit. He's already disappeared from sight, his figure blending into the background. He's going to let us know if we're clear to surface.

I'm too nervous to speak.

Too nervous to think.

I can do this we can do this we have no choice but to do this, is all I keep saying to myself.

"Let's go." I hear Kenji's voice from above our heads. Adam and I follow him up the last stretch of the ladder. We're taking one of the alternate exit routes out of Omega Point—one that only 7 people know about, according to Castle. We're taking as many precautions as necessary.

Adam and I manage to haul our bodies aboveground and I immediately feel the cold and Kenji's hand slip around my waist. Cold cold cold. It cuts through the air like little knives slicing across our skin. I look down at my feet and see nothing but a barely perceptible shimmer where my boots are supposed to be. I wiggle my fingers in front of my face.

Nothing.

I look around.

No Adam and no Kenji except for Kenji's invisible hand, now resting at the small of my back.

It worked. Adam made it work. I'm so relieved I want to sing.

"Can you guys hear me?" I whisper, happy no one can see me smiling.

"Yup."

"Yeah, I'm right here," Adam says.

"Nice work, Kent," Kenji says to him. "I know this can't be easy for you."

"It's fine," Adam says. "I'm fine. Let's go."

"Done."

We're like a human chain.

Kenji is between me and Adam and we're linked, holding hands as Kenji guides us through this deserted area. I have no idea where we are, and I'm starting to realize that I seldom do. This world is still so foreign to me, still so new. Spending so much time in isolation while the planet crumbled to pieces didn't do me any favors.

The farther we go, the closer we get to the main road and the closer we get to the compounds that are settled not a mile from here. I can see the boxy shape of their steel structures from where we're standing.

Kenji jerks to a halt.

Says nothing.

"Why aren't we moving?" I ask.

Kenji shushes me. "Can you hear that?"

"What?"

Adam pulls in a breath. "Shit. Someone's coming."

"A tank," Kenji clarifies.

"More than one," Adam adds.

"So why are we still standing here—"

"Wait, Juliette, hold on a second—"

And then I see it. A parade of tanks coming down the main road. I count 6 of them altogether.

Kenji unleashes a series of expletives under his breath.

"What is it?" I ask. "What's the problem?"

"There was only one reason Warner ever ordered us to take more than two tanks out at a time, on the same route," Adam says to me.

"What—"

"They're preparing for a fight."

I gasp.

"He knows," Kenji says. "Dammit! Of course he knows. Castle was right. He knows we're bringing backup. *Shit*."

"What time is it, Kenji?"

"We have about forty-five minutes."

"Then let's move," I tell him. "We don't have time to worry about what's going to happen afterward. Castle is prepared—he's anticipating something like this. We'll be okay. But if we don't get to that house on time, Winston and Brendan and everyone else might die today."

"*We* might die today," he points out.

"Yeah," I tell him. "That, too."

We're moving through the streets quickly now. Swiftly. Darting through the clearing toward some semblance of civilization and that's when I see it: the remnants of an achingly familiar universe. Little square houses with little square yards that are now nothing more than wild weeds decaying in the wind. The dead grass crunches under our feet, icy and uninviting. We count down the houses.

1542 Sycamore.

It must be this one. It's impossible to miss.

It's the only house on this entire street that looks fully functional. The paint is fresh, clean, a beautiful shade of robin's-egg blue. A small set of stairs leads up to the front porch, where I notice 2 white wicker rocking chairs and a huge planter full of bright blue flowers I've never seen before. I see a welcome mat made of rubber, wind chimes hanging from a wooden beam, clay pots and a small shovel tucked into a corner. It's everything we can never have anymore.

Someone *lives* here.

It's impossible that this exists.

I'm pulling Kenji and Adam toward the home, overcome with emotion, almost forgetting that we're no longer allowed to live in this old, beautiful world.

Someone is yanking me backward.

"This isn't it," Kenji says to me. "This is the wrong street. *Shit*. This is the wrong street—we're supposed to be two streets down—"

"But this house—it's—I mean, Kenji, someone *lives* here—"

"No one lives here," he says. "Someone probably set this up to throw us off—in fact, I bet that house is lined with C4. It's probably a trap designed to catch people wandering unregulated turf. Now come on"—he yanks at my hand again—"we have to hurry. We have seven minutes!"

And even though we're running forward, I keep looking back, waiting to see some sign of life, waiting to see someone step outside to check the mail, waiting to see a bird fly by.

And maybe I'm imagining it.

Maybe I'm insane.

But I could've sworn I just saw a curtain flutter in an upstairs window.

THIRTY-THREE

90 seconds.

The real 1542 Sycamore is just as dilapidated as I'd originally imagined it would be. It's a crumbling mess, its roof groaning under the weight of too many years' negligence. Adam and Kenji and I are standing just around the corner, out of sight even though we're technically still invisible. There is not a single person anywhere, and the entire house looks abandoned. I'm beginning to wonder if this was all just an elaborate joke.

75 seconds.

"You guys stay hidden," I tell Kenji and Adam, struck by sudden inspiration. "I want him to think I'm alone. If anything goes wrong, you guys can jump in, okay? There's too much of a risk that your presence will throw things off too quickly."

They're both quiet a moment.

"*Damn.* That's a good idea," Kenji says. "I should've thought of that."

I can't help but grin, just a little. "I'm going to let go now."

"Hey—good luck," Kenji says, his voice unexpectedly soft. "We'll be right behind you."

"Juliette—"

I hesitate at the sound of Adam's voice.

He almost says something but seems to change his mind. He clears his throat. Whispers, "Promise you'll be careful."

"I promise," I say into the wind, fighting back emotion. Not now. I can't deal with this right now. I have to focus.

So I take a deep breath.

Step forward.

Let go.

10 seconds and I'm trying to breathe

9

and I'm trying to be brave

8

but the truth is I'm scared out of my mind

7

and I have no idea what's waiting for me behind that door

6

and I'm pretty sure I'm going to have a heart attack

5

but I can't turn back now

4

because there it is

3

the door is right in front of me

2

all I have to do is knock

1

but the door flies open first.

"Oh good," he says to me. "You're right on time."

THIRTY-FOUR

"It's refreshing, really," he says. "To see that the youth still value things like punctuality. It's always so frustrating when people waste my time."

My head is full of missing buttons and shards of glass and broken pencil tips. I'm nodding too slowly, blinking like an idiot, unable to find the words in my mouth either because they're lost or because they never existed or simply because I have no idea what to say.

I don't know what I was expecting.

Maybe I thought he'd be old and slumped and slightly blind. Maybe he'd be wearing a patch on one eye and have to walk with a cane. Maybe he'd have rotting teeth and ragged skin and coarse, balding hair and maybe he'd be a centaur, a unicorn, an old witch with a pointy hat anything anything anything but this. Because this isn't possible. This is so hard for me to understand and whatever I was expecting was wrong so utterly, incredibly, horribly wrong.

I'm staring at a man who is absolutely, breathtakingly beautiful.

And he is a *man*.

He has to be at least 45 years old, tall and strong and silhouetted in a suit that fits him so perfectly it's almost unfair. His hair is thick, smooth like hazelnut spread; his jawline is sharp, the lines of his face perfectly symmetrical, his cheekbones hardened by life and age. But it's his eyes that make all the difference. His eyes are the most spectacular things I've ever seen.

They're almost aquamarine.

"Please," he says, flashing me an incredible smile. "Come in."

And it hits me then, right in that moment, because everything suddenly makes sense. His look; his stature; his smooth, classy demeanor; the ease with which I nearly forgot he was a villain—*this man.*

This is Warner's father.

I step into what looks like a small living room. There are old, lumpy couches settled around a tiny coffee table. The wallpaper is yellowed and peeling from age. The house is heavy with a strange, moldy smell that indicates the cracked glass windows haven't been opened in years, and the carpet is forest green under my feet, the walls embellished with fake wood panels that don't make sense to me at all. This house is, in a word, ugly. It seems ridiculous for a man so striking to be found inside of a house so horribly inferior.

"Oh wait," he says, "just one thing."

"Wha—"

He's pinned me against the wall by the throat, his hands carefully sheathed in a pair of leather gloves, already prepared to touch my skin to cut off my oxygen, choke me to death and I'm so sure I'm dying, I'm so sure that this is what it feels like to die, to be utterly immobilized, limp from the neck down. I try to claw at him, kicking at his body with the last of my energy until I'm giving up, forfeiting to my own stupidity, my last thoughts condemning me for being such an idiot, for thinking I could actually come in here and accomplish anything until I realize he's undone my holsters, stolen my guns, put them in his pockets.

He lets me go.

I drop to the floor.

He tells me to have a seat.

I shake my head, coughing against the torture in my lungs, wheezing into the dirty, musty air, heaving in strange, horrible gasps, my whole body in spasms against the pain. I've been inside for less than 2 minutes and he's already overpowered me. I have to figure out how to do something, how to get through this alive. Now's not the time to hold back.

I press my eyes shut for a moment. Try to clear my airways, try to find my head. When I finally look up I see he's already seated himself on one of the chairs, staring at me as though thoroughly entertained.

I can hardly speak. "Where are the hostages?"

"They're fine." This man whose name I do not know waves an indifferent hand in the air. "They'll be just fine. Are you sure you won't sit down?"

"What—" I try to clear my throat and regret it immediately, forcing myself to blink back the traitorous tears burning my eyes. “What do you want from me?”

He leans forward in his seat. Clasps his hands. “You know, I’m not entirely sure anymore.”

“What?”

“Well, you’ve certainly figured out that all of this”—he nods at me, around the room—“is just a distraction, right?” He smiles that same incredible smile. “Surely you’ve realized that my ultimate goal was to lure your people out into my territory? My men are waiting for just one word. One word from me and they will seek out and destroy all of your little friends waiting so patiently within this half-mile radius.”

Terror waves hello to me.

He laughs a little. “If you think I don’t know exactly what’s going on in my own *land*, young lady, you are quite mistaken.” He shakes his head. “I’ve let these freaks live too freely among us, and it was my mistake. They’re causing me too much trouble, and now it’s time to take them out.”

“I am one of those freaks,” I tell him, trying to control the tremble in my voice. “Why did you bring me here if all you want is to kill us? Why me? You didn’t have to single me out.”

“You’re right.” He nods. Stands up. Shoves his hands into his pockets. “I came here with a purpose: to clean up the mess my son made, and to finally put an end to the naive efforts of a group of idiotic aberrations. To erase the lot of you from this sorry world. But then,” he says, laughing a little, “just as I began drafting my plans, my son came to me and begged me not to kill you. Just you.” He stops. Looks up. "He actually *begged me* not to kill you." Laughs again. "It was just as pathetic as it was surprising.

"Of course then I knew I had to meet you," he says, smiling, staring at me like he might be enchanted. "'I must meet the girl who's managed to bewitch my boy!' I said to myself. This girl who's managed to make him lose sight of his pride—his *dignity*—long enough to beg me for a favor." A pause. "Do you know," he says to me, "when my son has ever asked me for a favor?" He cocks his head. Waits for me to answer.

I shake my head.

"Never." He takes a breath. "Never. Not once in nineteen years has he ever asked me for anything. Hard to believe, isn't it?" His smile is wider, brilliant. "I take full credit, of course. I raised him well. Taught him to be entirely self-reliant, self-possessed, unencumbered by the needs and wants that break most other men. So to hear these disgraceful, pleading words come out of his mouth?" He shakes his head. "Well. Naturally, I was intrigued. I had to see you for myself. I needed to understand what he'd seen, what was so special about you that it could've caused such a colossal lapse in judgment. Though, to be perfectly honest," he says, "I really didn't think you'd show up." He takes one hand out of his pocket, gestures with it as he speaks. "I mean I certainly hoped you would. But I thought if you did, you'd at least come with support—some form of backup. But here you are, wearing this spandex monstrosity"—he laughs out loud—"and you're all alone." He studies me. "Very stupid," he says. "But brave. I like that. I can admire bravery.

"Anyhow, I brought you here to teach my son a lesson. I had every intention of killing you," he says, assuming a slow, steady walk around the room. "And I preferred to do it where he would be sure to see it. War is messy," he adds, waving his hand. "It's easy to lose track of who's been killed and how they died and who killed whom, et cetera, et cetera. I wanted this particular death to be as clean and simple as the message it would convey. It's not good for him to form these kinds of attachments, after all. It's my duty as his father to put an end to that kind of nonsense."

I feel sick, so sick, so tremendously sick to my stomach. This man is far worse than I ever could have imagined.

My voice is one hard breath, one loud whisper when I speak. "So why don't you just kill me?"

He hesitates. Says, "I don't know. I had no idea you were going to be quite so lovely. I'm afraid my son never mentioned how beautiful you are. And it's always so difficult to kill a beautiful thing," he sighs. "Besides, you surprised me. You arrived on time. Alone. You were actually willing to sacrifice yourself to save the worthless creatures stupid enough to get themselves caught."

He takes a sharp breath. "Maybe we could keep you. If you don't prove useful, you might prove entertaining, at the very least." He tilts his head, thoughtful. "Though if we did keep you, I suppose you'd have to come back to the capital with me, because I can't trust my son to do anything right anymore. I've given him far too many chances."

"Thanks for the offer," I tell him. "But I'd really rather jump off a cliff."

His laughter is like a hundred little bells, happy and wholesome and contagious. "Oh my." He smiles, bright and warm and devastatingly sincere. He shakes his head. Calls over his shoulder toward what looks like it might be another room—maybe the kitchen, I can't be sure—and says, "Son, would you come in here, please?"

And all I can think is that sometimes you're dying, sometimes you're about to explode, sometimes you're 6 feet under and you're searching for a window when someone pours lighter fluid in your hair and lights a match on your face.

I feel my bones ignite.

Warner is here.

THIRTY-FIVE

He appears in a doorway directly across from where I'm now standing and he looks exactly as I remember him. Golden hair and perfect skin and eyes too bright for their faded shade of emerald. His is an exquisitely handsome face, one I now realize he's inherited from his father. It's the kind of face no one believes in anymore; lines and angles and easy symmetry that's almost offensive in its perfection. No one should ever want a face like that. It's a face destined for trouble, for danger, for an outlet to overcompensate for the excess it stole from an unsuspecting innocent.

It's overdone.

It's too much.

~~It frightens me.~~

Black and green and gold seem to be his colors. His pitch-black suit is tailored to his frame, lean but muscular, offset by the crisp white of his shirt underneath and complemented by the simple black tie knotted at his throat. He stands straight, tall, unflinching. To anyone else he would look imposing, even with his right arm still in a sling. He's the kind of boy who was only ever taught to be a man, who was told to erase the concept of childhood from his life's expectations. His lips do not dare to smile, his forehead does not crease in distress. He has been taught to disguise his emotions, to hide his thoughts from the world and to trust no one and nothing. To take what he wants by whatever means necessary. I can see all of this so clearly.

But he looks different to me.

His gaze is too heavy, his eyes, too deep. His expression is too full of something I don't want to recognize. He's looking at me like I succeeded, like I shot him in the heart and shattered him, like I left him to die after he told me he loved me and I refused to think it was even possible.

And I see the difference in him now. I see what's changed.

He's making no effort to hide his emotions from me.

My lungs are liars, pretending they can't expand just to have a laugh at my expense and my fingers are fluttering, struggling to escape the prison of my bones as if they've waited 17 years to fly away.

Escape, is what my fingers say to me.

Breathe, is what I keep saying to myself.

Warner as a child. Warner as a son. Warner as a boy who has only a limited grasp of his own life. Warner with a father who would teach him a lesson by killing the one thing he'd ever be willing to beg for.

Warner as a human being terrifies me more than anything else.

The supreme commander is impatient. "Sit down," he says to his son, motioning to the couch he was just sitting on.

Warner doesn't say a word to me.

His eyes are glued to my face, my body, to the harness

strapped to my chest; his gaze lingers on my neck, on the marks his father likely left behind and I see the motion in his throat, I see the difficulty he has swallowing down the sight in front of him before he finally rips himself away and walks into the living room. He's so like his father, I'm beginning to realize. The way he walks, the way he looks in a suit, the way he's so meticulous about his hygiene. And yet there is no doubt in my mind that he detests the man he fails so miserably not to emulate.

"So I would like to know," the supreme says, "how, exactly, you managed to get away." He looks at me. "I'm suddenly curious, and my son has made it very difficult to extract these details."

I blink at him.

"Tell me," he says. "How did you escape?"

I'm confused. "The first or the second time?"

"Twice! You managed to escape twice!" He's laughing heartily now; he slaps his knee. "Incredible. Both times, then. How did you get away both times?"

I wonder why he's stalling for time. I don't understand why he wants to talk when so many people are waiting for a war and I can't help but hope that Adam and Kenji and Castle and everyone else haven't frozen to death outside. And while I don't have a plan, I do have a hunch. I have a feeling our hostages might be hidden in the kitchen. So I figure I'll humor him for a little while.

I tell him I jumped out the window the first time. Shot Warner the second time.

The supreme is no longer smiling. "You *shot* him?"

I spare a glance at Warner to see his eyes are still fixed firmly on my face, his mouth still in no danger of moving. I have no idea what he's thinking and I'm suddenly so curious I want to provoke him.

"Yes," I say, meeting Warner's gaze. "I shot him. With his own gun." And the sudden tension in his jaw, the eyes that drop down to the hands he's gripping too tightly in his lap—he looks as if he's wrenched the bullet out of his body with his own 5 fingers.

The supreme runs a hand through his hair, rubs his chin. I notice he seems unsettled for the first time since I've arrived and I wonder how it's possible he had no idea how I escaped.

I wonder what Warner must have said about the bullet wound in his arm.

"What's your name?" I ask before I can stop myself, catching the words just a moment too late. I shouldn't be asking stupid questions but I hate that I keep referring to him as "the supreme," as if he's some kind of untouchable entity.

Warner's father looks at me. "My *name*?"

I nod.

"You may call me Supreme Commander Anderson," he says, still confused. "Why does that matter?"

"*Anderson?* But I thought your last name was Warner." I thought he had a first name I could use to distinguish between him and the Warner I've grown to know too well.

Anderson takes a hard breath, spares a disgusted glance at his son. "Definitely *not*," he says to me. "My son thought it would be a good idea to take his mother's last name, because that's exactly the kind of stupid thing he'd do. The mistake," he says, almost announcing it now, "that he always makes, time and time again—allowing his emotions to get in the way of his *duty*—it's pathetic," he says, spitting in Warner's direction. "Which is why as much as I'd like to let you live, my dear, I'm afraid you're too much of a distraction in his life. I cannot allow him to protect a person who has attempted to *kill* him." He shakes his head. "I can't believe I even have to have this conversation. What an embarrassment he's proven to be."

Anderson reaches into his pocket, pulls out a gun, aims it at my forehead.

Changes his mind.

"I'm sick of always cleaning up after you," he barks at Warner, grabbing his arm, pulling him up from the couch. He pushes his son directly across from me, presses the gun into his good hand.

"Shoot her," he says. "Shoot her right now."

THIRTY-SIX

Warner's gaze is locked onto mine.

He's looking at me, eyes raw with emotion and I'm not sure I even know him anymore. I'm not sure I understand him, I'm not sure I know what he's going to do when he lifts the gun with a strong, steady hand and points it directly at my face.

"Hurry up," Anderson says. "The sooner you do this, the sooner you can move on. Now *get this over with—*"

But Warner cocks his head. Turns around.

Points the gun at his father.

I actually gasp.

Anderson looks bored, irritated, annoyed. He runs an impatient hand across his face before he pulls out another gun—my other gun—from his pocket. It's unbelievable.

Father and son, both threatening to kill each other.

"Point the gun in the right direction, Aaron. This is ridiculous."

Aaron.

I almost laugh in the middle of this insanity.

Warner's first name is *Aaron.*

"I have no interest in killing her," ~~Warner Aaron~~ he says to his father.

"Fine." Anderson points the gun at my head again. "I'll do it then."

"Shoot her," Warner says, "and I will put a bullet through your skull."

It's a triangle of death. Warner pointing a gun at his father, his father pointing a gun at me. I'm the only one without a weapon and I don't know what to do.

If I move, I'm going to die. If I don't move, I'm going to die.

Anderson is smiling.

"How charming," he says. He's wearing an easy, lazy grin, his grip on the gun in his hand so deceptively casual. "What is it? Does she make you feel brave, boy?" A pause. "Does she make you feel strong?"

Warner says nothing.

"Does she make you wish you could be a better man?" A little chuckle. "Has she filled your head with dreams about your future?" A harder laugh.

"You have lost your mind," he says, "over a stupid *child* who's too much of a coward to defend herself even with the barrel of a gun pointed straight at her face. This," he says, pointing the gun harder in my direction, "is the silly little girl you've fallen in love with." He exhales a short, hard breath. "I don't know why I'm surprised."

A new tightness in his breathing. A new tightness in his grip around the gun in his hand. These are the only signs that Warner is even remotely affected by his father's words.

"How many times," Anderson asks, "have you threatened

to kill me? How many times have I woken up in the middle of the night to find you, even as a little boy, trying to shoot me in my sleep?" He cocks his head. "Ten times? Maybe fifteen? I have to admit I've lost count." He stares at Warner. Smiles again. "And how many times," he says, his voice so much louder now, "were you able to go through with it? How many times did you succeed? How many times," he says, "did you burst into tears, apologizing, clinging to me like some demented—"

"Shut your mouth," Warner says, his voice so low, so even, his frame so still it's terrifying.

"You are *weak*," Anderson spits, disgusted. "Too pathetically sentimental. Don't want to kill your own father? Too afraid it'll break your miserable heart?"

Warner's jaw tenses.

"Shoot me," Anderson says, his eyes dancing, bright with amusement. "I said *shoot me*!" he shouts, this time reaching for Warner's injured arm, grabbing him until his fingers are clenched tight around the wound, twisting his arm back until Warner actually gasps from the pain, blinking too fast, trying desperately to suppress the scream building inside of him. His grip on the gun in his good hand wavers, just a little.

Anderson releases his son. Pushes him so hard that Warner stumbles as he tries to maintain his balance. His face is chalk-white. The sling wrapped around his arm is seeping with blood.

"So much talk," Anderson says, shaking his head. "So much talk and never enough follow-through. You *embarrass* me," he says to Warner, face twisted in repulsion. "You make me *sick*."

A sharp crack.

Anderson backhands Warner in the face so hard Warner actually sways for a moment, already unsteady from all the blood he's losing. But he doesn't say a word.

He doesn't make a sound.

He stands there, bearing the pain, blinking fast, jaw so tight, staring at his father with absolutely no emotion on his face; there's no indication he's just been slapped but the bright red mark across his cheek, his temple, and part of his forehead. But his arm sling is more blood than cotton now, and he looks far too ill to be on his feet.

Still, he says nothing.

"Do you want to threaten me again?" Anderson is breathing hard as he speaks. "Do you still think you can defend your little girlfriend? You think I'm going to allow your stupid infatuation to get in the way of everything I've built? Everything I've worked toward?" Anderson's gun is no longer pointed at me. He forgets me long enough to press the barrel of his gun into Warner's forehead, twisting it, jabbing it against his skin as he speaks. "Have I taught you *nothing*?" he shouts. "Have you learned *nothing* from me—"

I don't know how to explain what happens next.

All I know is that my hand is around Anderson's throat and I've pinned him to the wall, so overcome by a blind, burning, all-consuming rage that I think my brain has already caught on fire and dissolved into ash.

I squeeze a little harder.

He's sputtering. He's gasping. He's trying to get at my arms, clawing limp hands at my body and he's turning red and blue and purple and I'm enjoying it. I'm enjoying it so, so much.

I think I'm smiling.

I bring my face less than an inch away from his ear and whisper, "Drop the gun."

He does.

I drop him and grab the gun at the same time.

Anderson is wheezing, coughing on the floor, trying to breathe, trying to speak, trying to reach for something to defend himself with and I'm amused by his pain. I'm floating in a cloud of absolute, undiluted hatred for this man and all that he's done and I want to sit and laugh until the tears choke me into a contented sort of silence. I understand so much now. So much.

"Juliette—"

"Warner," I say, so softly, still staring at Anderson's body slumped on the floor in front of me, "I'm going to need you to leave me alone right now."

I weigh the gun in my hands. Test my finger on the trigger. Try to remember what Kenji taught me about taking aim. About keeping my hands and arms steady. Preparing for the kickback—the recoil—of the shot.

I tilt my head. Take inventory of his body parts.

"You," Anderson finally manages to gasp, "you—"

I shoot him in the leg.

He's screaming. I think he's screaming. I can't really hear anything anymore. My ears feel stuffed full of cotton, like someone might be trying to speak to me or maybe someone is shouting at me but everything is muffled and I have too much to focus on right now to pay attention to whatever annoying things are happening in the background. All I know is the reverberation of this weapon in my hand. All I hear is the gunshot echoing through my head. And I decide I'd like to do it again.

I shoot him in the other leg.

There's so much screaming.

I'm entertained by the horror in his eyes. The blood ruining the expensive fabric of his clothes. I want to tell him he doesn't look very attractive with his mouth open like that but then I think he probably wouldn't care about my opinion anyway. I'm just a silly girl to him. Just a silly little girl, a stupid child with a pretty face who's too much of a coward, he said, too much of a coward to defend herself. And oh, wouldn't he like to *keep* me. Wouldn't he like to *keep* me as his little pet. And I realize no. I shouldn't bother sharing my thoughts with him. There's no point wasting words on someone who's about to die.

I take aim at his chest. Try to remember where the heart is.

Not quite to the left. Not quite in the center.

Just—*there*.

Perfect.

THIRTY-SEVEN

I am a thief.

I stole this notebook and this pen from one of the doctors, from one of his lab coats when he wasn't looking, and I shoved them both down my pants. This was just before he ordered those men to come and get me. The ones in the strange suits with the thick gloves and the gas masks with the foggy plastic windows hiding their eyes. They were aliens, I remember thinking. I remember thinking they must've been aliens because they couldn't have been human, the ones who handcuffed my hands behind my back, the ones who strapped me to my seat. They stuck Tasers to my skin over and over for no reason other than to hear me scream but I wouldn't. I whimpered but I never said a word. I felt the tears streak down my cheeks but I wasn't crying.

I think it made them angry.

They slapped me awake even though my eyes were open when we arrived. Someone unstrapped me without removing my handcuffs and kicked me in both kneecaps before ordering me to rise. And I tried. I tried but I couldn't and finally 6 hands shoved me out the door and my face was bleeding on the concrete for a while. I can't really remember the part where they dragged me inside.

I feel cold all the time.

I feel empty, like there is nothing inside of me but this broken heart, the only organ left in this shell. I feel the bleats echo within me, I feel the thumping reverberate around my skeleton. I have a heart, says science, but I am a monster, says society. And I know it, of course I know it. I know what I've done. I'm not asking for sympathy.

But sometimes I think—sometimes I wonder—if I were a monster, surely, I would feel it by now?

I would feel angry and vicious and vengeful. I'd know blind rage and bloodlust and a need for vindication.

Instead I feel an abyss within me that's so deep, so dark I can't see within it; I can't see what it holds. I do not know what I am or what might happen to me.

I do not know what I might do again.

THIRTY-EIGHT

An explosion.

The sound of glass shattering.

Someone yanks me back just as I pull the trigger and the bullet hits the window behind Anderson's head.

I'm spun around.

Kenji is shaking me, shaking me so hard I feel my head jerk back and forth and he's screaming at me, telling me we have to go, that I need to drop the gun, he's breathing hard and he's saying, "I'm going to need you to walk away, okay? Juliette? Can you understand me? I need you to back off right now. You're going to be okay—you're going to be all right—you're going to be fine, you just have to—"

"No, Kenji—" I'm trying to stop him from pulling me away, trying to keep my feet planted where they are because he doesn't understand. He needs to understand. "I have to kill him. I have to make sure he dies," I'm telling him. "I just need you to give me another second—"

"No," he says, "not yet, not right now," and he's looking at me like he's about to break, like he's seen something in my face that he wishes he'd never seen, and he says, "We can't. We can't kill him yet. It's too soon, okay?"

But it's not okay and I don't understand what's happening

but Kenji is reaching for my hand, he's prying the gun out of the fingers I didn't realize were wrapped so tightly around the handle. And I'm blinking. I feel confused and disappointed. I look down at my hands. At my suit. And I can't understand for a moment where all the blood came from.

I glance at Anderson.

His eyes are rolled back in his head. Kenji is checking his pulse. Looks at me, says, "I think he fainted." And my body has begun to shake so violently I can hardly stand.

What have I done.

I back away, needing to find a wall to cling to, something solid to hold on to and Kenji catches me, he's holding me so tightly with one arm and cradling my head with his other hand and I feel like I might want to cry but for some reason I can't. I can't do anything but endure these tremors rocking the length of my entire frame.

"We have to go," Kenji says to me, stroking my hair in a show of tenderness I know is rare for him. I close my eyes against his shoulder, wanting to draw strength from his warmth. "Are you going to be okay?" he asks me. "I need you to walk with me, all right? We'll have to run, too."

"Warner," I gasp, ripping out of Kenji's embrace, eyes wild. "Where's—"

He's unconscious.

A heap on the floor. Arms bound behind his back, an empty syringe tossed on the carpet beside him.

"I took care of Warner," Kenji says.

Suddenly everything is slamming into me all at the same

time. All the reasons why we were supposed to be here, what we were trying to accomplish in the first place, the reality of what I've done and what I was about to do. "Kenji," I'm gasping, "Kenji, where's Adam? What happened? Where are the hostages? Is everyone okay?"

"Adam is fine," he reassures me. "We slipped in the back door and found Ian and Emory." He looks toward the kitchen area. "They're in pretty bad shape, but Adam's hauling them out, trying to get them to wake up."

"What about the others? Brendan? A-and Winston?"

Kenji shakes his head. "I have no idea. But I have a feeling we'll be able to get them back."

"How?"

Kenji nods at Warner. "We're going to take this kid hostage."

"What?"

"It's our best bet," he says to me. "Another trade. A real one, this time. Besides, it'll be fine. You take away his guns, and this golden boy is harmless." He walks toward Warner's unmoving figure. Nudges him with the toe of his boot before hauling him up, flipping Warner's body over his shoulder. I can't help but notice that Warner's injured arm is now completely soaked through with blood.

"Come on," Kenji says to me, not unkindly, eyes assessing my frame like he's not sure if I'm stable yet. "Let's get out of here—it's insanity out there and we don't have much time before they move into this street—"

"What?" I'm blinking too fast. "What do you mean—"

Kenji looks at me, disbelief written across his features. "The *war,* princess. They're all fighting to the death out there—"

"But Anderson never made the call—he said they were waiting for a word from him—"

"No," Kenji says. "Anderson didn't make the call. Castle did."

Oh

God.

"Juliette!"

Adam is rushing into the house, whipping around to find my face until I run forward and he catches me in his arms without thinking, without remembering that we don't do this anymore, that we're not together anymore, that he shouldn't be touching me at all. "You're okay—you're *okay—*"

"LET'S GO," Kenji barks for the final time. "I know this is an emotional moment or whatever, but we have to get our asses the hell out of here. I swear, Kent—"

But Kenji stops.

His eyes drop.

Adam is on his knees, a look of fear and pain and horror and anger and terror etched into every line on his face and I'm trying to shake him, I'm trying to get him to tell me what's wrong and he can't move, he's frozen on the ground, his eyes glued to Anderson's body, his hands reaching out to touch the hair that was so perfectly set almost a moment ago and I'm begging him to speak to me, begging him to tell me what happened and it's like the world shifts in his eyes, like nothing will ever be right in this world and nothing can ever be good again and he parts his lips.

He tries to speak.

"My father," he says. "This man is my father."

THIRTY-NINE

"Shit."

Kenji presses his eyes shut like he can't believe this is happening. "Shit shit *shit*." He shifts Warner against his shoulders, wavers between being sensitive and being a soldier and says, "Adam, man, I'm sorry, but we really have to get out of here—"

Adam gets up, blinking back what I can only imagine are a thousand thoughts, memories, worries, hypotheses, and I call his name but it's like he can't even hear it. He's confused, disoriented, and I'm wondering how this man could possibly be his father when Adam told me his dad was dead.

Now is not the time for these conversations.

Something explodes in the distance and the impact rattles the ground, the windows, the doors of this house, and Adam seems to snap back to reality. He jumps forward, grabs my arm, and we're bolting out the door.

Kenji is in the lead, somehow managing to run despite the weight of Warner's body, limp, hanging over his shoulder, and he's shouting at us to stay close behind. I'm spinning, analyzing the chaos around us. The sounds of gunshots are too close too close too close.

"Where are Ian and Emory?" I ask Adam. "Did you get them out?"

"A couple of our guys were fighting not too far from here and managed to commandeer one of the tanks—I got them to carry those two back to Point," he tells me, shouting so I can hear him. "It was the safest transport possible."

I'm nodding, gasping for air as we fly through the streets and I'm trying to focus on the sounds around us, trying to figure out who's winning, trying to figure out if our numbers have been decimated. We round the corner.

You'd think it'd be a massacre.

50 of our people are fighting against 500 of Anderson's soldiers, who are unloading round after round, shooting at anything that could possibly be a target. Castle and the others are holding their ground, bloody and wounded but fighting back as best they can. Our men and women are armed and storming forward to match the shots of the opposition; others are fighting the only way they know how: one man has his hands to the ground, freezing the earth beneath the soldiers' feet, causing them to lose balance; another man is darting through the soldiers with such speed he's nothing but a blur, confusing the men and knocking them down and stealing their guns. I look up and see a woman hiding in a tree, throwing what must be knives or arrows in such rapid succession that the soldiers don't have a moment to react before they're hit from above.

Then there's Castle in the middle of it all, his hands outstretched over his head, collecting a whirlwind of particles, debris, scattered strips of steel and broken branches with nothing more than the coercion of his fingertips. The others have formed a human wall around him, protecting him as he forms a cyclone of such magnitude that even I can see he's straining to maintain control of it.

Then

he lets go.

The soldiers are shouting, screaming, running back and ducking for cover but most are too slow to escape the reach of so much destruction and they're down, impaled by shards of glass and stone and wood and broken metal but I know this defense won't last for long.

Someone has to tell Castle.

Someone has to tell him to go, to get out of here, that Anderson is down and that we have 2 of our hostages and Warner in tow. He has to get our men and women back to Omega Point before the soldiers get smart and someone throws a bomb big enough to destroy everything. Our numbers won't hold up for much longer and this is the perfect opportunity for them to get safe.

I tell Adam and Kenji what I'm thinking.

"But how?" Kenji shouts above the chaos. "How can we get to him? If we run through there we're dead! We need some kind of distraction—"

"What?" I yell back.

"A *distraction*!" he shouts. "We need something to throw off the soldiers long enough for one of us to grab Castle and give him the green light—we don't have much time—"

Adam is already trying to grab me, he's already trying to stop me, he's already begging me not to do what he thinks I'm going to do and I tell him it's okay. I tell him not to worry. I tell him to get the others to safety and promise him I'm going to be just fine but he reaches for me, he's pleading with his eyes and I'm so tempted to stay here, right next to him, but I break away. I finally know what I need to do; I'm finally ready to help; I'm finally kind of a little bit sure that maybe this time I might be able to control it and I have to try.

So I stumble back.

I close my eyes.

I let go.

I fall to my knees and press my palm to the ground and feel the power coursing through me, feel it curdling in my blood and mixing with the anger, the passion, the fire inside of me and I think of every time my parents called me a monster, a horrible terrifying mistake and I think of all the nights I sobbed myself to sleep and see all the faces that wanted me dead and then it's like a slide show of images reeling through my mind, men and women and children, innocent protesters run over in the streets; I see guns and bombs, fire and devastation, so much suffering suffering suffering and I steel myself. I flex my fist. I pull back my arm and

I

s h a t t e r

what's left of this earth.

FORTY

I'm still here.

I open my eyes and I'm momentarily astonished, confused, half expecting to find myself dead or brain-damaged or at the very least mangled on the ground, but this reality refuses to vanish.

The world under my feet is rumbling, rattling, shaking and thundering to life and my fist is still pressed into the ground and I'm afraid to let go. I'm on my knees, looking up at both sides of this battle and I see the soldiers slowing down. I see their eyes dart around. I see their feet slipping failing to stay standing and the snaps, the groans, the unmistakable cracks that are now creaking through the middle of the pavement cannot be ignored and it's like the jaws of life are stretching their joints, grinding their teeth, yawning themselves awake to witness our disgrace.

The ground looks around, its mouth gaping open at the injustice, the violence, the calculated ploys for power that stop for no one and nothing and are sated only by the blood of the weak, the screams of the unwilling. It's as if the earth thought to take a peek at what we've been doing all this time and it's terrifying just how disappointed it sounds.

Adam is running.

He's dashing through a crowd still gasping for air and an explanation for the earthquake under their feet and he tackles Castle, he pins him down, he's shouting to the men and the women and he ducks, he dodges a stray bullet, he pulls Castle to his feet and our people have begun to run.

The soldiers on the opposite side are stumbling over each other and tripping into a tangle of limbs as they try to outrun one another and I'm wondering how much longer I have to hold on, how much longer this must go on before it's sufficient, and Kenji shouts, "Juliette!"

And I spin around just in time to hear him tell me to let go.

So I do.

The wind the trees the fallen leaves all slip and slide back into place with one giant inhalation and everything stops and for a moment I can't remember what it's like to live in a world that isn't falling apart.

Kenji yanks me up by the arm and we're running, we're the last of our group to leave and he's asking me if I'm okay and I'm wondering how he's still carrying Warner, I'm thinking Kenji must be a hell of a lot stronger than he looks, and I'm thinking I'm too hard on him sometimes, I'm thinking I don't give him enough credit. I'm just beginning to realize that he's one of my favorite people on this planet and I'm so happy he's okay.

I'm so happy he's my friend.

I cling to his hand and let him lead me toward a tank abandoned on our side of the divide and suddenly I realize I can't see Adam, that I don't know where he's gone and I'm frantic, I'm screaming his name until I feel his arms around my waist, his words in my ear, and we're still diving for cover as the final shots sound in the distance.

We clamber into the tank.

We close the doors.

We disappear.

FORTY-ONE

Warner's head is on my lap.

His face is smooth and calm and peaceful in a way I've never seen it and I almost reach out to stroke his hair before I remember exactly how awkward this actually is.

~~Murderer on my lap~~

~~Murderer on my lap~~

~~Murderer on my lap~~

I look to my right.

Warner's legs are resting on Adam's knees and he looks just as uncomfortable as I am.

"Hang tight, guys," Kenji says, still driving the tank toward Omega Point. "I know this is about a million different kinds of weird, but I didn't exactly have enough time to think of a better plan."

He glances at the ~~2~~ 3 of us but no one says a word until

"I'm so happy you guys are okay." I say it like those 9 syllables have been sitting inside of me for too long, like they've been kicked out, evicted from my mouth, and only then do I realize exactly how worried I was that the 3 of us wouldn't make it back alive. "I'm so, so happy you're okay."

Deep, solemn, steady breathing all around.

"How are you feeling?" Adam asks me. "Your arm—you're all right?"

"Yeah." I flex my wrist and try not to wince. "I'm okay. These gloves and this metal thing actually helped, I think." I wiggle my fingers. Examine my gloves. "Nothing is broken."

"That was pretty badass," Kenji says to me. "You really saved us back there."

I shake my head. "Kenji—about what happened—in the house—I'm really sorry, I—"

"Hey, how about let's not talk about that right now."

"What's going on?" Adam asks, alert. "What happened?"

"Nothing," Kenji says quickly.

Adam ignores him. Looks at me. "What happened? Are you all right?"

"I just—I j-just—" I struggle to speak. "What happened—with Warner's da—"

Kenji swears very loudly.

My mouth freezes midmovement.

My cheeks burn as I realize what I've said. As I remember what Adam said just before we ran from that house. He's suddenly pale, pressing his lips together and looking away, out the tiny window of this tank.

"Listen . . ." Kenji clears his throat. "We don't have to talk about that, okay? In fact, I think I might rather *not* talk about that? Because that shit is just too weird for me to—"

"I don't know how it's even possible," Adam whispers. He's blinking, staring straight ahead now, blinking and blinking and blinking and "I keep thinking I must be dreaming," he says, "that I'm just hallucinating this whole thing. But then"—he drops his head in his hands, laughs a harsh laugh—"that is one face I will never forget."

"Didn't—didn't you ever meet the supreme commander?" I dare to ask. "Or even see a picture of him . . . ? Isn't that something you'd see in the army?"

Adam shakes his head.

Kenji speaks. "His whole kick was always being, like, invisible. He got some sick thrill out of being this unseen power."

"Fear of the unknown?"

"Something like that, yeah. I heard he didn't want his pictures anywhere—didn't make any public speeches, either—because he thought if people could put a face on him, it would make him vulnerable. Human. And he always got his thrills from scaring the shit out of everyone. Being the ultimate power. The ultimate threat. Like—how can you fight something if you can't even see it? Can't even find it?"

"That's why it was such a big deal for him to be here," I realize out loud.

"Pretty much."

"But you thought your dad was dead," I say to Adam. "I thought you said he was dead?"

"Just so you guys know," Kenji interjects, "I'm still voting for the *we don't have to talk about this* option. You know. Just so you know. Just putting that out there."

"I thought he was," Adam says, still not looking at me. "That's what they told me."

"Who did?" Kenji asks. Catches himself. Winces. "Shit. Fine. *Fine*. I'm curious."

Adam shrugs. "It's all starting to come together now. All the things I didn't understand. How messed up my life was with James. After my mom died, my dad was never around unless he wanted to get drunk and beat the crap out of someone. I guess he was living a completely different life somewhere else. That's why he used to leave me and James alone all the time."

"But that doesn't make sense," Kenji says. "I mean, not the parts about your dad being a dick, but just, like, the whole scope of it. Because if you and Warner are brothers, and you're eighteen, and Warner is nineteen, and Anderson has always been married to Warner's mom—"

"My parents were never married," Adam says, eyes widening as he speaks the last word.

"You were the love child?" Kenji says, disgusted. "I mean—you know, no offense to you—it's just, I do not want to think about Anderson having some kind of passionate love affair. That is just sick."

Adam looks like he's been frozen solid. "Holy shit," he whispers.

"But I mean, why even have a love affair?" Kenji asks. "I never understood that kind of crap. If you're not happy, just leave. Don't cheat. Doesn't take a genius to figure that shit out. I mean"—he hesitates—"I'm *assuming* it was a love affair," Kenji says, still driving and unable to see the look on Adam's face. "Maybe it wasn't a *love* affair. Maybe it was just another dude-being-a-jackass kind of th—" He catches himself, cringes. "Shit. See, this is why I do *not* talk to people about their personal problems—"

"It was," Adam says, barely breathing now. "I have no idea why he never married her, but I know he loved my mom. He never gave a damn about the rest of us," he says. "Just her. It was always about her. Everything was about her. The few times a month he was ever at home, I was always supposed to stay in my room. I was supposed to be very quiet. I had to knock on my own door and get permission before I could come out, even just to use the bathroom. And he used to get pissed whenever my mom would let me out. He didn't want to see me unless he had to. My mom had to sneak me my dinner just so he wouldn't go nuts about how she was feeding me too much and not saving anything for herself," he says. He shakes his head. "And he was even worse when James was born."

Adam blinks like he's going blind.

"And then when she died," he says, taking a deep breath, "when she died all he ever did was blame me for her death. He always told me it was my fault she got sick, and it was my fault she died. That I needed too much, that she didn't eat enough, that she got weak because she was too busy taking care of us, giving food to us, giving . . . everything to us. To me and James." His eyebrows pull together. "And I believed him for so long. I figured that was why he left all the time. I thought it was some kind of punishment. I thought I deserved it."

I'm too horrified to speak.

"And then he just . . . I mean he was never around when I was growing up," Adam says, "and he was always an asshole. But after she died he just . . . lost his mind. He used to come by just to get piss-drunk. He used to force me to stand in front of him so he could throw his empty bottles at me. And if I flinched—if I *flinched*—"

He swallows, hard.

"That's all he ever did," Adam says, his voice quieter now. "He would come over. Get drunk. Beat the shit out of me. I was fourteen when he stopped coming back." Adam stares at his hands, palms up. "He sent some money every month for us to survive on and then—" A pause. "Two years later I got a letter from our brand-new government telling me my father was dead. I figured he probably got wasted again and did something stupid. Got hit by a car. Fell into the ocean. Whatever. It didn't matter. I was happy he was dead, but I had to drop out of school. I enlisted because the money was gone and I had to take care of James and I knew I wouldn't find another job."

Adam shakes his head. "He left us with nothing, not a single penny, not even a piece of meat to live off of, and now I'm sitting here, in this tank, running from a global war my own *father* has helped orchestrate"—he laughs a hard, hollow laugh—"and the one other worthless person on this planet is lying unconscious in my lap." Adam is actually laughing now, laughing hard, disbelieving, his hand caught in his hair, tugging at the roots, gripping his skull. "And he's my *brother.* My own flesh and blood.

"My father had an entirely separate life I didn't know about and instead of being dead like he should be, he gave me a *brother* who almost tortured me to death in a *slaughterhouse*—" He runs an unsteady hand over the length of his face, suddenly cracking, suddenly slipping, suddenly losing control and his hands are shaking and he has to curl them into fists and he presses them against his forehead and says, "He has to die."

And I'm not breathing, not even a little bit, not even at all, when he says,

"My father," he says, "I have to kill him."

FORTY-TWO

~~I'm going to tell you a secret.~~

~~I don't regret what I did. I'm not sorry at all.~~

~~In fact, if I had a chance to do it again I know this time I'd do it right. I'd shoot Anderson right through the heart.~~

~~And I would enjoy it.~~

FORTY-THREE

I don't even know where to begin.

Adam's pain is like a handful of straw shoved down my throat. He has no parents but a father who beat him, abused him, abandoned him only to ruin the rest of the world and left him a brand-new brother who is exactly his opposite in every possible way.

Warner whose first name is no longer a mystery, Adam whose last name isn't actually Kent.

Kent is his middle name, Adam said to me. He said he didn't want to have anything to do with his father and never told people his real last name. He has that much, at least, in common with his brother.

That, and the fact that both of them have some kind of immunity to my touch.

Adam and Aaron Anderson.

Brothers.

I'm sitting in my room, sitting in the dark, struggling to reconcile Adam with his new sibling who is really nothing more than a boy, a child who hates his father and as a result, a child who made a series of very unfortunate decisions in life. 2 brothers. 2 very different sets of choices.

2 very different lives.

Castle came to me this morning—now that all the injured have been set up in the medical wing and the insanity has subsided—he came to me and he said, "Ms. Ferrars, you were very brave yesterday. I wanted to extend my gratitude to you, and thank you for what you did—for showing your support. I don't know that we would've made it out of there without you."

I smiled, struggled to swallow the compliment and assumed he was finished but then he said, "In fact, I'm so impressed that I'd like to offer you your first official assignment at Omega Point."

My first official assignment.

"Are you interested?" he asked.

I said yes yes yes of course I was interested, I was definitely interested, I was so very, very interested to finally have something to do—something to accomplish—and he smiled and he said, "I'm so happy to hear it. Because I can't think of anyone better suited to this particular position than you."

I beamed.

The sun and the moon and the stars called and said, "Turn down the beaming, please, because you're making it hard for us to see," and I didn't listen, I just kept on beaming. And then I asked Castle for the details of my official assignment. The one perfectly suited to me.

And he said

"I'd like you to be in charge of maintaining and interrogating our new visitor."

And I stopped beaming.

I stared at Castle.

"I will, of course, be overseeing the entire process," Castle continued, "so feel free to come to me with questions and concerns. But we'll need to take advantage of his presence here, and that means trying to get him to speak." Castle was quiet a moment. "He . . . seems to have an odd sort of attachment to you, Ms. Ferrars, and—forgive me—but I think it would behoove us to exploit it. I don't think we can afford the luxury of ignoring any possible advantages available to us. Anything he can tell us about his father's plans, or where our hostages might be, will be invaluable to our efforts. And we don't have much time," he said. "I'm afraid I'll need you to get started right away."

And I asked the world to open up, I said, world, please open up, because I'd love to fall into a river of magma and die, just a little bit, but the world couldn't hear me because Castle was still talking and he said, "Perhaps you can talk some sense into him? Tell him we're not interested in hurting him? Convince him to help us get our remaining hostages back?"

I said, "Oh," I said surely, "he's in some kind of holding cell? Behind bars or something?"

But Castle laughed, amused by my sudden, unexpected hilarity and said don't be silly, Ms. Ferrars, "We don't have anything like that here. I never thought we'd need to keep anyone captive at Omega Point. But yes, he's in his own room, and yes, the door is locked."

"So you want me to go inside of his room?" I asked. "With him? Alone?"

Calm! Of course I was calm. I was definitely absolutely everything that is the opposite of calm.

But then Castle's forehead tightened, concerned. "Is that a problem?" he asked me. "I thought—because he can't touch you—I actually thought you might not feel as threatened by him as the others do. He's aware of your abilities, is he not? I imagine he would be wise to stay away from you for his own benefit."

And it was funny, because there it was: a vat of ice, all over my head, dripping leaking seeping into my bones, and actually no, it wasn't funny at all, because I had to say, "Yes. Right. Yes, of course. I almost forgot. Of course he wouldn't be able to touch me," you're quite right, Mr. Castle, sir, what on earth was I thinking.

Castle was relieved, so relieved, as if he'd taken a dip in a warm pool he was sure would be frozen.

And now I'm here, sitting in exactly the same position I was in 2 hours ago and I'm beginning to wonder

how much longer

I can keep this secret to myself.

FORTY-FOUR

This is the door.

This one, right in front of me, this is where Warner is staying. There are no windows and there is no way to see inside of his room and I'm starting to think that this situation is the exact antonym of excellent.

Yes.

I am going to walk into his room, completely unarmed, because the guns are buried deep down in the armory and because I'm lethal, so why would I need a gun? No one in their right mind would lay a hand on me, no one but Warner, of course, whose half-crazed attempt at stopping me from escaping out of my window resulted in this discovery, his discovery that he can touch me without harming himself.

And I've said a word of this to exactly no one.

I really thought that perhaps I'd imagined it, just until Warner kissed me and told me he loved me and then, that's when I knew I could no longer pretend this wasn't happening. But it's only been about 4 weeks since that day, and I didn't know how to bring it up. I thought maybe I wouldn't have to bring it up. I really, quite desperately didn't *want* to bring it up.

And now, the thought of telling anyone, of making it known to Adam, of all people, that the one person he hates most in this world—second only to his own father—is the one other person who can touch me? That Warner has already touched me, that his hands have known the shape of my body and his lips have known the taste of my mouth—never mind that it wasn't something I actually wanted—I just can't do it.

Not now. Not after everything.

So this situation is entirely my own fault. And I have to deal with it.

I steel myself and step forward.

There are 2 men I've never met before standing guard outside Warner's door. This doesn't mean much, but it gives me a modicum of calm. I nod hello in the guards' direction and they greet me with such enthusiasm I actually wonder whether they've confused me with someone else.

"Thanks so much for coming," one of them says to me, his long, shaggy blond hair slipping into his eyes. "He's been completely insane since he woke up—throwing things around and trying to destroy the walls—he's been threatening to kill all of us. He says you're the only one he wants to talk to, and he's only just calmed down because we told him you were on your way."

"We had to take out all the furniture," the other guard adds, his brown eyes wide, incredulous. "He was breaking *everything*. He wouldn't even eat the food we gave him."

The antonym of excellent.

The antonym of excellent.

The antonym of excellent.

I manage a feeble smile and tell them I'll see what I can do to sedate him. They nod, eager to believe I'm capable of something I know I'm not and they unlock the door. "Just knock to let us know when you're ready to leave," they tell me. "Call for us and we'll open the door."

I'm nodding yes and sure and of course and trying to ignore the fact that I'm more nervous right now than I was meeting his father. To be alone in a room with Warner—to be alone with him and to not know what he might do or what he's capable of and I'm so confused, because I don't even know who he is anymore.

He's 100 different people.

He's the person who forced me to torture a toddler against my will. He's the child so terrorized, so psychologically tormented that he'd try to kill his own father in his sleep. He's the boy who shot a defecting soldier in the forehead; the boy who was trained to be a cold, heartless murderer by a man he thought he could trust. I see Warner as a child desperately seeking his dad's approval. I see him as the leader of an entire sector, eager to conquer me, to use me. I see him feeding a stray dog. I see him torturing Adam almost to death. And then I hear him telling me he loves me, feel him *kissing* me with such unexpected passion and desperation that I don't know I don't know I don't know what I'm walking into.

I don't know who he'll be this time. Which side of himself he'll show me today.

But then I think this must be different. Because he's in my territory now, and I can always call for help if something goes wrong.

He's not going to hurt me.

I hope.

FORTY-FIVE

I step inside.

The door slams shut behind me but the Warner I find inside this room is not one I recognize at all. He's sitting on the floor, back against the wall, legs outstretched in front of him, feet crossed at the ankles. He's wearing nothing but socks, a simple white T-shirt, and a pair of black slacks. His coat, his shoes, and his fancy shirt are all discarded on the ground. His body is toned and muscular and hardly contained by his undershirt; his hair is a blond mess, disheveled for what's probably the first time in his life.

But he's not looking at me. He doesn't even look up as I take a step closer. He doesn't flinch.

I've forgotten how to breathe again.

Then

"Do you have any idea," he says, so quietly, "how many times I've read this?" He lifts his hand but not his head and holds up a small, faded rectangle between 2 fingers.

And I'm wondering how it's possible to be punched in the gut by so many fists at the same time.

My notebook.

He's holding my notebook.

Of course he is.

I can't believe I'd forgotten. He was the last person to

touch my notebook; the last person to see it. He took it from me when he found that I'd hidden it in the pocket of my dress back on base. This was just before I escaped, just before Adam and I jumped out the window and ran away. Just before Warner realized he could touch me.

And now, to know that he's read my most painful thoughts, my most anguished confessions—the things I wrote while in complete and utter isolation, certain that I would die in that very cell, so certain no one would ever read the things I wrote down—to know that he's read these desperate whispers of my private mind.

I feel absolutely, unbearably naked.

Petrified.

So vulnerable.

He flips the notebook open at random. Scans the page until he stops. He finally looks up, his eyes sharper, brighter, a more beautiful shade of green than they've ever been and my heart is beating so fast I can't even feel it anymore.

And he begins to read.

"No—," I gasp, but it's too late.

"I sit here every day," he says. *"175 days I've sat here so far. Some days I stand up and stretch and feel these stiff bones, these creaky joints, this trampled spirit cramped inside my being. I roll my shoulders, I blink my eyes, I count the seconds creeping up the walls, the minutes shivering under my skin, the breaths I have to remember to take. Sometimes I allow my mouth to drop open, just a little bit; I touch my tongue to the backs of my teeth and the seam of my lips and I walk around this small space, I trail my fingers along the cracks in the concrete and wonder, I wonder what it would be like to speak out*

loud and be heard. I hold my breath, listen closely for anything, any sound of life and wonder at the beauty, the impossibility of possibly hearing another person breathing beside me."

He presses the back of his fist to his mouth for just a moment before continuing.

"I stop. I stand still. I close my eyes and try to remember a world beyond these walls. I wonder what it would be like to know that I'm not dreaming, that this isolated existence is not caged within my own mind.

"And I do," he says, reciting the words from memory now, his head resting back against the wall, eyes pressed shut as he whispers, *"I do wonder, I think about it all the time. What it would be like to kill myself. Because I never really know, I still can't tell the difference, I'm never quite certain whether or not I'm actually alive. So I sit here. I sit here every single day."*

I'm rooted to the ground, frozen in my own skin, unable to move forward or backward for fear of waking up and realizing that this is actually happening. I feel like I might die of embarrassment, of this invasion of privacy, and I want to run and run and run and run and run

"Run, I said to myself." Warner has picked up my notebook again.

"Please." I'm begging him. "Please s-stop—"

He looks up, looks at me like he can really see me, see into me, like he wants *me* to see into *him* and then he drops his eyes, he clears his throat, he starts over, he reads from my journal.

"Run, I said to myself. Run until your lungs collapse, until the

wind whips and snaps at your tattered clothes, until you're a blur that blends into the background.

"Run, Juliette, run faster, run until your bones break and your shins split and your muscles atrophy and your heart dies because it was always too big for your chest and it beat too fast for too long and run.

"Run run run until you can't hear their feet behind you. Run until they drop their fists and their shouts dissolve in the air. Run with your eyes open and your mouth shut and dam the river rushing up behind your eyes. Run, Juliette.

"Run until you drop dead.

"Make sure your heart stops before they ever reach you. Before they ever touch you.

"Run, I said."

I have to clench my fists until I feel pain, anything to push these memories away. I don't want to remember. I don't want to think about these things anymore. I don't want to think about what else I wrote on those pages, what else Warner knows about me now, what he must think of me. I can only imagine how pathetic and lonely and desperate I must appear to him. ~~I don't know why I care.~~

"Do you know," he says, closing the cover of the journal only to lay his hand on top of it. Protecting it. Staring at it. "I couldn't sleep for days after I read that entry. I kept wanting to know which people were chasing you down the street, who it was you were running from. I wanted to find them," he says, so softly, "and I wanted to rip their limbs off, one by one. I wanted to murder them in ways that would horrify you to hear."

I'm shaking now, whispering, "Please, please give that back to me."

He touches the tips of his fingers to his lips. Tilts his head back, just a little. Smiles a strange, unhappy smile. Says, "You must know how sorry I am. That I"—he swallows—"that I kissed you like that. I confess I had no idea you would shoot me for it."

And I realize something. "Your arm," I breathe, astonished. He wears no sling. He moves with no difficulty. There's no bruising or swelling or scars I can see.

His smile is brittle. "Yes," he says. "It was healed when I woke up to find myself in this room."

Sonya and Sara. They helped him. I wonder why anyone here would do him such a kindness. I force myself to take a step back. "Please," I tell him. "My notebook, I—"

"I promise you," he says, "I never would've kissed you if I didn't think you wanted me to."

And I'm so shocked that for a moment I forget all about my notebook. I meet his heavy gaze. Manage to steady my voice. "I told you I *hated* you."

"Yes," he says. He nods. "Well. You'd be surprised how many people say that to me."

"I don't think I would."

His lips twitch. "You tried to kill me."

"That amuses you."

"Oh yes," he says, his grin growing. "I find it fascinating." A pause. "Would you like to know why?"

I stare at him.

"Because all you ever said to me," he explains, "was that you didn't want to hurt anyone. You didn't want to *murder people.*"

"I don't."

"Except for me?"

I'm all out of letters. Fresh out of words. Someone has robbed me of my entire vocabulary.

"That decision was so easy for you to make," he says. "So simple. You had a gun. You wanted to run away. You pulled the trigger. That was it."

He's right.

I keep telling myself I have no interest in killing people but somehow I find a way to justify it, to rationalize it when I want to.

Warner. Castle. Anderson.

I wanted to kill every single one of them. And I would have.

What is happening to me.

I've made a huge mistake coming here. Accepting this assignment. Because I can't be alone with Warner. Not like this. Being alone with him is making my insides hurt in ways I don't want to understand.

I have to leave.

"Don't go," he whispers, eyes on my notebook again. "Please," he says. "Sit with me. Stay with me. I just want to see you. You don't even have to say anything."

Some crazed, confused part of my brain actually wants

to sit down next to him, actually wants to hear what he has to say before I remember Adam and what he would think if he knew, what he would say if he were here and could see I was interested in spending my time with the same person who shot him in the leg, broke his ribs, and hung him on a conveyor belt in an abandoned slaughterhouse, leaving him to bleed to death one minute at a time.

I must be insane.

Still, I don't move.

Warner relaxes against the wall. "Would you like me to read to you?"

I'm shaking my head over and over and over again, whispering, "Why are you doing this to me?"

And he looks like he's about to respond before he changes his mind. Looks away. Lifts his eyes to the ceiling and smiles, just a tiny bit. "You know," he says, "I could tell, the very first day I met you. There was something about you that felt different to me. Something in your eyes that was so tender. Raw. Like you hadn't yet learned how to hide your heart from the world." He's nodding now, nodding to himself about something and I can't imagine what it is. "Finding this," he says, his voice soft as he pats the cover of my notebook, "was so"—his eyebrows pull together—"it was so extraordinarily painful." He finally looks at me and he looks like a completely different person. Like he's trying to solve a tremendously difficult equation. "It was like meeting a friend for the very first time."

~~Why are my hands trembling.~~

He takes a deep breath. Looks down. Whispers, "I am so tired, love. I'm so very, very tired."

~~Why won't my heart stop racing.~~

"How much time," he says after a moment, "do I have before they kill me?"

"Kill you?"

He stares at me.

I'm startled into speaking. "We're not going to kill you," I tell him. "We have no intention of hurting you. We just want to use you to get back our men. We're holding you hostage."

Warner's eyes go wide, his shoulders stiffen. "What?"

"We have no reason to kill you," I explain. "We only need to barter with your life—"

Warner laughs a loud, full-bodied laugh. Shakes his head. Smiles at me in that way I've only ever seen once before, looking at me like I'm the sweetest thing he's ever decided to eat.

~~Those *dimples.*~~

"Dear, sweet, beautiful girl," he says. "Your team here has greatly overestimated my father's affection for me. I'm sorry to have to tell you this, but keeping me here is not going to give you the advantage you were hoping for. I doubt my father has even noticed I'm gone. So I would like to request that you please either kill me, or let me go. But I beg you not to waste my time by confining me here."

I'm checking my pockets for spare words and sentences but I'm finding none, not an adverb, not a preposition or even a dangling participle because there doesn't exist a single response to such an outlandish request.

Warner is still smiling at me, shoulders shaking in silent amusement.

"But that's not even a viable argument," I tell him. "No one *likes* to be held hostage—"

He takes a tight breath. Runs a hand through his hair. Shrugs. "Your men are wasting their time," he says. "Kidnapping me will never work to your advantage. This much," he says, "I can guarantee."

FORTY-SIX

Time for lunch.

Kenji and I are sitting on one side of the table, Adam and James on the other.

We've been sitting here for half an hour now, deliberating over my conversation with Warner. I conveniently left out the parts about my journal, though I'm starting to wonder if I should've mentioned it. I'm also starting to wonder if I should just come clean about Warner being able to touch me. But every time I look at Adam I just can't bring myself to do it. I don't even know *why* Warner can touch me. Maybe Warner is the fluke I thought Adam was. Maybe all of this is some kind of cosmic joke told at my expense.

I don't know what to do yet.

But somehow the extra details of my conversation with Warner seem too personal, too embarrassing to share. I don't want anyone to know, for example, that Warner told me he loves me. I don't want anyone to know that he has my journal, or that he's read it. Adam is the only other person who even knows it exists, and he, at least, was kind enough to respect my privacy. He's the one who saved my journal from the asylum, the one who brought it back to me in the first place. But he said he never read the things I wrote. He said he knew they must've been very private thoughts and that he didn't want to intrude.

Warner, on the other hand, has ransacked my mind.

I feel so much more apprehensive around him now. Just thinking about being near him makes me feel anxious, nervous, so vulnerable. I hate that he knows my secrets. My secret thoughts.

It shouldn't be him who knows anything about me at all.

It should be *him*. The one sitting right across from me. The one with the dark-blue eyes and the dark-brown hair and the hands that have touched my heart, my body.

And he doesn't seem okay right now.

Adam's head is down, his eyebrows drawn, his hands clenched together on the table. He hasn't touched his food and he hasn't said a word since I summarized my meeting with Warner. Kenji has been just as quiet. Everyone's been a bit more solemn since our recent battle; we lost several people from Omega Point.

I take a deep breath and try again.

"So what do you think?" I ask them. "About what he said about Anderson?" I'm careful not to use the word *dad* or *father* anymore, especially around James. I don't know what, if anything, Adam has said to James about the issue, and it's not my business to pry. Worse still, Adam hasn't said a word about it since we got back, and it's already been 2 days. "Do you think he's right that Anderson won't care if he's been taken hostage?"

James squirms around in his seat, eyes narrowed as he chews the food in his mouth, looking at the group of us like he's waiting to memorize everything we say.

Adam rubs his forehead. "That," he finally says, "might actually have some merit."

Kenji frowns, folds his arms, leans forward. "Yeah. It is kind of weird. We haven't heard a single thing from their side, and it's been over forty-eight hours."

"What does Castle think?" I ask.

Kenji shrugs. "He's stressed out. Ian and Emory were really messed up when we found them. I don't think they're conscious yet, even though Sonya and Sara have been working around the clock to help them. I think he's worried we won't get Winston and Brendan back at all."

"Maybe," Adam says, "their silence has to do with the fact that you shot Anderson in both his legs. Maybe he's just recovering."

I almost choke on the water I was attempting to drink. I chance a look at Kenji to see if he's going to correct Adam's assumption, but he doesn't even flinch. So I say nothing.

Kenji is nodding. Says, "Right. Yeah. I almost forgot about that." A pause. "Makes sense."

"You shot him in the legs?" James asks, eyes wide in Kenji's direction.

Kenji clears his throat but is careful not to look at me. I wonder why he's protecting me from this. Why he thinks it's better not to tell the truth about what really happened. "Yup," he says, and takes a bite of his food.

Adam exhales. Pushes up his shirtsleeves, studies the series of concentric circles inked onto his forearms, military mementos of a past life.

"But why?" James asks Kenji.

"Why what, kid?"

"Why didn't you kill him? Why just shoot him in the legs? Didn't you say he's the worst? The reason why we have all the problems we have now?"

Kenji is quiet for a moment. He's gripping his spoon, poking at his food. Finally he puts the spoon down. Motions for James to join him on our side of the table. I slide down to make room. "Come here," he says to James, pulling him tight against the right side of his body. James wraps his arms around Kenji's waist and Kenji drops his hand on James' head, mussing his hair.

I had no idea they were so close.

I keep forgetting that the 3 of them are roommates.

"So, okay. You ready for a little lesson?" he says to James.

James nods.

"It's like this: Castle always teaches us that we can't just cut off the head, you know?" He hesitates; collects his thoughts. "Like, if we just kill the enemy leader, then what? What would happen?"

"World peace," James says.

"Wrong. It would be mass chaos." Kenji shakes his head. Rubs the tip of his nose. "And chaos is a hell of a lot harder to fight."

"Then how do you win?"

"Right," Kenji says. "Well that's the thing. We can only take out the leader of the opposition when we're ready to take over—only when there's a new leader ready to take the place of the old one. People need someone to rally around, right? And we're not ready yet." He shrugs. "This was supposed to be a fight against Warner—taking *him* out wouldn't have been an issue. But to take out Anderson would be asking for absolute anarchy, all over the country. And anarchy means there's a chance someone else—someone even worse, possibly—could take control before we do."

James says something in response but I don't hear it.

Adam is staring at me.

He's staring at me and he's not pretending not to. He's not looking away. He's not saying a word. His gaze moves from my eyes to my mouth, focusing on my lips for a moment too long. Finally he turns away, just for a brief second before his eyes are fixed on mine again. Deeper. Hungrier.

My heart is starting to hurt.

I watch the hard movement in his throat. The rise and fall of his chest. The tense line of his jaw and the way he's sitting so perfectly still. He doesn't say anything, anything at all.

~~I want so desperately to touch him.~~

"Smartass." Kenji is chuckling, shaking his head as he reacts to something James just said. "You know that's not what I meant. Anyway," he sighs, "we're not ready to deal with that kind of insanity just yet. We take out Anderson when we're ready to take over. That's the only way to do this right."

Adam stands up abruptly. He pushes away his untouched bowl of food and clears his throat. Looks at Kenji. "So that's why you didn't kill him when he was right in front of you."

Kenji scratches the back of his head, uncomfortable. "Listen man, if I had any idea—"

"Forget it." Adam cuts him off. "You did me a favor."

"What do you mean?" Kenji asks. "Hey man—where're you going—"

But Adam is already walking away.

FORTY-SEVEN

I go after him.

I'm following Adam down an empty corridor as he exits the dining hall even though I know I shouldn't. I know I shouldn't be talking to him like this, shouldn't be encouraging the feelings I have for him but I'm worried. I can't help it. He's disappearing into himself, withdrawing into a world I can't penetrate and I can't even blame him for it. I can only imagine what he must be experiencing right now. These recent revelations would be enough to drive a weaker person absolutely insane. And even though we've managed to work together lately, it's always been during such high-stress situations that there's hardly been any time for us to dwell on our personal issues.

And I need to know that he's all right.

I can't just stop caring about him.

"Adam?"

He stops at the sound of my voice. His spine goes rigid with surprise. He turns around and I see his expression shift from hope to confusion to worry in a matter of seconds. "What's wrong?" he asks. "Is everything okay?"

Suddenly he's in front of me, all 6 feet of him, and I'm drowning in memories and feelings I've made no effort to forget. I'm trying to remember why I wanted to talk to him. Why I ever told him we couldn't be together. Why I would ever keep myself from a chance at even 5 seconds in his arms and he's saying my name, saying, "Juliette—what's wrong? Did something happen?"

I want so desperately to say yes, yes, horrible things have happened, and I'm sick, I'm so sick and tired and I really just want to collapse in your arms and forget the rest of the world. Instead I manage to look up, manage to meet his eyes. They're such a dark, haunting shade of blue. "I'm worried about you," I tell him.

And his eyes are immediately different, uncomfortable, closed off. "You're worried about me." He blows out a hard breath. Runs a hand through his hair.

"I just wanted to make sure you were okay—"

He's shaking his head in disbelief. "What are you doing?" he says. "Are you mocking me?"

"What?"

He's pounding a closed fist against his lips. Looking up. Looking like he's not sure what to say and then he speaks, his voice strained and hurt and confused and he says, "You broke up with me. You gave up on us—on our entire future together. You basically reached in and ripped my heart out and now you're asking me if I'm okay? How the hell am I supposed to be okay, Juliette? What kind of a question is that?"

I'm swaying in place.

"I didn't mean—" I swallow, hard. "I-I was t-talking about your—your dad—I thought maybe—oh, God, I'm sorry—you're right, I'm so stupid—I shouldn't have come, I sh-shouldn't—"

"Juliette," he says, so desperately, catching me around the waist as I back away. His eyes are shut tight. "Please," he says, "tell me what I'm supposed to do. How am I supposed to feel? It's one shitty thing right after another and I'm trying to be okay—God, I'm trying so hard but it's really freaking *difficult* and I miss"—his voice catches—"I miss you," he says. "I miss you so much it's killing me."

My fingers are clenched in his shirt.

My heart is hammering in the silence.

I see the difficulty he has in meeting my eyes when he whispers, "Do you still love me?"

And I'm straining every muscle in my body just to keep myself from reaching forward to touch him. "Adam—of course I still love you—"

"You know," he says, his voice rough with emotion, "I've never had anything like this before. I can barely remember my mom, and other than that it was just me and James and my piece-of-shit dad. And James has always loved me in his own way, but you—with *you*—" He falters. Looks down. "How am I supposed to go back?" he asks, so quietly. "How am I supposed to forget what it was like to be with you? To be loved by you?"

I don't even realize I'm crying until it's too late.

"You say you love me," he says. "And I know I love you." He looks up, meets my eyes. "So why the hell can't we be together?"

And I don't know how to say anything but "I'm s-sorry, I'm so sorry, you have no idea how sorry I am—"

"Why can't we just try?" He's gripping my shoulders now, his words urgent, anguished; our faces too dangerously close. "I'm willing to take whatever I can get, I swear, I just want to know I have you in my life—"

"We can't," I tell him. "It won't be enough, Adam, and you know it. One day we'll take a stupid risk or take a chance we shouldn't. One day we'll think it'll be okay and it won't. And it won't end well."

"But look at us now," he says. "We can make this work—I can be close to you without kissing you—I just need to spend a few more months training—"

"Your training might never be enough." I cut him off, knowing I need to tell him everything now. Knowing he has a right to know the same things I do. "Because the more I train, the more I learn exactly how dangerous I am. And you c-can't be near me. It's not just my skin anymore. I could hurt you just by holding your hand."

"What?" He blinks several times. "What are you talking about?"

I take a deep breath. Press my palm flat against the side of the tunnel before digging my fingers in and dragging them right through the stone. I punch my fist into the wall and grab a handful of rough rock, crush it in my hand, allow it to sift as sand through my fingers to the floor.

Adam is staring at me. Astonished.

"I'm the one who shot your father," I tell him. "I don't

know why Kenji was covering for me. I don't know why he didn't tell you the truth. But I was so blinded by this—this all-consuming *rage*—I just wanted to kill him. And I was torturing him," I whisper. "I shot him in his legs because I was taking my time. Because I wanted to enjoy that last moment. That last bullet I was about to put through his heart. And I was so close. I was so close, and Kenji," I tell him, "Kenji had to pull me away. Because he saw that I'd gone insane.

"I'm out of control." My voice is a rasp, a broken plea. "I don't know what's wrong with me or what's happening to me and I don't even know what I'm capable of yet. I don't know how much worse this is going to get. Every day I learn something new about myself and every day it terrifies me. I've done terrible things to people," I whisper. I swallow back the sob building in my throat. "And I'm not okay," I tell him. "I'm not okay, Adam. I'm not okay and I'm not safe for you to be around."

He's staring at me, so stunned he's forgotten how to speak.

"Now you know that the rumors are true," I whisper. "I am crazy. And I am a monster."

"No," he breathes. "No—"

"Yes."

"No," he says, desperate now. "That's not true—you're stronger than this—I know you are—I know *you*," he says. "I've known your heart for ten years," he says, "and I've seen what you had to live through, what you had to go through, and I'm not giving up on you now, not because of this, not because of something like this—"

"How can you say that? How can you still believe that, after everything—after all of this—"

"You," he says to me, his hands gripping me tighter now, "are one of the bravest, strongest people I've ever met. You have the best heart, the best intentions—" He stops. Takes a tight, shaky breath. "You're the best person I've ever known," he says to me. "You've been through the worst possible experiences and you survived with your humanity still intact. How the hell," he says, his voice breaking now, "am I supposed to let go of you? How can I walk away from you?"

"Adam—"

"No," he says, shaking his head. "I refuse to believe that this is the end of us. Not if you still love me. Because you're going to get through this," he says, "and I will be waiting for you when you're ready. I'm not going anywhere. There won't be another person for me. You're the only one I've ever wanted and that's never," he says, "that's *never* going to change."

"How touching."

Adam and I freeze. Turn around slowly to face the unwelcome voice.

He's right there.

Warner is standing right in front of us, his hands tied behind his back, his eyes blazing bright with anger and hurt and disgust. Castle comes up behind him to lead him in whatever whichever wherever direction and he sees where Warner is stuck, still, staring at us, and Adam is like one block of marble, not moving, not making any effort to breathe or speak or look away. I'm fairly certain I'm burning so bright I've burnt to a crisp.

"You're so lovely when you're blushing," Warner says to me. "But I really wish you wouldn't waste your affections on someone who has to beg for your love." He cocks his head at Adam. "How sad for you," he says. "This must be terribly embarrassing."

"You sick bastard," Adam says to him, his voice like steel.

"At least I still have my dignity."

Castle shakes his head, exasperated. Pushes Warner forward. "Please get back to work—both of you," he shouts at us as he and Warner make their way past. "You're wasting valuable time standing out here."

"You can go to hell," Adam shouts at Warner.

"Just because I'm going to hell," Warner says, "doesn't mean you'll ever deserve her."

And Adam doesn't answer.

He just watches, eyes focused, as Warner and Castle disappear around the corner.

FORTY-EIGHT

James joins us during our training session before dinner.

He's been hanging out with us a lot since we got back, and we all seem happier when he's around. There's something about his presence that's so disarming, so welcome. It's so good to have him back.

I've been showing him how easily I can break things now.

The bricks are nothing. It feels like crushing a piece of cake. The metal pipes bend in my hands like plastic straws. Wood is a little tricky because if I break it the wrong way I can catch a splinter, but just about nothing is difficult anymore. Kenji has been thinking of new ways to test my abilities; lately he's been trying to see if I can project—if I can focus my power from a distance.

Not all abilities are designed for projection, apparently. Lily, for example, has that incredible photographic memory. But she'd never be able to project that ability onto anyone else.

Projection is, by far, the most difficult thing I've ever attempted to do. It's extremely complicated and requires both mental and physical exertion. I have to be wholly in control of my mind, and I have to know exactly how my brain communicates with whichever invisible bone in my body is responsible for my gift. Which means I have to know how to locate the source of my ability—and how to focus it into one concentrated point of power I can tap into from anywhere.

It's hurting my brain.

"Can I try to break something, too?" James is asking. He grabs one of the bricks off the stack and weighs it in his hands. "Maybe I'm super strong like you."

"Have you ever *felt* super strong?" Kenji asks him. "Like, you know, abnormally strong?"

"No," James says, "but I've never tried to break anything, either." He blinks at Kenji. "Do you think maybe I could be like you guys? That maybe I have some kind of power, too?"

Kenji studies him. Seems to be sorting some things out in his head. Says, "It's definitely possible. Your brother's obviously got something in his DNA, which means you might, too."

"Really?" James is practically jumping up and down.

Kenji chuckles. "I have no idea. I'm just saying it might be *possi*—no," he shouts, "James—"

"Oops." James is wincing, dropping the brick to the floor and clenching his fist against the gash bleeding in the palm of his hand. "I think I pressed too hard and it slipped," he says, struggling not to cry.

"You *think*?" Kenji is shaking his head, breathing fast. "Damn, kid, you can't just go around slicing your hand open like that. You're going to give me a freaking heart attack.

Come here," he says, more gently now. "Let me take a look."

"It's okay," James says, cheeks flushed, hiding his hand behind his back. "It's nothing. It'll go away soon."

"That kind of cut is not just going to go away," Kenji says. "Now let me take a look at it—"

"Wait." I interrupt him, caught by the intense look on James' face, the way he seems to be so focused on the clenched fist he's hiding. "James—what do you mean it'll 'go away'? Do you mean it's going to get better? On its own?"

James blinks at me. "Well yeah," he says. "It always gets better really quickly."

"What does? What gets better really quickly?" Kenji is staring too now, already catching on to my theory and throwing looks at me, mouthing *Holy shit* over and over again.

"When I get hurt," James says, looking at us like we've lost our minds. "Like if you cut yourself," he says to Kenji, "wouldn't it just get better?"

"It depends on the size of the cut," Kenji tells him. "But for a gash like the one on your hand?" He shakes his head. "I'd need to clean it to make sure it didn't get infected. Then I'd have to wrap it up in gauze and some kind of ointment to keep it from scarring. And then," he says, "it would take at least a couple days for it to scab up. And then it would begin to heal."

James is blinking like he's never heard of something so absurd in his life.

"Let me see your hand," Kenji says to him.

James hesitates.

"It's all right," I tell him. "Really. We're just curious."

Slowly, so slowly, James shows us his clenched fist. Even more slowly, he uncurls his fingers, watching our reactions the whole time. And exactly where just a moment ago there was a huge gash, now there's nothing but perfect pink skin and a little pool of blood.

"Holy shit on a cracker," Kenji breathes. "Sorry," he says to me, jumping forward to grab James' arm, barely able to rein in his smiles, "but I need to get this guy over to the medical wing. That okay? We can pick up again tomorrow—"

"But I'm not hurt anymore," James protests. "I'm okay—"

"I know, kid, but you're going to want to come with me."

"But why?"

"How would you like," he says, leading James out the door, "to start spending some time with two very pretty girls. . . ."

And they're gone.

And I'm laughing.

Sitting in the middle of the training room all by myself when I hear 2 familiar knocks at my door.

I already know who it's going to be.

"Ms. Ferrars."

I whip around, not because I'm surprised to hear Castle's voice, but because I'm surprised at the intonation. His eyes are narrowed, his lips tight, his eyes sharp and flashing in this light.

He is very, very angry.

Crap.

"I'm sorry about the hallway," I tell him, "I didn't—"

"We can discuss your public and wildly inappropriate displays of affection at a later time, Ms. Ferrars, but right now I have a very important question to ask you and I would advise you to be honest, as acutely honest as is physically possible."

"What"—I can hardly breathe—"what is it?"

Castle narrows his eyes at me. "I have just had a conversation with Warner, who says he is able to touch you without consequence, and that this information is something you are well aware of."

And I think, Wow, I did it. I actually managed to die of a stroke at age 17.

"I need to know," Castle hurries on, "whether or not this information is true and I need to know right now."

There's glue all over my tongue, stuck to my teeth, my lips, the roof of my mouth, and I can't speak, I can't move, I'm pretty sure I just had a seizure or an aneurysm or heart failure or something equally as awful but I can't explain any of this to Castle because I can't move my jaw even an inch.

"Ms. *Ferrars.* I don't think you understand how important this question is. I need an answer from you, and I need it thirty seconds ago."

"I . . . I—"

"Today, I need an answer *today, right now, this very moment*—"

"Yes," I choke out, blushing through my skull, horribly

ashamed, embarrassed, horrified in every possible way and the only thing I can think of is Adam Adam Adam how will Adam respond to this information *now,* why does this have to happen *now,* why did Warner say anything at all and I want to kill him for sharing the secret that was mine to tell, mine to hide, mine to hoard.

Castle looks like he's a balloon that fell in love with a pushpin that got too close and ruined him forever. "So it's true, then?"

I drop my eyes. "Yes, it's true."

He falls to the floor right across from me, astonished. "How is it even possible, do you think?"

Because Warner is Adam's brother, I don't tell him.

And I don't tell him because it is *Adam's* secret to tell and I will not talk about it until he does, even though I desperately want to tell Castle that the connection must be in their blood, that they both must share a similar kind of gift or Energy, or oh oh *oh*

Oh God.

Oh no.

Warner is one of us.

FORTY-NINE

"It changes everything."

Castle isn't even looking at me. "This—I mean—this means so many things," he says. "We'll have to tell him everything and we'll have to test him to be sure, but I'm fairly positive it's the only explanation. And he would be welcome to take refuge here if he wanted it—I would have to give him a regular room, allow him to live among us as an equal. I cannot keep him here as a prisoner, at the very least—"

"*What*—but, Castle—why? He's the one who almost killed Adam! And Kenji!"

"You have to understand—this news might change his entire outlook on life." Castle is shaking his head, one hand almost covering his mouth, his eyes wide. "He might not take it well—he might be thrilled—he might lose his mind completely—he might wake up a new man in the morning. You would be surprised what these kinds of revelations will do to people.

"Omega Point will always be a place of refuge for our kind," he continues. "It's an oath I made to myself many years ago. I cannot deny him food and shelter if, for example, his father were to cast him out entirely."

This can't be happening.

"But I don't understand," Castle says suddenly, looking up at me. "Why didn't you say anything? Why not report this information? This is important for us to know and it doesn't condemn you in any way—"

"I didn't want Adam to know," I admit out loud for the first time, my voice 6 broken bits of shame strung together. "I just . . ." I shake my head. "I didn't want him to know."

Castle actually looks sad for me. He says, "I wish I could help you keep your secret, Ms. Ferrars, but even if I wanted to, I'm not sure Warner will."

I focus on the mats laid out on the floor. My voice sounds tiny when I ask, "Why did he even tell you? How did that even come up in conversation?"

Castle rubs his chin, thoughtful. "He told me of his own accord. I volunteered to take him on his daily rounds—walking him to the restroom, et cetera—because I wanted to follow up and ask him questions about his father and see what he knew about the state of our hostages. He seemed perfectly fine. In fact, he looked much better than he was when he first showed up. He was compliant, almost polite. But his attitude changed rather dramatically after we stumbled upon you and Adam in the hall. . . ." His voice trails off, his eyes snap up, his mind working quickly to fit all the pieces together and he's gaping at me, staring at me in a way that is entirely foreign to Castle, in a way that says he is utterly, absolutely baffled.

I'm not sure if I should be offended.

"He's in love with you," Castle whispers, a dawning, groundbreaking realization in his voice. He laughs, once, hard, fast. Shakes his head. "He held you captive and managed to fall in love with you in the process."

I'm staring at the mats like they're the most fascinating things I've ever seen in my life.

"Oh, Ms. Ferrars," Castle says to me. "I do not envy you your predicament. I can see now why this situation must be uncomfortable for you."

I want to say to him, You have no idea, Castle. You have no idea because you don't even know the entire story. You don't know that they're *brothers*, brothers who *hate* each other, brothers who only seem to agree on one thing, and that one thing happens to be killing their own father.

But I don't say any of those things. I don't say anything, in fact.

I sit on these mats with my head in my hands and I'm trying to figure out what else could possibly go wrong. I'm wondering how many more mistakes I'll have to make before things finally fall into place.

If they ever will.

FIFTY

I'm so humiliated.

I've been thinking about this all night and I came to a realization this morning. Warner must've told Castle on purpose. Because he's playing games with me, because he hasn't changed, because he's still trying to get me to do his bidding. He's still trying to get me to be his project and he's trying to hurt me.

I won't allow it.

I will not allow Warner to lie to me, to manipulate my emotions to get what he wants. I can't believe I felt pity for him—that I felt weakness, tenderness for him when I saw him with his father—that I believed him when he told me his thoughts about my journal. I'm such a gullible fool.

I was an idiot to ever think he might be capable of human emotion.

I told Castle that maybe he should put someone else on this assignment now that he knows Warner can touch me; I told him it might be dangerous now. But he laughed and he laughed and he laughed and he said, "Oh, Ms. Ferrars, I'm quite, *quite* certain you will be able to defend yourself. In fact, you're probably much better equipped against him than any of us. Besides," he added, "this is an ideal situation. If he truly is in love with you, you must be able to use that to our advantage somehow. We need your help," he said to me, serious again. "We need all the help we can find, and right now you're the one person who might be able to get the answers we need. Please," he said. "Try to find out anything you can. Anything at all. Winston and Brendan's lives are at risk."

And he's right.

So I'm shoving my own concerns aside because Winston and Brendan are out there, hurting somewhere, and we need to find them. And I'm going to do whatever I can to help.

Which means I have to talk to Warner again.

I have to treat him just like the prisoner that he is. No more side conversations. No falling for his efforts to confuse me. Not again and again and again. I'm going to be better. Smarter.

And I want my notebook back.

The guards are unlocking his room for me and I'm marching in, I'm sealing the door shut behind me and I'm getting ready to give him the speech I've already prepared when I stop in place.

I don't know what I was expecting.

Maybe I thought I'd catch him trying to break a hole in the wall or maybe he'd be plotting the demise of every person at Omega Point or I don't know I don't know I don't know anything because I only know how to fight an angry body, an insolent creature, an arrogant monster, and I do not know what to do with this.

He's sleeping.

Someone put a mattress in here, a simple rectangle of average quality, thin and worn but better than the ground, at least, and he's lying on top of it in nothing but a pair of black boxer briefs.

His clothes are on the floor.

His pants, his shirts, his socks are slightly damp, wrinkled, obviously hand-washed and laid out to dry; his coat is folded neatly over his boots, and his gloves are resting right next to each other on top of his coat.

He hasn't moved an inch since I stepped into this room.

He's resting on his side, his back to the wall, his left arm tucked under his face, his right arm against his torso, his entire body ~~perfect~~ bare, strong, smooth, and smelling faintly of soap. I don't know why I can't stop staring at him. I don't know what it is about sleep that makes our faces appear so soft and innocent, so peaceful and vulnerable, but I'm trying to look away and I can't. I'm losing sight of my own purpose, forgetting all the brave things I said to myself before I stepped in here. Because there's something about him—there's *always* been something about him that's intrigued me and I don't understand it. I wish I could ignore it but I can't.

Because I look at him and wonder if maybe it's just me? Maybe I'm naive?

But I see layers, shades of gold and green and a person who's never been given a chance to be human and I wonder if I'm just as cruel as my own oppressors if I decide that society is right, that some people are too far gone, that sometimes you can't turn back, that there are people in this world who don't deserve a second chance and I can't I can't I can't

I can't help but disagree.

I can't help but think that 19 is too young to give up on someone, that 19 years old is just the beginning, that it's too soon to tell anyone they will never amount to anything but evil in this world.

I can't help but wonder what my life would've been like if someone had taken a chance on me.

So I back away. I turn to leave.

I let him sleep.

I stop in place.

I catch a glimpse of my notebook lying on the mattress next to his outstretched hand, his fingers looking as if they've only just let go. It's the perfect opportunity to steal it back if I can be stealthy enough.

I tiptoe forward, forever grateful that these boots I wear are designed to make no sound at all. But the closer I inch toward his body, the more my attention is caught by something on his back.

A little rectangular blur of black.

I creep closer.

Blink.

Squint.

Lean in.

It's a tattoo.

No pictures. Just 1 word. 1 word, typed into the very center of his upper back. In ink.

IGNITE

And his skin is shredded with scars.

Blood is rushing to my head so quickly I'm beginning to feel faint. I feel sick. Like I might actually, truly upturn the contents of my stomach right now. I want to panic, I want to shake someone, I want to know how to understand the emotions choking me because I can't even imagine, can't even imagine, can't even *imagine* what he must've endured to carry such suffering on his skin.

His entire back is a map of pain.

Thick and thin and uneven and terrible. Scars like roads that lead to nowhere. They're gashes and ragged slices I can't understand, marks of torture I never could have expected. They're the only imperfections on his entire body, imperfections hidden away and hiding secrets of their own.

And I realize, not for the first time, that I have no idea who Warner really is.

"Juliette?"

I freeze.

"What are you doing here?" His eyes are wide, alert.

"I—I came to talk to you—"

"Jesus," he gasps, jumping away from me. "I'm very flattered, love, but you could've at least given me a chance to put my pants on." He's pulled himself up against the wall but makes no effort to grab his clothes. His eyes keep darting from me to the pants on the floor like he doesn't know what to do. He seems determined not to turn his back to me.

"Would you mind?" he says, nodding to the clothes next to my feet and affecting an air of nonchalance that does little to hide the apprehension in his eyes. "It gets chilly in here."

But I'm staring at him, staring at the length of him, awed by how incredibly flawless he looks from the front. Strong, lean frame, toned and muscular without being bulky. He's fair without being pale, skin tinted with just enough sunlight to look effortlessly healthy. The body of a perfect boy.

What a lie appearances can be.

What a terrible, terrible lie.

His gaze is fixed on mine, his eyes green flames that will not extinguish and his chest is rising and falling so fast, so fast, so fast.

"What happened to your back?" I hear myself whisper.

I watch as the color drains from his face. He looks away, runs a hand across his mouth, his chin, down the back of his neck.

"Who hurt you?" I ask, so quietly. I'm beginning to recognize the strange feeling I get just before I do something terrible. Like right now. Right now I feel like I could kill someone for this.

"Juliette, please, my clothes—"

"Was it your father?" I ask, my voice a little sharper. "Did he do this to you—"

"It doesn't matter." Warner cuts me off, frustrated now.

"Of course it matters!"

He says nothing.

"That tattoo," I say to him, "that word—"

"Yes," he says, though he says it quietly. Clears his throat.

"I don't . . ." I blink. "What does it mean?"

Warner shakes his head, runs a hand through his hair.

"Is it from a book?"

"Why do you care?" he asks, looking away again. "Why are you suddenly so interested in my life?"

I don't know, I want to tell him. I want to tell him I don't know but that's not true.

Because I feel it. I feel the clicks and the turns and the creaking of a million keys unlocking a million doors in my mind. It's like I'm finally allowing myself to see what I really think, how I really feel, like I'm discovering my own secrets for the first time. And then I search his eyes, search his features for something I can't even name. And I realize I don't want to be his enemy anymore.

"It's over," I say to him. "I'm not on base with you this time. I'm not going to be your weapon and you'll never be able to change my mind about that. I think you know that now." I study the floor. "So why are we still fighting each other? Why are you still trying to manipulate me? Why are you still trying to get me to fall for your tricks?"

"I have no idea," he says, looking at me like he's not sure I'm even real, "no idea what you're talking about."

"Why did you tell Castle you could touch me? That wasn't your secret to share."

"Right." He exhales a deep breath. "Of course." Seems to return to himself. "Listen, love, could you at least toss me my jacket if you're going to stay here and ask me all these questions?"

I toss him his jacket. He catches it. Slides down to the floor. And instead of putting his jacket on, he drapes it over his lap. Finally, he says, "Yes, I did tell Castle I could touch you. He had a right to know."

"That wasn't any of his business."

"Of course it's his business," Warner says. "The entire world he's created down here thrives on exactly that kind of information. And you're here, living among them. He should know."

"He doesn't need to know."

"Why is it such a big deal?" he asks, studying my eyes too carefully. "Why does it bother you so much for someone to know that I can touch you? Why does it have to be a secret?"

I struggle to find the words that won't come.

"Are you worried about Kent? You think he'd have a problem knowing I can touch you?"

"I didn't want him to find out like this—"

"But why does it matter?" he insists. "You seem to care so much about something that makes no difference in your personal life. It wouldn't," he says, "make any difference in your personal life. Not if you still claim to feel nothing but hatred for me. Because that's what you said, isn't it? That you hate me?"

I fold myself to the floor across from Warner. Pull my knees up to my chest. Focus on the stone under my feet. "I don't hate you."

Warner seems to stop breathing.

"I think I understand you sometimes," I tell him. "I really do. But just when I think I finally get you, you surprise me. And I never really know who you are or who you're going to be." I look up. "But I know that I don't hate you anymore. I've tried," I say, "I've tried so hard. Because you've done so many terrible, terrible things. To innocent people. To *me*. But I know too much about you now. I've seen too much. You're too human."

His hair is so gold. His eyes so green. His voice is tortured when he speaks. "Are you saying," he says, "that you want to be my friend?"

"I-I don't know." I'm so petrified, so, so petrified of this possibility. "I didn't think about that. I'm just saying that I don't know"—I hesitate, breathe—"I don't know how to hate you anymore. Even though I want to. I really want to and I know I should but I just can't."

He looks away.

And he smiles.

It's the kind of smile that makes me forget how to do everything but blink and blink and I don't understand what's happening to me. I don't know why I can't convince my eyes to find something else to focus on.

I don't know why my heart is losing its mind.

He touches my notebook like he's not even aware he's doing it. His fingers run the length of the cover once, twice, before he registers where my eyes have gone and he stops.

"You wrote these words?" He touches the notebook again. "Every single one?"

I nod.

He says, "Juliette."

I stop breathing.

He says, "I would like that very much. To be your friend," he says. "I'd like that."

And I don't really know what happens in my brain.

Maybe it's because he's broken and I'm foolish enough to think I can fix him. Maybe it's because I see myself, I see 3, 4, 5, 6, 17-year-old Juliette abandoned, neglected, mistreated, abused for something outside of her control and I think of Warner as someone who's just like me, someone who was never given a chance at life. I think about how everyone already hates him, how hating him is a universally accepted fact.

Warner is horrible.

There are no discussions, no reservations, no questions asked. It has already been decided that he is a despicable human being who thrives on murder and power and torturing others.

But I want to know. I need to know. I have to know.

If it's really that simple.

Because what if one day I slip? What if one day I fall through the cracks and no one is willing to pull me back? What happens to me then?

So I meet his eyes. I take a deep breath.

And I run.

I run right out the door.

FIFTY-ONE

Just a moment.

Just 1 second, just 1 more minute, just give me another hour or maybe the weekend to think it over it's not so much it's not so hard it's all we ever ask for it's a simple request.

But the moments the seconds the minutes the hours the days and years become one big mistake, one extraordinary opportunity slipped right through our fingers because we couldn't decide, we couldn't understand, we needed more time, we didn't know what to do.

We don't even know what we've done.

We have no idea how we even got here when all we ever wanted was to wake up in the morning and go to sleep at night and maybe stop for ice cream on the way home and that one decision, that one choice, that one accidental opportunity unraveled everything we've ever known and ever believed in and what do we do?

What do we do
from here?

FIFTY-TWO

Things are getting worse.

The tension among the citizens of Omega Point is getting tighter with each passing hour. We've tried to make contact with Anderson's men to no avail—we've heard nothing from their team or their soldiers, and we have no updates on our hostages. But the civilians of Sector 45—the sector Warner used to be in charge of, the sector he used to oversee—are beginning to grow more and more unsettled. Rumors about us and our resistance are spreading too quickly.

The Reestablishment tried to cover up the news of our recent battle by calling it a standard attack on rebel party members, but the people are getting smarter. Protests are breaking out among them and some are refusing to work, standing up to authority, trying to escape the compounds, and running back to unregulated territory.

It never ends well.

The losses have been too many and Castle is anxious to do something. We all have a feeling we're going to be heading out again, and soon. We haven't received any reports that Anderson is dead, which means he's probably just biding his time—or maybe Adam is right, and he's just recovering. But whatever the reason, Anderson's silence can't be good.

"What are you doing here?" Castle says to me.

I've just collected my dinner. I've just sat down at my usual table with Adam and Kenji and James. I blink at Castle, confused.

Kenji says, "What's going on?"

Adam says, "Is everything all right?"

Castle says, "My apologies, Ms. Ferrars, I didn't mean to interrupt. I confess I'm just a bit surprised to see you here. I thought you were currently on assignment."

"Oh." I startle. Glance at my food and back at Castle again. "I—well yes, I am—but I've talked to Warner twice already—I actually just saw him yesterday—"

"Oh, that's excellent news, Ms. Ferrars. Excellent news." Castle clasps his hands together; his face is the picture of relief. "And what have you been able to discover?" He looks so hopeful that I actually begin to feel ashamed of myself.

Everyone is staring at me and I don't know what to do. I don't know what to say.

I shake my head.

"Ah." Castle drops his hands. Looks down. Nods to himself. "So. You've decided that your two visits have been more than sufficient?" He won't look at me. "What is your professional opinion, Ms. Ferrars? Do you think it would be best to take your time in this particular situation? That Winston and Brendan will be relaxing comfortably until you find an opportunity in your busy schedule to interrogate the only person who might be able to help us find them? Do you think that y—"

"I'll go right now." I grab my tray and jump up from table, nearly tripping over myself in the process. "I'm sorry—I'm just—I'll go right now. I'll see you guys at breakfast," I whisper, and run out the door.

Brendan and Winston

Brendan and Winston

Brendan and Winston, I keep telling myself.

I hear Kenji laughing as I leave.

I'm not very good at interrogation, apparently.

I have so many questions for Warner but none of them have to do with our hostage situation. Every time I tell myself I'm going to ask the right questions, Warner somehow manages to distract me. It's almost like he knows what I'm going to ask and is already prepared to redirect the conversation.

It's confusing.

"Do you have any tattoos?" he's asking me, smiling as he leans back against the wall in his undershirt; pants on, socks on, shoes off. "Everyone seems to have tattoos these days."

This is not a conversation I ever thought I'd have with Warner.

"No," I tell him. "I've never had an opportunity to get one. Besides, I don't think anyone would ever want to get that close to my skin."

He studies his hands. Smiles. Says, "Maybe someday."

"Maybe," I agree.

A pause.

"So what about your tattoo?" I ask. "Why *IGNITE*?"

His smile is bigger now. Dimples again. He shakes his head, says, "Why not?"

"I don't get it." I tilt my head at him, confused. "You want to remind yourself to catch on fire?"

He smiles, presses back a laugh. "A handful of letters doesn't always make a word, love."

"I . . . have no idea what you're talking about."

He takes a deep breath. Sits up straighter. "So," he says. "You used to read a lot?"

I'm caught off guard. It's a strange question, and I can't help but wonder for a moment if it's a trick. If admitting to such a thing might get me into trouble. And then I remember that Warner is *my* hostage, not the other way around. "Yes," I say to him. "I used to."

His smile fades into something a bit more serious, calculated. His features are carefully wiped clean of emotion. "And when did you have a chance to read?"

"What do you mean?"

He shrugs slowly, glances at nothing across the room. "It just seems strange that a girl who's been so wholly isolated her entire life would have much access to literature. Especially in this world."

I say nothing.

He says nothing.

I breathe a few beats before answering him.

"I . . . I never got to choose my own books," I tell him, and I don't know why I feel so nervous saying this out loud, why I have to remind myself not to whisper. "I read whatever was available. My schools always had little libraries and my parents had some things around the house. And later . . ." I hesitate. "Later, I spent a couple of years in ~~hospitals and psychiatric wards and~~ a juvenile d-detention center." My face enflames as if on cue, always ready to be ashamed of my past, of who I've been and continue to be.

But it's strange.

While one part of me struggles to be so candid, another part of me actually feels comfortable talking to Warner. Safe. Familiar.

Because he already knows everything about me.

He knows every detail of my 17 years. He has all of my medical records, knows all about my incidents with the police and the painful relationship I ~~have~~ had with my parents. And now he's read my notebook, too.

There's nothing I could reveal about my history that would surprise him; nothing about what I've done would shock or horrify him. I don't worry that he'll judge me or run away from me.

And this realization, perhaps more than anything else, rattles my bones.

~~And gives me some sense of relief.~~

"There were always books around," I continue, somehow unable to stop now, eyes glued to the floor. "In the detention center. A lot of them were old and worn and didn't have covers, so I didn't always know what they were called or who wrote them. I just read anything I could find. Fairy tales and mysteries and history and poetry. It didn't matter what it was. I would read it over and over and over again. The books . . . they helped keep me from losing my mind altogether . . ." I trail off, catching myself before I say much more. Horrified as I realize just how much I want to confide in him. In Warner.

Terrible, terrible Warner who tried to kill Adam and Kenji. Who made me his toy.

I hate that I should feel safe enough to speak so freely around him. I hate that of all people, Warner is the one person I can be completely honest with. I always feel like I have to protect Adam from me, from the horror story that is my life. I never want to scare him or tell him too much for fear that he'll change his mind and realize what a mistake he's made in trusting me; in showing me affection.

But with Warner there's nothing to hide.

I want to see his expression; I want to know what he's thinking now that I've opened up, offered him a personal look at my past, but I can't make myself face him. So I sit here, frozen, humiliation perched on my shoulders and he doesn't say a word, doesn't shift an inch, doesn't make a single sound. Seconds fly by, swarming the room all at once and I want to swat them all away; I want to catch them and shove them into my pockets just long enough to stop time.

Finally, he interrupts the silence.

"I like to read, too," he says.

I look up, startled.

He's leaned back against the wall, one hand caught in his hair. He runs his fingers through the golden layers just once. Drops his hand. Meets my gaze. His eyes are so, so green.

"You like to read?" I ask.

"You're surprised."

"I thought The Reestablishment was going to destroy all of those things. I thought it was illegal."

"They are, and it will be," he says, shifting a little. "Soon, anyway. They've destroyed some of it already, actually." He looks uncomfortable for the first time. "It's ironic," he says, "that I only really started reading when the plan was in place to destroy everything. I was assigned to sort through some lists—give my opinion on which things we'd keep, which things we'd get rid of, which things we'd recycle for use in campaigns, in future curriculum, et cetera."

"And you think that's okay?" I ask him. "To destroy what's left of culture—all the languages—all those texts? Do you agree?"

He's playing with my notebook again. "There . . . are many things I'd do differently," he says, "if I were in charge." A deep breath. "But a soldier does not always have to agree in order to obey."

"What would you do differently?" I ask. "If you were in charge?"

He laughs. Sighs. Looks at me, smiles at me out of the corner of his eye. "You ask too many questions."

"I can't help it," I tell him. "You just seem so different now. Everything you say surprises me."

"How so?"

"I don't know," I say. "You're just . . . so calm. A little less crazy."

He laughs one of those silent laughs, the kind that shakes his chest without making a sound, and he says, "My life has been nothing but battle and destruction. Being here?" He looks around. "Away from duties, responsibilities. Death," he says, eyes intent on the wall. "It's like a vacation. I don't have to think all the time. I don't have to do anything or talk to anyone or be anywhere. I've never had so many hours to simply *sleep*," he says, smiling. "It's actually kind of luxurious. I think I'd like to get held hostage more often," he adds, mostly to himself.

And I can't help but study him.

I study his face in a way I've never dared to before and I realize I don't have the faintest idea what it must be like to live his life. He told me once that I didn't have a clue, that I couldn't possibly understand the strange laws of his world, and I'm only just beginning to see how right he was. Because I don't know anything about that kind of bloody, regimented existence. But I suddenly want to know.

I suddenly want to understand.

I watch his careful movements, the effort he makes to look unconcerned, relaxed. But I see how calculated it is. How there's a reason behind every shift, every readjustment of his body. He's always listening, always touching a hand to the ground, the wall, staring at the door, studying its outline, the hinges, the handle. I see the way he tenses—just a little bit—at the sound of small noises, the scratch of metal, muffled voices outside the room. It's obvious he's always alert, always on edge, ready to fight, to react. It makes me wonder if he's ever known tranquillity. Safety. If he's ever been able to sleep through the night. If he's ever been able to go anywhere without constantly looking over his own shoulder.

His hands are clasped together.

He's playing with a ring on his left hand, turning and turning and turning it around his pinkie finger. I can't believe it's taken me so long to notice he's wearing it; it's a solid band of jade, a shade of green pale enough to perfectly match his eyes. And then I remember, all at once, seeing it before.

Just one time.

The morning after I'd hurt Jenkins. When Warner came to collect me from his room. He caught me staring at his ring and quickly slipped his gloves on.

It's déjà vu.

He catches me looking at his hands and quickly clenches his left fist, covers it with his right.

"Wha—"

"It's just a ring," he says. "It's nothing."

"Why are you hiding it if it's nothing?" I'm already so much more curious than I was a moment ago, too eager for any opportunity to crack him open, to figure out what on earth goes on inside of his head.

He sighs.

Flexes and unflexes his fingers. Stares at his hands, palms down, fingers spread. Slips the ring off his pinkie and holds it up to the fluorescent light; looks at it. It's a little O of green. Finally, he meets my eyes. Drops the ring into the palm of his hand and closes a fist around it.

"You're not going to tell me?" I ask.

He shakes his head.

"Why not?"

He rubs the side of his neck, massages the tension out of the lowest part, the part that just touches his upper back. I can't help but watch. Can't help but wonder what it would feel like to have someone massage the pain out of my body that way. His hands look so strong.

I've just about forgotten what we were talking about when he says, "I've had this ring for almost ten years. It used to fit my index finger." He glances at me before looking away again. "And I don't talk about it."

"Ever?"

"No."

"Oh." I bite down on my bottom lip. Disappointed.

"Do you like Shakespeare?" he asks me.

An odd segue.

I shake my head. "All I know about him is that he stole my name and spelled it wrong."

Warner stares at me for a full second before he bursts into laughter—strong, unrestrained gales of laughter—trying to rein it in and failing.

I'm suddenly uncomfortable, nervous in front of this strange boy who laughs and wears secret rings and asks me about books and poetry. "I wasn't trying to be funny," I manage to tell him.

But his eyes are still full of smiles when he says, "Don't worry. I didn't know much about him until roughly a year ago. I still don't understand half the things he says, so I think we're going to get rid of most of it, but he did write a line I really liked."

"What was it?"

"Would you like to see it?"

"*See* it?"

But Warner is already on his feet, unbuttoning his pants and I'm wondering what could possibly be happening, worried I'm being tricked into some new sick game of his when he stops. Catches the horrified look on my face. Says, "Don't worry, love. I'm not getting naked, I promise. It's just another tattoo."

"Where?" I ask, frozen in place, wanting and not wanting to look away.

He doesn't answer.

His pants are unzipped but hanging low on his waist. His boxer-briefs are visible underneath. He tugs and tugs on the elastic band of his underwear until it sits just below his hipbone.

I'm blushing through my hairline.

I've never seen such an intimate area of any boy's body before, and I can't make myself look away. My moments with Adam were always in the dark and always interrupted; I never saw this much of him not because I didn't want to, but because I never had a chance to. And now the lights are on and Warner's standing right in front of me and I'm so caught, so intrigued by the cut of his frame. I can't help but notice the way his waist narrows into his hips and disappears under a piece of fabric. I want to know what it would be like to understand another person without those barriers.

To know a person so thoroughly, so privately.

I want to study the secrets tucked between his elbows and the whispers caught behind his knees. I want to follow the lines of his silhouette with my eyes and the tips of my fingers. I want to trace rivers and valleys along the curved muscles of his body.

My thoughts shock me.

There's a desperate heat in the pit of my stomach I wish I could ignore. There are butterflies in my chest I wish I could explain away. There's an ache in my core that I'm unwilling to name.

~~Beautiful.~~

~~He's so *beautiful.*~~

I must be insane.

"It's interesting," he says. "It feels very . . . relevant, I think. Even though it was written so long ago."

"What?" I rip my eyes away from his lower half, desperately trying to keep my imagination from drawing in the details. I look back at the words tattooed onto his skin and focus this time. "Oh," I say. "Yes."

It's 2 lines. Font like a typewriter inked across the very bottom of his torso.

hell is empty
and all the devils are here

Yes. Interesting. Yes. Sure.

I think I need to lie down.

"Books," he's saying, pulling his boxer-briefs up and rezipping his pants, "are easily destroyed. But words will live as long as people can remember them. Tattoos, for example, are very hard to forget." He buttons his button. "I think there's something about the impermanence of life these days that makes it necessary to etch ink into our skin," he says. "It reminds us that we've been marked by the world, that we're still alive. That we'll never forget."

"Who *are* you?"

I don't know this Warner. I'd never be able to recognize this Warner.

He smiles to himself. Sits down again. Says, "No one else will ever need to know."

"What do you mean?"

"I know who I am," he says. "That's enough for me."

I'm silent a moment. I frown at the floor. "It must be great to go through life with so much confidence."

"You are confident," he says to me. "You're stubborn and resilient. So brave. So strong. So inhumanly beautiful. You could conquer the world."

I actually laugh, look up to meet his eyes. "I cry too much. And I'm not interested in conquering the world."

"That," he says, "is something I will never understand." He shakes his head. "You're just scared. You're afraid of what you're unfamiliar with. You're too worried about disappointing people. You stifle your own potential," he says, "because of what you think others expect of you—because you still follow the rules you've been given." He looks at me, hard. "I wish you wouldn't."

"I wish you'd stop expecting me to use my power to kill people."

He shrugs. "I never said you had to. But it will happen along the way; it's an inevitability in war. Killing is statistically impossible to avoid."

"You're joking, right?"

"Definitely not."

"You can always avoid killing people, Warner. You avoid killing them by *not* going to war."

But he grins, so brilliantly, not even paying attention. "I love it when you say my name," he says. "I don't even know why."

"Warner isn't your name," I point out. "Your name is Aaron."

His smile is wide, so wide. "God, I love that."

"Your name?"

"Only when you say it."

"Aaron? Or Warner?"

His eyes close. He tilts his head back against the wall. Dimples.

Suddenly I'm struck by the reality of what I'm doing here. Sitting here, spending time with Warner like we have so many hours to waste. Like there isn't a very terrible world outside of these walls. I don't know how I manage to keep getting distracted and I promise myself that this time I won't let the conversation veer out of control. But when I open my mouth he says

"I'm not going to give you your notebook back."

My mouth falls closed.

"I know you want it back," he says, "but I'm afraid I'm going to have to keep it forever." He holds it up, shows it to me. Grins. And then puts it in his pocket. The one place I'd never dare to reach.

"Why?" I can't help but ask. "Why do you want it so much?"

He spends far too long just looking at me. Not answering my question. And then he says

"On the darkest days you have to search for a spot of brightness, on the coldest days you have to seek out a spot of warmth; on the bleakest days you have to keep your eyes onward and upward and on the saddest days you have to leave them open to let them cry. To then let them dry. To give them a chance to wash out the pain in order to see fresh and clear once again."

"I can't believe you have that memorized," I whisper.

He leans back again. Closes his eyes again. Says, *"Nothing in this life will ever make sense to me but I can't help but try to collect the change and hope it's enough to pay for our mistakes."*

"I wrote that, too?" I ask him, unable to believe it's possible he's reciting the same words that fell from my lips to my fingertips and bled onto a page. Still unable to believe he's now privy to my private thoughts, feelings I captured with a tortured mind and hammered into sentences I shoved into paragraphs, ideas I pinned together with punctuation marks that serve no function but to determine where one thought ends and another begins.

This blond boy has my secrets in his mouth.

"You wrote a lot of things," he says, not looking at me. "About your parents, your childhood, your experiences with other people. You talked about hope and redemption and what it would be like to see a bird fly by. You wrote about pain. And what it's like to think you're a monster. What it was like to be judged by everyone before you'd even spoken two words to them." A deep inhale. "So much of it was like seeing myself on paper," he whispers. "Like reading all the things I never knew how to say."

And I wish my heart would just shut up shut up shut up shut up.

"Every single day I'm sorry," he says, his words barely a breath now. "Sorry for believing the things I heard about you. And then for hurting you when I thought I was helping you. I can't apologize for who I am," he says. "That part of me is already done; already ruined. I gave up on myself a long time ago. But I am sorry I didn't understand you better. Everything I did, I did because I wanted to help you to be stronger. I wanted you to use your anger as a tool, as a weapon to help harness the strength inside of you; I wanted you to be able to fight the world. I provoked you on purpose," he says. "I pushed you too far, too hard, did things to horrify and disgust you and I did it all on purpose. Because that's how I was taught to steel myself against the terror in this world. That's how I was trained to fight back. And I wanted to teach you. I knew you had the potential to be more, so much more. I could see greatness in you."

He looks at me. Really, really looks at me.

"You're going to go on to do incredible things," he says. "I've always known that. I think I just wanted to be a part of it."

And I try. I try so hard to remember all the reasons why I'm supposed to hate him, I try to remember all the horrible things I've seen him do. But I'm tortured because I understand too much about what it's like to be tortured. To do things because you don't know any better. To do things because you think they're right because you were never taught what was wrong.

Because it's so hard to be kind to the world when all you've ever felt is hate.

Because it's so hard to see goodness in the world when all you've ever known is terror.

And I want to say something to him. Something profound and complete and memorable but he seems to understand. He offers me a strange, unsteady smile that doesn't reach his eyes but says so much.

Then

"Tell your team," he says, "to prepare for war. Unless his plans have changed, my father will be ordering an attack on civilians the day after tomorrow and it will be nothing short of a massacre. It will also be your only opportunity to save your men. They are being held captive somewhere in the lower levels of Sector 45 Headquarters. I'm afraid that's all I can tell you."

"How did you—"

"I know why you're here, love. I'm not an idiot. I know why you're being forced to spend time with me."

"But why offer the information so freely?" I ask him. "What reason do you have to help us?"

There's a flicker of change in his eyes that doesn't last long enough for me to examine it. And though his expression is carefully neutral, something in the space between us feels different all of a sudden. Charged.

"Go," he says. "You must tell them now."

FIFTY-THREE

Adam, Kenji, Castle, and I are camped out in his office trying to discuss strategy.

Last night I ran straight to Kenji—who then took me to Castle—to tell him what Warner told me. Castle was both relieved and horrified, and I think he still hasn't digested the information yet.

He told me he was going to meet with Warner in the morning, just to follow up, just to see if Warner would be willing to elaborate at all (he wasn't), and that Kenji, Adam, and I should meet him in his office at lunch.

So now we're all crammed into his small space, along with 7 others. The faces in this room are many of the same ones I saw when we journeyed into The Reestablishment's storage compound; that means they're important, integral to this movement. And it makes me wonder when I ever became a part of Castle's core group at Omega Point.

I can't help but feel a little proud. A little thrilled to be someone he relies on. To be contributing.

And it makes me wonder how much I've changed in such a short period of time. How different my life has become, how much stronger and how much weaker I feel now. It makes me wonder whether things would've turned out differently if Adam and I had found a way to stay together. If I ever would've ventured outside of the safety he introduced to my life.

I wonder about a lot of things.

But when I look up and catch him staring at me, my wonders disappear; and I'm left with nothing but the pains of missing him. Left wishing he wouldn't look away the moment I look up.

This was my miserable choice. I brought it upon myself.

Castle is sitting at his desk, elbows propped up on the table, chin resting on clasped hands. His eyebrows are furrowed, his lips pursed, his eyes focused on the papers in front of him.

He hasn't said a word in 5 minutes.

Finally, he looks up. Looks at Kenji, who is sitting right in front of him, between me and Adam. "What do you think?" he says. "Offensive or defensive?"

"Guerrilla warfare," Kenji says without hesitation. "Nothing else."

A deep breath. "Yes," Castle says. "I thought so too."

"We need to be split up," Kenji says. "Do you want to assign groups, or should I?"

"I'll assign the preliminary groups. I'd like you to look them over and suggest changes, if any."

Kenji nods.

"Perfect. And weapons—"

"I'll oversee that," Adam says. "I can make sure everything is clean, loaded, ready to go. I'm already familiar with the armory."

I had no idea.

"Good. Excellent. We'll assign one group to try and get on base to find Winston and Brendan; everyone else will spread out among the compounds. Our mission is simple: save as many civilians as possible. Take out only as many soldiers as is absolutely necessary. Our fight is not against the men, but against their leaders—we must never forget that. Kenji," he says, "I'd like you to oversee the groups entering the compounds. Do you feel comfortable doing that?"

Kenji nods.

"I will lead the group onto base," Castle says. "While you and Mr. Kent would be ideal for infiltrating Sector 45, I'd like you to stay with Ms. Ferrars; the three of you work well together, and we could use your strengths on the ground. Now," he says, spreading out the papers in front of him, "I've been studying these blueprints all ni—"

Someone is banging on the glass window in Castle's door.

He's a youngish man I've never seen before, with bright, light-brown eyes and hair cropped so close to the crown I can't even make out the color. His eyes are pulled together, his forehead tight, tense. "Sir!" he's shouting, he's *been* shouting, I realize, but his voice is muffled and only then does it dawn on me that this room must be soundproof, if only just a little bit.

Kenji jumps out of his chair, yanks the door open.

"Sir!" The man is out of breath. It's clear he ran all the way here. "Sir, please—"

"Samuel?" Castle is up, around his desk, charging forward to grip this boy's shoulders, trying to focus his eyes. "What is it—what's wrong?"

"Sir," Samuel says again, this time more normally, his breathing almost within his grasp. "We have a—a situation."

"Tell me everything—now is not the time to hold back if something has happened—"

"It's nothing to do with anything topside, sir, it's just—" His eyes dart in my direction for one split second. "Our . . . visitor—he—he is not cooperating, sir, he's—he's giving the guards a lot of trouble—"

"What kind of trouble?" Castle's eyes are two slits.

Samuel drops his voice. "He's managed to make a dent in the door, sir. He's managed to dent the *steel door*, sir, and he's threatening the guards and they're beginning to worry—"

"Juliette."

No.

"I need your help," Castle says without looking at me. "I know you don't want to do this, but you're the only one he'll listen to and we can't afford this distraction, not right now." His voice is so thin, so stretched it sounds as if it might actually crack. "Please do what you can to contain him, and when you deem it safe for one of the girls to enter, perhaps we can find a way to sedate him without endangering them in the process."

My eyes flick up to Adam almost accidentally. He doesn't look happy.

"Juliette." Castle's jaw tightens. "Please. Go now."

I nod. Turn to leave.

"Get ready," Castle adds as I walk out the door, his voice too soft for the words he speaks next. "Unless we have been deceived, the supreme will be massacring unarmed civilians tomorrow, and we can't afford to assume Warner has given us false information. We leave at dawn."

FIFTY-FOUR

The guards let me into Warner's room without a single word.

My eyes dart around the now partially furnished space, heart pounding, fists clenching, blood racing racing racing. Something is wrong. Something has happened. Warner was perfectly fine when I left him last night and I can't imagine what could've inspired him to lose his mind like this but I'm scared.

Someone has given him a chair. I realize now how he was able to dent the steel door. No one should've given him a chair.

Warner is sitting in it, his back to me. Only his head is visible from where I'm standing.

"You came back," he says.

"Of course I came back," I tell him, inching closer. "What's wrong? Is something wrong?"

He laughs. Runs a hand through his hair. Looks up at the ceiling.

"What happened?" I'm so worried now. "Are you—did something happen to you? Are you okay?"

"I need to get out of here," he says. "I need to leave. I can't be here anymore."

"Warner—"

"Do you know what he said to me? Did he tell you what he said to me?"

Silence.

"He just walked into my room this morning. He walked right in here and said he wanted to have a conversation with me." Warner laughs again, loud, too loud. Shakes his head. "He told me I can change. He said I might have a *gift* like everyone else here—that maybe I have an *ability*. He said I can be different, love. He said he *believes* I can be *different* if I *want* to be."

Castle told him.

Warner stands up but doesn't turn around all the way and I see he's not wearing a shirt. He doesn't even seem to mind that I can see the scars on his back, the word *IGNITE* tattooed on his body. His hair is messy, untamed, falling into his face and his pants are zipped but unbuttoned and I've never seen him so disheveled before. He presses his palms against the stone wall, arms outstretched; his body is bowed, his head down as if in prayer. His entire body is tense, tight, muscles straining against his skin. His clothes are in a pile on the floor and his mattress is in the middle of the room and the chair he was just sitting in is facing the wall, staring at nothing at all and I realize he's begun to lose his mind in here.

"Can you believe that?" he asks me, still not looking in my direction. "Can you believe he thinks I can just wake up one morning and be *different*? Sing happy songs and give money to the poor and beg the world to forgive me for what

I've done? Do you think that's possible? Do you think I can change?"

He finally turns to face me and his eyes are laughing, his eyes are like emeralds glinting in the setting sun and his mouth is twitching, suppressing a smile. "Do you think I could be *different*?" He takes a few steps toward me and I don't know why it affects my breathing. Why I can't find my mouth.

"It's just a question," he says, and he's right in front of me and I don't even know how he got there. He's still looking at me, his eyes so focused and so simultaneously unnerving, brilliant, blazing with something I can never place.

My heart it will not be still it refuses to stop skipping skipping skipping

"Tell me, Juliette. I'd love to know what you really think of me."

"Why?" Barely a whisper in an attempt to buy some time.

Warner's lips flicker up and into a smile before they fall open, just a bit, just enough to twitch into a strange, curious look that lingers in his eyes. He doesn't answer. He doesn't say a word. He only moves closer to me, studying me and I'm frozen in place, my mouth stuffed full of the seconds he doesn't speak and I'm fighting every atom in my body, every stupid cell in my system for being so attracted to him.

Oh.

God.

~~I am so horribly attracted to him.~~

The guilt is growing inside of me in stacks, settling on

my bones, snapping me in half. It's a cable twisted around my neck, a caterpillar crawling across my stomach. It's the night and midnight and the twilight of indecision. It's too many secrets I no longer contain.

~~I don't understand why I want this.~~

I am a terrible person.

And it's like he *sees* what I'm thinking, like he can feel the change happening in my head, because suddenly he's different. His energy slows down, his eyes are deep, troubled, tender; his lips are soft, still slightly parted and now the air in this room is too tight, too full of cotton and I feel the blood rushing around in my head, crashing into every rational region of my brain.

I wish someone would remind me how to breathe.

"Why can't you answer my question?" He's looking so deeply into my eyes that I'm surprised I haven't buckled under the intensity and I realize then, right in this moment I realize that everything about him is intense. Nothing about him is manageable or easy to compartmentalize. He's too much. Everything about him is too much. His emotions, his actions, his anger, his aggression.

~~His love.~~

He's dangerous, electric, impossible to contain. His body is rippling with an energy so extraordinary that even when he's calmed down it's almost palpable. It has a presence.

But I've developed a strange, frightening faith in who Warner really is and who he has the capacity to become. I want to find the 19-year-old boy who would feed a stray dog. I want to believe in the boy with a tortured childhood and an abusive father. I want to understand him. I want to unravel him.

I want to believe he is more than the mold he was forced into.

"I think you can change," I hear myself saying. "I think anyone can change."

And he smiles.

It's a slow, delighted smile. The kind of smile that breaks into a laugh and lights up his features and makes him sigh. He closes his eyes. His face is so touched, so amused. "It's just so sweet," he says. "So unbearably sweet. Because you really believe that."

"Of course I do."

He finally looks at me when he whispers, "But you're wrong."

"What?"

"I'm heartless," he says to me, his words cold, hollow, directed inward. "I'm a heartless bastard and a cruel, vicious being. I don't care about people's feelings. I don't care about their fears or their futures. I don't care about what they want or whether or not they have a family, and I'm not sorry," he says. "I've never been sorry for anything I've done."

It actually takes me a few moments to find my head. "But you apologized to me," I tell him. "You apologized to me just last night—"

"You're different," he says, cutting me off. "You don't count."

"I'm not different," I tell him. "I'm just another person, just like everyone else. And you've proven you have the capacity for remorse. For compassion. I know you can be kind—"

"That's not who I am." His voice is suddenly hard, suddenly too strong. "And I'm not going to change. I can't erase the nineteen miserable years of my life. I can't misplace the memories of what I've done. I can't wake up one morning and decide to live on borrowed hopes and dreams. Someone else's promises for a brighter future.

"And I won't lie to you," he says. "I've never given a damn about others and I don't make sacrifices and I do not compromise. I am not good, or fair, or decent, and I never will be. I can't be. Because to try to be any of those things would be *embarrassing.*"

"How can you think that?" I want to shake him. "How can you be ashamed of an attempt to be better?"

But he's not listening. He's laughing. He's saying, "Can you even picture me? Smiling at small children and handing out presents at birthday parties? Can you picture me helping a stranger? Playing with the neighbor's dog?"

"Yes," I say to him. "Yes I can." I've already seen it, I don't say to him.

"No."

"Why not?" I insist. "Why is that so hard to believe?"

"That kind of life," he says, "is impossible for me."

"But why?"

Warner clenches and unclenches 5 fingers before

running them through his hair. "Because I feel it," he says, quieter now. "I've always been able to feel it."

"Feel what?" I whisper.

"What people think of me."

"What . . . ?"

"Their feelings—their energy—it's—I don't know what it is," he says, frustrated, stumbling backward, shaking his head. "I've always been able to tell. I know how everyone hates me. I know how little my father cares for me. I know the agony of my mother's heart. I know that you're not like everyone else." His voice catches. "I know you're telling the truth when you say you don't hate me. That you want to and you can't. Because there's no ill will in your heart, not toward me, and if there was I would know. Just like I know," he says, his voice husky with restraint, "that you felt something when we kissed. You felt the same thing I did and you're ashamed of it."

I'm dripping panic everywhere.

"How can you know that?" I ask him. "H-how—you can't just *know* things like that—"

"No one has ever looked at me like you do," he whispers. "No one ever talks to me like you do, Juliette. You're different," he says. "You're so different. You would understand me. But the rest of the world does not want my sympathies. They don't want my smiles. Castle is the only man on Earth who's been the exception to this rule, and his eagerness to trust and accept me only shows how weak this resistance is. No one here knows what they're doing and they're all going to get themselves slaughtered—"

"That's not *true*—that can't be true—"

"Listen to me," Warner says, urgently now. "You must understand—the only people who matter in this wretched world are the ones with real power. And you," he says, "*you* have power. You have the kind of strength that could shake this planet—that could conquer it. And maybe it's still too soon, maybe you need more time to recognize your own potential, but I will always be waiting. I will always want you on my side. Because the two of us—the two of us," he says, he stops. He sounds breathless. "Can you imagine?" His eyes are intent on mine, eyebrows drawn together. Studying me. "Of course you can," he whispers. "You think about it all the time."

I gasp.

"You don't belong here," he says. "You don't belong with these people. They will drag you down with them and get you *killed*—"

"I have no other choice!" I'm angry now, indignant. "I'd rather stay here with those who are trying to help—trying to make a difference! At least they're not murdering innocent people—"

"You think your new friends have never killed before?" Warner shouts, pointing at the door. "You think Kent has never killed anyone? That Kenji has never put a bullet through a stranger's body? They were *my* soldiers!" he says. "I saw them do it with my own eyes!"

"They were trying to survive," I tell him, shaking,

fighting to ignore the terror of my own imagination. "Their loyalties were never with The Reestablishment—"

"My loyalties," he says, "do not lie with The Reestablishment. My loyalties lie with those who know how to live. I only have two options in this game, love." He's breathing hard. "Kill. Or be killed."

"No," I tell him, backing away, feeling sick. "It doesn't have to be like that. You don't have to live like that. You could get away from your father, from that life. You don't have to be what he wants you to be—"

"The damage," he says, "is already done. It's too late for me. I've already accepted my fate."

"No—Warner—"

"I'm not asking you to worry about me," he says. "I know exactly what my future looks like and I'm okay with it. I'm happy to live in solitude. I'm not afraid of spending the rest of my life in the company of my own person. I do not fear loneliness."

"You don't have to have that life," I tell him. "You don't have to be alone."

"I will not stay here," he says. "I just wanted you to know that. I'm going to find a way out of here and I'm going to leave as soon as I have the chance. My vacation," he says, "has officially come to an end."

FIFTY-FIVE

Tick tock.

Castle called an impromptu meeting to brief everyone on the details of tomorrow's fight; there are less than 12 hours until we leave. We've gathered in the dining hall because it's the easiest place to seat everyone at once.

We had 1 final meal, a handful of forced conversation, 2 tense hours filled with brief, spastic moments of laughter that sounded more like choking. Sara and Sonya were the last to sneak into the hall, both spotting me and waving a quick hello before they sat down on the other side of the room. Then Castle began to speak.

Everyone will need to fight.

All able-bodied men and women. The elderly unable to enter battle will stay back with the youngest ones, and the youngest ones will include James and his old group of friends.

James is currently crushing Adam's hand.

Anderson is going after the people, Castle says. The people have been rioting, raging against The Reestablishment now more than ever. Our battle gave them hope, Castle says to us. They'd only heard rumors of a resistance, and the battle concretized those rumors. They are looking to us to support them, to stand by them, and now, for the first time, we will be fighting with our gifts out in the open.

On the compounds.

Where the civilians will see us for what we are.

Castle is telling us to prepare for aggression on both sides. He says that sometimes, especially when frightened, people will not react positively to seeing our kind. They prefer the familiar terror as opposed to the unknown or the inexplicable, and our presence, our public display might create new enemies.

We have to be ready for that.

"Then why should we care?" someone shouts from the back of the room. She gets to her feet and I notice her sleek black hair, one heavy sheet of ink that stops at her waist. Her eyes are glittering under the fluorescent lights. "If they're only going to hate us," she says, "why should we even defend them? That's ridiculous!"

Castle takes a deep breath. "We cannot fault them all for the foolishness of one."

"But it's not just one, is it?" a new voice chimes in. "How many of them are going to turn on us?"

"We have no way of knowing," Castle says. "It could be one. It could be none. I am merely advising you to be cautious. You must never forget that these civilians are innocent and unarmed. They are being murdered for their disobedience—for merely speaking out and asking for fair treatment. They are starved and they've lost their homes, their families. Surely, you must be able to relate. Many of you still have family lost, scattered across the country, do you not?"

There's a general murmur among the crowd.

"You must imagine that it is your mother. Your father. Your brothers and sisters among them. They are hurting and they are beaten down. We have to do what little we can to help. It's the only way. We are their only hope."

"What about our men?" Another person gets to his feet. He must be in his late 40s, round and robust, towering over the room. "Where is the guarantee that we will get Winston and Brendan back?"

Castle's gaze drops for only a second. I wonder if I'm the only one who noticed the pain flit in and out of his eyes. "There is no guarantee, my friend. There never is. But we will do our best. We will not give up."

"Then what good was it to take the kid hostage?" he protests. "Why not just kill him? Why are we keeping him alive? He's done us no good and he's eating our food and using resources that should go to the rest of us!"

The crowd bursts into an aggravated frenzy, angry, insane with emotions. Everyone is shouting at once, shouting things like, "Kill him!" and "That'll show the supreme!" and "We have to make a statement!" and "He deserves to die!"

There's a sudden constriction in my heart. I've almost begun to hyperventilate and I realize, for the very first time, that the thought of Warner dead is anything but appealing to me.

It horrifies me.

I look to Adam for a different kind of reaction but I don't know what I was expecting. I'm stupid to be surprised at the tension in his eyes, his forehead, the stiff set of his lips. I'm stupid to have expected anything but hatred from Adam. Of course Adam hates Warner. Of course he does.

Warner tried to *murder* him.

Of course he, too, wants Warner dead.

I think I'm going to be sick.

"Please!" Castle shouts. "I know you're upset! Tomorrow is a difficult thing to face, but we can't channel our aggression onto one person. We have to use it as fuel for our fight and we have to remain united. We cannot allow anything to divide us. Not now!"

6 ticks of silence.

"I won't fight until he's dead!"

"We kill him tonight!"

"Let's get him now!"

The crowd is a roar of angry bodies, determined, ugly faces so scary, so savage, so twisted in inhuman rage. I hadn't realized that the people of Omega Point were harboring so much resentment.

"STOP!" Castle's hands are in the air, his eyes on fire. Every table and chair in the room has begun to rattle. People are looking around, scattered and scared, unnerved.

They're still unwilling to undermine Castle's authority. At least for now.

"Our hostage," Castle begins, "is no longer a hostage."

Impossible.

It's *impossible.*

It's not *possible.*

"He has come to me, just tonight," Castle says, "and asked for sanctuary at Omega Point."

My brain is screaming, raging against the 14 words Castle has just confessed.

It can't be true. Warner said he was going to leave. He said he was going to find a way to get *out*.

But Omega Point is even more shocked than I am. Even Adam is shaking with anger beside me. I'm afraid to look at his face.

"SILENCE! PLEASE!" Castle holds out another hand to quell the explosion of protests.

He says, "We have recently discovered that he, too, has a gift. And he says he wants to join us. He says he will fight with us tomorrow. He says he will fight against his father and help us find Brendan and Winston."

Chaos

Chaos

Chaos

explodes in every corner of the room.

"He's a liar!"

"Prove it!"

"How can you believe him?"

"He's a traitor to his own people! He'll be a traitor to us!"

"I'll never fight beside him!"

"I'll kill him first!"

Castle's eyes narrow, flashing under the fluorescent

lights, and his hands move through the air like whisks, gathering up every plate, every spoon, every glass cup in the room and he holds them there, right in midair, daring someone to speak, to shout, to disagree.

"You will not touch him," he says quietly. "I took an oath to help the members of our kind and I will not break it now. Think of yourselves!" he shouts. "Think of the day you found out! Think of the loneliness, the isolation, the terror that overcame you! Think of how you were cast off by your families and your friends! You don't think he could be a changed man? How have *you* changed, friends? You judge him now! You judge one of your own who asks for amnesty!"

Castle looks disgusted.

"If he does anything to compromise any of us, if he does one single thing to disprove his loyalty—only then are you free to pass judgment upon his person. But we first give him a chance, do we not?" He is no longer bothering to hide his anger. "He says he will help us find our men! He says he will fight against his father! He has valuable information we can use! Why should we be unwilling to take a chance? He is no more than a child of nineteen! He is only one and we are many more!"

The crowd is hushed, whispering amongst itself and I hear snippets of conversation and things like "naive" and "ridiculous" and "he's going to get all of us killed!" but no one speaks up and I'm relieved. I can't believe what I'm feeling right now and I wish I didn't care at all about what happens to Warner.

I wish I could want him dead. I wish I felt nothing for him.

But I can't. I can't. I can't.

"How do you know?" someone asks. A new voice, a calm voice, a voice struggling to be rational.

The voice sitting right beside me.

Adam gets to his feet. Swallows, hard. Says, "How do you know he has a gift? Have you tested him?"

And he looks at me, Castle looks at me, he stares at me as if to will me to speak and I feel like I've sucked all of the air out of this room, like I've been thrown into a vat of boiling water, like I will never find my heartbeat ever again and I am begging praying hoping and wishing he will not say the words he says next but he does.

Of course he does.

"Yes," Castle says. "We know that he, like you, can touch Juliette."

FIFTY-SIX

It's like spending 6 months just trying to inhale.

It's like forgetting how to move your muscles and reliving every nauseous moment in your life and struggling to get all the splinters out from underneath your skin. It's like that one time you woke up and tripped down a rabbit hole and a blond girl in a blue dress kept asking you for directions but you couldn't tell her, you had no idea, you kept trying to speak but your throat was full of rain clouds and it's like someone has taken the ocean and filled it with silence and dumped it all over this room.

It's like this.

No one is speaking. No one is moving. Everyone is staring.

At me.

At Adam.

At Adam staring at me.

His eyes are wide, blinking too fast, his features shifting in and out of confusion and anger and pain and confusion so much confusion and a touch of betrayal, of suspicion, of so much more confusion and an extra dose of pain and I'm gaping like a fish in the moments before it dies.

I wish he would say something. I wish he would at least

ask or accuse or demand *something* but he says nothing, he only studies me, stares at me, and I watch as the light goes out of his eyes, as the anger gives way to the pain and the extraordinary impossibility he must be experiencing right now and he sits down.

He does not look in my direction.

"Adam—"

He's up. He's up. He's up and he's charging out of the room and I scramble to my feet, I chase him out the door and I hear the chaos erupt in my wake, the crowd dissolving into anger all over again and I almost slam right into him, I'm gasping and he spins around and he says

"I don't understand." His eyes are so hurt, so deep, so blue.

"Adam, I—"

"He's touched you." It's not a question. He can hardly meet my eyes and he looks almost embarrassed by the words he speaks next. "He's touched your skin."

If only it were just that. If only it were that simple. If only I could get these currents out of my blood and Warner out of my head and *why am I so confused*

"Juliette."

"Yes," I tell him, I hardly move my lips. The answer to his nonquestion is yes.

Adam touches his fingers to his mouth, looks up, looks away, makes a strange, disbelieving sound. "When?"

I tell him.

I tell him when it happened, how it all began, I tell him

how I was wearing one of the dresses Warner always made me wear, how he was fighting to stop me before I jumped out the window, how his hand grazed my leg and how he touched me and nothing happened.

I tell him how I tried to pretend it was all just a figment of my imagination until Warner caught us again.

I don't tell him how Warner told me he missed me, how he told me he loved me and he kissed me, how he kissed me with such wild, reckless intensity. I don't tell him that I pretended to return Warner's affections just so I could slip my hands under his coat to get the gun out of his inside pocket. I don't tell him that I was surprised, shocked, even, at how it felt to be in his arms, and that I pushed away those strange feelings because I hated Warner, because I was so horrified that he'd shot Adam that I wanted to kill him.

All Adam knows is that I almost did. That I almost killed Warner.

And now Adam is blinking, digesting the words I'm telling him, innocent of the things I've kept to myself.

~~I really am a monster.~~

"I didn't want you to know," I manage to say. "I thought it would complicate things between us—after everything we've had to deal with—I just thought it would be better to ignore it and I don't know." I fumble, fail for words. "It was stupid. I was stupid. I should have told you and I'm sorry. I'm so sorry. I didn't want you to find out like this."

Adam is breathing hard, rubbing the back of his head before running a hand through his hair and he says, "I don't—I don't get it—I mean—do we know why he can touch you? Is it like me? Can he do what I do? I don't—*God,* Juliette, and you've been spending all that time alone with him—"

"Nothing happened," I tell him. "All I did was talk to him and he never tried to touch me. And I have no idea why he can touch me—I don't think anyone does. He hasn't started testing with Castle yet."

Adam sighs and drags a hand across his face and says, so quietly only I can hear him, "I don't even know why I'm surprised. We share the same goddamn DNA." He swears under his breath. Swears again. "Am I ever going to catch a break?" he asks, raising his voice, talking to the air. "Is there ever going to be a time when some shitty thing isn't being thrown in my face? Jesus. It's like this insanity is never going to end."

I want to tell him that I don't think it ever will.

"Juliette."

I freeze at the sound of his voice.

I squeeze my eyes shut tight, so tight, refusing to believe my ears. Warner cannot be here. Of course he's not here. It's not even *possible* for him to be out here but then I remember. Castle said he's no longer a hostage.

Castle must've let him out of his room.

Oh.

Oh no.

This can't be happening. Warner is not standing so close to me and Adam right now, not again, not like this not after everything this *cannot* be happening

but Adam looks over my shoulder, looks behind me at the person I'm trying so hard to ignore and I can't lift my eyes. I don't want to see what's about to happen.

Adam's voice is like acid when he speaks. "What the hell are you doing here?"

"It's good to see you again, Kent." I can actually hear Warner smile. "We should catch up, you know. Especially in light of this new discovery. I had no idea we had so much in common."

You really, truly have no idea, I want to say out loud.

"You sick piece of shit," Adam says to him, his voice low, measured.

"Such unfortunate language." Warner shakes his head. "Only those who cannot express themselves intelligently would resort to such crude substitutions in vocabulary." A pause. "Is it because I intimidate you, Kent? Am I making you nervous?" He laughs. "You seem to be struggling to hold yourself together."

"I will *kill you*—" Adam charges forward to grab Warner by the throat just as Kenji slams into him, into both of them, shoving them apart with a look of absolute disgust on his face.

"What the *hell* do you two think you're doing?" His eyes are blazing. "I don't know if you've noticed but you're standing right in front of the doorway and you're scaring the *shit* out of the little kids, Kent, so I'm going to have to ask you to calm your ass down." Adam tries to speak but Kenji cuts him off. "Listen, I don't have a clue what Warner is doing out of his room, but that's not my call to make. Castle is in charge around here, and we have to respect that. You can't go around killing people just because you feel like it."

"This is the same guy who tried to torture me to death!" Adam shouts. "He had his men beat the shit out of you! And I have to live with him? Fight with him? Pretend everything is fine? Has Castle *lost his mind*—"

"Castle knows what he's doing," Kenji snaps. "You don't need to have an opinion. You will defer to his judgment."

Adam throws his hands in the air, furious. "I don't believe this. This is a *joke*! Who does this? Who treats hostages like they're on some kind of retreat?" he shouts again, making no effort to keep his voice down. "He could go back and give away every detail of this place—he could give away our exact location!"

"That's impossible," Warner says. "I have no idea where we are."

Adam turns on Warner so quickly that I spin around just as fast, just to catch the action. Adam is shouting, saying something, looking like he might attack Warner right here in this moment and Kenji is trying to restrain him but I can hardly hear what's going on around me. The blood is pounding too hard in my head and my eyes are forgetting to blink because Warner is looking at me, only me, his eyes so focused, so intent, so heart-wrenchingly deep it renders me completely still.

Warner's chest is rising and falling, strong enough that I can see it from where I'm standing. He's not paying attention to the commotion beside him, the chaos of the dining hall or Adam trying to pummel him into the ground; he's not moved a single inch. He will not look away and I know I have to do it for him.

I turn my head.

Kenji is yelling at Adam to calm down about something and I reach out, I grab Adam's arm, I offer him a small smile and he stills. "Come on," I tell him. "Let's go back inside. Castle isn't finished yet and we need to hear what he's saying."

Adam makes an effort to regain control of himself. Takes a deep breath. Offers me a quick nod and allows me to lead him forward. I'm forcing myself to focus on Adam so I can pretend Warner isn't here.

Warner isn't a fan of my plan.

He's now standing in front of us, blocking our path and I look at him despite my best intentions only to see something I've never seen before. Not to this degree, not like this.

Pain.

"Move," Adam snaps at him, but Warner doesn't seem to notice.

He's looking at me. He's looking at my hand clenched around Adam's covered arm and the agony in his eyes is breaking my knees and I can't speak, I shouldn't speak, I wouldn't know what to say even if I could speak and then he says my name. He says it again. He says, "Juliette—"

"Move!" Adam barks again, this time losing restraint and pushing Warner with enough strength to knock him to the floor. Except Warner doesn't fall. He trips backward, just a little, but the movement somehow triggers something within him, some kind of dormant anger he's all too eager to unleash and he's charging forward, ready to inflict damage and I'm trying to figure out what to do to make it stop, I'm trying to come up with a plan and I'm stupid.

I'm stupid enough to step in the middle.

Adam grabs me to try and pull me back but I'm already pressing a palm to Warner's chest and I don't know what I'm thinking but I'm not thinking at all and that seems to be the problem. I'm here, I'm caught in the milliseconds standing between 2 brothers willing to destroy one another and it's not even me who manages to do anything at all.

It's Kenji.

He grabs both boys by the arms and tries to pry them apart but the sudden sound that rips through his throat is a torture and a terror I wish I could tear out of my skull.

He's down.

He's on the ground.

He's choking, gasping, writhing on the floor until he goes limp, until he can hardly breathe and then he's still, too still, and I think I'm screaming, I keep touching my lips to see where this sound is coming from and I'm on my knees. I'm trying to shake him awake but he's not moving, he's not responding and I have no idea what just happened.

I have no idea if Kenji is dead.

FIFTY-SEVEN

I'm definitely screaming.

Arms are pulling me up off the floor and I hear voices and sounds I don't care to recognize because all I know is that this can't happen, not to Kenji, not to my funny, complicated friend who keeps secrets behind his smiles and I'm ripping away from the hands holding me back and I'm blind, I'm bolting into the dining hall and a hundred blurry faces blend into the background because the only one I want to see is wearing a navy-blue blazer and headful of dreads tied into a ponytail.

"Castle!" I'm screaming. I'm still screaming. I may have fallen to the floor, I'm not sure, but I can tell my kneecaps are starting to hurt and I don't care I don't care I don't care—

"Castle! It's Kenji—he's—*please*—"

I've never seen Castle run before.

He charges through the room at an inhuman speed, past me and into the hall. Everyone in the room is up, frantic, some shouting, panicked, and I'm chasing Castle back into the tunnel and Kenji is still there. Still limp. Still.

Too still.

"Where are the girls?" Castle is shouting. "Someone—get the girls!" He's cradling Kenji's head, trying to pull

Kenji's heavy body into his arms and I've never heard him like this before, not even when he talked about our hostages, not even when he talked about what Anderson has done to the civilians. I look around and see the members of Omega Point standing all around us, pain carved into their features and so many of them have already started crying, clutching at each other and I realize I never fully recognized Kenji. I didn't understand the reach of his authority. I'd never really seen just how much he means to the people in this room.

How much they love him.

I blink and Adam is one of 50 different people trying to help carry Kenji and now they're running, they're hoping against hope and someone is saying, "They've gone to the medical wing! They're preparing a bed for him!" And it's like a stampede, everyone rushing after them, trying to find out what's wrong and no one will look at me, no one will meet my eyes and I pull myself away, out of sight, around the corner, into the darkness. I taste the tears as they fall into my mouth, I count each salty drop because I can't understand what happened, how it happened, how this is even possible because I wasn't touching him, I couldn't have been touching him please please please I couldn't have touched him but then I freeze. Icicles form along my arms as I realize:

I'm not wearing my gloves.

I forgot my gloves. I was in such a rush to get here tonight that I just jumped out of the shower and left my gloves in my room and it doesn't seem real, it doesn't seem possible that I could've done this, that I could've forgotten, that I could be responsible for yet another life lost and I just I just I just

I fall to the floor.

"Juliette."

I look up. I jump up.

I say, "Stay away from me" and I'm shaking, I'm trying to push the tears back but I'm shrinking into nothingness because I'm thinking this must be it. This must be my ultimate punishment. I deserve this pain, I deserve to have killed one of my only friends in the world and I want to shrivel up and disappear forever. "Go away—"

"Juliette, *please,*" Warner says, coming closer. His face is cast in shadow. This tunnel is only half lit and I don't know where it leads. All I know is that I do not want to be alone with Warner.

Not now. Not ever again.

"I said stay away from me." My voice is trembling. "I don't want to talk to you. Please—just leave me alone!"

"I can't abandon you like this!" he says. "Not when you're crying!"

"Maybe you wouldn't understand that emotion," I snap at him. "Maybe you wouldn't care because killing people means nothing to you!"

He's breathing hard. Too fast. "What are you talking about?"

"I'm talking about Kenji!" I explode. "I did that! It's my

fault! It's my fault you and Adam were fighting and it's my fault Kenji came out to stop you and it's my fault—" My voice breaks once, twice. "It's my fault he's dead!"

Warner's eyes go wide. "Don't be ridiculous," he says. "He's not dead."

I'm agony.

I'm sobbing about what I've done and how of course he's dead, didn't you see him, he wasn't even moving and I killed him and Warner remains utterly silent. He doesn't say a single thing as I hurl awful, horrible insults at him and accuse him of being too coldhearted to understand what it's like to grieve. I don't even realize he's pulled me into his arms until I'm nestled against his chest and I don't fight it. I don't fight it at all. I cling to him because I need this warmth, I miss feeling strong arms around me and I'm only just beginning to realize how quickly I came to rely on the healing properties of an excellent hug.

How desperately I've missed this.

And he just holds me. He smooths back my hair, he runs a gentle hand down my back, and I hear his heart beat a strange, crazy beat that sounds far too fast to be human.

His arms are wrapped entirely around me when he says, "You didn't kill him, love."

And I say, "Maybe you didn't see what I saw."

"You are misunderstanding the situation entirely. You didn't do anything to hurt him."

I shake my head against his chest. "What are you talking about?"

"It wasn't you. I know it wasn't you."

I pull back. Look up into his eyes. "How can you know something like that?"

"Because," he says. "It wasn't you who hurt Kenji. It was me."

FIFTY-EIGHT

"What?"

"He's not dead," Warner says, "though he is severely injured. I suspect they should be able to revive him."

"What"—I'm panicking, panicking in my bones—"what are you talking about—"

"Please," Warner says. "Sit down. I'll explain." He folds himself onto the floor and pats the place beside him. I don't know what else to do and my legs are now officially too shaky to stand on their own.

My limbs spill onto the ground, both our backs against the wall, his right side and my left side divided only by a thin inch of air.

1

2

3 seconds pass.

"I didn't want to believe Castle when he told me I might have a . . . a *gift,*" Warner says. His voice is pitched so low that I have to strain to hear it even though I'm only inches away. "A part of me hoped he was trying to drive me mad for his own benefit." A small sigh. "But it did make a bit of sense, if I really thought about it. Castle told me about Kent, too," Warner says. "About how he can touch you and how they've discovered why. For a moment I wondered if perhaps I had a similar ability. One just as pathetic. Equally as useless." He laughs. "I was extremely reluctant to believe it."

"It's not a useless ability," I hear myself saying.

"Really?" He turns to face me. Our shoulders are almost touching. "Tell me, love. What can he do?"

"He can disable things. Abilities."

"Right," he says, "but how will that ever *help* him? How could it ever help him to disable the powers of his own people? It's absurd. It's *wasteful*. It won't help at all in this war."

I bristle. Decide to ignore that. "What does any of this have to do with Kenji?"

He turns away from me again. His voice is softer when he says, "Would you believe me if I told you I could sense your energy right now? Sense the tone and weight of it?"

I stare at him, study his features and the earnest, tentative note in his voice. "Yes," I tell him. "I think I'd believe you."

Warner smiles in a way that seems to sadden him. "I can sense," he says, taking a deep breath, "the emotions you're feeling most strongly. And because I know you, I'm able to put those feelings into context. I know the fear you're feeling right now, for example, is not directed toward me, but toward yourself, and what you think you've done to Kenji. I sense your hesitation—your reluctance to believe that it wasn't your fault. I feel your sadness, your grief."

"You can really feel that?" I ask.

He nods without looking at me.

"I never knew that was possible," I tell him.

"I didn't either—I wasn't aware of it," he says. "Not for a very long time. I actually thought it was normal to be so acutely aware of human emotions. I thought perhaps I was more perceptive than most. It's a big factor in why my father allowed me to take over Sector 45," he tells me. "Because I have an uncanny ability to tell whenever someone is hiding something, or feeling guilty, or, most importantly, lying." A pause. "That," he says, "and because I'm not afraid to deliver consequences if the occasion calls for it.

"It wasn't until Castle suggested there might be something more to me that I really began to analyze it. I nearly lost my mind." He shakes his head. "I kept going over it, thinking of ways to prove and disprove his theories. Even with all my careful deliberation, I dismissed it. And while I am a bit sorry—for your sake, not for mine—that Kenji had to be stupid enough to interfere tonight, I think it was actually quite serendipitous. Because now I finally have proof. Proof that I was wrong. That Castle," he says, "was right."

"What do you mean?"

"I took your Energy," he tells me, "and I didn't know I could. I could feel it all very vividly when the four of us connected. Adam was inaccessible—which, by the way, explains why I never suspected him of being disloyal. His emotions were always hidden; always blocked off. I was naive and assumed he was merely robotic, devoid of any real personality or interests. He eluded me and it was my own fault. I trusted myself too much to be able to anticipate a flaw in my system."

And I want to say, Adam's ability isn't so useless after all, is it?

But I don't.

"And Kenji," Warner says after a moment. He rubs his forehead. Laughs a little. "Kenji was . . . very smart. A lot smarter than I gave him credit for—which, as it turns out, was exactly his tactic. Kenji," he says, blowing out a breath, "was careful to be an obvious threat as opposed to a discreet one.

"He was always getting into trouble—demanding extra portions at meals, fighting with the other soldiers, breaking curfew. He broke simple rules in order to draw attention to himself. In order to trick me into seeing him as an irritant and nothing more. I always felt there was something off about him, but I attributed it to his loud, raucous behavior and his inability to follow rules. I dismissed him as a poor soldier. Someone who would never be promoted. Someone who would always be recognized as a waste of time." He shakes his head. Raises his eyebrows at the ground. "Brilliant," he says, looking almost impressed. "It was brilliant. His only mistake," Warner adds after a moment, "was being too openly friendly with Kent. And that mistake nearly cost him his life."

"So—what? You were trying to finish him off tonight?" I'm still so confused, trying to make an attempt to refocus the conversation. "Did you hurt him on purpose?"

"Not on purpose." Warner shakes his head. "I didn't actually know what I was doing. Not at first. I've only ever just *sensed* Energy; I never knew I could *take* it. But I touched yours simply by touching you—there was so much adrenaline among the group of us that yours practically threw itself at me. And when Kenji grabbed my arm," he says, "you and I, we were still connected. And I . . . somehow I managed to redirect your power in his direction. It was quite accidental but I felt it happen. I felt your power rush into me. Rush out of me." He looks up. Meets my eyes. "It was the most extraordinary thing I've ever experienced."

I think I'd fall down if I weren't already sitting.

"So you can take—you can just take other people's powers?" I ask him.

"Apparently."

"And you're sure you didn't hurt Kenji on purpose?"

Warner laughs, looks at me like I've just said something highly amusing. "If I had wanted to kill him, I would have. And I wouldn't have needed such a complicated setup to accomplish it. I'm not interested in theatrics," he says. "If I want to hurt someone, I won't require much more than my own two hands."

I'm stunned into silence.

"I'm actually amazed," Warner says, "how you manage to contain so much without finding ways to release the excess. I could barely hold on to it. The transfer from my body to Kenji's was not only immediate, it was necessary. I couldn't tolerate the intensity for very long."

"And I can't hurt you?" I blink at him, astonished. "At all? My power just goes *into* you? You just absorb it?"

He nods. Says, "Would you like to see?"

And I'm saying yes with my head and my eyes and my lips and I've never been more terrified to be excited in my life. "What do I have to do?" I ask him.

"Nothing," he says, so quietly. "Just touch me."

My heart is beating pounding racing running through my body and I'm trying to focus. Trying to stay calm. This is going to be fine, I say to myself. It's going to be fine. It's just an experiment. There's no need to get so excited about being able to touch someone again, I keep saying to myself.

~~But oh, I am so, so excited.~~

He holds out his bare hand.

I take it.

I wait to feel something, some feeling of weakness, some depletion of my Energy, some sign that a transfer is taking place from my body to his but I feel nothing at all. I feel exactly the same. But I watch Warner's face as his eyes close and he makes an effort to focus. Then I feel his hand tighten around mine and he gasps.

His eyes fly open and his free hand goes right through the floor.

I jerk back, panicked. I'm tipping sideways, my hands catching me from behind. I must be hallucinating. I must be hallucinating the hole in the floor not 4 inches from where Warner is still sitting on the ground. I must've been hallucinating when I saw his resting palm press too hard and go right through. I must be hallucinating everything. All of this. I'm dreaming and I'm sure I'm going to wake up soon. That must be it.

"Don't be afraid—"

"H-how," I stammer, "how did you d-do that—"

"Don't be frightened, love, it's all right, I promise—it's new for me, too—"

"My—my power? It doesn't—you don't feel any pain?"

He shakes his head. "On the contrary. It's the most incredible rush of adrenaline—it's unlike anything I've ever known. I actually feel a little light-headed," he says, "in the best possible way." He laughs. Smiles to himself. Drops his head into his hands. Looks up. "Can we do it again?"

"No," I say too quickly.

He's grinning. "Are you sure?"

"I can't—I just, I still can't believe you can touch me. That you really—I mean"—I'm shaking my head—"there's no catch? There are no conditions? You touch me and no one gets hurt? And not only does no one get hurt, but you *enjoy* it? You actually *like* the way it feels to touch me?"

He's blinking at me now, staring like he's not sure how to answer my question.

"Well?"

"Yes," he says, but it's a breathless word.

"Yes, what?"

I can hear how hard his heart is beating. I can actually hear it in the silence between us. "Yes," he says. "I like it."

Impossible.

"You never have to be afraid of touching me," he says. "It won't hurt me. It can only give me strength."

I want to laugh one of those strange, high-pitched, delusional laughs that signals the end of a person's sanity. Because this world, I think, has a terrible, terrible sense of humor. It always seems to be laughing at me. At my expense. Making my life infinitely more complicated all the time. Ruining all of my best-laid plans by making every choice so difficult. Making everything so confusing.

I can't touch the boy I love.

But I can use my touch to strengthen the boy who tried to kill the one I love.

No one, I want to tell the world, is laughing.

"Warner." I look up, hit with a sudden realization. "You have to tell Castle."

"Why would I do that?"

"Because he has to know! It would explain Kenji's situation and it could help us tomorrow! You'll be fighting with us and it might come in handy—"

Warner laughs.

He laughs and laughs and laughs, his eyes brilliant, gleaming even in this dim light. He laughs until it's just a hard breath, until it becomes a gentle sigh, until it dissolves into an amused smile. And then he grins at me until he's grinning to himself, until he looks down and his gaze drops to my hand, the one lying limp on my lap and he hesitates just a moment before his fingers brush the soft, thin skin covering my knuckles.

I don't breathe.

I don't speak.

I don't even move.

He's hesitant, like he's waiting to see if I'll pull away and I should, I know I should but I don't. So he takes my hand. Studies it. Runs his fingers along the lines of my palm, the creases at my joints, the sensitive spot between my thumb and index finger and his touch is so tender, so delicate and gentle and it feels so good it hurts, it actually hurts. And it's too much for my heart to handle right now.

I snatch back my hand in a jerky, awkward motion, face flushing, pulse tripping.

Warner doesn't flinch. He doesn't look up. He doesn't even seem surprised. He only stares at his now empty hands as he speaks. "You know," he says, his voice both strange and soft, "I think Castle is little more than an optimistic fool. He tries too hard to welcome too many people and it's going to backfire, simply because it's impossible to please everyone." A pause. "He is the perfect example of the kind of person who doesn't know the rules of this game. Someone who thinks too much with his heart and clings too desperately to some fantastical notion of hope and peace. It will never help him," he sighs. "In fact, it will be the end of him, I'm quite sure of it.

"But there is something about you," Warner says, "something about the way *you* hope for things." He shakes his head. "It's so naive that it's oddly endearing. You like to believe people when they speak," he says. "You prefer kindness." He smiles, just a little. Looks up. "It amuses me."

All at once I feel like an idiot. "You're not fighting with us tomorrow."

Warner is smiling openly now, his eyes so warm. "I'm going to leave."

"You're going to leave." I'm numb.

"I don't belong here."

I'm shaking my head, saying, "I don't understand—how can you leave? You told Castle you're going to fight with us tomorrow—does he know you're leaving? Does anyone know?" I ask him, searching his face. "What do you have planned? What are you going to do?"

He doesn't answer.

"What are you going to *do*, Warner—"

"Juliette," he whispers, and his eyes are urgent, tortured all of a sudden. "I need to ask you somethi—"

Someone is bolting down the tunnels.

Calling my name.

Adam.

FIFTY-NINE

I jump up, frantic, and tell Warner I'll be right back.

I'm saying don't leave yet, don't go anywhere just yet I'll be right back but I don't wait for his response because I'm on my feet and I'm running toward the lighted hallway and I almost slam right into Adam. He steadies me and pulls me tight, so close, always forgetting not to touch me like this and he's anxious and he says, "Are you okay?" and "I'm so sorry," and "I've been looking for you everywhere," and "I thought you'd come down to the medical wing," and "it wasn't your fault, I hope you know that—"

It keeps hitting me in the face, in the skull, in the spine, this knowledge of just how much I care about him. How much I know he cares about me. Being close to him like this is a painful reminder of everything I had to force myself to walk away from. I take a deep breath.

"Adam," I ask, "is Kenji okay?"

"He's not conscious yet," he says to me, "but Sara and Sonya think he's going to be okay. They're going to stay up with him all night, just to be sure he makes it through in one piece." A pause. "No one knows what happened," he says. "But it wasn't you." His eyes lock mine in place. "You know that, right? You didn't even touch him. I know you didn't."

And even though I open my mouth a million times to say, It was Warner. Warner did it. He's the one who did this to Kenji, you have to get him and catch him and stop him he is lying to all of you! He's going to escape tomorrow! I don't say any of it and I don't know why.

I don't know why I'm protecting him.

I think part of me is afraid to say the words out loud, afraid to make them true. I still don't know whether or not Warner is really going to leave or even how he's going to escape; I don't know if it's even possible. And I don't know if I can tell anyone about Warner's ability yet; I don't think I want to explain to Adam that while he and the rest of Omega Point were tending to Kenji, I was hiding in a tunnel with Warner—our enemy and hostage—holding his hand and testing out his new power.

I wish I weren't so confused.

I wish my interactions with Warner would stop making me feel so guilty. Every moment I spend with him, every conversation I have with him makes me feel like I've somehow betrayed Adam, even though technically we're not even together anymore. My heart still feels so tied to Adam; I feel bound to him, like I need to make up for already having hurt him so much. I don't want to be the reason for the pain in his eyes, not again, and somehow I've decided that keeping secrets is the only way to keep him from getting hurt. But deep down, I know this can't be right. Deep down, I know it could end badly.

But I don't know what else to do.

"Juliette?" Adam is still holding me tight, still so close and warm and wonderful. "Are you okay?"

And I'm not sure what makes me ask it, but suddenly I need to know.

"Are you ever going to tell him?"

Adam pulls back, just an inch. "What?"

"Warner. Are you ever going to tell him the truth? About the two of you?"

Adam is blinking, stunned, caught off guard by my question. "No," he finally says. "Never."

"Why not?"

"Because it takes a lot more than blood to be family," he says. "And I want nothing to do with him. I'd like to be able to watch him die and feel no sympathy, no remorse. He's the textbook definition of a monster," Adam says to me. "Just like my dad. And I'll drop dead before I recognize him as my brother."

Suddenly I'm feeling like I might fall over.

Adam grabs my waist, tries to focus my eyes. "You're still in shock," he says. "We need to get you something to eat—or maybe some water—"

"It's okay," I tell him. "I'm okay." I allow myself to enjoy one last second in his arms before I break away, needing to breathe. I keep trying to convince myself that Adam is right, that Warner has done terrible, awful things and I shouldn't forgive him. I shouldn't smile at him. I shouldn't even talk to him. And then I want to scream because I don't think my brain can handle the split personality I seem to be developing lately.

I tell Adam I need a minute. I tell him I need to stop by the bathroom before we head over to the medical wing and he says okay, he says he'll wait for me.

He says he'll wait for me until I'm ready.

And I tiptoe back into the dark tunnel to tell Warner that I have to leave, that I won't be coming back after all, but when I squint into the darkness I can't see a thing.

I look around.

He's already gone.

SIXTY

We don't have to do anything at all to die.

We can hide in a cupboard under the stairs our whole life and it'll still find us. Death will show up wearing an invisible cloak and it will wave a magic wand and whisk us away when we least expect it. It will erase every trace of our existence on this earth and it will do all this work for free. It will ask for nothing in return. It will take a bow at our funeral and accept the accolades for a job well done and then it will disappear.

Living is a little more complex. There's one thing we always have to do.

Breathe.

In and out, every single day in every hour minute and moment we must inhale whether we like it or not. Even as we plan to asphyxiate our hopes and dreams still we breathe. Even as we wither away and sell our dignity to the man on the corner we breathe. We breathe when we're wrong, we breathe when we're right, we breathe even as we slip off the ledge toward an early grave. It cannot be undone.

So I breathe.

I count all the steps I've climbed toward the noose hanging from the ceiling of my existence and I count out the number of times I've been stupid and I run out of numbers.

Kenji almost died today.

Because of me.

It's still my fault that Adam and Warner were fighting. It's still my fault that I stepped between them. It's still my fault that Kenji felt the need to pull them apart and if I hadn't been caught in the middle Kenji never would've been hurt.

And I'm standing here. Staring at him.

He's barely breathing and I'm begging him. I'm begging him to do the one thing that matters. The only thing that matters. I need him to hold on but he's not listening. He can't hear me and I need him to be okay. I need him to pull through. I need him to breathe.

I need him.

Castle didn't have much more to say.

Everyone was standing around, some wedged into the medical wing, others standing on the other side of the glass, watching silently. Castle gave a small speech about how we need to stick together, how we're a family and if we don't have each other then who do we have? He said we're all scared, sure, but now is the time for us to support one another. Now is the time to band together and fight back. Now is the time, he said, for us to take back our world.

"Now is the time for us to live," he said.

"We'll postpone tomorrow's departure just long enough for everyone to have a final breakfast together. We cannot go into battle divided," he said. "We have to have faith in ourselves and in each other. Take a little more time in the morning to find peace with yourselves. After breakfast we leave. As one."

"What about Kenji?" someone asked, and I was startled to hear the familiar voice.

James. He was standing there with his fists clenched, tearstains streaked across his face, his bottom lip trembling even as he fought to hide the pain in his voice.

My heart split clean in half.

"What do you mean?" Castle asked him.

"Will he fight tomorrow?" James demanded, sniffing back the last of his tears, fists beginning to shake. "He wants to fight tomorrow. He told me he wants to fight tomorrow."

Castle's face creased as it pulled together. He took his time responding. "I . . . I'm afraid I don't think Kenji will be able to join us tomorrow. But perhaps," he said, "perhaps you could stay and keep him company?"

James didn't respond. He only stared at Castle. Then he stared at Kenji. He blinked several times before pushing through the crowd to clamber onto Kenji's bed. Burrowed into his side and promptly fell asleep.

We all took that as our cue to leave.

Well. Everyone but me, Adam, Castle, and the girls. I find it interesting that everyone refers to Sonya and Sara as "the girls," as if they're the only girls in this entire place. They're not. I don't even know how they got that nickname and while a part of me wants to know, another part of me is too exhausted to ask.

I curl into my seat and stare at Kenji, who is struggling to breathe in and out. I prop my head up on my fist, fighting the sleep weaving its way into my consciousness. I don't deserve to sleep. I should stay here all night and watch over him. I would, too, if I could touch him without destroying his life.

"You two should really get to bed."

I jolt awake, jerking up, not realizing I'd actually dozed off for a second. Castle is staring at me with a soft, strange look on his face.

"I'm not tired," I lie.

"Go to bed," he says. "We have a big day tomorrow. You need to sleep."

"I can walk her out," Adam says. He moves to stand up. "And then I can be right back—"

"Please." Castle cuts him off. "Go. I'll be fine with the girls."

"But you need to sleep more than we do," I tell him.

Castle smiles a sad smile. "I'm afraid I won't be getting any sleep tonight."

He turns to look at Kenji, his eyes crinkling in happiness or pain or something in between. "Did you know," Castle says to us, "that I've known Kenji since he was a small boy? I found him shortly after I'd built Omega Point. He grew up here. When I first met him he was living in an old shopping cart he'd found on the side of the highway." Castle pauses. "Has he ever told you that story?"

Adam sits back down. I'm suddenly wide-awake. "No,"

we both say at the same time.

"Ah—forgive me." Castle shakes his head. "I shouldn't waste your time with these things," he says. "I think there's too much on my mind right now. I'm forgetting which stories to keep to myself."

"No—please—I want to know," I tell him. "Really."

Castle stares into his hands. Smiles a little. "There's not much to it," he says. "Kenji has never talked to me about what happened to his parents, and I try not to ask. All he ever had was a name and an age. I stumbled upon him quite accidentally. He was just a boy sitting in a shopping cart. Far from civilization. It was the dead of winter and he was wearing nothing but an old T-shirt and a pair of sweatpants a few sizes too big for him. He looked like he was freezing, like he could use a few meals and place to sleep. I couldn't just walk away," Castle says. "I couldn't just leave him there. So, I asked him if he was hungry."

He stops, remembering.

"Kenji didn't say a single thing for at least thirty seconds. He simply stared at me. I almost walked away, thinking I'd frightened him. But then, finally, he reached out, grabbed my hand, placed it in his palm and shook it. Very hard. And then he said, 'Hello, sir. My name is Kenji Kishimoto and I am nine years old. It's very nice to meet you.'" Castle laughs out loud, his eyes shining with an emotion that betrays his smiles. "He must've been starving, the poor kid. He always," Castle says, blinking up at the ceiling now, "he always had a strong, determined sort of personality. So much pride.

Unstoppable, that boy."

We're all silent for a while.

"I had no idea," Adam says, "that you two were so close."

Castle stands up. Looks around at us and smiles too brightly, too tightly. Says, "Yes. Well, I'm sure he's going to be just fine. He'll be just fine in the morning, so you two should definitely get some sleep."

"Are you su—"

"Yes, please, get to bed. I'll be fine here with the girls, I promise."

So we get up. We get up and Adam manages to lift James from Kenji's bed and into his arms without waking him. And we walk out.

I glance back.

I see Castle fall into his chair and drop his head into his hands and rest his elbows on his knees. I see him reach out a shaky hand to rest on Kenji's leg and I wonder at how much I still don't know about these people I live with. How little I've allowed myself to become a part of their world.

And I know I want to change that.

SIXTY-ONE

Adam walks me to my room.

It's been lights-out for about an hour now, and, with the exception of faint emergency lights glowing every few feet, everything is, quite literally, out. It's absolute blackness, and even still, the guards on patrol manage to spot us only to warn us to go straight to our separate quarters.

Adam and I don't really speak until we reach the mouth of the women's wing. There's so much tension, so many unspoken worries between us. So many thoughts about today and tomorrow and the many weeks we've already spent together. So much we don't know about what's already happening to us and what will eventually happen to us. Just looking at him, being so close and being so far away from him—it's painful.

I want so desperately to bridge the gap between our bodies. I want to press my lips to every part of him and I want to savor the scent of his skin, the strength in his limbs, in his heart. I want to wrap myself in the warmth and reassurance I've come to rely on.

But.

In other ways, I've come to realize that being away from him has forced me to rely on myself. To allow myself to be scared and to find my own way through it. I've had to train without him, fight without him, face Warner and Anderson and the chaos of my mind all without him by my side. And I feel different now. I feel stronger since putting space between us.

And I don't know what that means.

All I know is that it'll never be safe for me to rely on someone else again, to *need* constant reassurance of who I am and who I might someday be. I can love him, but I can't depend on him to be my backbone. I can't be my own person if I constantly require someone else to hold me together.

My mind is a mess. Every single day I'm confused, uncertain, worried I'm going to make a new mistake, worried I'm going to lose control, worried I'm going to lose myself. But it's something I have to work through. Because for the rest of my life, I'll always, always be stronger than everyone around me.

But at least I'll never have to be scared anymore.

"Are you going to be okay?" Adam asks, finally dispelling the silence between us. I look up to find that his eyes are worried, trying to read me.

"Yes," I tell him. "Yes. I'm going to be fine." I offer him a tight smile, but it feels wrong to be this close to him without being able to touch him at all.

Adam nods. Hesitates. Says, "It's been one hell of a night."

"And it'll be one hell of day tomorrow, too," I whisper.

"Yeah," he says quietly, still looking at me like he's trying to find something, like he's searching for an answer to an unspoken question and I wonder if he sees something different in my eyes now. He grins a small grin. Says, "I should probably go," and nods at James bundled in his arms.

I nod, not sure what else to do. What to say.

So much is uncertain.

"We'll get through this," Adam says, answering my silent thoughts. "All of it. We're going to be okay. And Kenji will be fine." He touches my shoulder, allows his fingers to trail down my arm and stop just short of my bare hand.

I close my eyes, try to savor the moment.

And then his fingers graze my skin and my eyes fly open, my heart racing in my chest.

He's staring at me like he might've done much more than touch my hand if he weren't holding James against his chest.

"Adam—"

"I'm going to find a way," he says to me. "I'm going to find a way to make this work. I promise. I just need some time."

I'm afraid to speak. Afraid of what I might say, what I might do; afraid of the hope ballooning inside of me.

"Good night," he whispers.

"Good night," I say.

I'm beginning to think of hope as a dangerous, terrifying thing.

SIXTY-TWO

I'm so tired when I walk into my room that I'm only half conscious as I change into the tank top and pajama pants I sleep in. They were a gift from Sara. It was her recommendation that I change out of my suit while I sleep; she and Sonya think it's important to give my skin direct contact with fresh air.

I'm about to climb under the covers when I hear a soft knock at my door.

Adam

is my first thought.

But then I open the door. And promptly close it.

I must be dreaming.

"Juliette?"

Oh. God.

"What are you *doing* here?" I shout-whisper through the closed door.

"I need to speak with you."

"Right now. You need to speak with me right now."

"Yes. It's important," Warner says. "I heard Kent telling you that those twin girls would be in the medical wing tonight and I figured it would be a good time for us to speak privately."

"You heard my conversation with Adam?" I begin to panic, worried he might've heard too much.

"I have zero interest in your conversation with Kent," he says, his tone suddenly flat, neutral. "I left just as soon as I heard you'd be alone tonight."

"Oh." I exhale. "How did you even get in here without guards stopping you?"

"Maybe you should open the door so I can explain."

I don't move.

"Please, love, I'm not going to do anything to hurt you. You should know that by now."

"I'm giving you five minutes. Then I have to sleep, okay? I'm exhausted."

"Okay," he says. "Five minutes."

I take a deep breath. Crack the door open. Peek at him.

He's smiling. Looking entirely unapologetic.

I shake my head.

He slips past me and sits down directly on my bed.

I close the door, make my way across the room from him, and sit on Sonya's bed, suddenly all too aware of what I'm wearing and how incredibly exposed I feel. I cross my arms over the thin cotton clinging to my chest—even though I'm sure he can't actually see me—and make an effort to ignore the cold chill in the air. I always forget just how much the suit does to regulate my body temperature so far belowground.

Winston was a genius to design it for me.

Winston.

Winston and Brendan.

Oh how I hope they're okay.

"So . . . what is it?" I ask Warner. I can't see a single thing in this darkness; I can hardly make out the form of his silhouette. "You just left earlier, in the tunnel. Even though I asked you to wait."

A few beats of silence.

"Your bed is so much more comfortable than mine," he says quietly. "You have a pillow. And an actual blanket?" He laughs. "You're living like a queen in these quarters. They treat you well."

"Warner." I'm feeling nervous now. Anxious. Worried. Shivering a little and not from the cold. "What's going on? Why are you here?"

Nothing.

Still nothing.

Suddenly.

A tight breath.

"I want you to come with me."

The world stops spinning.

"When I leave tomorrow," he says. "I want you to come with me. I never had a chance to finish talking to you earlier and I thought asking you in the morning would be bad timing all around."

"You want me to come with you." I'm not sure I'm still breathing.

"Yes."

"You want me to run away with you." This can't possibly be happening.

A pause. "Yes."

"I can't believe it." I'm shaking my head over and over and over again. "You really have lost your mind."

I can almost hear him smile in the dark. "Where's your face? I feel like I'm talking to a ghost."

"I'm right here."

"Where?"

I stand up. "I'm here."

"I still can't see you," he says, but his voice is suddenly much closer than it was before. "Can you see me?"

"No," I lie, and I'm trying to ignore the immediate tension, the electricity humming in the air between us.

I take a step back.

I feel his hands on my arms, I feel his skin against my skin and I'm holding my breath. I don't move an inch. I don't say a word as his hands drop to my waist, to the thin material making a poor attempt to cover my body. His fingers graze the soft skin of my lower back, right underneath the hem of my shirt and I'm losing count of the number of times my heart skips a beat.

I'm struggling to get oxygen in my lungs.

~~I'm struggling to keep my hands to myself.~~

"Is it even possible," he whispers, "that you can't feel this fire between us?" His hands are traveling up my arms again, his touch so light, his fingers slipping under the straps of my shirt and it's ripping me apart, it's aching in my core, it's a pulse beating in every inch of my body and I'm trying to convince myself not to lose my head when I feel the straps fall down and everything stops.

The air is still.

My skin is scared.

Even my thoughts are whispering.

2

4

6 seconds I forget to breathe.

Then I feel his lips against my shoulder, soft and scorching and tender, so gentle I could almost believe it's the kiss of a breeze and not a boy.

Again.

This time on my collarbone and it's like I'm dreaming, reliving the caress of a forgotten memory and it's like an ache looking to be soothed, it's a steaming pan thrown in ice water, it's a flushed cheek pressed to a cool pillow on a hot hot hot night and I'm thinking *yes,* I'm thinking *this,* I'm thinking *thank you thank you thank you*

before I remember his mouth is on my body and I'm doing nothing to stop him.

He pulls back.

My eyes refuse to open.

His finger t-touches my bottom lip.

He traces the shape of my mouth, the curves the seam the dip and my lips part even though I asked them not to and he steps closer. I feel him so much closer, filling the air around me until there's nothing but him and his body heat, the smell of fresh soap and something unidentifiable, something sweet but not, something real and hot, something that smells like *him,* like it belongs to him, like he was poured into the bottle I'm drowning in and I don't even realize I'm leaning into him, inhaling the scent of his neck until I find his fingers are no longer on my lips because his hands are around my waist and he says

"You," and he whispers it, letter by letter he presses the word into my skin before he hesitates.

Then.

Softer.

His chest, heaving harder this time. His words, almost gasping this time. "You *destroy* me."

I am falling to pieces in his arms.

My fists are full of unlucky pennies and my heart is a jukebox demanding a few nickels and my head is flipping quarters heads or tails heads or tails heads or tails heads or tails

"Juliette," he says, and he mouths the name, barely speaking at all, and he's pouring molten lava into my limbs and I never even knew I could melt straight to death.

"I want you," he says. He says "I want all of you. I want you inside and out and catching your breath and aching for me like I ache for you." He says it like it's a lit cigarette lodged in his throat, like he wants to dip me in warm honey and he says "It's never been a secret. I've never tried to hide that from you. I've never pretended I wanted anything less."

"You—you said you wanted f-friendship—"

"Yes," he says, he swallows, "I did. I do. I do want to be your friend." He nods and I register the slight movement in the air between us. "I want to be the friend you fall hopelessly in love with. The one you take into your arms and into your bed and into the private world you keep trapped in your head. I want to be that kind of friend," he says. "The one who will memorize the things you say as well as the shape of your lips when you say them. I want to know every curve, every freckle, every shiver of your body, *Juliette*—"

"No," I gasp. "Don't—don't s-say that—"

I don't know what I'll do if he keeps talking I don't know what I'll do and I don't trust myself

"I want to know where to touch you," he says. "I want to know how to touch you. I want to know how to convince you to design a smile just for me." I feel his chest rising, falling, up and down and up and down and "Yes," he says. "I do want to be your friend." He says "I want to be your best friend in the entire world."

I can't think.

I can't *breathe*

"I want so many things," he whispers. "I want your mind. Your strength. I want to be worth your time." His fingers graze the hem of my top and he says "I want this up." He tugs on the waist of my pants and says "I want these down." He touches the tips of his fingers to the sides of my body and says, "I want to feel your skin on fire. I want to feel your heart racing next to mine and I want to know it's racing because of me, because you want me. Because you never," he says, he breathes, "never want me to stop. I want every second. Every inch of you. I want all of it."

And I drop dead, all over the floor.

"Juliette."

I can't understand why I can still hear him speaking because I'm dead, I'm already dead, I've died over and over and over again

He swallows, hard, his chest heaving, his words a breathless, shaky whisper when he says "I'm so—I'm so desperately in love with you—"

I'm rooted to the ground, spinning while standing, dizzy in my blood and in my bones and I'm breathing like I'm the first human who's ever learned to fly, like I've been inhaling the kind of oxygen only found in the clouds and I'm trying but I don't know how to keep my body from reacting to him, to his words, to the ache in his voice.

He touches my cheek.

Soft, so soft, like he's not sure if I'm real, like he's afraid if he gets too close I'll just oh, look she's gone, she's just disappeared. His 4 fingers graze the side of my face, slowly, so slowly before they slip behind my head, caught in that in-between spot just above my neck. His thumb brushes the apple of my cheek.

He keeps looking at me, looking into my eyes for help, for guidance, for some sign of a protest like he's so sure I'm going to start screaming or crying or running away but I won't. I don't think I could even if I wanted to because I don't want to. I want to stay here. Right here. I want to be paralyzed by this moment.

He moves closer, just an inch. His free hand reaches up

to cup the other side of my face.

He's holding me like I'm made of feathers.

He's holding my face and looking at his own hands like he can't believe he's caught this bird who's always so desperate to fly away. His hands are shaking, just a little bit, just enough for me to feel the slight tremble against my skin. Gone is the boy with the guns and the skeletons in his closet. These hands holding me have never held a weapon. These hands have never touched death. These hands are perfect and kind and tender.

And he leans in, so carefully. Breathing and not breathing and hearts beating between us and he's so close, he's so close and I can't feel my legs anymore. I can't feel my fingers or the cold or the emptiness of this room because all I feel is him, everywhere, filling everything and he whispers

"Please."

He says "Please don't shoot me for this."

And he kisses me.

His lips are softer than anything I've ever known, soft like a first snowfall, like biting into cotton candy, like melting and floating and being weightless in water. It's sweet, it's so effortlessly sweet.

And then it changes.

"Oh *God*—"

He kisses me again, this time stronger, desperate, like he has to have me, like he's dying to memorize the feel of my lips against his own. The taste of him is making me crazy; he's all heat and desire and peppermint and I want more.

I've just begun reeling him in, pulling him into me when he breaks away.

He's breathing like he's lost his mind and he's looking at me like something has broken inside of him, like he's woken up to find that his nightmares were just that, that they never existed, that it was all just a bad dream that felt far too real but now he's awake and he's safe and everything is going to be okay and

I'm falling.

I'm falling apart and into his heart and I'm a disaster.

He's searching me, searching my eyes for something, for yeses or nos or maybe a cue to keep going and all I want is to drown in him. I want him to kiss me until I collapse in his arms, until I've left my bones behind and floated up into a new space that is entirely our own.

No words.

Just his lips.

Again.

Deep and urgent like he can't afford to take his time anymore, like there's so much he wants to feel and there aren't enough years to experience it all. His hands travel the length of my back, learning every curve of my figure and he's kissing my neck, my throat, the slope of my shoulders and his breaths come harder, faster, his hands suddenly threaded in my hair and I'm spinning, I'm dizzy, I'm moving and reaching up behind his neck and clinging to him and it's ice-cold heat, it's an ache that attacks every cell in my body. It's a wanting so desperate, a need so exquisite that it rivals everything, every happy moment I ever thought I knew.

I'm against the wall.

He's kissing me like the world is rolling right off a cliff, like he's trying to hang on and he's decided to hold on to me, like he's starving for life and love and he's never known it could ever feel this good to be close to someone. Like it's the first time he's ever felt anything but hunger and he doesn't know how to pace himself, doesn't know how to eat in small bites, doesn't know how to do anything anything anything in moderation.

My pants fall to the floor and his hands are responsible.

I'm in his arms in my underwear and a tank top that's doing little to keep me decent and he pulls back just to look at me, to drink in the sight of me and he's saying "you're so beautiful" he's saying "you're so unbelievably beautiful" and he pulls me into his arms again and he picks me up, he carries me to my bed and suddenly I'm resting against my pillows and he's straddling my hips and his shirt is no longer on his body and I have no idea where it went. All I know is that I'm looking up and into his eyes and I'm thinking there isn't a single thing I would change about this moment.

He has a hundred thousand million kisses and he's giving them all to me.

He kisses my top lip.

He kisses my bottom lip.

He kisses just under my chin, the tip of my nose, the length of my forehead, both temples, my cheeks, all across my jawline. Then my neck, behind my ears, all the way down my throat and

his hands

slide

down

my body. His entire form is moving down my figure, disappearing as he shifts downward and suddenly his chest is hovering above my hips; suddenly I can't see him anymore. I can only make out the top of his head, the curve of his shoulders, the unsteady rise and fall of his back as he inhales, exhales. He's running his hands down and around my bare thighs and up again, up past my ribs, around my lower back and down again, just past my hip bone. His fingers hook around the elastic waist of my underwear and I gasp.

His lips touch my bare stomach.

It's just a whisper of a kiss but something collapses in my skull. It's a feather-light brush of his mouth against my skin in a place I can't quite see. It's my mind speaking in a thousand different languages I don't understand.

And I realize he's working his way up my body.

He's leaving a trail of fire along my torso, one kiss after another, and I really don't think I can take much more of this; I really don't think I'll be able to survive this. There's a whimper building in my throat, begging to break free and I'm locking my fingers in his hair and I'm pulling him up, onto me, on top of me.

I need to kiss him.

I'm reaching up only to slip my hands down his neck, over his chest and down the length of his body and I realize I've never felt this, not to this degree, not like every moment is about to explode, like every breath could be our last, like every touch is enough to ignite the world. I'm forgetting everything, forgetting the danger and the horror and the terror of tomorrow and I can't even remember *why* I'm forgetting, *what* I'm forgetting, that there's something I already seem to have forgotten. It's too hard to pay attention to anything but his eyes, burning; his skin, bare; his body, perfect.

He's completely unharmed by my touch.

He's careful not to crush me, his elbows propped up on either side of my head, and I think I must be smiling at him because he's smiling at me, but he's smiling like he might be petrified; he's breathing like he's forgotten he's supposed to, looking at me like he's not sure how to do this, hesitating like he's unsure how to let me see him like this. Like he has no idea how to be so vulnerable.

But here he is.

And here I am.

Warner's forehead is pressed against mine, his skin flushed with heat, his nose touching my own. He shifts his weight to one arm, uses his free hand to softly stroke my cheek, to cup my face like it's spun from glass and I realize I'm still holding my breath and I can't even remember the last time I exhaled.

His eyes shift down to my lips and back again. His gaze is heavy, hungry, weighed down by emotion I never thought him capable of. I never thought he could be so full, so human, so real. But it's there. It's right there. Raw, written across his face like it's been ripped out of his chest.

He's handing me his heart.

And he says one word. He whispers one thing. So urgently.

He says, "Juliette."

I close my eyes.

He says, "I don't want you to call me Warner anymore."

I open my eyes.

"I want you to know me," he says, breathless, his fingers pushing a stray strand of hair away from my face. "I don't want to be Warner with you," he says. "I want it to be different now. I want you to call me Aaron."

And I'm about to say yes, of course, I completely understand, but there's something about this stretch of silence that confuses me; something about this moment and the feel of his name on my tongue that unlocks other parts of my brain and there's something there, something pushing and pulling at my skin and trying to remind me, trying to tell me and

it slaps me in the face

it punches me in the jaw

it dumps me right into the ocean.

"Adam."

My bones are full of ice. My entire being wants to vomit. I'm tripping out from under him and pulling myself away and I almost fall right to the floor and this feeling, this feeling, this overwhelming *feeling* of absolute self-loathing sticks in my stomach like the slice of a knife too sharp, too thick, too lethal to keep me standing and I'm clutching at myself, I'm trying not to cry and I'm saying no no no this can't happen this can't be *happening* I love Adam, my heart is with Adam, I can't do this to him

and Warner looks like I've shot him all over again, like I've wedged a bullet in his heart with my bare hands and he gets to his feet but he can hardly stand. His frame is shaking and he's looking at me like he wants to say something but every time he tries to speak he fails.

"I'm s-sorry," I stammer, "I'm so sorry—I never meant for this to happen—I wasn't *thinking*—"

But he's not listening.

He's shaking his head over and over and over and he's looking at his hands like he's waiting for the part where someone tells him this isn't real and he whispers "What's happening to me? Am I dreaming?"

And I'm so sick, I'm so confused, because I want him, I want him and I want Adam, too, and I want too much and I've never felt more like a monster than I have tonight.

The pain is so plain on his face and it's killing me.

I feel it. I feel it killing me.

I'm trying so hard to look away, to forget, to figure out how to erase what just happened but all I can think is that life is like a broken tire swing, an unborn child, a fistful of wishbones. It's all possibility and potential, wrong and right steps toward a future we're not even guaranteed and I, I am so wrong. All of my steps are wrong, always wrong. I am the incarnation of error.

Because this never should have happened.

This was a mistake.

"You're choosing him?" Warner asks, barely breathing, still looking as if he might fall over. "Is that what just happened? You're choosing Kent over me? Because I don't think I understand what just happened and I need you to say something, I need you to tell me what the hell is happening to me right now—"

"No," I gasp. "No, I'm not choosing anyone—I'm not—I'm n-not—"

But I am. And I don't even know how I got here.

"Why?" he says. "Because he's the safer choice for you? Because you think you *owe* him something? You are making a mistake," he says, his voice louder now. "You're scared. You don't want to make the difficult choice and you're running away from me."

"Maybe I just d-don't want to be with you."

"I know you want to be with me!" he explodes.

"You're wrong."

Oh my God what am I saying I don't even know where I'm finding these words, where they're coming from or which tree I've plucked them from. They just keep growing in my mouth and sometimes I bite down too hard on an adverb or a pronoun and sometimes the words are bitter, sometimes they're sweet, but right now everything tastes like romance and regret and liar liar pants on fire all the way down my throat.

Warner is still staring.

"Really?" He struggles to rein in his temper and takes a step closer, so much closer, and I can see his face too clearly, I can see his lips too clearly, I can see the anger and the pain and the disbelief etched into his features and I'm not so sure I should be standing anymore. I don't think my legs can carry me much longer.

"Y-yes." I pluck another word from the tree lying in my mouth, lying lying lying on my lips.

"So I'm wrong." He says the sentence quietly, so, so quietly. "I'm wrong that you want me. That you want to be with me." His fingers graze my shoulders, my arms; his hands slide down the sides of my body, tracing every inch of me and I'm pressing my mouth shut to keep the truth from falling out but I'm failing and failing and failing because the only truth I know right now is that I'm mere moments from losing my mind.

"Tell me something, love." His lips are whispering against my jaw. "Am I blind, too?"

I am actually going to die.

"I will not be your clown!" He breaks away from me. "I will not allow you to make a mockery of my feelings for you! I could respect your decision to *shoot me*, Juliette, but doing this—doing—doing what you just did—" He can hardly speak. He runs a hand across his face, both hands through his hair, looking like he wants to scream, to break something, like he's really, truly about to lose his mind. His voice is a rough whisper when he finally speaks. "It's the play of a coward," he says. "I thought you were so much better than that."

"I'm not a coward—"

"Then be honest with yourself!" he says. "Be honest with me! Tell me the truth!"

My head is rolling around on the floor, spinning like a wooden top, circling around and around and around and I can't make it stop. I can't make the world stop spinning and my confusion is bleeding into guilt which quickly evolves into anger and suddenly it's bubbling raging rising to the surface and I look at him. I clench my shaking hands into fists. "The truth," I tell him, "is that I never know what to think of you! Your actions, your behavior—you're never consistent! You're horrible to me and then you're kind to me and you tell me you love me and then you hurt the ones I care most about!

"And you're a liar," I snap, backing away from him. "You say you don't care about what you do—you say you don't care about other people and what you've done to them but I don't believe it. I think you're hiding. I think the real you is hiding underneath all of the destruction and I think you're better than this life you've chosen for yourself. I think you can change. I think you could be different. And I feel sorry for you!"

These words these stupid stupid words they won't stop spilling from my mouth.

"I'm sorry for your horrible childhood. I'm sorry you

have such a miserable, worthless father and I'm sorry no one ever took a chance on you. I'm sorry for the terrible decisions you've made. I'm sorry that you feel trapped by them, that you think of yourself as a monster who can't be changed. But most of all," I tell him, "most of all I'm sorry that you have no mercy for yourself!"

Warner flinches like I've slapped him in the face.

The silence between us has slaughtered a thousand innocent seconds and when he finally speaks his voice is barely audible, raw with disbelief.

"You pity me."

My breath catches. My resolve wavers.

"You think I'm some kind of broken project you can repair."

"No—I didn't—"

"You have no *idea* what I've done!" His words are furious as he steps forward. "You have no idea what I've seen, what I've had to be a part of. You have no idea what I'm capable of or how much mercy I deserve. I know my own heart," he snaps. "I know who I am. Don't you dare pity me!"

Oh my legs are definitely not working.

"I thought you could love me for *me*," he says. "I thought you would be the one person in this godforsaken world who would accept me as I am! I thought you, of all people, would understand." His face is right in front of mine when he says, "I was wrong. I was so horribly, horribly wrong."

He backs away. He grabs his shirt and he turns to leave and I should let him go, I should let him walk out the door and out of my life but I can't, I catch his arm, I pull him back and I say, "Please—that's not what I meant—"

He spins around and he says, "I do not want your *sympathy!*"

"I wasn't trying to hurt you—"

"The truth," he says, "is a painful reminder of why I prefer to live among the lies."

I can't stomach the look in his eyes, the wretched, awful pain he's making no effort to conceal. I don't know what to say to make this right. I don't know how to take my words back.

I know I don't want him to leave.

Not like this.

He looks as if he might speak; he changes his mind. He takes a tight breath, presses his lips together as if to stop the words from escaping and I'm about to say something, I'm about to try again when he pulls in a shaky breath, when he says, "Good-bye, Juliette."

And I don't know why it's killing me, I can't understand my sudden anxiety and I need to know, I have to say it, I have to ask the question that isn't a question and I say "I won't see you again."

I watch him struggle to find the words, I watch him turn to me and turn away and for one split second I see what's happened, I see the difference in his eyes, the shine of emotion I never would've dreamed him capable of and I know, I understand why he won't look at me and I can't believe it. I want to fall to the floor as he fights himself, fights to speak, fights to swallow back the tremor in his voice when he says, "I certainly hope not."

And that's it.

He walks out.

I'm split clean in half and he's gone.

He's gone forever.

SIXTY-THREE

Breakfast is an ordeal.

Warner has disappeared and he's left a trail of chaos in his wake.

No one knows how he escaped, how he managed to get out of his room and find his way out of here and everyone is blaming Castle. Everyone is saying he was stupid to trust Warner, to give him a chance, to believe he might have changed.

Angry is an insult to the level of aggression in here right now.

But I'm not going to be the one to tell everyone that Warner was already out of his room last night. I'm not going to be the one to tell them that he probably didn't have to do much to find the exit. I won't explain to them that he's not an idiot.

I'm sure he figured it out easily enough. I'm sure he found a way to get past the guards.

Now everyone is ready to fight, but for all the wrong reasons. They want to murder Warner: first for all he's done; second for betraying their trust. More frightening still, everyone is worried that he'll give away all of our most sensitive information. I have no idea what Warner managed to discover about this place before he left, but nothing that happens now can possibly be good.

No one has even touched their breakfasts.

We're all dressed, armed, ready to face what could be an almost instant death, and I'm feeling little more than entirely numb. I didn't sleep at all last night, my heart and mind plagued and conflicted and I can't feel my limbs, I can't taste the food I'm not eating and I can't see straight, I can't focus on the things I'm supposed to be hearing. All I can think about are all the casualties ~~and Warner's lips on my neck, his hands on my body, the pain and passion in his eyes~~ and the many possible ways I could die today. I can only think about ~~Warner touching me, kissing me, torturing me with his heart and~~ Adam sitting beside me, not knowing what I've done.

It probably won't even matter after today.

Maybe I'll be killed and maybe all the agony of these past 17 years will have been for naught. Maybe I'll just fall right off the face of the Earth, gone forever, and all of my adolescent angst will have been a ridiculous afterthought, a laughable memory.

But maybe I'll survive.

Maybe I'll survive and I'll have to face the consequences of my actions. I'll have to stop lying to myself; I'll have to actually make a decision.

I have to face the fact that I'm battling feelings for someone who has no qualms about putting a bullet in another man's head. I have to consider the possibility that I might really be turning into a monster. A horrible, selfish creature who cares only about herself.

Maybe Warner was right all along.

Maybe he and I really are perfect for each other.

Just about everyone has filed out of the dining hall. People are saying last-minute good-byes to the old and the young ones they're leaving behind. James and Adam had a lengthy good-bye just this morning. Adam and I have to head out in about 10 minutes.

"Well damn. Who died?"

I spin around at the sound of his voice. Kenji is up. He's in this room. He's standing next to our table and he looks like he's about to fall right over but he's *awake*. He's alive.

He's breathing.

"Holy crap." Adam is gaping. "Holy *shit*."

"Good to see you too, Kent." Kenji grins a crooked grin. He nods at me. "You ready to kick some ass today?"

I tackle him.

"WHOA—hey—thank you, yeah—that's—uh—" He clears his throat. Tries to shift away from me and I flinch, pull back. I'm covered everywhere except for my face; I'm wearing my gloves and my reinforced knuckles, and my suit is zipped up to my neck. Kenji never usually shies away from me.

"Hey, uh, maybe you should hold off on touching me for a little while, yeah?" Kenji tries to smile, tries to make it sound like he's joking, but I feel the weight of his words, the tension and the sliver of fear he's trying so hard to hide. "I'm not too steady on my feet just yet."

I feel the blood rush out of me, leaving me weak in the knees and needing to sit down.

"It wasn't her," Adam says. "You know she didn't even touch you."

"I *don't* know that, actually," Kenji says. "And it's not like I'm blaming her—I'm just saying maybe she's projecting and doesn't know it, okay? Because last I checked, I don't think we have any other explanations for what happened last night. It sure as hell wasn't you," he says to Adam, "and shit, for all we know, Warner being able to touch Juliette could just be a fluke. We don't know anything about him yet." A pause. He looks around. "Right? Unless Warner pulled some kind of magical rabbit out of his ass while I was busy being dead last night?"

Adam scowls. I don't say a word.

"Right," Kenji says. "That's what I thought. So. I think it's best if, unless absolutely necessary, I stay away." He turns to me. "Right? No offense, right? I mean, I did nearly just die. I think you could cut me some slack."

I can hardly hear my own voice when I say, "Yeah, of course." I try to laugh. I try to figure out why I'm not telling them about Warner. Why I'm still protecting him. ~~Probably because I'm just as guilty as he is.~~

"So *anyway,*" Kenji says. "When are we leaving?"

"You're insane," Adam tells him. "You're not going anywhere."

"Bullshit I'm not."

"You can barely stand up on your own!" Adam says.

And he's right. Kenji is clearly leaning on the table for support.

"I'd rather die out there than sit in here like some kind of idiot."

"Kenji—"

"Hey," Kenji says, cutting me off. "So I heard through the very loud grapevine that Warner got his ass the hell out of here last night. What's that about?"

Adam makes a strange sound. It's not quite a laugh. "Yeah," he says. "Who even knows. I never thought it was a good idea to keep him hostage here. It was an even stupider idea to trust him."

"So first you insult my idea, and then you insult Castle's, huh?" Kenji's eyebrow is cocked.

"They were bad calls," Adam says. "Bad ideas. Now we have to pay for it."

"Well how was I supposed to know Anderson would be so willing to let his own son rot in hell?"

Adam flinches and Kenji backpedals.

"Oh, hey—I'm sorry, man—I didn't mean to say it like that—"

"Forget it." Adam cuts him off. His face is suddenly hard, suddenly cold, closed off. "Maybe you should get back to the medical wing. We're leaving soon."

"I'm not going anywhere but *out of here*."

"Kenji, please—"

"Nope."

"You're being unreasonable. This isn't a joke," I tell him. "People are going to die today."

But he laughs at me. Looks at me like I've said something obliquely entertaining. "I'm sorry, are you trying to teach *me* about the realities of war?" He shakes his head. "Are you forgetting that I was a soldier in Warner's army? Do you have any idea how much crazy shit we've seen?" He gestures between himself and Adam. "I know exactly what to expect today. Warner was *insane*. If Anderson is even twice as bad as his son, then we are diving right into a bloodbath. I can't leave you guys hanging like that."

But I'm caught on one sentence. One word. I just want to ask. "Was he really that bad . . . ?"

"Who?" Kenji is staring at me.

"Warner. Was he really that ruthless?"

Kenji laughs out loud. Laughs louder. Doubles over. He's practically wheezing when he says, "Ruthless? Juliette, the guy is sick. He's an animal. I don't think he even knows what it means to be human. If there's a hell out there, I'm guessing it was designed especially for him."

It's so hard to pull this sword out of my stomach.

A rush of footsteps.

I turn around.

Everyone is supposed to exit the tunnels in a single-file line in an attempt to maintain order as we leave this underground world. Kenji and Adam and I are the only fighters who haven't joined the group yet.

We all get to our feet.

"Hey—so, does Castle know what you're doing?" Adam is looking at Kenji. "I don't think he'd be okay with you going out there today."

"Castle wants me to be happy," Kenji says matter-of-factly. "And I won't be happy if I stay here. I've got work to do. People to save. Ladies to impress. He'd respect that."

"What about everyone else?" I ask him. "Everyone was so worried about you—have you even seen them yet? To at least tell them you're okay?"

"Nah," Kenji says. "They'd probably shit a brick if they knew I was going up. I thought it'd be safer to keep it quiet. I don't want to freak anyone out. And Sonya and Sara—poor kids—they're passed the hell out. It's my fault they're so exhausted, and they're still talking about heading out today. They want to fight even though they're going to have a lot of work to do once we're done with Anderson's army. I've been trying to convince them to stay here but they can be so damn stubborn. They need to save their strength," he says, "and they've already wasted too much of it on me."

"It's not a *waste*—," I try to tell him.

"Anywayyy," Kenji says. "Can we please get going? I know you're all about hunting down Anderson," he says to Adam, "but personally? I would love to catch Warner. Put a bullet through that worthless piece of crap and be done with it."

Something punches me in the gut so hard I'm afraid I'm actually going to be sick. I'm seeing spots, struggling to keep myself standing, fighting to ignore the image of Warner dead, his body crumpled in red.

"Hey—you okay?" Adam pulls me to the side. Takes a good look at my face.

"I'm okay," I lie to him. Nod too many times. Shake my head once or twice. "I just didn't get enough sleep last night, but I'll be fine."

He hesitates. "Are you sure?"

"I'm positive," I lie again. I pause. Grab his shirt. "Hey—just be careful out there, okay?"

He exhales a heavy breath. Nods once. "Yeah. You too."

"Let's go let's go let's go!" Kenji interrupts us. "Today is our day to die, ladies."

Adam shoves him. A little.

"Oh, so now you're abusing the crippled kid, huh?" Kenji takes a moment to steady himself before punching Adam in the arm. "Save your angst for the battlefield, bro. You're going to need it."

A shrill whistle sounds in the distance.

It's time to go.

SIXTY-FOUR

It's raining.

The world is weeping at our feet in anticipation of what we're about to do.

We're all supposed to split off into clusters, fighting in tight groups so we can't all be killed at once. We don't have enough people to fight offensively so we have to be stealthy. And though I feel a pang of guilt for admitting it, I'm so happy Kenji decided to come with us. We would've been weaker without him.

But we have to get out of the rain.

We're already soaked through, and while Kenji and I are wearing suits that offer at least a modicum of protection against the natural elements, Adam is wearing nothing but crisp cotton basics, and I'm worried we won't last long like this. All members of Omega Point have already scattered. The immediate area above the Point is still nothing but a barren stretch of land that leaves us vulnerable upon exiting.

Lucky for us, we have Kenji. The 3 of us are already invisible.

Anderson's men aren't far from here.

All we know is that ever since Anderson arrived, he's

been going out of his way to make a point about his power and the iron grip of The Reestablishment. Any voice of opposition, no matter how weak or feeble, no matter how unthreatening or innocuous, has been silenced. He's angry that we've inspired rebellion and now he's trying to make a statement. What he really wants is to destroy all of *us*.

The poor civilians are just caught in his friendly fire.

Gunshots.

We automatically move toward the sound echoing in the distance. We aren't saying a word. We understand what we need to do and how we have to operate. Our only mission is to get as close as possible to the devastation and then to take out as many of Anderson's men as we can. We protect the innocent. We support our fellow Point men and women.

We try very hard not to die.

I can make out the compounds creeping closer in the distance, but the rain is making it difficult to see. All the colors are bleeding together, melting into the horizon, and I have to strain to discern what lies ahead of us. I instinctively touch the guns attached to the holsters on my back and I'm momentarily reminded of my last encounter with Anderson—my *only* encounter with the horrible, despicable man—and I wonder what's happened to him. I wonder if maybe Adam was right when he said that Anderson might be severely wounded, that perhaps he's still struggling to recuperate. I wonder if Anderson will make an appearance on the battlefield. I wonder if perhaps he's too much of a coward to fight in his own wars.

The screams tell us we're getting closer.

The world around us is a blurry landscape of blues and grays and mottled hues and the few trees still standing have a hundred shaky, quivering arms ripping through their trunks, reaching up to the sky as if in prayer, begging for relief from the tragedy they've been rooted in. It's enough to make me feel sorry for the plants and animals forced to bear witness to what we've done.

They never asked for this.

Kenji guides us toward the outskirts of the compounds and we slip forward to stand flush against the wall of one of the little square houses, huddled under the extra bit of roof that, at least for a moment, grants us reprieve from the clenched fists falling from the sky.

Wind is gnawing at the windows, straining against the walls. Rain is popping against the roof like popcorn against a pane of glass.

The message from the sky is clear: we are pissed.

We are pissed and we will punish you and we will make you pay for the blood you spill so freely. We will not sit idly by, not anymore, not ever again. We will *ruin* you, is what the sky says to us.

How could you do this to me? it whispers in the wind.

I gave you everything, it says to us.

Nothing will ever be the same again.

I'm wondering why I still can't see any sign of the army. I don't see anyone else from Omega Point. I don't see anyone at all. In fact, I'm starting to feel like this compound is a little too peaceful.

I'm about to suggest we move when I hear a door slam open.

"This is the last of them," someone shouts. "She was hiding out over here." A soldier is dragging a crying woman out from the compound we're huddled against and she's screaming, she's begging for mercy and asking about her husband and the soldier barks at her to shut up.

I have to keep the emotions from spilling out of my eyes, my mouth.

I do not speak.

I do not breathe.

Another soldier jogs over from somewhere I can't see. He shouts some kind of approving message and makes a motion with his hands that I don't understand. I feel Kenji stiffen beside me.

Something is wrong.

"Toss her in with everyone else," the second soldier shouts. "And then we'll call this area clear."

The woman is hysterical. She's screeching, clawing at the soldier, telling him she's done nothing wrong, she doesn't understand, where is her husband, she's been looking for her daughter everywhere and what is happening, she cries, she screams, she flails her fists at the man gripping her like an animal.

He presses the barrel of his gun to her neck. "If you don't shut up, I'll shoot you right now."

She whimpers once, twice, and then she's limp. She's fainted in his arms and the soldier looks disgusted as he pulls her out of sight toward wherever they're keeping everyone else. I have no idea what's happening. I don't understand what's happening.

We follow them.

The wind and the rain pick up in pace and there's enough noise in the air and distance between us and the soldiers that I feel safe to speak. I squeeze Kenji's hand. He's still the glue between me and Adam, projecting his powers to keep us all invisible. "What do you think is going on?" I ask.

He doesn't answer right away.

"They're rounding them up," he says after a moment. "They're creating groups of people to kill all at once."

"The woman—"

"Yeah." I hear him clear his throat. "Yeah, she and whoever else they think might be connected to the protests. They don't just kill the inciters," he tells me. "They kill the friends and the family members, too. It's the best way to keep people in line. It never fails to scare the shit out of the few left alive."

I have to swallow back the vomit threatening to overpower me.

"There has to be a way to get them out of there," Adam says. "Maybe we can take out the soldiers in charge."

"Yeah, but listen, you guys know I'm going to have to let go of you, right? I'm already kind of losing strength; my Energy is fading faster than normal. So you'll be visible,"

Kenji says. "You'll be a clearer target."

"But what other choice do we have?" I ask.

"We could try to take them out sniper-style," Kenji says. "We don't have to engage in direct combat. We have that option." He pauses. "Juliette, you've never been in this kind of situation before. I want you to know I'd respect your decision to stay out of the direct line of fire. Not everyone can stomach what we might see if we follow those soldiers. There's no shame or blame in that."

I taste metal in my mouth as I lie. "I'll be okay."

He's quiet a moment. "Just—all right—but don't be afraid to use your abilities to defend yourself," he says to me. "I know you're all weird about not wanting to hurt people or whatever, but these guys aren't messing around. They *will* try to kill you."

I nod even though I know he can't see me. "Right," I say. "Yeah." But I'm panicked through my mind.

"Let's go," I whisper.

SIXTY-FIVE

I can't feel my knees.

There are 27 people lined up, standing side by side in the middle of a big, barren field. Men and women and children of all different ages. All different sizes. All standing before what could be called a firing squad of 6 soldiers. The rain is rushing down around us, hard and angry, pelting everything and everyone with teardrops as hard as my bones. The wind is absolutely frantic.

The soldiers are deciding what to do. How to kill them. How to dispose of the 27 sets of eyes staring straight ahead. Some are sobbing, some are shaking from fear and grief and horror, others still are standing perfectly straight, stoic in the face of death.

One of the soldiers fires a shot.

The first man crumples to the ground and I feel like I've been whipped in the spine. So many emotions rush in and out of me in the span of a few seconds that I'm afraid I might faint; I'm clinging to consciousness with an animal desperation and trying to swallow back the tears, trying to ignore the pain spearing through me.

I can't understand why no one is moving, why we're not moving, why none of the civilians are moving even just to jump out of the way and it occurs to me, it dawns on me that running, trying to escape or trying to fight back is simply not a viable option. They are utterly overpowered. They have no guns. No ammunition of any kind.

But I do.

I have a gun.

I have 2, in fact.

This is the moment, this is where we have to let go, this is where we fight alone, just the 3 of us, 3 ancient kids fighting to save 26 faces or we die trying. My eyes are locked on a little girl who can't be much older than James, her eyes so wide, so terrified, the front of her pants already wet from fear and it rips me to pieces, it *kills* me, and my free hand is already reaching for my gun when I tell Kenji I'm ready.

I watch the same soldier focus his weapon on the next victim when Kenji releases us.

3 guns are up, aimed to fire, and I hear the bullets before they're released into the air; I see one find its mark in a soldier's neck and I have no idea if it's mine.

It doesn't matter now.

There are still 5 soldiers left to face, and now they can see us.

We're running.

We're dodging the bullets aimed in our direction and I see Adam dropping to the ground, I see him shooting with perfect precision and still failing to find a target. I look around for Kenji only to find that he's disappeared and I'm so happy for it; 3 soldiers go down almost instantly. Adam takes advantage of the remaining soldiers' distraction and takes out a fourth. I shoot the fifth from behind.

I don't know whether or not I've killed him.

We're screaming for the people to follow us, we're herding them back to the compounds, yelling for them to stay down, to stay out of sight; we tell them help is coming and we'll do whatever we can to protect them and they're trying to reach out to us, to touch us, to thank us and take our hands but we don't have time. We have to hurry them to some semblance of safety and move on to wherever the rest of this decimation is taking place.

I still haven't forgotten the one man we weren't able to save. I haven't forgotten number 27.

I never want that to happen again.

We're bolting across the many miles of land dedicated to these compounds now, not bothering to keep ourselves hidden or to come up with a definitive plan. We still haven't spoken. We haven't discussed what we've done or what we might do and we only know that we need to keep moving.

We follow Kenji.

He weaves his way through a demolished cluster of compounds and we know something has gone horribly wrong. There's no sign of life anywhere. The little metal boxes that used to house civilians are completely destroyed and we don't know if there were people inside when this happened.

Kenji tells us we have to keep looking.

We move deeper through the regulated territory, these pieces of land dedicated to human habitation, until we hear a rush of footsteps, the sound of a softly churning mechanical sound.

The tanks.

They run on electricity so they're less conspicuous as they move through the streets, but I'm familiar enough with these tanks to be able to recognize the electric thrum. Adam and Kenji do too.

We follow the noise.

We're fighting against the wind trying push us away and it's almost as if it knows, as if the wind is trying to protect us from whatever is waiting on the other side of this compound. It doesn't want us to have to see this. It doesn't want us to have to die today.

Something explodes.

A raging fire rips through the atmosphere not 50 feet from where we're standing. The flames lick the earth, lapping up the oxygen, and even the rain can't douse the devastation all at once. The fire whips and sways in the wind, dying down just enough, humbled into submission by the sky.

We need to be wherever that fire is.

Our feet fight for traction on the muddy ground and I don't feel the cold as we run, I don't feel the wet, I only feel the adrenaline coursing through my limbs, forcing me to move forward, gun clenched too tight in my fist, too ready to aim, too ready to fire.

But when we reach the flames I almost drop my weapon.

I almost fall to the floor.

I almost can't believe my eyes.

SIXTY-SIX

Dead dead dead is everywhere.

So many bodies mixed and meshed into the earth that I have no idea whether they're ours or theirs and I'm beginning to wonder what it means, I'm beginning to doubt myself and this weapon in my hand and I can't help but wonder about these soldiers, I wonder how they could be just like Adam, just like a million other tortured, orphaned souls who simply needed to survive and took the only job they could get.

My conscience has declared war against itself.

I'm blinking back tears and rain and horror and I know I need to move my legs, I know I need to push forward and be brave, I have to fight whether I like it or not because we can't let this happen.

I'm tackled from behind.

Someone pins me down and my face is buried in the ground and I'm kicking, I'm trying to scream but I feel the gun wrenched out of my grip, I feel an elbow in my spine and I know Adam and Kenji are gone, they're deep in battle and I know I'm about to die. I know it's over and it doesn't feel real, somehow, it feels like this is a story someone else is telling, like death is a strange, distant thing you've only ever seen happen to people you've never known and surely it doesn't happen to me, to you, to any of the rest of us.

But here it is.

It's a gun in the back of my head and a boot pressed down on my back and it's my mouth full of mud and it's a million worthless moments I never really lived and it's all right in front of me. I see it so clearly.

Someone flips me over.

The same someone who held a gun to my head is now pointing it at my face, inspecting me as if trying to read me and I'm confused, I don't understand his angry gray eyes or the stiff set of his mouth because he's not pulling the trigger. He's not killing me and this, this more than anything else is what petrifies me.

I need to take off my gloves.

My captor shouts something I don't catch because he's not talking to me, he's not looking in my direction because he's calling to someone else and I use his moment of distraction to yank off the steel knuckle brace on my left hand only to toss it to the ground. I have to get my glove off. I have to get my glove off because it's my only chance for survival but the rain has made the leather too wet and it's sticking to my skin, refusing to come off easily and the soldier spins back too soon. He sees what I'm trying to do and he yanks me to my feet, pulls me into a headlock and presses the gun to my skull. "I know what you're trying to do, you little freak," he says. "I've heard about you. You move even an inch and I will kill you."

Somehow, I don't believe him.

I don't think he's supposed to shoot me, because if he wanted to, he would've done it already. But he's waiting for something. He's waiting for something I don't understand and I need to act fast. I need a plan but I have no idea what to do and I'm only clawing at his covered arm, at the muscle he's bound around my neck and he shakes me, shouts at me to stop squirming and he pulls me tighter to cut off my air supply and my fingers are clenched around his forearm, trying to fight the viselike grip he has around me and I can't breathe and I'm panicked, I'm suddenly not so sure he's not going to kill me and I don't even realize what I've done until I hear him scream.

I've crushed all the bones in his arm.

He falls to the floor, he drops his gun to grab at his arm, and he's screaming with a pain so excruciating I'm almost tempted to feel remorse for what I've done.

Instead, I run.

I've only gotten a few feet before 3 more soldiers slam into me, alerted by what I've done to their comrade, and they see my face and they're alight with recognition. One of them appears vaguely familiar, almost as if I've seen his shaggy brown hair before, and I realize: they know me. These soldiers knew me when Warner held me captive. Warner had made a complete spectacle out of me. Of course they'd recognize my face.

And they're not letting me go.

The 3 of them are pushing me face-first into the ground,

pinning down my arms and legs until I'm fairly certain they've decided to rip my limbs off. I'm trying to fight back, I'm trying to get my mind in the right place to focus my Energy, and I'm just about to knock them back but then

a sharp blow to my head and I'm rendered almost entirely unconscious.

Sounds are mixing together, voices are becoming one big mess of noise and I can't see colors, I don't know what's happening to me because I can't feel my legs anymore. I don't even know if I'm walking or if I'm being carried but I feel the rain. I feel it fall fast down the planes of my face until I hear the sound of metal on metal, I hear a familiar electric thrum and then the rain stops, it disappears from the sky and I only know 2 things and I only know 1 of those things for certain

I am in a tank.

I am going to die.

SIXTY-SEVEN

I hear wind chimes.

I hear wind chimes being blown into hysteria by a wind so violent as to be a legitimate threat and all I can think is that the tinkling sounds seem so incredibly familiar to me. My head is still spinning but I have to stay as aware as possible. I have to know where they're taking me. I have to have some idea of where I am. I need to have a point of reference and I'm struggling to keep my head straight without making it known that I'm not unconscious.

The soldiers don't speak.

I was hoping to at least glean a bit of information from the conversations they might have but they do not say a word to one another. They are like machines, like robots programmed to follow through with a specific assignment, and I wonder, I'm so curious, I can't figure out why I had to be dragged away from the battlefield to be killed. I wonder why my death has to be so special. I wonder why they're carrying me out of the tank toward the chaos of an angry wind chime and I dare to open my eyes just a sliver and I nearly gasp.

It's the house.

It's the house, the house on unregulated turf, the one

painted the perfect shade of robin's-egg blue and the only traditional, functioning home within a 500-mile radius. It's the same house Kenji told me must be a trap, it's the house where I was so sure I'd meet Warner's father, and then it hits me. A sledgehammer. A bullet train. A rush of realization crushing my brain.

Anderson must be here. He must want to kill me himself.

I am a special delivery.

They even ring the doorbell.

I hear feet shuffling. I hear creaks and groans. I hear the wind snapping through the world and then I see my future, I see Anderson torturing me to death in every possible way and I wonder how I'm going to get myself out of this. Anderson is too smart. He will probably chain me to the floor and cut off my hands and feet one at a time. He is likely going to want to enjoy this.

He answers the door.

"Ah! Gentlemen. Thank you very much," he says. "Please follow me." And I feel the soldier carrying me shift his weight under my damp, limp, suddenly heavy body. I'm starting to feel a cold chill seep into my bones and I realize I've been running through the pouring rain for too long.

I'm shaking and it's not from fear.

I'm burning and it's not from anger.

I'm so delirious that even if I had the strength to defend myself I'm not sure I'd be able to do it right. It's amazing how many different ways I could meet my end today.

Anderson smells rich and earthy; I can smell him even though I'm being carried in someone else's arms, and the scent is disturbingly pleasant. He closes the front door behind us just after advising the waiting soldiers to return to work. Which is essentially an order for them to go kill more people.

I think I'm starting to hallucinate.

I see a warm fireplace like the kind I've only ever read about. I see a cozy living room with soft, plush couches and a thick oriental rug gracing the floor. I see a mantel with pictures on it that I can't recognize from here and Anderson is telling me to wake up, he's saying you need to take a bath, you've gotten yourself quite dirty haven't you, and that won't do, will it? I'm going to need you to be awake and fully coherent or this won't be much fun at all, he says, and I'm fairly certain I'm losing my mind.

I feel the thud thud thud of heavy footsteps climbing a stairwell and realize my body is moving with it. I hear a door whine open, I hear the shuffle of other feet and there are words being spoken that I can't distinguish anymore. Someone says something to someone and I'm dropped onto a cold, hard floor.

I hear myself whimper.

"Be careful not to touch her skin," is the only sentence I can make out in a single thread. Everything else is "bathe" and "sleep" and "in the morning" and "no, I don't think so" and "very good," and I hear another door slam shut. It's the one right next to my head.

Someone is trying to take my suit off.

I snap up so quickly it's painful; I feel something sear through me, through my head until it hits me square in the eye and I know I'm a mix of so many things right now. I can't remember the last time I ate anything and I haven't truly slept in over 24 hours. My body is soaked through, my head is pounding with pain, my body has been twisted and stepped on, and I'm aching in a million different ways. But I will not allow any strange man to take my clothes off. I'd rather be dead.

But the voice I hear isn't male at all. It sounds soft and gentle, motherly. She's speaking to me in a language I don't understand but maybe it's just my head that can't understand anything at all. She makes soothing noises, she rubs her hands in small circles on my back. I hear a rush of water and feel the heat rise up around me and it's so warm, it feels like steam and I think this must be a bathroom, or a tub, and I can't help but think that I haven't taken a hot shower since I was back at the headquarters with Warner.

I try to open my eyes and fail.

It's like two anvils are sitting on my eyelids, like everything is black and messy and confusing and exhausting and I can only make out the general circumstances of my situation. I see through little more than slits; I see only the gleaming porcelain of what I assume is a bathtub and I crawl over despite the protests in my ear and clamber up.

I topple right into the hot water fully clothed, gloves and boots and suit intact and it's an unbelievable pleasure I didn't expect to experience.

My bones begin to thaw and my teeth are slowing their chatter and my muscles are learning to relax. My hair floats up around my face and I feel it tickle my nose.

I sink beneath the surface.

I fall asleep.

SIXTY-EIGHT

I wake up in a bed made of heaven and I'm wearing clothes that belong to a boy.

I'm warm and comfortable but I can still feel the creak in my bones, the ache in my head, the confusion clouding my mind. I sit up. I look around.

I'm in someone's bedroom.

I'm tangled in blue-and-orange bedsheets decorated with little baseball mitts. There's a little desk with a little chair set off to the side and there's a set of drawers, a collection of plastic trophies in perfectly straight rows on top. I see a simple wooden door with a traditional brass knob that must lead outside; I see a sliding set of mirrors that must be hiding a closet. I look to my right to find a little bedside table with an alarm clock and a glass of water and I grab it.

It's almost embarrassing how quickly I inhale the contents.

I climb out of bed only to find that I'm wearing a pair of navy gym shorts that are hanging so low on my hips I'm afraid they're going to fall off. I'm wearing a gray T-shirt with some kind of logo on it and I'm swimming in the extra material. I have no socks. No gloves. No underwear.

I have nothing.

I wonder if I'm allowed to step outside and I decide it's worth a shot. I have no idea what I'm doing here. I have no idea why I'm not dead yet.

I freeze in front of the mirrored doors.

My hair has been washed well and it falls in thick, soft waves around my face. My skin is bright and, with the exception of a few scratches, relatively unscathed. My eyes are wide; an odd, vibrant mix of green and blue blinking back at me, surprised and surprisingly unafraid.

But my neck.

My neck is one mess of purple, one big bruise that discolors my entire appearance. I hadn't realized just how tightly I was being choked to death yesterday—I think it was yesterday—and I only now realize just how much it hurts to swallow. I take a sharp breath and push past the mirrors. I need to find a way to get out of here.

The door opens at my touch.

I look around the hallway for any sign of life. I don't have any idea what time of day it is or what I've gotten myself into. I don't know if anyone exists in this house except for Anderson—and whoever it was that helped me in the bathroom—but I have to assess my situation. I have to figure out exactly how much danger I'm in before I can devise a plan to fight my way out.

I try to tiptoe quietly down the stairs.

It doesn't work.

The stairs creak and groan under my weight and I hardly

have a chance to backpedal before I hear him call my name. He's downstairs.

Anderson is downstairs.

"Don't be shy," he says. I hear the rustle of something that sounds like paper. "I have food for you and I know you must be starving."

My heart is suddenly beating in my throat. I wonder what choices I have, what options I have to consider and I decide I can't hide from him in his own hideout.

I meet him downstairs.

He's the same beautiful man he was before. Hair perfect and polished, clothing crisp, clean, expertly pressed. He's sitting in the living room in an overstuffed chair with a blanket draped over his lap. I notice a gorgeous, rustic-looking, intricately carved walking stick leaning against the armrest. He has a stack of papers in his hand.

I smell coffee.

"Please," he says to me, not at all surprised by my strange, wild appearance. "Have a seat."

I do.

"How are you feeling?" he asks.

I look up. I don't answer him.

He nods. "Yes, well, I'm sure you're very surprised to see me here. It's a lovely little house, isn't it?" He looks around. "I had this preserved shortly after I moved my family to what is now Sector 45. This sector was supposed to be mine, after all. It turned out to be the ideal place to store my wife." He waves a hand. "Apparently she doesn't do very well in the compounds," he says, as if I'm supposed to have any idea what he's talking about.

Store his wife?

I don't know why I allow anything out of his mouth to surprise me.

Anderson seems to catch my confusion. He looks amused. "Am I to understand that my love-struck boy didn't tell you about his beloved mother? He didn't go on and on and on about his pathetic love for the creature that gave birth to him?"

"What?" is the first word I speak.

"I am truly shocked," Anderson says, smiling like he's not shocked at all. "He didn't bother to mention that he has a sick, ailing mother who lives in this house? He didn't tell you that's why he wanted the post here, in this sector, so desperately? No? He didn't tell you anything about that?" He cocks his head. "I am just so shocked," he lies again.

I'm trying to keep my heart rate down, trying to figure out why on earth he's telling me this, trying to stay one step ahead of him, but he's doing a damn good job of confusing the hell out of me.

"When I was chosen as supreme commander," he goes on, "I was going to leave Aaron's mother here and take him with me to the capital. But the boy didn't want to leave his mother behind. He wanted to take care of her. He didn't want to leave her. He needed to *be* with her like some stupid *child*," he says, raising his voice at the end, forgetting himself for a moment. He swallows. Regains his composure.

And I'm waiting.

Waiting for the anvil he's preparing to drop on my head.

"Did he tell you how many other soldiers wanted be in charge of Sector 45? How many fine candidates we had to choose from? He was only eighteen years old!" He laughs. "Everyone thought he'd gone mad. But I gave him a chance," Anderson says. "I thought it might be good for him to take on that kind of responsibility."

Still waiting.

A deep, contented sigh. "Did he ever tell you," Anderson says, "what he had to do to prove he was worthy?"

There it is.

"Did he ever tell you what I made him do to earn it?"

I feel so dead inside.

"No," Anderson says, eyes bright, too bright. "I suspect he didn't want to mention that part, did he? I bet he didn't include that part of his past, did he?"

I don't want to hear this. I don't want to know this. I don't want to listen anymore—

"Don't worry," Anderson says. "I won't spoil it for you. Best to let him share those details with you himself."

I'm not calm anymore. I'm not calm and I've officially begun to panic.

"I'll be heading back to base in just a bit," Anderson says, sorting through his papers, not seeming to mind having an entirely one-sided conversation with me. "I can't stand to be under the same roof as his mother for very long—I do not get on well with the ill, unfortunately—but this has turned out to be a convenient little camp under the present circumstances. I've been using it as a base from which to oversee all that's going on at the compounds."

The battle.

The fighting.

The bloodshed and Adam and Kenji and Castle and everyone I've left behind

How could I forget

The horrifying, terrifying possibilities are flashing through my mind. I have no idea what's happened. If they're okay. If they know I'm still alive. If Castle managed to get Brendan and Winston back.

If anyone I know has died.

My eyes are crazed, darting around. I get to my feet, convinced that this is all just an elaborate trap, that perhaps someone is going to maul me from behind or someone is waiting in the kitchen with a cleaver, and I can't catch my breath, I'm wheezing and I'm trying to figure out what to do what to do what to do and I say "What am I doing here? Why did you bring me here? Why haven't you killed me yet?"

Anderson looks at me. He cocks his head. He says, "I am very upset with you, Juliette. Very, very unhappy." He says, "You have done a very bad thing."

"What?" seems to be the only question I know how to ask. "What are you talking about?" For one crazy moment I wonder if he knows about what happened with Warner. I almost feel myself blush.

But he takes a deep breath. Grabs the cane resting against his chair. He has to use his entire upper body to get to his feet. He's shaking, even with the cane to support him.

He's crippled.

He says, "You did this to me. You managed to overpower me. You shot me in my legs. You almost shot me in the heart. And you kidnapped my son."

"No," I gasp, "that wasn't—"

"You did this to me." He cuts me off. "And now I want compensation."

SIXTY-NINE

Breathing. I have to remember to keep breathing.

"It's quite extraordinary," Anderson says, "what you were able to do entirely on your own. There were only three people in that room," he says. "You, me, and my son. My soldiers were watching that entire area for anyone else who might've come with you, and they said you were utterly alone." A pause. "I actually thought you'd come with a team, you see. I didn't think you'd be brave enough to meet me by yourself. But then you single-handedly disarmed me and stole back your hostages. You had to carry two men—not including my son—out to safety. How you managed to do it is entirely beyond my comprehension."

And it hits me: this choice is simple.

I either tell him the truth about Kenji and Adam and risk having Anderson go after them, or I take the fall.

So I meet Anderson's eyes.

I nod. I say, "You called me a stupid little girl. You said I was too much of a coward to defend myself."

He looks uncomfortable for the very first time. Seems to realize that I could probably do the same thing to him again, right now if I wanted.

And I think, yes, I probably could. What an excellent idea.

But for now, I'm still strangely curious to see what he wants from me. Why he's talking to me. I'm not worried about attacking him right away; I know that I have an advantage over him now. I should be able to overtake him easily.

Anderson clears his throat.

"I was planning on returning to the capital," he says. He takes a deep breath. "But it's clear that my work here is not yet finished. Your people are making things infinitely more complicated and it's becoming harder and harder to simply kill all the civilians." A pause. "Well, no, actually, that's not true. It's not hard to kill them, it's only that it's becoming impractical." He looks at me. "If I were to kill them all, I wouldn't have any left to rule over, would I?"

He actually laughs. Laughs as if he's said something funny.

"What do you want with me?" I ask him.

He takes a deep breath. He's smiling. "I must admit, Juliette—I'm thoroughly impressed. You alone were able to overpower me. You had enough foresight to think of taking my son hostage. You saved two of your own men. You caused an *earthquake* to save the rest of your team!" He laughs. He laughs and laughs and laughs.

I don't bother telling him that only 2 of those things are true.

"I see now that my son was right. You *could* be invaluable to us, especially right now. You know the inside of their headquarters better than anything Aaron is able to remember."

So Warner has been to see his father.

He's shared our secrets. Of course he has. I can't imagine why I'm so surprised.

"You," Anderson says to me, "could help me destroy all of your little friends. You could tell me everything I need to know. You could tell me all about the other freaks, what they're capable of, what their strengths and weaknesses are. You could take me to their hideout. You would do whatever I asked you to do."

I want to spit in his face.

"I would sooner *die*," I tell him. "I'd rather be burned alive."

"Oh, I highly doubt that," he says. He shifts his weight onto the cane to better hold himself up. "I think you'd change your mind if you actually had the opportunity to feel the skin melt off your face. But," he says, "I am not unkind. I certainly won't rule it out as an option, if you're really that interested."

Horrible, horrible man.

He smiles, wide, satisfied by my silence. "Yes, I didn't think so."

The front door flies open.

I don't move. I don't turn around. I don't know if I want to see what's about to happen to me but then I hear Anderson greet his visitor. Invite him in. Ask him to say hello to their new guest.

Warner steps into my line of vision.

I'm suddenly weak through the bone, sick and slightly

mortified. Warner doesn't say a word. He's wearing his perfect suit with his perfect hair and he looks exactly like the Warner I first met; the only difference now is the look in his eyes. He's staring at me in a state of shock so debilitating he actually looks ill.

"You kids remember each other, right?" Anderson is the only one laughing.

Warner is breathing like he's hiked several mountains, like he can't understand what he's seeing or why he's seeing it and he's staring at my neck, at what must be the ugly blotchy bruise staining my skin and his face twists into something that looks like anger and horror and heartbreak. His eyes drop to my shirt, to my shorts, and his mouth falls open just enough for me to notice before he's reining himself in, wiping the emotions off his face. He's struggling to stay composed but I can see the rapid motions of his chest rising and falling. His voice isn't nearly as strong as it could be when he says, "What is she doing here?"

"I've had her collected for us," Anderson says simply.

"For what?" Warner asks. "You said you didn't want her—"

"Well," Anderson says, considering. "That's not entirely true. I could certainly benefit from having her around, but I decided at the last moment that I wasn't interested in her company anymore." He shakes his head. Looks down at his legs. Sighs. "It's just so *frustrating* to be crippled like this," he says, laughing again. "It's just so unbelievably *frustrating*. But," he says, smiling, "at least I've found a fast and easy way to fix it. To put it all back to normal, as they say. It'll be just like magic."

Something about his eyes, the sick smile in his voice, the way he says that last line makes me feel ill. "What do you mean?" I ask, almost afraid to hear his response.

"I'm surprised you even have to ask, my dear. I mean, honestly—did you really think I wouldn't notice my son's brand-new shoulder?" He laughs. "Did you think I wouldn't find it strange to see him come home not only unharmed, but entirely *healed*? No scars, no tenderness, no weakness—as if he'd never been shot at all! It's a miracle," he says. "A miracle, my son informs me, that was performed by two of your little freaks."

"No."

Horror is building inside of me, blinding me.

"Oh yes." He glances at Warner. "Isn't that right, son?"

"No," I gasp. "Oh, God—what have you done—WHERE ARE THEY—"

"Calm yourself," Anderson says to me. "They are perfectly unharmed. I simply had them collected, just as I had you collected. I need them to stay alive and healthy if they're going to heal me, don't you think?"

"Did you know about this?" I turn to Warner, frantic. "Did you do this? Did you know—"

"No—Juliette," he says, "I swear—this wasn't my idea—"

"You are both getting agitated over nothing," Anderson says, waving a lazy hand in our direction. "We have more important things to focus on right now. More pressing issues to deal with."

"What," Warner asks, "are you talking about?" He doesn't seem to be breathing.

"Justice, son." Anderson is staring at me now. "I'm talking about justice. I like the idea of setting things right. Of putting order back into the world. And I was waiting for you to arrive so I could show you exactly what I mean. This," he says, "is what I should've done the first time." He glances at Warner. "Are you listening? Pay close attention now. Are you watching?"

He pulls out a gun.

And shoots me in the chest.

SEVENTY

My heart has exploded.

I'm thrown backward, tripping over my own feet until I hit the floor, my head slamming into the carpeted ground, my arms doing little to break my fall. It's pain like I've never known it, pain I never thought I could feel, never would have even imagined. It's like dynamite has gone off in my chest, like I've been lit on fire from the inside out, and suddenly everything slows down.

So this, I think, is what it feels like to die.

I'm blinking and it seems to take forever. I see an unfocused series of images in front of me, colors and bodies and lights swaying, stilted movements all blurred together. Sounds are warped, garbled, too high and too low for me to hear clearly. There are icy, electric bursts surging through my veins, like every part of my body has fallen asleep and is trying to wake up again.

There's a face in front of me.

I try to concentrate on the shape, the colors, try to bring everything into focus but it's too difficult and suddenly I can't breathe, suddenly I feel like there are knives in my throat, holes punched into my lungs, and the more I blink, the less clearly I'm able to see. Soon I'm only able to take in the tightest breaths, tiny little gasps that remind me of when I was a child, when the doctors told me I suffered from asthma attacks. They were wrong, though; my shortness of breath had nothing to do with asthma. It had to do with panic and anxiety and hyperventilation. But this feeling I'm feeling right now is very similar to what I experienced then. It's like trying to take in oxygen by breathing through the thinnest straw. Like your lungs are just closing up, gone for the holidays. I feel the dizziness take over, the light-headed feeling take over. And the pain, the pain, the *pain*. The pain is terrible. The pain is the worst. The pain never seems to stop.

Suddenly I'm blind.

I feel rather than see the blood, feel it leaking out of me as I blink and blink and blink in a desperate attempt to regain my vision. But I can see nothing but a haze of white. I hear nothing but the pounding in my eardrums and the short, the short, the short frantic gasp gasp gasps of my own breath and I feel hot, so hot, the blood of my body still so fresh and warm and pooling underneath me, all around me.

Life is seeping out of me and it makes me think about death, makes me think about how short a life I lived and how little I lived it. How I spent most of my years cowering in fear, never standing up for myself, always trying to be what someone else wanted. For 17 years I tried to force myself into a mold that I hoped would make other people feel comfortable, safe, unthreatened.

And it never helped.

I will have died having accomplished nothing. I am still no one. I am nothing more than a silly little girl bleeding to death on a psychotic man's floor.

And I think, if I could do it over again, I'd do it so differently.

I'd be better. I'd make something of myself. I'd make a difference in this sorry, sorry world.

And I'd start by killing Anderson.

It's too bad I'm already so close to dead.

SEVENTY-ONE

My eyes open.

I'm looking around and wondering at this strange version of an afterlife. Odd, that Warner is here, that I still can't seem to move, that I still feel such extraordinary pain. Stranger still to see Sonya and Sara in front of me. I can't even pretend to understand their presence in this picture.

I'm hearing things.

Sounds are beginning to come in more clearly, and, because I can't lift my head to look around, I try instead to focus on what they're saying.

They're arguing.

"You have to!" Warner shouts.

"But we can't—we can't t-touch her," Sonya is saying, choking back tears. "There's no way for us to help her—"

"I can't believe she's actually dying," Sara gasps. "I didn't think you were telling the truth—"

"She's not dying!" Warner says. "She is not going to die! Please, listen, I'm telling you," he says, desperate now, "you can help her—I've been trying to explain to you," he says, "all you have to do is touch me and I can take your power—I can be the transfer, I can control it and redirect your Energy—"

"That's not possible," Sonya says. "That's not—Castle never said you could do that—he would've told us if you could do that—"

"Jesus, please, just listen to me," he says, his voice breaking. "I'm not trying to trick you—"

"You kidnapped us!" they both shout at the same time.

"That wasn't me! I wasn't the one who kidnapped you—"

"How are we supposed to trust you?" Sara says. "How do we know you didn't do this to her yourself?"

"Why don't you care?" He's breathing so hard now. "How can you not care? Why don't you care that she's bleeding to death—I thought you were her friends—"

"Of course we care!" Sara says, her voice catching on the last word. "But how can we help her now? Where can we take her? Who can we take her to? No one can touch her and she's lost so much blood already—just look at he—"

A sharp intake of breath.

"Juliette?"

Footsteps stomp stomp stomp the ground. Rushing around my head. All the sounds are banging into each other, colliding again, spinning around me. I can't believe I'm not dead yet.

I have no idea how long I've been lying here.

"Juliette? JULIETTE—"

Warner's voice is a rope I want to cling to. I want to catch it and tie it around my waist and I want him to haul me out of this paralyzed world I'm trapped in. I want to tell him not to worry, that it's fine, that I'm going to be okay because

I've accepted it, I'm ready to die now, but I can't. I can't say anything. I still can't breathe, can hardly shape my lips into words. All I can do is take these torturous little gasps and wonder why the hell my body hasn't given up yet.

All of a sudden Warner is straddling my bleeding body, careful not to allow any of his weight to touch me, and he shoves up my shirtsleeves. Grabs ahold of my bare arms and says, "You are going to be okay. We're going to fix this—they're going to help me fix this and you—you're going to be fine." Deep breaths. "You're going to be perfect. Do you hear me? Juliette, can you hear me?"

I blink at him. I blink and blink and blink at him and find I'm still fascinated by his eyes. Such a startling shade of green.

"Each one of you, grab my arms," he shouts to the girls, his hands still gripped firmly around my shoulders. "Now! Please! I'm *begging you*—"

And for some reason they listen.

Maybe they see something in him, see something in his face, in his features. Maybe they see what I see from this disjointed, foggy perspective. The desperation in his expression, the anguish carved into his features, the way he looks at me, like he might die if I do.

And I can't help but think this is an interesting parting gift from the world.

That at least, in the end, I didn't die alone.

SEVENTY-TWO

I'm blind again.

Heat is pouring into my being with such intensity it's literally taken over my vision. I can't feel anything but hot, hot, searing hot heat flooding my bones, my nerves, my skin, my cells.

Everything is on fire.

At first I think it's the same heat in my chest, the same pain from the hole where my heart used to be, but then I realize this heat doesn't actually hurt. It's a soothing kind of heat. So potent, so intense, but somehow it's welcome. My body does not want to reject it. Does not want to flinch away from it, is not looking for a way to protect itself from it.

I actually feel my back lift off the floor when the fire hits my lungs. I'm suddenly gasping in huge, raging hyperventilated breaths, taking in lungfuls of air like I might cry if I don't. I'm drinking oxygen, devouring it, choking on it, taking it in as quickly as possible, my entire body heaving as it strains to return to normal.

My chest feels like it's being stitched back together, like the flesh is regenerating itself, healing itself at an inhuman rate and I'm blinking and breathing and I'm moving my head and trying to see but it's still so blurry, still unclear but it's getting easier. I can feel my fingers and my toes and the life in my limbs and I can actually hear my heart beating again and suddenly the faces above me come into focus.

All at once the heat is gone.

The hands are gone.

I collapse back onto the floor.

And everything goes black.

SEVENTY-THREE

Warner is sleeping.

I know this because he's sleeping right next to me. It's dark enough that it takes me several tries to blink my eyes open and understand that I'm not blind this time. I catch a glimpse out the window and find the moon filled to the brim, pouring light into this little room.

I'm still here. In Anderson's house. In what probably used to be Warner's bedroom.

And he's asleep on the pillow right next to me.

His features are so soft, so ethereal in the moonlight. His face is deceptively calm, so unassuming and innocent. And I think of how impossible it is that he's here, lying next to me. That I'm here, lying next to him.

That we're lying in his childhood bed together.

That he saved my life.

Impossible is such a stupid word.

I shift hardly at all and Warner reacts immediately, sitting straight up, chest heaving, eyes blinking. He looks at me, sees that I'm awake, that my eyes are open, and he freezes in place.

There are so many things I want to say to him. So many things I have to tell him. So many things I need to do now, that I need to sort through, that I have to decide.

But for now, I only have one question.

"Where's your father?" I whisper.

It takes Warner a moment to find his voice. He says, "He's back on base. He left right after"—he hesitates, struggles for a second—"right after he shot you."

Incredible.

He left me bleeding all over his living room floor. What a nice little present for his son to clean up. What a nice little lesson for his son to learn. Fall in love, and you get to watch your love get shot.

"So he doesn't know I'm here?" I ask Warner. "He doesn't know I'm alive?"

Warner shakes his head. "No."

And I think, *Good*. That's very good. It'll be so much better if he thinks I'm dead.

Warner is still looking at me. Looking and looking and looking at me like he wants to touch me but he's afraid to get too close. Finally, he whispers, "Are you okay, love? How do you feel?"

And I smile to myself, thinking of all the ways I could answer that question.

I think of how my body is more exhausted, more defeated, more drained than it's ever been in my life. I think about how I've had nothing but a glass of water in 2 days. How I've never been more confused about people, about who they seem to be and who they actually are, and I think about how I'm lying here, sharing a bed in a house we were told doesn't exist anymore, with one of the most hated and feared people of Sector 45. And I think about how that terrifying creature has the capacity for such tenderness, how he saved my life. How his own father shot me in the chest. How only hours earlier I was lying in a pool of my own blood.

I think about how my friends are probably still locked in battle, how Adam must be suffering not knowing where I am or what's happened to me. How Kenji is still pulling the weight of so many. How Brendan and Winston might still be lost. How the people of Omega Point might all be dead. And it makes me think.

I feel better than I ever have in my entire life.

I'm amazed by how different I feel now. How different I know things will be now. I have so many things to do. So many scores to settle. So many friends who need my help.

Everything has changed.

Because once upon a time I was just a child.

Today I'm still just a child, but this time I've got an iron will and 2 fists made of steel and I've aged 50 years. Now I finally have a clue. I've finally figured out that I'm strong enough, that maybe I'm a touch brave enough, that maybe this time I can do what I was meant to do.

This time I am a force.

A deviation of human nature.

I am living, breathing proof that nature is officially screwed, afraid of what it's done, what it's become.

And I'm stronger. I'm angrier.

I'm ready to do something I'll definitely regret and this

time I don't care. I'm done being nice. I'm done being nervous. I'm not afraid of anything anymore.

Mass chaos is in my future.

And I'm leaving my gloves behind.

Lose yourself in the exhilarating return to the #1 global bestselling Shatter Me universe, set ten years after the fall of The Reestablishment.

SHATTER ME: SERIES TWO

BOOK ONE

ROSABELLE

CHAPTER 1

When I open the cupboard, the shelves are empty.

This is no surprise, of course; the shelves have been empty for weeks. It's for Clara's sake that I make a show of opening them every morning, pretending there might be more than the same skittering cockroach living inside.

I close the cabinet door, then turn to face her. Clara never leaves the bed unless I carry her; today she's sitting up and staring out the icy window, her pale eyes made paler by the blast of early morning light. Her hand trembles as she twitches the threadbare curtain, and a blue glare briefly illuminates the glass.

"We're out of bread," I announce. "I'm heading out."

Some days Clara lets me leave without asking questions. Other days she asks me how I pay for the food I bring home. Today she says, "I dreamed of Mama last night."

I keep my face impassive. "Again?"

Clara turns toward me, so gaunt her eyes appear sunken in her face. "She wasn't well, Rosa. She was suffering."

I step into my boots, shaking my head as I move into a shaft of light. "It was only a dream," I say to her. "The dead don't suffer."

Clara looks away again. "You always say that."

"And you stare at her photograph too much," I say, knotting my laces. My right hand doesn't shake today, and I experience a rush of relief as I straighten, then a flash of terror as I note the dwindling fire in the hearth—and the disappearing pile of firewood beside it. I force the terror down. "Besides," I add, "you hardly knew her."

"Well, you hardly speak of her," Clara counters with a sigh.

Through the window I glimpse a redheaded woodpecker and watch, transfixed, as it hammers its beak into a mossy trunk. It's been just over a decade since the fall of The Reestablishment—just over a decade since we've lived here, on Ark Island—and I, too, wish I could bash my head over and over against a hard surface every day. I take a sharp breath, ignoring the ever-present ache of hunger.

It's still strange to see the birds.

They fill the sky with sound and color, rattling roofs and branches. All around us evergreens spiral skyward, never surrendering to the seasons. It's always damp here; viridescent; cold. Lakes shimmer unprovoked. Distant mountain ranges seem painted in watercolors, layers of teeth made translucent by fog. The warm and well-fed have been known to call this land beautiful.

"I won't be long," I say, buttoning myself into Papa's old coat. Years ago I cut off the military insignias with a dull blade, earning myself a scar in the process. "I'll see about rebuilding the fire when I get back."

"Okay," Clara says quietly. Then: "Sebastian came by yesterday."

I stiffen.

Very slowly I reanimate, wrapping my mother's tattered scarf too tightly around my neck. I was allowed to work at the mill yesterday, and by the time I got home Clara had been asleep.

"He came to deliver the mail," she says.

"The mail," I echo. "He came all this way just to deliver the mail."

Clara nods, then reaches under her pillow to retrieve a folded newspaper and a thick, unmarked envelope, both of which she holds out in offering. I tuck the two into my coat pocket without glancing at either.

"Thank you," I say softly. I imagine, for a moment, how it might feel to slit Sebastian's throat.

Clara tilts her head at me. "He said you missed last week's meeting."

"You were sick."

"I told him that."

I look toward the door. "You don't need to tell him anything."

"He still wants to marry you, Rosa."

I lift my head sharply. "How do you know about that?"

"Would it be so terrible?" She ignores my question, shivering violently. "Don't you like him? I thought you liked him."

I turn to face our little kitchen, the small stove, the rickety table and chairs we never use. The wooden plaque hanging above the sink.

Our society
REESTABLISHED
Our future
REDEFINED

My eyes unfocus.

I was ten when I came home to find a black bear tearing through the last of our food. Clara was three; Mama had been dead three days. I don't remember killing the bear or burying what remained of my mother.

I remember the blood.

I remember the weeks it took to scrub the floorboards. The bars of Clara's crib. The ceiling. Mama's last words to me had been *close your eyes, Rosa,* except that she'd closed her eyes and I'd kept mine open. She put the gun in her mouth just hours after we heard that Papa would no longer be executed for war crimes. He'd traded all of us in for a half-life, selling secrets to the enemy in exchange for a slow rot in prison. I used to think Mama killed herself because she couldn't withstand the shame. Now I'm certain it was because she knew she'd be forced to pay for Papa's treason.

Maybe she thought they'd spare her children.

I grab the bear pelt from its hook and drape it around Clara's trembling limbs. She hates the pelt. She says the bear's pain still lingers in the cottage, that it makes her retch even after all these years. So when she allows the fur to settle on her shoulders without protest, I know the situation is dire.

"If you married Sebastian, things would be better," Clara says, suppressing another shiver. She pauses to cough, and the hacking sound drives a hole through my head. "They'd lift the sanctions. You wouldn't have to pretend we have food in our cupboards every morning."

Slowly, I meet her eyes.

I remember when Clara was born, when I'd looked at her and wondered whether Mama had given birth to a doll. Only later did I realize I must've looked just as strange when I was born: all ghost and glass. I study her often when she sleeps, or when the illness overtakes her so completely she slips into a coma. At thirteen, she's tender and optimistic; nothing like I was at her age. Still, despite the seven years between us, she and I are physically similar: shockingly pale; hair so blond it's nearly white; eyes a disorienting shade of cold. Staring at Clara is like staring into the past, at what I used to be, who I could've been.

I was soft once, too.

"I really think he loves you," she says, her eyes brightening with feeling. "You should've heard the way he talked about you— Rosa, wait—"

I don't say goodbye to my sister.

I reach for the automatic rifle tucked away in the entry, pulling the strap over my head before tugging a battered balaclava over my face. I step into the cold, and thick flakes catch in my eyelashes just as the front door slams shut behind me, the sound briefly drowning out his voice. It's my only explanation for being startled.

"Rosabelle," he says, cutting in front of me with a smile. "Still dead inside?"

ROSABELLE

CHAPTER 2

I sidestep Lieutenant Soledad, absently running my hand along the cold weapon slung across my chest. Soledad is no longer a lieutenant the way he once was; the title is a relic of another time. In this newly imagined world he's the head of our island's security, which makes him nothing more than a glorified busybody. And a tyrant.

I nod at familiar faces as they pass, their eyes anxiously tracking between myself and Soledad, who's fallen into step beside me. Snow is beginning to stick to the ground; spirals of smoke curl away from stacked chimneys, smudging the skies like errant brushstrokes. I adjust the balaclava on my face; the wool is old and itchy. I am impatient.

"I thought our appointment was for tomorrow," I say flatly.

"I thought I'd surprise you," he says. "Impromptu interrogations often yield interesting results."

I come to a halt, turning to face him.

I remember when Soledad was young and fit and full of bravado—when he served under my father, the chief commander and regent of Sector 52. Now he's somehow barrel-chested but soft; stooped. His skin is waxy, his hair thinning. He wears the stale air of another time, the only lingering evidence of that epoch imprinted on his face. A soft blue glow pulses at his temples, his dark eyes occasionally brightening, then dimming.

Unbidden, my right arm trembles.

Quietly I change course for the day, feeling the pressure of a single, physical key tucked inside in the false pocket sewn into Papa's old coat. The only lock I own is bolted to the shed camouflaged in the wilds beyond the cottage—which I meant to visit first, and which I'll now have to avoid. No one in the pit knows about the lock because the lock is illegal; the homes in the pit are meant to be borderless. Our minds, too, are meant to be open at all times for inspection. It was the way of our parents, the way of The Reestablishment.

Surveillance is security, Papa used to say. *Only criminals need privacy.*

I glance at Soledad, who still wears his old military fatigues, the front pocket adorned with the tricolored emblem of a buried era. He lost an arm during the post-revolution skirmishes and wears his prosthetic proudly, one sleeve rolled up to reveal the silver gleam of muscular machinery.

"So," he says. "We can set up here, or we can head back to central. Your choice."

I cast a furtive glance around the pit, which comprises a cluster of cottages, square windows aglow in the gray morning light. People scurry along, heads down, avoiding eye contact with Soledad, who's never paid the pit a visit without doing some damage. Those who live here have been sanctioned—cut off from the community for any number of infractions—but no one has lived here longer than Clara and me, who've never known another home on the island. In the chaotic weeks after our supreme commanders were slaughtered, Papa sent us here with Mama, promising to follow as soon as he could. It turned out Papa had stayed behind on purpose, voluntarily surrendering to the rebels. As a reward, we were sanctioned upon arrival.

"Do we have to do this now?" I ask, thinking of Clara, shivering and starved. "I'd rather keep our appointment for tomorrow."

"Why, you have plans this morning?" He says this like it's a joke. "You're not allowed a shift at the mill today."

A sharp pang of hunger cuts through me then, nearly taking my breath away. "Just some things to do."

Soledad grabs my chin and I suppress a flinch, steadying myself as he forces me to look at him. He stares into my eyes for a long beat before letting go, and I kill the flare of revulsion in my chest, compelling my racing heart to slow.

I remind myself that I am dead inside.

"So strange not to know what you're thinking," he says, a notch forming between his brows. "All these years and I still haven't gotten used to it. Makes it hard to believe you're always telling the truth."

Another slight tremor moves through my right hand. I'm the only person here unconnected to the Nexus. Even Clara was brought online before Papa was arrested. Just before the end, all civilians under the directive of The Reestablishment had been connected to the neural network, a program quickly dismantled by the new regime. Soledad and the others like to remind us that the reason we lost the war was because the rebels hadn't been chipped.

I have no acceptable excuse.

"Pity we can't seem to get you online again," Soledad says finally. "Things might've been easier for you."

Memories flare to life: cold metal; muted screams; drug-induced nightmares. With Mama dead, there was no one to beg them to stop. No one who cared whether their experiments would eventually kill me.

"I couldn't agree more," I lie.

Soledad shifts his weight. Blue veins of light pulse through his metal arm, silver fingers flashing as they flex and curl. "So," he says. "Why'd you miss the meeting last week?"

Just like that, an unofficial interrogation has begun. Here, in the freezing cold. While my neighbors watch.

Clara, I realize, can probably see us from the window.

There's a sudden chorus of shouts and my heart stutters, steadying only when I spot Zadie's twin boys, Jonah and Micah, tackling each other in the snow. One of them punches the other in the gut, this accomplishment punctuated by peals of laughter. I catch the drifting scent of breakfast meat from a nearby cottage and my knees nearly give out.

I return my eyes to Soledad. "Clara was sick."

"Coma?"

"No." I look away. "She spent most of the night throwing up."

"Food?"

"Blood," I clarify.

"Right." Soledad laughs. He sizes me up through Papa's overlarge coat. "That makes more sense, considering the fact that you're both starving."

"We're not starving." Another lie.

A fresh circus of sound short-circuits my nervous system. A murder of crows lands heavily on a nearby roof, eerie calls clamoring, wings flapping. I'm watching them, fascinated a moment by an iridescent sheen of black feathers when two earsplitting shots ring out.

I stiffen on impulse then force myself to thaw, my fingers to unclench, my pulse to slow.

"Fucking birds," Soledad mutters.

He walks over to the duo of fallen bodies, then stomps on their small, hollow bones, smearing blood and feathers into the snow. I blink, exhaling softly into the cold. I've been dead inside for years, I remind myself.

Most people here hate the birds for what they represent. The birds mean that The Reestablishment has been dethroned, that the project has all but failed. The New Republic and its traitorous leaders—the children of our fallen supreme commanders—have been a ripe source of hatred for as long as I can remember.

Clara, I realize, will have questions about the gunshots.

"I've got real work for you, if you're interested," says Soledad, now wiping his boots on a clean patch of ground.

I look up. Realization is swift. "You didn't come here for an interrogation."

Soledad smiles at me, but his eyes are unreadable. "Never misses a thing, this one. I've always hated that about you."

"How many this time?" I ask, my heart beginning a traitorous rhythm.

"We've got four altogether. Three have been processed already. New one came through last night and he's definitely—" Soledad's eyes brighten, glazing over in an inhuman shade of blue. Suddenly he whips around, marches over to the twins still grappling in snow, grabs one of them—Micah—by the scruff of his neck, and shoves him, angrily, to the ground. "You've just lost your rations for the week."

Jonah darts forward. "But— We were only playing around—"

"He was going to take your eye out," Soledad barks, then jerks his head in a familiar motion.

Micah screams.

Jonah stills, but his eyes are fixed on his brother, who's lying on the ground, now silent and twitching violently. There's the slam of a door, a sudden cry, and his mother, Zadie, comes running. Soledad shakes his head in disgust, and Micah is released from his paralysis. With some effort, the boy revives in his mother's arms.

"Sorry, sir," says Micah, his chest heaving. "I didn't mean—"

Soledad directs his next words to Zadie. "If you can't get these two idiots to stop acting like animals, you'll spend another year in the pit. Is that clear?"

Heads appear, then disappear, in neighboring windows.

Zadie nods, mumbling something inarticulate, then grabs her boys and bolts.

In the quiet aftermath Soledad returns to my side, scanning me for a reaction, but I'm careful, as always, to betray no emotion. It's the only way I've survived here, where I'm surveilled not only by the system but also through the eyes of everyone I encounter—even my own sister.

Surveillance is security, Rosa.

Only criminals need privacy.

Only criminals need privacy.

For so many years I used to believe everything my father said.

Those were the years when Soledad was a friend to our family; the years we lived in a warm, comfortable home, when food was abundant, when Nanny would dress me in silks before braiding my hair. I'd sneak downstairs during my mother's dinner parties just to hear the sound of her laughter.

"How many more before you'll lift the sanctions?" I ask, ripping the balaclava off my head. I feel the static of my hair; the compression of my chest. Brisk wind batters my face but the icy air is welcome against my heated skin.

Soledad shakes his head. "I can't answer that. Your father is still alive, still feeding secrets to the enemy. For as long as we can't know your mind, you'll always be a question mark." He shrugs, then looks away. "We all make sacrifices for the security of our nation, Rosabelle. For the security of our future. This is your sacrifice—and it may never end."

He returns his eyes to me.

"Look," he says. "You can kill them all at once or one at a time. I'll let you decide. When you're done, I'll see about getting Clara some medicine."

"And food," I say too quickly, then pause, taking a moment to compose my face. "And firewood."

"All at once, then," he says, narrowing his eyes.

"All at once," I agree. "And right now."

Soledad raises his eyebrows. "You sure? One of them won't stop screaming. She had a bad reaction to the sedative."

I feel unseasonably warm. Overdressed. I distract myself by stuffing the balaclava into Papa's coat pocket, and the thick envelope from earlier kisses me with a paper cut. The pain focuses my thoughts.

It's not necessary to kill them like this.

We have among our ranks some of the best medics and scientists in the world; we possess far more advanced and humane ways to kill the rare spies who manage to breach Ark Island.

Of course, murdering them isn't meant to be humane.

"Do you care how I kill them?" I ask, and my voice is mercifully steady.

The electric hum of the helicopter pulls my attention skyward. Clara will see it. She'll know what it means.

"I don't care how you do it." Soledad smiles now; a real smile. "You've always been creative."

JAMES

CHAPTER 3

"Okay. All right. This is fine. You're fine," I say, pacing up and down the short length of my prison cell. I hesitate, then look around for the hundredth time.

I mean, I'm guessing this is a prison cell.

It's clean, which is weird. It's also well-lit, fully illuminated by a light source I can't identify. The walls and floors are made of gleaming steel—so glossy I can see myself from every direction—and the warped reflections keep freaking me out. I have no idea how long I've been in here. Every once in a while a weird mist is released into the room, and each time I lose what feels like a few hours.

My brilliant plan is not exactly going to plan.

"Look," I say, pointing at a melted blur of my face. "There's no reason to panic. You've still got your own pants on, plus all your original body parts, and if you were supposed to die here, no one would care if you had to use the bathroom, okay? They'd let you die in a heap of your own shit—"

As if on cue, a mechanical whirr precedes the reveal of an aperture in the ground. I've been here long enough to have learned that every time I say the word *bathroom* a panel slides away to reveal a bottomless black pit, the opening of which is lined with metal teeth that all but promise to bite off your dick. I've never been so terrified and relieved to take a piss in my life. I fucking hate it here.

I tried shouting other things, too; things like *Get me out of here* and *Motherfucker* and *Ice cream sundae,* and all I got was more mist in my face.

I wonder if anyone back home has realized I'm gone.

"Of course they have, moron," I mutter.

Adam is going to be pissed. Warner is going to be super pissed. Juliette might already be crying. If I survive this, Kenji will probably kill me himself.

A week ago it seemed like a good idea, trying to break into Ark Island. This shithole is the last refuge of The Reestablishment—the last gasp of a fascist psychopathic government that basically wants to enslave the world—and no one's ever been able to penetrate their defenses. Back in the womb of home and family, where I'm still treated like a baby who doesn't know how to wipe his own ass, doing something like this seemed genius. If I could do the one thing even the famous Aaron Warner Anderson couldn't do, maybe they'd finally respect me. Maybe they'd finally look at me like a man and not a ten-year-old boy who used to cry for his big brother every night.

"Great job, idiot." I bang my head against the wall.

If I ever make it back home, they'll never let me do anything again. My own half brother is basically running the world with his wife, and I'll be reduced to desk work. Back in diapers. All my security clearances revoked.

I let out a nervous laugh, then push both hands through my hair. I don't know how Juliette did solitary confinement for nearly a year. Before she single-handedly orchestrated the downfall of The Reestablishment, she'd suffered in ways I could never imagine. Now, looking around this gleaming hellscape, I realize I've never appreciated her enough. I thought I couldn't love her more than I already do—hell, she and Warner helped raise me—but imagining how The Reestablishment tortured her—

Nah. I can't go there. Not here. Not now.

"Shower!" I shout at the wall.

Nothing happens.

"Piece of shit!" I shout at the wall.

The toilet hole opens again.

"Listen," I say angrily, "if you're not going to kill me, the least you could do is offer me some snacks—"

The words have barely left my mouth when I'm startled by memory. Propelled into motion, I search my pockets until I find it—a little plastic pouch of gummy bears, half-melted.

I can't help but smile.

These assholes stripped every weapon off my body but left me the candy. I'd swiped it from five-year-old Gigi's snack bag on my way out the door; a moment that now feels like a lifetime ago. I rip the packet open, then stare at the melted gummies for half a second, the artificial scent of various fruit flavors generating sense recognition so strong my heart nearly gives out.

"Hey," I say, narrowing my eyes at my liquid reflection. "Pull yourself together."

I empty the bag of gummies into my mouth, then stuff the plastic into my pocket. I'm still chewing when I say, "You're going to go home. You're going to see everyone again. You're—"

The room begins to vibrate with a soft, mechanical rumble, and the words die in my throat. I stiffen and back up, shielding my eyes as one of the walls disappears, then reappears in a flare so bright I can't clock the change.

Suddenly, I have a visitor.

I knew The Reestablishment had seriously advanced tech—we've been studying their work for a decade—but this girl materializes as if out of thin air. We're face-to-face, trapped by steel in all directions, and she's standing so inhumanly still that for a second I think I'm hallucinating. She looks like an elfin creature out of a fairy tale, so slight she's practically a beam of light. White-blond hair, icy eyes. Skin like glass.

Really, absurdly gorgeous.

My heart beats a little too hard as I blink and straighten, fake candy flavors coming alive on my tongue at the worst moment. My mouth is full of half-chewed gummy bears. I'm trying to chew without looking like I'm chewing. Jesus.

The tiny elf takes a step toward me, and I flinch.

"State your name and date of birth," she says quietly, her cold eyes appraising me.

Something about the way she tilts her head—that, and the smooth, measured sound of her voice—and suddenly I understand. This beautiful weirdo isn't a real person. She's artificial intelligence.

I exhale, irritation doing the counterintuitive work of relaxing my body.

The fact that she's a robot makes things easier. First of all, I'm not going to talk to a fucking robot. I might be an idiot, but I'm not uninformed. I know how much The Reestablishment loves surveillance. I know that this cell is being watched. They love mind games. Love to torture. If they wanted me dead, they'd have sent a real person to mess with my head at least a little before killing me. Instead, this thing is probably recording and analyzing my vitals while doing a background check. I bet it's mining some database right now, figuring out that Aaron Warner Anderson is my half brother; that Juliette Ferrars is his wife; that I'm the youngest son of Paris Anderson, the dead, ex–supreme commander of North America. They've caught themselves a big fish.

Mentally, I kick myself in the face.

"I gave you a directive," she says, and takes another step closer.

I chew a little more, trying to swallow without killing myself. "Look, if the computer in your head doesn't already know who I am just by scanning my face, I'm not going to answer your questions. So if you're here to extract information, you're shit out of luck. Maybe just send in the guy who's supposed to torture me."

She hesitates, surprise coloring her features so briefly I nearly miss it. Fascinating, lifelike tech.

She blinks those strange eyes at me before saying, softly, "Are you *eating* something?"

"Gummy bears," I say with my mouth full.

She blinks again. There's something so human about the way she studies me then that it gives me goose bumps.

"I don't understand," she says.

"Gummy bears? It's, like, a chewy candy—"

"You're not afraid to die?"

"Uh." I stop chewing. "What?"

And then she moves toward me, closing the gap between us in two strides, and I realize with a sudden, palpable fear—

This is a real woman. Not a robot.

I'm so distracted by this fact, so alarmed by the warmth of her small hand as she touches my face that, at first, I don't even notice the knife she's pressed to my throat.